Christmas
at the
Movies

Anne Marie was raised in the US, but has lived and worked in London for over 20 years. She works as a children's books editor and is the author of *The Six Tales of Christmas*.

Christmas
at the
Movies

Anne Marie Ryan

ORION

An Orion paperback

First published in Great Britain in 2025
by Orion Fiction, an imprint of The Orion Publishing Group Ltd,
Carmelite House, 50 Victoria Embankment
London EC4Y 0DZ

An Hachette UK company

The authorised representative in the EEA is Hachette Ireland,
8 Castlecourt Centre, Dublin 15, D15 XTP3,
Ireland (email: info@hbgi.ie)

1 3 5 7 9 10 8 6 4 2

A CIP catalogue record for this book
is available from the British Library.

ISBN (Paperback) 978 1 3987 2150 0
ISBN (eBook) 978 1 3987 2151 7

Typeset by Born Group
Printed and bound in Great Britain by Clays Ltd, Elcograf S.p.A.

www.orionbooks.co.uk

For anyone who has ever gone to the movies with me, especially Gabby, Debra, Jacqueline, Sophia and Anna, who napped through baby-friendly screenings with me at Watermans.

24th December 1995

James O'Hara pulled his overcoat closed against the cold wind as he hurried across Leicester Square. The cuckoo clock outside the Swiss Centre chimed the hour, reminding him that he was running late for the film. He hated missing the trailers so he quickened his pace, navigating around last-minute Christmas shoppers clutching Hamley's bags full of toys, tipsy groups of office workers spilling out of pubs and people rushing to Charing Cross to catch trains home for the holidays.

He stepped into the warmth of the cinema lobby and pulled off his hat. His wavy, sandy-coloured hair crackled with static electricity as he pushed it out of his face.

'One for *Babette's Feast*,' he said to the girl at the ticket booth. Her name badge said: *Erica – I'm Happy to Help* and she wore a reindeer antler headband over her shaved head. But her sour demeanour suggested that she was anything but thrilled to be working on Christmas Eve. And who could blame her? 'Hope I'm not late,' James said, smiling. He had a video of the Danish film at home, but he was looking forward to seeing it on the big screen.

'That's on at midnight,' Erica said, unenthusiastically.

Damn! He must have got the time wrong when he'd checked the cinema listings. 'What's playing now?' he asked.

Erica pointed to a poster with Sandra Bullock on it. It looked like a romantic comedy, which wasn't his favourite genre. But he'd come all the way into town, the pubs would be packed, and it was freezing outside . . .

As James was deciding what to do, the cinema door opened, letting in a blast of cold air. A girl strode into the foyer. Around the same age as him, she was bundled up in a parka and wore a fluffy purple beret. Her hair was brown, apart from one streak of purple at the front that matched her beret. Her nose had a smattering of freckles and a diamond stud that twinkled under the cinema's fluorescent lights, but it wasn't as bright as her smile.

$W = A\star V$. The equation for the rate of electrical work popped into his head. This girl could power a whole generator with her megawatt smile.

'Brrr!' She shivered, pulling off her gloves and rubbing her hands together to warm them. 'It's freezing out there.' She stood behind James.

'You can go ahead of me,' he said, gesturing for her to take his place at the counter. She was nearly as tall as him, so he could look right into her eyes, which were light brown flecked with gold. 'I'm still deciding.'

'Thanks.' As she stepped past him, he inhaled a familiar warm and spicy scent – like oranges mixed with cinnamon and cloves. What did it remind him of . . . ?

Suddenly, it hit him – she smelled like Christmas.

'One for *While You Were Sleeping*,' she said.

Erica handed the girl her ticket, then James watched her stride into the cinema. Her long legs were encased in black tights that had a ladder down one leg and ended in a pair of scuffed Doc Marten boots.

'Take a picture, it will last longer,' muttered Erica.

Flustered at having been caught staring, James handed Erica a five-pound note. 'One, please,' he said quickly. If the film was awful, he could always nap. He'd pulled several late nights on the trot finishing off his computer engineering coursework before the end of term.

Apart from the fact that it showed an interesting mix of second-run blockbusters, obscure foreign films, arthouse movies and raucous screenings of *The Rocky Horror Picture Show*, the Prince Charles was also the cheapest cinema in all of London, which was why James frequented it regularly. It meant he could afford to go to the cinema several times a week, even on his meagre student grant.

Taking his ticket from the sullen Erica, James went into the auditorium and looked around to see where the girl had sat down. It wasn't hard to spot her as the cinema was practically empty, apart from a few couples and an old man snoring loudly in the back row. She was sitting on her own, smack bang in the centre of the auditorium. That was where James liked to sit too, but if he sat right next to her in a practically empty cinema he'd look like a creep. Besides, someone would undoubtedly join her before the film started.

So James sat down two rows behind her, at the end of the aisle. He was close enough that he could see her profile. The silver hoops in her earlobes glinted in the light from the projector as she wriggled out of her parka. As she settled back in her red velvet seat, he caught another whiff of her spicy Christmas scent.

James had missed the adverts, but luckily not the trailers. His ex-girlfriend, Kim, thought watching trailers was a waste of time, but the advertisements for forthcoming films always filled James with happy anticipation. It was good to have something to look forward to. Kim hadn't even been that into the movies themselves, which was probably why they'd split up at the end of the second year. 'You're obsessed with films,' she'd complained. 'Why can't we ever go clubbing or to a gig, instead of always going to the sodding cinema?' But James could never see the appeal of bobbing around with sweaty strangers in a dark, smoke-filled nightclub. You couldn't have a proper conversation without shouting to be heard over the music. Unsurprisingly, Kim had left him for a guitarist in an indie band.

Some people thought going to the cinema on your own was strange, but not James. You weren't truly alone when you were sitting in the cinema; it was a communal experience. Everyone was united in the dark theatre – laughing at the funny bits, gasping at the jumpy scares, crying at the sad scenes. It was a collective ritual, a bit like going to church – not that he'd been to mass lately.

But tonight was Christmas Eve, and it felt lonely to be on his own. The nearly empty auditorium was a reminder that most other people had other places to be. His mates from uni had all gone home for the holidays, and his dad, Sean, was working a late shift at Pinewood, where he was Head Carpenter. He was building a set for a new Tom Cruise movie that was shooting in the new year.

As he sat alone in the cinema, James found himself wishing he had someone to hold hands with. Someone to share a bucket of popcorn with. Someone to discuss the film with in the pub afterwards. He'd been so busy with his studies that he hadn't dated anyone since Kim had dumped him. It had got to the point where even his dad kept hinting about whether there were any nice girls on his course. (In short, no. There were only two girls in the computer engineering department and they both had boyfriends.)

Judging from the trailers, 1996 was going to be a bumper year for movies. There was a new Coen brothers movie coming out, and a ground-breaking animated film called *Toy Story* that had already opened in the US. James couldn't wait to see it – the animation had been done entirely by computer, for the first time ever.

'Computers are taking over the world,' his father had grumbled. 'Soon they'll have robots building sets and they won't need chippies like me.'

'I don't think you need to worry, Dad,' James had reassured him, though the guys in the robotics department at Imperial were working on some amazing technology.

The feature presentation began. Set in Chicago at Christmastime, the film was about Lucy, a lonely young woman who was pretending to be engaged to a man in a coma.

As you do, thought James, rolling his eyes.

But the girl with the purple streak in her hair was clearly loving the film. Her shoulders shook with laughter at a funny scene on the screen. Soon, James found himself paying almost as much attention to her as to the movie itself. His eyes kept drifting to her face as he watched her reactions. He thought she was more beautiful than any of the actresses on the screen. He looked forward to the bits that made her giggle, because her laugh was so contagious it made him chuckle too.

About halfway through the film, someone in the audience started whispering loudly and rustling a packet of sweets. The girl turned around to glare at them and, as she did so, locked eyes with James. They both shook their heads, united in their silent disapproval. Then she winked at James. God, was she beautiful.

Feeling heat rise to his cheeks, James felt grateful that his tell-tale blush was hidden by the dark. As she turned back to the film, her Christmassy scent wafted over to him again. James closed his eyes and inhaled deeply. He wondered if she smelled like that all year round.

The movie ended with Lucy finally revealing the truth – that she had deceived everyone so she could spend Christmas as part of a family. But – surprise, surprise – Lucy got her 'happily ever after' anyway, having fallen in love with the brother of the man in the coma.

James could hear the girl sniffling at the happy ending. Despite the film's blatant emotional manipulation, there was a lump in James's throat as well.

James remained in his seat as the closing credits scrolled down the screen. It wasn't just because he was hoping to time his exit with the girl's, it was a habit his father had instilled in him. Even though the names rolled past quickly and in small type, the credits were where the film's unsung heroes – the grips, the sound engineers, the camera operators, the prop makers and the carpenters – got their brief moment of glory on the silver screen.

When the house lights came on, the girl remained seated. James stood and *sloooowly* gathered up his coat, hoping she would do the same. And then he heard . . . more sniffling.

Surely she wasn't still crying over the film? He hesitated for a moment, wondering if he should check if she was OK.

It's none of your business, James, he told himself. If she was upset, she probably didn't want to be bothered.

He started to walk out, then his conscience pricked at him. He could hear his mother's voice in his head, reminding him that Christmas could be a hard time for many people. Before James's family had eaten their festive meal, his mum had always served Christmas dinner at St Joseph's church hall to those who didn't have anywhere else to go. James hated the thought that his mum might be looking down from heaven and see him ignoring someone in need.

Go and check on her, he could hear her urging.

6

He turned around and walked down the aisle to where the girl was sitting. Her head was bowed, long brown hair spilling forwards.

'Hey, are you OK?' he asked, crouching down.

Startled, she looked up and self-consciously wiped her eyes with her sleeve. 'Oh, hi,' she said, sounding embarrassed. 'I didn't know anyone else was still in here. I'm just feeling a bit sorry for myself.'

'Why's that?' asked James.

'It's Christmas Eve and I'm on my own at the movies.' She gave a humourless laugh. 'I don't even have a fake boyfriend in a coma to hang out with.'

'I'm happy to volunteer,' offered James, hoping to coax a smile out of her. 'That film was so saccharine, I'm at risk of slipping into a diabetic coma.'

The girl's eyes widened in surprise. 'You didn't like it?'

'I mean . . .' James hesitated, not sure whether to temper his review to avoid offending her. 'The plot was a bit far-fetched. The whole thing was based on a misunderstanding that could have been cleared up in about two seconds.'

'You're missing the point,' the girl retorted passionately. '*Of course* it was predictable. Romantic comedies are *supposed* to be predictable! You know from the start that they're going to fall in love at the end.'

'I guess,' said James. He didn't like romcoms for exactly that reason. They were predictable.

'There was such a spark between Sandra Bullock and Bill Pullman. It reminded me of old screwball comedies – you know, like *His Girl Friday* or *Bringing Up Baby*. Watching them, you just knew it was love at first sight.' Her brown eyes flashed as she spoke, her tears apparently forgotten. She spoke so quickly, she could have been in an old screwball comedy herself.

Did anyone really fall in love at first sight outside of the movies? wondered James.

'You two need to leave,' said Erica from the ticket booth, entering the auditorium. She was holding a broom and a dustpan.

'Sorry!' The girl stood and picked up her parka. 'We'll get out of your way.'

'Here, let me,' said James, helping the girl put her coat on. As she flipped her hair over the collar, he inhaled that Christmassy smell again.

'So you're at Imperial?' she asked as they walked down the aisle together.

'Third year,' replied James. 'How did you know?'

She pointed to his chest. James looked down and saw that he was wearing his college scarf.

Duh.

'I'm in my first year at UCL. Sarah,' she said, offering her hand. Her nails had chipped purple vanish on them.

'James,' he said, shaking it and not wanting to let it go.

They stood in the foyer for a moment, putting on their gloves and hats.

Sarah dropped one of her gloves on the ground. James stooped to pick it up and when he handed it to her, there was zap of static electricity as their hands touched again.

'Guess we've got a spark too,' she said, laughing.

'Actually, that's just electrons colliding.'

You idiot! Why couldn't he flirt like a normal person. He'd spent way too much time with only other engineering nerds for company.

'I'll take your word for it,' said Sarah, smiling as she put on her gloves. 'I'm not a scientist, I'm reading English.'

James pointed to a poster for Ang Lee's *Sense and Sensibility* hanging outside of the cinema. 'I bet you've seen that then.'

'I loved it so much I saw it twice.' Sarah beamed. 'Have you seen his *Eat Drink Man Woman*?'

James was impressed. This girl clearly knew a lot about cinema. 'Yeah, it's great – I'm not surprised it won an Oscar.'

'All that delicious food . . .' said Sarah. James watched, transfixed, as she pulled a lip balm out of her coat pocket and applied some to her lips. They were full, but slightly chapped. 'I feel hungry right now just thinking about it.'

God, he felt hungry too. He wondered how her lips would taste.

'Want some?' Sarah said, mistaking his reason for staring and offering him the tube of lip balm.

James shook his head and felt himself starting to blush again, the curse of his pale, Celtic complexion. He glanced down the street. The Prince Charles was right on the edge of Chinatown, where restaurants would be open late. Would it be weird to suggest going for a bite to eat? They had only just met, but sharing a movie together on Christmas Eve, in a nearly empty cinema, had felt oddly intimate. He wasn't sure he could tear himself away from her, even if he wanted to.

'Do you fancy getting some noodles?' he said.

He was rewarded with a dazzling smile. 'That sounds amazing. I can't face going back to halls. I'm just about the only person sticking around over the holidays.'

'Great,' remarked James, unable to stop a huge grin spreading across his face.

Be cool, James, he told himself. This girl was way out of his league. It wasn't a proper date. She just didn't want to be alone on Christmas Eve.

James took her to a nearby restaurant called Wong Kei, popular with students. The food was famously cheap and the waiters were notoriously rude. The only nod towards the festive season was some tired tinsel decorations hanging from the ceiling. James and Sarah climbed the stairs and took a table by the window, looking out onto the red lanterns of Wardour Street that swayed in the wind.

'What do you want to eat?' barked a waiter, looking fed up despite the fact that the restaurant was practically empty.

They ordered and then smiled at each other awkwardly across the table. Sarah slipped her chopsticks out of their wrapper and folded the paper into a concertina.

'So . . . why are you spending Christmas in halls?' James asked her.

'Well, I was supposed to spend it with my boyfriend's family . . .' said Sarah.

James forced himself to hold back a sigh. She had a boyfriend. Of course she did.

'But then I found out he was cheating on me with someone in his hall.' With a wry smile, she snapped her wooden chopsticks apart.

'Oh, no,' said James, inwardly rejoicing. 'I'm sorry to hear that.'

'Don't be,' replied Sarah with a shrug. 'We'd been together since sixth form. He's studying in Leeds, and the whole long-distance thing wasn't really working. Anyway, it was too late to make other plans. My parents are on sabbatical in the US – they're professors.'

The waiter brought their beers, plonking them unceremoniously on the table.

'To new . . . friends,' said James, raising his bottle.

Sarah blushed, clinked her bottle against his and took a sip.

'So, um, what do your parents teach?' James asked, trying to distract himself from her long, elegant neck as she swallowed her drink.

'They're both anthropologists. Mum's a cultural anthropologist and Dad's a linguistic anthropologist. But I won't bore you with the difference.'

'You could never bore me,' said James truthfully.

Sarah met his gaze, the gold in her eyes seeming to sparkle, and everything else – the noise from the kitchen, the click of chopsticks, the low murmur of the other diners – faded away. It was as if they were the only two people in the restaurant. James felt like she could see right into his soul.

'Your food,' said the waiter, breaking the spell and piling an array of dishes onto the white tablecloth.

Famished, they feasted on crispy spring rolls, deliciously greasy chicken chow mein and fried rice flecked with lurid green peas and bright pink pork.

'What about you?' Sarah asked him, dipping a spring roll in chilli sauce. 'Why didn't you go home for Christmas?'

'London *is* home,' he explained, taking a sip of his beer. 'I grew up in Ealing.'

He'd stayed in London for uni because Imperial's engineering department was one of the best in the world. And because he didn't want to be too far from his dad. It had been just the two of them ever since his mum had passed away when he was fifteen.

Sarah's face brightened with recognition. 'I've never been there, but I love all the old Ealing comedies. *The Lavender Hill Mob, The Ladykillers, Passport to Pimlico . . .*'

James and Sarah traded film recommendations – classic and contemporary – and quoted favourite lines until not even a grain of rice remained. Apart from his dad, he'd never met anyone else quite as obsessed with cinema.

'I'm impressed,' said James. 'You know a lot about movies.'

'I want to make them one day,' confided Sarah.

'You're an actor?' he asked. That wasn't surprising – she certainly had the looks for it.

Sarah shook her head. 'No, I'm a writer – or at least trying to be. I'm working on a screenplay.' She raised an eyebrow teasingly. 'You won't like it – it's a romantic comedy.'

'Oh, I don't know. I might be warming up to romcoms.' James was starting to think he'd been too quick to write off a whole genre.

They both reached for the last spring roll, their fingers touching.

'You have it,' said James gallantly.

'No, that's OK,' she said.

Neither of them pulled their hand away. As they looked in each other's eyes, James moved his index finger ever so slightly, stroking hers. Sarah curled her finger around his in response, so they were linked.

'So, James,' said Sarah, her voice low. 'What do *you* want?'

You.

But he knew she was asking what he wanted to do after graduation. It was a question he asked himself nearly every day. With only two more terms left, he was on track to get a first. He'd always been good at maths and science. Words, on the other hand, were tricky for him. He was dyslexic, and it was hard for him to keep the words from jumping about on the page. That was one of the reasons he loved cinema so much – it was a way to enjoy stories told in pictures.

'I'm applying for master's degrees. But can I tell you a secret?'

Sarah nodded and leant forward in anticipation. Her face was so close, James longed to close the gap with a kiss. Instead, he confided something he'd never told anyone else before – not even Kim. But he instinctively knew that Sarah would understand.

'I want to own my own cinema.' It didn't sound like a very lofty ambition. Everyone knew that videos were killing off cinemas. But they were his happy place and James couldn't think of anything he wanted more.

Except, maybe, the girl sitting across the table from him.

Sarah let out a dreamy sigh. 'That sounds heavenly. Just imagine being able to watch movies all day long . . .'

James *had* imagined it. He even knew what he would call his cinema – the Picture Palace.

'Shit!' Pulling her hand away, Sarah jumped to her feet. 'What time is it?'

James checked his watch. 'Nearly midnight.'

Sarah started putting on her coat. 'I should be getting back to Camden before the Tube stops running.'

Dismayed, James put notes on the table to settle the bill. He didn't want the night to end. He couldn't risk this beautiful, passionate, intelligent girl disappearing from his life, Cinderella-style, at the stroke of midnight. Maybe love at first sight *wasn't* just something in the movies.

'Do you fancy seeing another movie?' he asked her, trying not to sound desperate. 'There's a midnight showing of *Babette's Feast* at the Prince Charles. I can walk you back to your halls afterwards.'

It would mean a long night-bus home for him. It didn't matter – after just one night in her company, he already knew he'd walk to the ends of the earth for this girl.

Sarah hesitated, toying with the purple strand of her hair.

'It's not a romcom,' James babbled. 'But it *is* heartwarming. And Christmassy, well, sort of. And there's a rum baba in it that's guaranteed to make you want dessert.'

Please say yes . . . please say yes . . .

Sarah zipped up her parka. 'We'd better get going, then, if we need to buy cinema sweets.' She grinned and held out her hand for him to take. 'I *really* hate missing the trailers.'

Chapter 1

Present Day

The lobby of the Plumdale Picture Palace was overrun with babies – babies in slings, babies in car seats and babies on their exhausted-looking mothers' hips. Some of the mums were sipping coffees and chatting to each other among the vintage cinema posters. These days, there were a fair number of dads too, armed with well stocked nappy bags and bottles of milk. The cinema's weekly Wednesday morning 'Baby and Me' screenings were always well-attended, even if the film was inevitably accompanied by a soundtrack of crying infants.

A baby girl with a shock of brown hair, huge blue eyes and deliciously chubby thighs gave Sarah O'Hara a gummy smile.

'What a little cutie,' said Sarah, making a silly face at the baby as she sold a ticket to her mother. The baby giggled and kicked her legs in delight. She reminded Sarah of her daughter, Holly, when she was a baby. She was nearly sixteen now and those days were a distant memory, as were the smiles – at least, Holly rarely bestowed them on her mother these days. Somehow, over the past year or so, Sarah had gone from being her daughter's favourite person to Public Enemy Number One.

'It's just a stage,' her best friend, Pari, Holly's godmother, had reassured her. 'I was horrible to my mother when I was a teenager and I bet you were too. She'll come back to you.'

But when, Sarah couldn't help wondering. She gazed round at the young parents cuddling their adorable infants and felt a pang of envy. It was so much easier when they were that age, despite the broken nights, sore boobs and smelly nappies. When she could make her children laugh by pulling a silly face and make everything better with a kiss. Even the terrible twos were a breeze compared with the teenaged years . . .

Sarah finished selling drinks and refreshments, then scuttled around to the other side of the counter to open the door to the auditorium and let the parents inside. The plush red velvet seats, ornate proscenium arch and gold fan-shaped light fittings on the stucco walls never failed to take her breath away. Nearly two decades ago, she and James had lovingly restored the Picture Palace to its former art deco glory. It had been a ruin when they'd bought it, disused since the early 70s, but eventually they had made it worthy of its name.

As the feature presentation began, she noticed that the auditorium was a bit too hot so she turned the thermostat down a touch. Then she slipped out to do some work in the office. Checking her to-do list, Sarah rubbed her temples wearily. She'd slept badly – again – and was already exhausted. The ancient sofa in the office looked very inviting, but there was no time for a nap. She needed to make a staff rota for the month ahead, order sweets and drinks for the concession stand, and schedule the programme for December. She'd once naively assumed owning a cinema would mean watching movies all day long. *Ha!*

The desk was cluttered with posters for upcoming attractions and catalogues from suppliers. She picked up a brochure and flicked through it. Last week, one of the speakers in the auditorium had blown during a screening. Fortunately, James had managed to rewire the system to a different speaker before the next showing. It was fortunate her husband could turn his hand to most repairs, because things were constantly breaking down in the cinema, from troublesome taps to temperamental ticket printers. Seeing the price of a new sound system, she winced and closed the brochure.

Maybe Santa will bring us a new one, thought Sarah.

That was yet another thing she needed to sort out – Christmas. She hadn't even begun to think about shopping yet, not to mention planning the festive film festival that the cinema ran every December.

Sarah's phone rang and her stomach clenched when she saw that it was from Severn Valley secondary school. What was it this time? Had Holly bunked off school again? Or got yet another detention?

'Hello, Mrs O'Hara? This is Stephen Wu, Nick's form tutor.'

Instantly, Sarah was on red alert. 'Is Nick ill?' she asked, her hand scrabbling in her bag to find her car keys so she could race to the school and collect him.

'No, don't worry, Nick's perfectly well. I just wanted to have a chat about how he's settling in to secondary school.'

Ahhh . . .

'Nick's a very bright boy,' said Mr Wu, 'but he seems quite anxious and hasn't made friends yet.'

Sarah's heart clenched with worry as she thought of her twelve-year-old son, looking lost in his too-big school blazer (they'd bought it large so he could grow into it). Moving from the security of the tiny village primary school to the regional secondary school had been a difficult transition for him, unlike his outgoing older sister. Nick begged his parents not to make him go to school most mornings.

Sarah's heart broke when she sent him off to catch the bus, even though she knew it was the right thing to do.

'You're only ever as happy as your unhappiest child,' her older sister, Meg, who had three kids of her own, had once told Sarah. Truer words had never been spoken.

'Nick is highly sensitive,' explained Sarah. 'He finds it hard to cope in an overly stimulating environment, especially if it's new. Noisy situations, crowded spaces, strong smells, bright lights – they can all trigger him.'

'I see,' murmured Mr Wu. 'I wasn't aware that Nick was on the special educational needs register.'

'He's not,' said Sarah. 'But his primary school made accommodations for him.'

She'd had to fight tooth and nail to get the school to do that, as Nick didn't have a medical condition. Luckily, Mr Wu seemed much more cooperative.

'What would help Nick?' asked the teacher.

'Is there somewhere quiet he could go if he's feeling overwhelmed and needs a break?'

'The library is usually quiet,' suggested Mr Wu. 'I'll have a word with Nick and his other teachers, and see what we can arrange.'

'Thank you,' said Sarah.

No sooner had she ended the call, she received another one.

'Hi, Mum,' Sarah answered, trying – but failing – to keep the worry out of her voice.

'What's wrong?' asked Geraldine with a mother's sixth sense.

'It's Nick,' replied Sarah. 'The school just called. They're concerned because he's having trouble settling in.'

'Children are so mollycoddled these days.' Geraldine tutted. 'Benign neglect is good for children. You and your sister turned out just fine.'

'These days, it's frowned upon to let your kids raise themselves,' said Sarah tartly.

Sarah and Meg were textbook 1980s latchkey kids, as their ambitious parents were busy furthering their academic careers. Ironically, for someone with such a hands-off approach to parenting, Geraldine's main field of research had been community and families. When she'd had children of her own, Sarah had made a conscious decision to put them first, always. But her mum had disapproved of the fact that Sarah had given up her television career.

'When I was still working, I would sometimes get the parents of university students phoning to query their child's mark, or asking me to grant them an extension on an essay. Ridiculous!' Her mum sighed deeply down the phone. 'But I miss it so much. Teaching, being around interesting young people, being relevant.'

Geraldine had recently retired from Bristol University and moved into a community for seniors on the outskirts of Plumdale. Sarah's mother had always been fiercely independent, but after developing health complications due to long Covid, it just wasn't possible for her to live on her own. Moving in with Sarah wasn't an option – there was barely enough space in the cottage for the four of them. And Meg, who'd lived in Edinburgh since university, had her hands full with her own family and thriving dental clinic. So Sarah had found Valley Vistas, a gorgeous complex with modern flats and beautiful gardens, within walking distance of the village centre. Geraldine had strenuously resisted moving there, even when they'd tried to persuade her that she'd see loads more of them. In the end, she'd had a fall and that was what had sealed the deal – she needed to live somewhere with a lift.

It was so unlike Geraldine – who had marched for women's rights and reclaimed her life after a bitter divorce

– to sound defeated. 'Of course you're still relevant,' Sarah reassured her.

'I'm just so lonely,' said Geraldine, her voice cracking with emotion. 'I don't know what to do with myself all day.'

'Why don't you get to know some of the other residents at Valley Vistas?' suggested Sarah. 'There are lots of activities you can get involved with.' It wasn't the first time she'd made the suggestions, and she could predict what her mother was going to say next. They'd had a similar conversation nearly every day since her mother had moved in.

'I don't want to hang around with boring old people,' moaned Geraldine. 'All they do is talk about their medical conditions.'

Sarah stifled a frustrated sigh. 'Well, how about you come over to dinner tomorrow night?'

'That would be lovely.' The speed with which she accepted the invitation and rang off made Sarah suspect it had been her mother's main reason for phoning.

I should have Mum over more often, she thought guiltily, even though her mother joined them for dinner at least twice a week.

She jotted down a reminder to pick up something from the butcher's for dinner tomorrow, and to tidy the house. Then she slid the rubber band off a rolled-up film poster. She stretched the elastic between her thumb and her forefinger, pulling it taut. That's how she felt these days – like a rubber band, about to snap. Between the cinema and home, her mum and the kids, she was stretched to breaking point. From remembering birthdays, making doctor's appointments and finding missing socks, to filling out school forms, ironing uniforms and keeping the fridge filled, everything to do with running the family seemed to land on Sarah's plate. She worked less hours at the cinema than James did, but the emotional labour of running the family was never-ending.

Suddenly, Sarah felt a wave of anxiety engulf her like a riptide. Intense heat crept up her torso, rising to her face. In seconds, her arms and chest were drenched in sweat.

Here we go again . . .

Grabbing the poster, she hurried outside. The cold air felt blissful as it blasted her overheated body. She closed her eyes, took a few deep breaths and waited for her internal thermometer to stop thinking she was in a sauna. Sarah rested her damp forehead against the glass door.

Opening her eyes again, she saw her reflection in the glass – a tall woman in jeans, a striped sweater and white trainers. Her brown hair was in a messy bun, there were bags under her eyes and a groove between her eyebrows even when she wasn't frowning. Her sister's dental practice offered Botox, and Meg had encouraged her to try it, but Sarah had so far resisted.

Maybe I should, she thought, smoothing the groove with her finger. *I look so old.*

Turning away from her reflection, she unfurled the poster and hung it in a glass case outside the cinema. As she did so, a name jumped out at her. The screenwriter was Jack Greenstreet, someone she'd worked with at the BBC.

Sarah stared at the poster, amazed that her former colleague had penned a blockbuster starring Eddie Redmayne.

Good for him, thought Sarah, trying not to feel envious.

How long had it been since she'd done any writing herself? Years and years. Could she even legitimately call herself a writer any more?

When they'd quit their jobs in London to buy the cinema, the plan had been to hire a full-time manager so

Sarah would be able to finish her screenplay. But somehow that had never happened. Then the kids had arrived, and in between running the cinema and raising a young family, there was never any time to write. The kids weren't little any more, but there *still* wasn't any time to write. Not now that she had her mum to look after as well.

Sarah didn't regret the time she'd devoted to her family; her kids were her most important – and rewarding – creation. But a tiny part of her wondered if it could have been her name on a movie poster, if only she had kept at it. If only she had *made* the time to write.

Sarah shook her head. There was no point dwelling on the past. She'd ended up working in movies, just not quite in the way she'd imagined.

Shutting the glass case, she turned and saw that volunteers from the Plumdale Beautification Society were busy decorating the market square for Christmas. Not that the village needed much beautification. The perfectly preserved buildings lining the high street were made of golden Cotswold stone and nestled in a picturesque valley of rolling hills. Plumdale had just about everything you could want – two nice pubs at either end of the high street, an organic butcher's, a baker's, and, yes, even a candlestick maker's. Cotswold Candles, a few doors down from the cinema, had recently opened, selling tapers made of locally sourced beeswax and other overpriced knick-knacks. Even the postboxes in the village were well turned out, sporting knitted toppers made by members of the local craft circle. The one outside the cinema was jauntily adorned with knitted snowmen.

'Hiya, Sarah,' called a man in jeans, scuffed work boots and a plaid shirt. He was halfway up a ladder, putting lights on the Christmas tree.

Sarah crossed the road to say hello. 'The market square looks good, Ian.' The volunteers had hung wreaths with red bows on every lamp post. She could still remember what she'd said to James their first Christmas in the village: 'It looks like the set of a Hallmark movie!'

'We can't let Stowford win the Cotswolds Christmas Village title again,' he said, glancing at the cinema pointedly.

Plumdale and its neighbour, Stowford, were perennial rivals for the crown of prettiest village in the Cotswolds. Sarah thought both villages were equally beautiful – not that she'd admit it to Ian, who had lived in Plumdale his entire life and would consider it tantamount to treason.

'We haven't got around to decorating the cinema yet,' Sarah said. 'But we will. I promise.'

Christmas was yet another thing to add to her bottomless to-do list.

Just then, Ian dropped the star he was putting on the top of the tree. Sarah went to pick it up, but Hermione de la Mere – the candle shop's owner – got there first. She had just stepped out of the beauty salon, where her long blonde hair had been blow-dried into a cascade of bouncy waves. Sarah was pretty sure they were both in their late forties, but Hermione, in her tan cashmere poncho, white jeans and Barbour wellies, looked much younger.

Botox, she could hear Meg's voice saying in her head. That, and not having kids.

'Here you are.' Hermione handed the star up to Ian.

'Make a wish,' he teased.

'Pardon?' said Hermione, sounding confused.

'On the star,' replied Ian, placing it on top of the tree. He came down and smiled at Hermione, his elbow resting on one of the ladder's rungs. 'It's good luck to wish upon a star.'

'Do you two know each other?' asked Sarah.

They both shook their heads.

'Ian, this is Hermione, owner of Cotswold Candles.'

'Oh, dear!' Ian shook his finger in playful admonishment. 'Your shop's not decorated for Christmas either.'

'Ian owns the antique shop and is the president of the Plumdale Beautification Society.' Sarah lowered her voice to a stage whisper. 'He takes his responsibilities *very* seriously.'

'I'm afraid I'm just not feeling very Christmassy this year,' said Hermione. 'It's my first since getting divorced. I'm dreading being alone.'

Although Hermione had lived in the village nearly as long as Sarah, they'd always mixed with different crowds. Hermione had been married to a wealthy banker – a stalwart of the local polo set. According to village gossip, he'd left Hermione for one of the grooms at the stable. In the aftermath, they'd sold their house and Hermione had opened her shop, moving into the flat above it.

'Maybe the Twelve Films of Christmas will help you find your festive spirit,' said Ian.

'Oh, yes! Good idea. What movies are you showing this year?' asked Hermione.

'If I told you, it wouldn't be a surprise,' said Sarah, smiling mysteriously.

Over the month of December, the Picture Palace screened a festival of surprise Christmas films. It was like a cinematic advent calendar – the audience didn't know what they were going to see until the movie started. But with only two weeks to go until December, Sarah and James still hadn't picked the twelve movies – they hadn't even had a moment to discuss it.

'It's such a lovely tradition,' said Hermione.

Tickets for the Christmas films were free, with an optional donation to a different charity at every screening. For some local families, it was the only time they could afford to go to the cinema. The Christmas film festival was Sarah and her husband's way of giving back to the community that had embraced them so warmly from the cinema's very beginning.

Ian climbed down the ladder. 'I've got some spare wreaths.' He pointed at a pile of greenery. 'Shall I hang one on your shop's door?'

'That's very kind of you,' said Hermione.

As Ian and Hermione headed to the candle shop, Sarah went back inside the cinema and searched for James. She finally tracked her husband down in the projection room at the top of the cinema. The small, stuffy room housed both the projector and the sound system – a tall column of amps that controlled the speakers and their output.

James was fiddling with the controls on the projector, surrounded by bowls of ice.

'What on earth are you doing?' she asked him over the noise of the projector's fan.

James barely glanced up. 'The extraction fan is over-heating. I'm hoping the ice cools it down.'

Great, thought Sarah. Now their most expensive piece of equipment was on the fritz. Yet another thing to worry about.

'Don't worry – I'm dealing with it,' said James, tinkering with the equipment.

'Ian reminded us about decorating the cinema for Christmas,' said Sarah.

'I know, I know,' replied James distractedly.

'And the school rang.'

James looked up. 'What's wrong now?'

She filled him in on her conversation with Mr Wu.

James frowned, running his hand through his hair. 'Let's not panic. It's early days. And it sounds like the school is being supportive.'

'It's been nearly a term.' Sarah's eyebrows knitted together with worry. 'I hate that Nick doesn't have any friends.'

'We can't always be fighting Nick's battles for him,' said James. 'And I'm not sure hiding out in the library is going to help him make friends.'

'Well, what else was I supposed to do?' demanded Sarah, her temper flaring. James sounded like her mother. 'Nothing?'

'It took him a while to settle into primary school as well. He'll make friends in his own time,' countered James. 'We don't have to blow this out of proportion.'

He turned his attention back to the projector, and anger coiled inside Sarah.

It infuriated her that James was being so relaxed about this. Why did she have to always worry about everything for the both of them? Feeling herself starting to sweat again, she looked at the ice longingly.

'If it had been up to you, we'd never have had Nick assessed in the first place.' She glared at her husband accusingly. 'I guess that was blowing it out of proportion too?'

James held up his hand. 'Hey – that's not fair.'

'You're right,' she replied, shaking her head. 'I'm sorry. I'm just in a bad mood.' She felt ashamed that she'd raked up an old disagreement. James had resisted getting Nick for neurodiversity but had agreed when he'd realised how important it had been to her.

'We're on the same side, hon,' said James. 'We both want what's best for Nick.'

'I know,' said Sarah.

'I expect you're just tired.' James pushed his floppy hair out of his face, a gesture Sarah had once found beyond endearing. It was mostly grey now, and there were crow's feet around his blue eyes, but there was still a boyish air about her husband.

Men have it easy, thought Sarah. She was fairly certain her husband had never contemplated dying his hair or getting Botox on his wrinkles.

'You haven't been sleeping very well, have you?'

Sarah shook her head wearily. She kept waking up in the middle of the night, pyjamas and sheets soaked through with sweat. The washing machine had never worked harder. Once she was awake, she couldn't fall back asleep, as worries about the kids, and her mum, and the cinema spiralled through her head.

'You don't think it could be—'

'No,' said Sarah, cutting him off. 'I'm fine. Just tired. And stressed because of, well . . . everything.'

Everyone felt anxious sometimes. That was normal. At least, that's what she kept telling herself.

'If you're sure . . .' said James, not sounding convinced.

'We'd better get back downstairs,' said Sarah, not liking where the conversation was heading. She hurried out of the projection room and arrived in the lobby just as the film ended.

Parents streamed out of the auditorium and into the lobby, which was decorated with framed film memorabilia. Sarah gathered up her dustpan and broom, bracing herself for the usual carnage after the Baby and Me screenings – teething biscuit crumbs, lost dummies, tiny socks and discarded teddies. The baby-friendly movies had been her idea – a brainwave when she'd been expecting Holly. She was proud of how popular the screenings had become.

Near the back of the cinema, a mother with a sleek bob was sound asleep. A baby in a sling, with a shock of jet-black hair, dozed against her chest, long lashes resting against his chubby cheeks. They looked so peaceful, it felt cruel to wake her, but there was another movie starting shortly.

Reaching out, Sarah touched the woman's shoulder lightly. She just murmured and nestled deeper into her seat. Sarah smiled – she'd often slept through Baby and Me screenings when her kids had been tiny. The seats were so comfy, it was hard not to nod off in the warm, dark auditorium.

'Hey,' Sarah whispered. 'Time to wake up.'

The woman's eyes opened and she sat up with a start. 'Oh, my goodness,' she said, blinking. 'I was out like a light.'

Sarah smiled. 'It happens a lot. I'm sure some parents come to the cinema hoping their baby will sleep so they can nap too.'

'I really wanted to see the movie,' protested the woman. 'But I'm just so tired. Henry is really colicky in the evenings.' She stroked her baby's downy head.

Sarah nodded sympathetically. 'I've been there.' Nick had been a fussy baby, too. She extended her hand, to help the woman to her feet. 'I'm Sarah, by the way. My husband and I own the cinema. I don't think I've seen you at the Baby and Me screenings before.'

'Iris,' said the woman. She studied Sarah intently. 'It's weird – I feel like we've met before, but I only moved here at the end of the summer.'

Sarah shrugged. 'I guess I just have one of those faces.'

James used to say she was beautiful, but the last time she'd had a haircut he hadn't even noticed. Sometimes Sarah felt invisible. Even when she was standing right in front of her husband, he didn't seem to see her any more.

Iris gathered up her things, including a still-full cup of coffee. 'I didn't even get to drink it — I was out like a light before the trailers even finished.'

'Let me treat you to another one.'

'Oh, you don't need to do that,' said Iris.

'I insist,' said Sarah, as they walked into the lobby. She glanced down at the sleeping baby. 'How old is Henry?'

'Five months.'

James had come downstairs and was manning the concession stand, serving hot drinks to the post-movie crowd.

'I'm taking a quick break,' Sarah told her husband, slipping behind the counter.

He nodded distractedly, while ringing up an order.

Sarah went over to the coffee machine and made lattes for herself and Iris. The machine wheezed asthmatically as it brewed their drinks. Then she carried them over to the café area, where Iris had grabbed a free table. Most of the other tables were filled with parents chatting and feeding their babies.

'So what brought you to Plumdale?' asked Sarah as she sat down opposite Iris.

'My husband,' Iris replied. 'We're from Hong Kong, but he went to boarding school in the Cotswolds. A job came up in the area and he jumped at the opportunity to come back here.'

'The Cotswolds must seem so provincial compared to Hong Kong.' Sarah took a sip of her coffee, savouring the jolt of caffeine.

'We wanted a change from big city life,' explained Iris. 'We thought it would be nice for Henry to grow up in the countryside, with fresh air and plenty of space.'

That was part of the reason she and James had moved to Plumdale too.

'The only thing I insisted on was a village with a cinema,' added Iris. 'I'm a massive film buff and wouldn't want to live anywhere I couldn't go to the movies.'

'Same here,' said Sarah.

'My parents live near an amazing vintage cinema in Kowloon.' Iris sipped her coffee. 'This place reminds me of it a bit.'

'The Lux?' asked Sarah.

'Yes!' said Iris, surprised. 'You know it?'

Sarah smiled and nodded. She and James had visited the cinema on holiday, years ago. 'I bet you miss having your family nearby.'

'Yes,' I haven't met many other local mums yet. It's been a bit lonely admitted Iris.

Henry woke up and started fussing.

'He's hungry,' said Iris. 'Do you mind if I feed him?'

'Of course not,' said Sarah.

Iris took the baby out of his sling and placed him on her breast. His tiny fingers clutched at his mother's jumper as he nursed. When Henry had had his fill, Iris held him over her shoulder to burp him.

'He looks so happy,' said Sarah, as the baby cooed contentedly on his mother's lap. 'You're obviously doing a great job.'

To Sarah's horror, tears began to spill down Iris's cheeks, plopping onto baby Henry's head.

'Oh, no,' said Sarah, handing Iris a napkin. 'I didn't mean to upset you.'

'I don't know why I'm crying,' said Iris, dabbing her eyes. 'That was such a nice thing to say. I just feel like I don't have a clue what I'm doing. I'm so scared I'm doing this wrong.'

Sarah's heart went out to the young woman, so far from home, from her own mother. She patted Iris's arm reassuringly. 'There is no right or wrong way to be a mum – we're all just doing the best we can.'

'It's just so hard,' said Iris, stroking Henry's tufty hair. 'I just worry about him all the time.'

Sarah didn't have the heart to tell her that that would probably never change. She worried about Nick and Holly constantly. 'It's the toughest job in the world.'

'I know I'm lucky to have this time with Henry, but I miss my other job too. The one I did back in Hong Kong.'

'What was that?' Sarah asked.

'I'm an illustrator and graphic designer,' replied Iris. 'I worked in comic books. I really miss the creativity.'

Sarah could understand that. She still missed being creative, too. It had once been such a big part of who she was. She gestured to the café's walls, which were hung with paintings and photographs by local artists, all for sale. 'Let me know if you'd ever like to display your work here. We change the display every month.'

'Thanks. I haven't drawn anything since he was born, but I'm hoping to get back to it.'

'You should,' said Sarah adamantly. 'Make time for it. Don't lose touch with that creative part of yourself.'

Like me . . .

Iris started to put Henry back in the sling. 'I should go home and get dinner started.'

So should I, thought Sarah. She hoped she'd remembered to defrost the sausages she was planning to cook for dinner. A mother's work was never done.

Sarah helped Iris put her coat on. 'I hope I'll see you back here for Baby and Me next week. I can introduce you to some of the other parents who come regularly.'

'That would be wonderful,' said Iris with a grateful smile.

As Sarah walked Iris out, she caught sight of the poster she'd hung up earlier. She hated to admit it, but her former colleague's success had really got under her skin. She couldn't ignore the feeling of resentment and frustration bubbling up inside her – the feeling that she had somehow sold herself short.

Maybe I should dig out my screenplay, she thought. It was in a drawer, somewhere. Then she shook her head. No, who was she kidding. She wasn't a writer any more. That was a whole other lifetime ago, before she was 'Holly's mum' or 'Nick's mum' or 'James's wife'.

When she'd been still just Sarah.

30th June 1999

'What are you still doing working?' said a voice. 'It's officially the weekend.'

Sarah looked up and saw her best friend, Pari Johal, standing by her desk. The BBC drama department was practically empty, the clock on the wall reading 6.10 p.m. She'd been so engrossed in her work she hadn't noticed her colleagues departing for the weekend.

'I'm still not happy with the last scene,' fretted Sarah, chewing on her red pen. She was editing an episode of a popular television series called *The Vicarage Mysteries*, about a vicar in the Cotswolds who solved crimes. The episode concerned a poisoning at a cake sale. 'It just doesn't make sense. How could the killer have known the victim was going to buy the poisoned lemon drizzle cake?'

'It will keep until Monday.' Pari tugged the script out of Sarah's hands. 'We're going out. It's payday and we need to celebrate your promotion.' She perched on the end of Sarah's desk and picked up a box of freshly printed business cards. Taking one out, she read it aloud: 'Sarah Goodwin — Script Editor.'

Sarah loved how her new title sounded. She grinned at her friend. 'Drinks are on me,' she said, shoving the script into her handbag.

A head poked out of one of the offices and a slim young man with dark, slicked-back hair approached them. 'Well, well, well,' he said, leering at Sarah. 'If it isn't my two favourite ladettes.'

Rupert had been in their graduate intake as well and had already been fast-tracked to the commissioning team. It helped that his uncle played golf with the director general. He looked Sarah up and down, taking in her long legs in their sheer black tights and ballet flats. She tugged the hem of her skirt self-consciously.

'Congratulations on your promotion, Sarah,' he said, putting his arm around her. 'I put in a good word for you. I'm heading down to my parents' place this weekend, if you want to get out of the city for a bit. I'm sure a creative girl like yourself could think of a way to thank me—'

'Get lost, Rupert,' said Pari.

'I wasn't talking to you.' He sneered. 'I know you've probably got an arranged marriage lined up. Or, wait a minute, are you a lesbian? You certainly look like one in that outfit.'

Pari was wearing combat trousers, trainers and a cropped T-shirt that showed off her belly-button piercing.

Sarah extricated herself from Rupert's arm. 'Um, thanks, but I've got plans.' She couldn't afford to be rude to him. Not if she wanted to keep her job.

The girls linked arms and headed for the lift. Once the doors had shut, Sarah shuddered. 'Ugh. What a slimeball.

I worked my butt off for that promotion. How dare he make it sound like I only got it because of him.'

'He's a triple threat,' said Pari. 'Sexist, racist *and* homophobic.'

'He'll probably be running this place in a few years,' said Sarah. Their male superiors adored Rupert, whose main talents seemed to be name-dropping and taking credit for other people's ideas.

'Not if we feed him a poisoned lemon drizzle cake,' quipped Pari.

Sarah looked at their reflection in the lift door. She towered over Pari, who had recently got a pixie cut. Pari worried that it made her look like a ten-year-old boy, but Sarah had assured her that it was the height of fashion. They made an unlikely pair, and not just because of the height difference. Wanting to look professional, Sarah had taken her nose ring out, grown out her purple streak and bought herself a suit. But her fearless friend was never less than her authentic self at work – which was probably why she hadn't been promoted yet.

She and Pari had become the very best of friends after arriving at the BBC as graduate trainees. Pari, an aspiring stand-up comedian with a law degree from Cambridge – where she'd performed in Footlights – had started as a joke writer for a chat show. Sarah had been an assistant in the drama department. They'd quickly banded together against the posh public schoolboys who'd comprised most of their fellow trainees. Together, they'd endured wandering hands and inappropriate comments. And they'd had to work twice as hard as their male peers to get noticed for their talents.

'It's just office banter,' said Sarah's mentor, Rosemary, when she'd mentioned Rupert's relentless overtures. 'You don't know how lucky you are – women weren't even allowed to wear trousers back when I started here.'

So Sarah did her best to ignore it. She didn't bother complaining again, just made sure she was never in the lift alone with him.

'Where should we head?' Sarah asked as they left Television Centre.

'Let's go to Pharmacy,' suggested Pari.

It was such a nice evening that they walked from the BBC's headquarters in White City to Notting Hill Gate. Smokers and drinkers clustered around tables on the pavement outside pubs festooned with hanging baskets, as tourists flocked towards Portobello Road.

'This area has been so busy ever since that Julia Roberts movie came out,' complained Pari. She had grown up in nearby Shepherd's Bush, before that corner of west London had been gentrified.

Sarah, the world's biggest romcom fan, had adored *Notting Hill*.

She wished she could live there, in a pretty pastel house. But instead, she and Pari had been sharing a flat in Acton for the past year. It had damp walls, draughty windows and a barking dog next door, but they'd filled it with houseplants, books and colourful tapestries. Sarah loved her bedroom, which had a futon and a desk she'd found in a charity shop. When she was sitting at it, working on her screenplay, she had a beautiful view of Acton Park. The flat was perfectly situated halfway between Sarah's job at Television Centre and James's dad's flat in Ealing. James was still living at home to save up for a deposit on a place of his own.

Sarah liked James's father, Sean. He was a quiet, gentle soul. But he smoked like a chimney, and James's childhood bedroom was only big enough for a single bed, so James usually slept over at her place a few nights a week. As fun as it was to live with Pari, Sarah hoped that James would ask her to move in with him when he eventually bought a flat. They'd been going out together for three and a half years – since her first year of uni – and Sarah was more than ready to take the next step of living together. She loved the thought of making a home with James. Sometimes, when she went shopping, she lingered over the soft furnishings and fantasised about picking out cushions and china together. Not that she would ever admit her daydreams of domestic bliss to Pari, who would probably tease her about betraying her feminist principles.

Sarah and Pari went inside the restaurant, which had a stark white interior decorated to look like a chemist's shop. Acid jazz played softly in the background. They ordered Cosmopolitans, making them feel like characters in *Sex and the City*, which they watched together every Wednesday night over a takeaway.

'Here's to not having to make the tea any more!' said Sarah, clinking glasses with her friend. They had both made more than their fair share of hot drinks over the past two years.

'How are you going to spend your massive pay rise?' asked Pari, sipping her cocktail.

Sarah laughed. Her salary increase had been negligible, but she was proud of the title she'd worked so hard to get. She didn't mind putting in long hours because she absolutely loved her job. She loved crafting stories, helping writers make their work even better. Sarah had a knack for spotting what wasn't working in a script and finding creative solutions to problems. In a weird way, it was similar to what James did – except he looked for bugs in software and found ways to fix them.

'I was thinking of maybe getting a DVD player for the flat,' said Sarah.

'Do you really need one?' asked Pari. 'You and James are always going to the cinema.'

Their dinners arrived, looking like works of art. Pari's spaghetti was moulded in the shape of a haystack, perched on a delicate puddle of tomato sauce. Sarah's pork medallion was surrounded by baby vegetables and colourful dots of sauces arranged artfully on a square white plate. There was a tower of perfectly rectangular chips stacked on the side.

'It's almost too pretty to eat,' said Sarah.

'Then I'll eat it for you,' said Pari, cheekily pulling out a chip from the bottom of the tower and bringing the whole stack tumbling down.

'Hey!' protested Sarah in mock indignation.

'How's *The Ghost Writer* coming along?' asked Pari.

'It's nearly finished,' replied Sarah. 'I'm going to do some work on it this weekend.' In her free time, she was writing a screenplay. The story was about a romance author with writer's block, who fell intensely in love with the ghost of a nineteenth-century duke haunting the house where she was staying. The ghost told her the story of his life, which the author used as inspiration for her novel. But as soon as the book was written, the ghost vanished. She'd shown one of her colleagues − a writer named Jack − some scenes and he'd praised them, saying she had 'a great ear for dialogue'.

'I'd love to read it when it's done,' said Pari.

A buzzing noise came from her handbag. Pari took out her Nokia mobile phone, which James had helped her set up. He wanted Sarah to get a mobile, too, but she really couldn't see the point. What phone call couldn't wait until you got home?

Pari grinned as she put her phone back in her bag. 'That was the Chuckle Hut. Their usual compère has the flu, so I'm going to fill in tonight.' She was trying out new material for a one-woman show about her Punjabi upbringing, which she was planning to take to the Edinburgh Festival. Sarah was in awe of how her friend put hecklers in their place and kept going without missing a beat even when people called out the most awful abuse. It was even harder to be a woman on the comedy circuit than it was at the BBC.

'Do you have time for dessert?' asked Sarah.

'Always.'

They shared a decadent chocolate pudding with a molten middle.

'Want me to comp you a ticket for the show tonight?' asked Pari.

'I can't – I'm meeting James in town,' said Sarah. 'We're going to see *An Affair to Remember*. Can you believe he's never seen it before?'

'Um, yeah – because I've never seen it either,' remarked Pari.

Sarah gasped in mock horror. 'It's about a couple who fall in love on a cruise liner,' she explained. 'They're both in relationships, so they agree to meet at the top of the Empire State Building in six months' time.'

'So what happens? Do they get together or not?'

'On the way to meet him, she gets hit by a car and ends up disabled. Not wanting to burden him, she never gets in touch. But he comes to her apartment on Christmas Eve anyway and figures out what happened.' Sarah sighed deeply. 'Not even tragedy can get in the way of their being together because they're soulmates.'

Pari spooned up the last of the chocolate sauce. 'I'm not sure I believe in soulmates.'

'You just haven't met yours yet,' countered Sarah. 'Maybe tonight will be the night.'

'I don't think I'm going to find him at the Chuckle Hut,' said Pari drily. The men Pari met at comedy clubs tended to have questionable personal hygiene and, after a few dates, became threatened by the fact that she was much funnier than they were.

'I didn't expect to find my soulmate at the cinema,' said Sarah. 'So you never know.'

Some people thought it was strange that she had been with the same guy for so long, but the jerks Pari dated and the sleazeballs at work like Rupert made her realise how lucky she was to have found James, her soulmate. He was smart, funny and handsome – and most of all *kind*.

Pari wiped her mouth with her napkin. 'Don't get me wrong, I'd love to have what you have. And goodness knows my mum would love me to get married to a nice guy like James – well, a Punjabi version of him. But if it doesn't happen, I'm OK with that too. I'm happy being single.'

After settling the bill and wishing Pari luck for her gig, Sarah walked to the Tube station. The Underground was stuffy in the summer heat, so she was sweating by the time she arrived at the British Film Institute.

James was waiting for her inside the lobby. 'Hello, beautiful,' he said when he spotted her. 'I got the tickets already.'

'Sorry I'm late,' she said, panting. She went up on her tiptoes to kiss him. 'Did you come straight from work?'

James nodded. He had been working lots of overtime as well. Everyone in the software industry was worried about the Y2K bug. James and his colleagues at the computer engineering consultancy where he worked were racing against the clock as the new millennium approached. They were pre-emptively working to rectify old software programmes that wouldn't be able to cope when 1999 turned to 2000.

'Is the world still grinding to a halt in six months?' Sarah asked him.

Scaremongering newspapers had been predicting disaster. James's dad had already stocked up on canned food and toilet paper, to be on the safe side.

'Not if I can help it,' replied James.

'My hero,' said Sarah, kissing him again, this time more deeply.

'You're tipsy.' His blue eyes regarded her with amusement.

'A bit,' admitted Sarah. Mostly she was just happy. Life was good. She had a job she loved, lived in the coolest city in the world and had a boyfriend she adored.

They took their seats just as the movie began. The air-conditioned cinema felt wonderfully cool, as the movie swept Sarah back to the Golden Age of Hollywood. As usual, the ending had her in tears. James took a handkerchief out of his pocket and silently passed it over to her. That was another thing she loved about him – his thoughtfulness. James knew her well enough to know that she would cry at the movie, so he'd come prepared.

'It's so romantic.' Sarah rubbed her eyes on the hankie, leaving streaks of mascara on the white cotton.

When she'd managed to compose herself, they stepped outside into the balmy night.

'Let's take a walk,' she said, not wanting to face the heat of the Underground. As they strolled down the embankment, hand in hand, Sarah hummed the theme song from the movie.

Not far from the cinema, the Millennium Wheel was under construction – a gigantic observation wheel to mark the new millennium.

'Hard to believe it will be done by New Year's Eve,' Sarah said.

'A mate of mine from Imperial is working on the engineering team. It's going to be cantilevered. There's an A-frame to support the wheel, with supporting cables and a spindle to counterbalance the hub.'

'It's so sexy when you talk science at me,' teased Sarah.

James grinned. 'I'll get us tickets when it opens.'

In just six months' time, it would be the twenty-first century. Well, assuming the world didn't come to an end on New Year's Eve.

Letting go of James's hand, Sarah went over to the railing and looked across the sparkling river at the Houses of Parliament. The twenty-first century – it sounded like something out of a science-fiction movie. She wondered what the future held. Would they all be driving around in flying cars? Would people be living on the moon? Would robots do all their chores?

She looked down the river, at the skyscrapers that had recently cropped up in Canary Wharf. A bit further along the South Bank, a new modern-art museum was scheduled to open in an old power station. On the brink of the new century, London buzzed with energy and creativity.

'I can't imagine wanting to live anywhere else, can you?' asked Sarah, gazing at the city's twinkling lights.

When James didn't reply, Sarah turned to him.

To her surprise, he was down on one knee. Taking the cinema ticket stub out of his pocket, he curled it around Sarah's finger like a ring. 'Sarah Goodwin, will you marry me?' he asked her.

In stunned silence, Sarah looked down at her finger.

Words tumbled out of James in a rush. 'Maybe you think we're too young, but I don't see the point in waiting.

That movie just goes to show – anything can happen in six months. But I'm not going to change my mind about you in six months, six years or even six decades, if we're lucky enough to live that long.' Suddenly looking worried, James stood up. 'I know that you weren't expecting this. I understand if you need to think about it—'

'Yes,' she said, throwing her arms around him. 'Of course I'll marry you.'

James hugged her tightly. 'I love you, Sarah.'

'I love you too,' she whispered in his ear.

'I have an actual ring for you,' he said. 'I was going to wait until Christmas to propose, but that movie really got to me. I just didn't want to wait a second longer to tell you that I want to spend the rest of my life with you.'

Their lips came together and Sarah knew without a doubt that whatever the twenty-first century held, James would be by her side, driving along in their flying car or taking a holiday on the moon. Or even just watching movies together until they got old.

James was her person and she was his. Always and forever.

Chapter 2

Present Day

'Help yourself to tea and biscuits in the café,' said James, holding the cinema door open for the pensioners slowly making their way out of the auditorium. The cinema's discounted Thursday afternoon Golden Oldies screenings were always well attended. This week's film had been the Fellini masterpiece, *La Dolce Vita*.

'Are you sure about that?' Sarah had asked him when he'd told her what he was showing. 'It's a pretty racy film – we don't want anyone having a heart attack.'

James had chuckled. 'This lot lived through the swinging sixties; I think they can handle it. Besides, we have a defibrillator in the lobby.'

When everyone was out of the auditorium, James fetched his toolbox and made his way to the café. After the Golden Oldies screenings, he ran a weekly repair shop. People could bring along anything they needed mending, and James did his best to fix it.

Three elderly woman made a beeline for the free biscuits that James had set out.

A woman with a grey bob rubbed her hands together in delight. 'Ooh, goodie, there are chocolate digestives this week.' Olwyn Powell was a former primary school teacher from the neighbouring village.

'Oh, I shouldn't,' said Pam Cusack, a short, plump woman with white hair. She was pushing a walker and wearing a sweatshirt that said *I'd Rather Be Reading*. Now retired, she had been Plumdale's librarian for decades. 'The doctor says I need to get my blood sugar down.' She watched as her friend helped herself to a biscuit. 'But maybe just one won't hurt . . .'

Olwyn munched her chocolate biscuit. 'Your paintings look great, Vi.'

Vivian Georgitis – Vi for short – was a petite woman with a hot-pink pixie cut. From a distance, in her skinny jeans and trainers, she looked like a teenager. Only her deeply lined face, from summers sunbathing in her husband's native Greece, made it evident that she was well into her eighties. Vi's boldly coloured abstract paintings were currently on display in the café this month. 'Thanks. I hope I sell a few. That will pay for the grandkids' Christmas presents,' said Vi.

A spry little man in his seventies came over to James. He had a tonsure of white hair and a moustache that called to mind an emperor tamarin. His shoes were perfectly polished and he wore a waistcoat and bow tie. The only incongruous aspect of his dapper appearance was the tape wrapped around the arm of his spectacles.

'Shall I mend your glasses for you, Roger?' James offered.

'Oh, that would be splendid, dear boy,' said Roger, handing them over. 'I'd do it myself, except I'm blind as a bat without them.'

James put on his own reading glasses first, then got to work replacing the tiny screw. 'Did you enjoy the film?'

'Oh, yes. I remember the first time I saw it,' replied Roger. 'I was so smitten with Marcello Mastroianni that I booked a holiday to Rome in hopes that I'd meet him – or at least someone who looked like him.'

Pam giggled. 'And did you?'

'No, but I hung around Cinecittà Studios and had a fling with a rather gorgeous gaffer named Antonio,' said Roger, winking at his friends. 'I didn't speak a word of Italian and he didn't speak any English, but after a bottle or two of Chianti we understood each other perfectly.'

Vi gave a throaty laugh. 'Wine – the international language of love!'

Tittering, the three ladies went to sit down at a table.

'Now, James, I thought you should know that the picture was ever so slightly off-kilter,' Roger confided.

'Oh, dear, I'll have to adjust the aspect ratio on the projector,' said James. 'Thanks for letting me know.'

Roger had been the cinema's first employee. He had been the head projectionist at a cinema in London's Leicester Square, but had followed his partner to the Cotswolds when Omar had taken a job teaching maths at the local secondary school. Roger had taught James how to operate the projector, which they'd nicknamed Groucho Marx, when the cinema had first opened. James understood the science behind movies, but the way the projector transformed a series of still images into moving pictures had always seemed to him a type of magic. Roger had taught him how to change reels of film smoothly, so the optical illusion wasn't spoiled mid-film.

Roger had retired when the cinema had switched to a digital projection system.

Now theatre management software programmed everything to run automatically – from when the projector lamp turned on to when the trailers played. But Roger still came to the Picture Palace regularly, to make sure that his high standards were being maintained.

'I didn't see you here last week,' said James. 'I showed *Citizen Kane*.'

44

'I was visiting my nephew in Oxford. We went to see the new Wes Anderson film at the local multiplex.' Roger shook his head disparagingly. 'It made my blood boil − £12.50 for a ticket and they can't even be bothered to mask the screen.'

James winced. It was a pet peeve they shared, a sign that a cinema didn't care at all about the audience's viewing experience.

'Must have been nice to see Jonny, though,' said James.

Roger nodded. 'Yes, it was. I get lonely, you know.' His eyes filled with tears and he dabbed at them with a paisley-printed handkerchief from the pocket of his waistcoat.

Omar had passed away two years ago and Roger was still grieving the loss of his soulmate. James didn't know how he'd cope if he lost Sarah. He'd known she was The One from the very first time they met. They had always been a team, throughout their long and happy marriage.

Or at least, he *thought* it was a happy marriage.

Their disagreement from the day before popped into his head as he cleaned the lenses of Roger's glasses.

Every couple argues sometimes, he told himself. It's normal.

And yet, he couldn't help feeling worried. Sarah had seemed so angry and he wasn't sure why.

James handed Roger back his glasses, now repaired. 'You know you're always welcome here, Roger,' he said. 'Pop in for a cup of tea any time.'

Roger wandered off to get a biscuit.

'James, dear,' said one of the cinema's patrons. 'Would you mind taking a look at one of my wheels − it's a bit sticky.'

'No problem,' replied James amiably. 'Probably just needs a bit of WD40.' He got satisfaction from fixing things and the people he helped were always very grateful.

He got the walker running smoothly, changed the batteries in someone's hearing aid, then showed Pam how to use her new smartphone.

'Oh, how wonderful,' enthused Pam, as he explained how to use the camera and video functions.

'You can also set alarms to remind you when to take medicines,' said James, talking Pam through the clock features.

'You youngsters are so good with technology,' said Olwyn admiringly.

James chuckled. He certainly didn't feel like a youngster. He had turned fifty on his last birthday. He was now the age his mother had been when she'd passed away suddenly from a stroke. His father had died quite young as well. James had been all too aware of his own mortality after his milestone birthday. He'd stopped eating biscuits and started taking long bike rides to get his heart pumping. Every morning, his legs pedalled as fast as they could down country lanes, feeling like he was racing against Death. He could practically feel the Grim Reaper, in a yellow jersey, spandex cycling shorts and helmet, breathing down his neck.

When he had finished all his repairs, James went to put his toolbox away. The weekly repair shop was just one of the ways in which the Picture Palace was so much more than just a place to watch films. It was a community space, for everyone from little kids to their elderly grandparents.

Owning his own cinema had always been James's dream. But it was getting tougher and tougher to keep that dream alive. People had stopped going to the cinema during the Covid lockdowns, and ticket sales still hadn't returned to pre-pandemic levels. Perhaps they never would. Streaming services meant that people didn't need to leave their living rooms to watch the latest releases. With sky-rocketing energy prices and cost of living at an all time high, it had never been a more challenging time to own a cinema. Even the nationwide cinema chains were closing branches and going out of business. So what hope did a tiny independent with only one screen have?

But Plumdale *needed* a cinema. It was the beating heart of the village. No matter how hard it was, James knew he couldn't let his community down. People like Pam and Roger were counting on him. So he was determined to keep the cinema going, even though these days it felt like a Herculean task.

When he came back out to the lobby, he found Sarah and her mum.

'Sorry I missed the Golden Oldies,' said Sarah. 'But I've brought my own.'

'Hilarious,' said her mother, rolling her eyes.

James's mother-in-law had long, snow-white hair. Tall and slim like her daughter, she was wearing a woven tunic and a beaded necklace. Her sharp eyes peered at James through glasses with bright red frames.

'Did you know that some Native American tribes practised senicide?' Geraldine asked him, in lieu of a greeting.

'Senicide?' asked James, indulging her. His mother-in-law was never happier than when she was giving a lecture.

'Killing the elderly when resources were scarce,' explained Geraldine.

'Things aren't so bad that we need to feed you to the wolves, Geraldine,' replied James. 'Sarah's bought lamb chops for dinner.'

'Now, in Ecuador, the Huaorani people believe that elderly people are shamans with magical powers,' continued Geraldine, ignoring his teasing.

'In that case, maybe you can magic us up a new sound system,' joked James. 'Ours is on the blink.'

'Throw in a new projector too, while you're at it,' added Sarah.

'If I had magic powers, I'd conjure myself young again,' said Geraldine. 'So I wouldn't be stuck in the middle of nowhere, bored out of my mind.'

'Oh, Mum,' said Sarah sadly, a groove appearing in her forehead as she frowned.

James thought that if he had magic powers, he'd use them to make his wife's worries disappear.

He glanced over at Pam, Vi, Roger and Olwyn, chatting over hot drinks in the café area. Maybe he didn't need magic powers . . .

'A few of our regulars live at Valley Vistas,' said James. 'They're very nice.'

'Nice,' said Geraldine, rolling her eyes.

'Come and meet some of them now,' he said, taking his mother-in-law's arm and steering her over to the others before she could object.

'What a fab-u-lous necklace,' exclaimed Roger as they approached. 'Is it from Morocco?'

'Why, yes, it is,' said Geraldine, looking pleased. 'You have a good eye.'

'That's where my late husband was from,' explained Roger.

'I was a visiting professor at the University of Rabat for a semester,' said Geraldine.

'Everyone, this is Sarah's mum,' announced James. 'Geraldine recently moved to Valley Vistas.'

'We're neighbours!' exclaimed Vi. 'Pam and I live there too.'

'How are you finding village life, Geraldine?' asked Roger.

'A bit dull, I'm afraid,' said Geraldine stiffly.

'Oh, there's plenty of fun to be had, you just have to make your own.' Pam pulled a silver hip flask out of her handbag and held it up, her eyes twinkling.

'You should join us for Golden Oldies next week,' said Olwyn. 'James is showing *The Godfather*.'

'Perhaps I will,' replied Geraldine. 'I've always had a soft spot for Al Pacino.'

'Who doesn't,' said Roger and everyone laughed.

James went over to the concession stand to check on the stock levels. The boy working behind the counter had curly hair and wore a T-shirt that said *Sal's Famous Pizzeria* on it.

James pointed at his shirt. '*Do The Right Thing*?'

'Yeah,' said Aaron. 'I've been watching a lot of old Spike Lee movies lately.'

James nodded approvingly.

Aaron, who was in the final year of sixth form, worked at the cinema weekends and after school. An avid cinephile, he wanted to direct movies one day. He was a good kid and a hard worker.

James went into the stockroom to get more popcorn boxes. As he was coming out, Holly ran into the cinema, her school backpack slung over her shoulder. Her uniform skirt was rolled up to show off her long legs. Every morning Sarah reminded her that it was against school uniform rules, and every morning Holly retorted that the rules were sexist. Multiple lunchtime detentions were the price their feisty daughter had paid for her principles.

James caught Aaron staring at Holly. James still thought of his daughter as his little girl, but over the past year she had blossomed into a beautiful young woman. Embarrassed, Aaron quickly averted his gaze and started vigorously polishing the counter.

'I've got huge news!' announced Holly dramatically. She slid her backpack off her shoulder and dropped it on the floor. Her cheeks were flushed from the cold outside and her blue eyes flashed with excitement.

'Taylor Swift is doing a gig in Plumdale?' teased James.

'No,' said Holly. 'It's even more exciting than that. Noa Drakos is making a movie right here in Plumdale!'

James and Sarah exchanged surprised looks. Now that *was* big news.

'Who on earth is that?' asked Geraldine.

'He's a famous director, Grandma,' explained Holly.

'A very *handsome* famous director,' added Roger.

'You know the one, Mum,' prompted Sarah. 'He won an Oscar for *ANZAC*, about the two soldiers who fall in love while fighting in the Battle of Gallipoli?'

'Oh, yes,' said Geraldine. 'I didn't care for the battle scenes – too gory for me.'

'It's a masterpiece,' said Roger. 'He used thousands of extras to recreate those battles.'

'It's a great film,' agreed James. He'd followed the Australian film-maker's career with interest, ever since seeing his debut, a low-budget indie inspired by his mixed Greek and Polynesian heritage.

'He hasn't made anything recently, has he?' asked Roger.

'No,' replied James. 'His last few movies haven't done as well.'

Holly bit her lip. 'Speaking of extras . . . They're doing an open casting for small parts next week. Can I go?'

'When is it?' asked Sarah.

Holly tugged at her skirt nervously, avoiding her parents' eyes. 'Well, that's the thing . . . It's on Tuesday morning, so I'd have to miss school – and then a few more days for the shoot if I get chosen.'

James and Sarah exchanged concerned looks. They both knew that Holly couldn't afford to miss any more lessons. Not if she wanted to pass maths and science.

'I don't think that's a good idea,' said James. 'This is your GCSE year.'

Sarah nodded. 'You've got mocks after Christmas. You can't miss school unless it's something important.'

'This *is* important,' insisted Holly. 'It could be my big break. Mocks aren't real exams – the clue's in the name. Besides, why do I even need to study subjects like chemistry and maths? I know I want to act.'

James's daughter had always loved performing – ever since a scene-stealing turn as a sheep in her nursery nativity. When she'd realised her bleating had made the audience laugh, she'd milked it for all it was worth.

'Yes, but even actors need to get their GCSEs,' said Sarah. 'It's a tough profession, so it's good to have qualifications to fall back on.'

'Oh, wow, thanks,' said Holly sarcastically. 'So you're saying you don't think I'm good enough?'

'That's not what I meant—'

'Yes, it is!' exploded Holly. 'That's literally what you mean.'

'Holly, calm down,' said James, trying to keep the peace.

'Don't tell me what to do! I'm nearly sixteen!' shouted Holly. 'I'm practically an adult. I should be able to make my own decisions!'

'I'm sorry,' said Sarah. 'But the answer is still no.'

'I hate you!' Holly glowered at her mother. 'Just because you regret giving up on your dream doesn't mean I'm going to give up on mine!' Picking up her backpack, she stormed out of the lobby.

Sarah looked stricken, as if Holly had slapped her in the face.

'She didn't mean that,' said James. He went to give Sarah a hug, but she shrugged him away.

'She's right,' she said.

'What?'

'Holly has no respect for me because I stopped writing. I gave up on my career.' Sarah choked the words out.

Geraldine raised her eyebrow and James knew she was struggling to bite her tongue. His mother-in-law had objected when Sarah had quit her job at the BBC.

'Don't be daft. Of course she respects you. It's just normal teenaged stuff,' he appeased. 'It's a stage all adolescents go through.'

'Well, actually, Margaret Mead's study, *Coming of Age in Samoa,* showed that adolescence in the South Pacific wasn't marked by conflict and rebellion,' remarked Geraldine.

'Not helpful, Geraldine,' said James. Sarah had told him all about the clashes she'd had with her mother when she'd been a rebellious teenager. He put his hands on his wife's shoulders. 'I'll speak with Holly. Get her to apologise.'

'A forced apology is meaningless,' said Sarah miserably. She looked as if she was going to cry. James wanted to comfort her, but wasn't sure how. 'Will you be home for dinner?' she asked him.

'I wish I could be,' said James. 'But I need to stay here until closing.'

'*Quelle surprise*,' muttered Sarah. 'I'll deal with Holly on my own. As usual.'

Taking her mother's arm, she headed for the door.

'Sarah!' James called after her. 'Wait!'

But she didn't turn around.

He wanted to join them for dinner. Of course he did! But it just wasn't possible. They'd had to cut back on staff costs, but there always needed to be at least two people on duty for health-and-safety reasons. James couldn't afford to take on a night manager, so most nights it fell to him to work late. What else could he do? Didn't Sarah understand that he was just barely keeping the place afloat? That he was trying to provide for his family?

They'd had several full-time employees when they'd first opened the cinema, but now they could only afford part-time staff like Aaron. So James wasn't just the cinema's general manager, he also sold tickets, made coffees, restocked toilet paper in the bathroom, scooped popcorn and swept up spilled kernels after the show had finished. He did whatever needed to be done.

And right now, the café area needed tidying. A cleaning company came in every night, but it was up to staff to keep the cinema looking good during the day. So James swept up the biscuit crumbs and collected the empty teacups that the Golden Oldies had left behind.

Once the next movie was underway, James slipped into the auditorium to do a screen check. The picture was still slightly off-kilter and the sound was crackling. He winced.

So far, he had managed to repair the sound system's problems. At some point soon, though, they'd need to install a new system. And those didn't come cheap . . .

He went into the office and checked his emails. The code for a new action-adventure film opening tomorrow was in his inbox. Back when they had first opened the cinema, films would be delivered in heavy metal canisters. Now, all he needed was a code to unlock the content.

There was also a message from the manager of a cinema in Evesham. The Picture Palace and a few other independent cinemas in the Cotswolds had formed a consortium to share resources. They were all struggling, and banding together would hopefully make them stronger. Because of his IT background, James had volunteered to build a website for the group. Though he wasn't exactly sure when he was going to find the time to do it.

The final new message was from the managing director of Valley Vistas. James clicked on it in nervous anticipation, assuming the email was about something his mother-in-law had done. But instead it was an enquiry about whether he would consider selling the cinema to turn it into more retirement flats.

James stared at the message in surprise. They had been approached by interested parties before, but had always turned them down. Nobody was ever bothered about keeping the Picture Palace a cinema.

He quickly typed a response: *Sorry, we're not interested in selling.*

To sell the cinema would be to admit defeat. He and Sarah had put all of their savings – and all of his dad's savings – into this place. He'd persuaded Sarah to leave London and her successful career at the BBC, for the sake of his dream. If he failed now, then what had it all been for? No, he had to keep going, for his family, for the community. He had to press on, even if it felt like he had the weight of the world on his shoulders.

James closed his email. A screensaver photo of the whole family beaming on a sandy beach filled the laptop screen. Nick, only about five, was holding a bucket. Holly was wearing seaweed on her head, as if it was a long mermaid wig, and striking a dramatic pose. Sarah was laughing, her hair blowing in the wind. It had been taken on holiday in France years ago, when they could still afford to take holidays. A holiday that had started badly, but they'd got through it as a team. James studied the picture. When was the last time he'd seen Sarah smile like that, making the gold flecks in her eyes sparkle?

It wasn't just their argument today, or the one yesterday. Things had felt off between them for a while now, like a film where the sound and picture were out of sync. *We just haven't been spending enough time together,* thought James. They were always so busy with the cinema and the kids – and now Geraldine as well. Whenever he'd tried to talk to Sarah about the growing distance between them, she'd claimed she was just tired. It was true that she was sleeping badly. But James knew his wife. There was more to it than that; he was sure of it.

When the film was over, James went up to the projection room and rebooted the system. He tested the output and nodded with satisfaction. That had fixed the problem – for now. James had always been good at fixing things. He just wished he knew how to fix whatever was wrong between him and Sarah.

As he turned the dial on an amp, he glanced at the gold wedding band on his left hand. He still loved his wife just as much as he had on the day he'd married her. If only there was a way he could reboot their relationship . . .

11th May 2003

'You couldn't have asked for better weather,' said Pari, peering out of the mullioned window of Merricourt Manor.

Still in her dressing gown, Sarah joined her friend on the window seat of the bridal suite and looked out onto the landscaped grounds, where azaleas and rhododendrons were in full bloom, in vibrant shades from vivid violet to a pale pink – the same hue as Pari's bridesmaid dress. Beyond them rolled the gentle green hills of the Cotswolds.

'It's so pretty around here,' said Sarah. She had chosen the venue, a stately home that had been converted into a hotel, after spending a night there while visiting the set of

The Vicarage Mysteries. The nearby village of Plumdale was charming, full of quaint pubs, tea rooms and antique shops. There was even a gorgeous old art deco cinema, although it had shut down years before and was now derelict.

'Yeah, but I can't imagine leaving London,' replied Pari, pouring two glasses of champagne. 'There's not much of a comedy scene around here. Although, on the way here I passed a village called North Piddle, and another called Twatley, so there's plenty of good material.'

Like Sarah, Pari still worked at the Beeb, writing material for people who were more famous, but less funny, than her.

Two years earlier, Sarah and James had bought a flat in up-and-coming Hackney. They'd spent weekends renovating it – or rather James had, with his dad's help. Sarah loved the flat, which they'd decorated with vintage movie posters. She'd tamed the small garden at the back and filled it with pots of flowers. Lately, though, she'd been feeling worn down by her daily commute across London and her long hours at work. Now a senior script editor at the BBC, Sarah was the go-to editor for tricky rewrites and had a reputation for being able to make any story stronger. Sarah was proud to be trusted with the department's most challenging projects, but the pressure was intense.

'You didn't invite Rupert, did you?' asked Pari.

'Ew. Of course not,' said Sarah. Her boss was as odious as ever. Even her engagement ring hadn't deterred him from making unwanted overtures.

'Sorry I'm late,' said Meg, hurrying into the bridal suite. Her pink dress had an empire waist, to accommodate a large baby bump.

Sarah hugged her sister. 'Oh! I just felt her kick!'

'Or him,' said Meg. 'Let's see your dress.'

Sarah took off her dressing gown to reveal an elegant ivory off-the-shoulder gown. A beautician had come earlier in the morning to do her hair and make-up. She'd curled Sarah's long hair and topped it with a tiara.

'Oh, wow!' gushed Meg. She stroked one of Sarah's curls. 'Hey, remember when you dyed that purple streak in your hair.'

'I thought I was soooo cool.' Sarah chuckled. 'I got my nose ring around the same time.'

'Mum was going to make you take it out, until you argued that you'd been inspired by her research on the Berber tribe.'

'Well played.' Pari raised her glass to Sarah.

'I'm hoping Mum and Dad behave today,' said Sarah, touching up her lipstick.

Today would be the first time her parents would see each other since their divorce had been finalised. Their split had been acrimonious, after her father, Charles, had had an affair with one of Geraldine's graduate students. Things had started going downhill after Geraldine had won a prestigious fellowship they'd both wanted. Sarah's father simply could not cope with his wife's academic career eclipsing his. The affair was just the last straw.

'Speak of the devil,' said Meg as Geraldine came into the bridal suite.

Their mum was holding a gift and wearing a green silk dress she'd had made in China. She wore bright pink jewellery and her long white hair was in a chignon, topped by fuchsia fascinator with a spray of feathers jutting from it. The whole effect made her look like a tropical bird.

Geraldine gave both of her daughters a kiss. 'How is the blushing bride? Is this the part where I fill you in on the birds and the bees?'

'It's a bit late for that, Mum,' said Sarah, laughing. At thirteen, when she'd got her first period, her mother had been more interested in telling her about the puberty rituals of various African tribes than in talking about sex education. Fortunately, Sarah had already gleaned everything she needed to know from Judy Bloom books.

Geraldine made a beeline for the champagne and poured herself a glass.

Meg glanced longingly at the champagne. 'I wish I could have some.'

'Well, why don't you?' said Geraldine. 'This is a celebration.'

Meg cradled her belly. 'Um, hello, I'm pregnant?'

'A few glasses won't hurt the baby.' Geraldine took a long swig. 'I had the odd drink when I was pregnant with you.'

'Explains a lot,' quipped Sarah.

Her older sister gave her a playful shove.

'Too bad the baby isn't here already,' said Geraldine. 'We could have an *An Chuang* ceremony. That's what the Chinese do – they put a baby on the marriage bed to ensure a newly-wed couple's fertility. Wedding traditions are so fascinating, aren't they?'

'Look what Pari did for me last night,' said Sarah. She raised the hem of her wedding dress and showed her mother and sister the beautiful henna designs on her bare feet.

'In Sikh culture, henna symbolises good luck and prosperity,' explained Pari. 'The night before the wedding, there's a ceremony where the bride is decorated with henna.'

'Oh, how marvellous,' said Geraldine.

Sarah slipped her feet into white slippers embellished with tiny pearls.

'I wish I'd gone for flats too.' Meg sighed as she flopped down onto the bed. 'My feet are already swelling up.'

'I can't believe you're finally making it down the aisle.' Geraldine adjusted Sarah's tiara. 'You must hold the record for the longest engagement in history.'

'Well, we needed to wait until you were back in the UK,' replied Sarah. Her mother had spent a whole year on sabbatical as part of her fellowship. She'd travelled around Asia researching courtship and marriage.

Their long engagement had also given Sarah and James time to save up for their wedding. Fortunately, the software company James worked for was doing well, and his role and salary had grown along with the company. He and his colleagues were currently preparing to float the company on the stock market.

'Did you know that the Mosuo people in south-western China don't practise any form of marriage at all?' Geraldine downed the rest of her champagne. 'It's a matriarchal society. Women live with their mothers and sisters, and have sexual relationships with multiple men.'

'That actually sounds kind of fun,' said Pari. She had sworn off dating any more of her fellow comedians. Sarah had encouraged her to join one of the new online dating services, but Pari said she wanted to be single for a bit, so she could focus on her comedy.

'Oh, yes,' said Geraldine, refilling her glass. 'Men are *totally irrelevant* in Mosuo society.'

Sarah and her sister exchanged worried looks.

'Mum, please try to be happy for me,' said Sarah nervously. She knew today was going to be hard for her mother.

'I *am* happy for you, darling,' said Geraldine. 'Here – open your present.' She handed Sarah the gift that she'd come in with.

Sarah opened it up and took out a shimmering white scarf, made of the finest silk. It slipped through her fingers like liquid.

'Oooh!' exclaimed Pari and Meg.

'It's a *khata*, from Tibet,' explained Geraldine. 'Couples receive them on their wedding day because it symbolises how they will be wrapped in love and affection.'

Sarah draped the scarf around her shoulders and gave her mother a hug. 'Thanks, Mum. It's gorgeous.'

'I hope you and James will be very happy together,' said Geraldine.

Sarah stroked the soft fabric. James *did* make her feel wrapped in love. Sarah was confident that they would never end up like her parents. They barely ever argued, and, when they did, they never went to bed angry. James was the love of her life; whatever married life held for them, they would face it together.

'Right!' said Pari, draining her glass of champagne. 'Let's get this wedding on the road!'

The ceremony was held in Plumdale Catholic church. Every pew in St Mark's was filled with family and friends from work and university. On James's side, aunts, uncles and cousins from Ireland had travelled over for the wedding.

Sarah's dad was waiting for her on the church porch. His girlfriend, Tiffany, was seated well away from Geraldine. Sarah hadn't wanted to invite her, but her dad had insisted. 'We're a package deal,' he'd announced.

'Ready?' he asked her now.

Sarah nodded. Then she shook her head, suddenly overcome with nerves. 'I'm scared, Dad.'

'Marriage *is* scary,' he said. 'Even though it didn't work out between your mum and me, I'll never regret the years we spent together because we had you and Meg. I'm so proud of you, Pumpkin. I love you very much.'

Sarah looked down at her bouquet and took a deep breath, willing herself not to cry. 'I love you too, Dad.'

'Now, come on – let's go and give the people what they're waiting for.'

Sarah's dad took her arm and walked her down the aisle.

Sarah's heart skipped a beat as she saw James, waiting for her at the altar. He looked so handsome in his morning suit, his unruly hair gelled back for the occasion.

'Hello, beautiful,' he whispered when she reached his side.

Instantly, Sarah's wedding-day jitters dissipated. Being around James, even in front of a whole church of people, felt like being home.

The wedding service flew by in a blur of readings, hymns, incense and confetti. Afterwards, they returned to Merricourt Manor, for a photo shoot among the rhododendrons.

'I'm actually tying the knot myself soon,' Charles said, as she and James posed for a photo flanked by both of her parents. 'I've asked Tiffany to marry me.'

Really, Dad? thought Sarah. *This couldn't have waited?*

She could feel her mother's body stiffen next to her and sensed storm signals, despite the clear blue skies.

'Is that legal? Are you sure she's old enough?' said Geraldine caustically.

Sarah kept a grin plastered on her face for the photographer as James squeezed her hand reassuringly.

Photos over, they went inside the manor's restaurant for the wedding breakfast.

Once the plates had been cleared away, it was time for the speeches. Sarah's dad reminisced about how Sarah used to re-enact the wedding scene from *The Sound of Music*, using a white bed sheet as her veil. 'Marriage is a beautiful, sacred bond.'

'Not to you, it wasn't!' shouted Geraldine. She had been drinking steadily all day and looked worse for wear, her fascinator listing precariously.

'I know James will be a wonderful husband and cherish my darling daughter,' said Charles.

'It won't be hard to be a better husband than *you* were,' heckled Geraldine.

'Mum!' hissed Sarah, feeling her cheeks flush with embarrassment.

'I wish Sarah and James a lifetime of wedded bliss,' continued Charles, glaring at his ex-wife.

'Ha!' snorted Geraldine, standing up and swaying towards the toilets.

Meg got up and waddled after her. Sarah watched them go anxiously.

James's best man, his best friend from uni, gave a speech that compared Sarah and James's relationship to an ionic bond.

'Um, is that supposed to be a compliment?' whispered Sarah.

'Very much so,' answered James, stroking her arm reassuringly. 'He's calling us a pair of electrons who have a strong bond.'

Pari delivered her maid-of-honour speech as if it were the voiceover for a romcom trailer. 'From a chance first meeting at a cinema to a wedding in the Cotswolds, this is the romance of the year, sure to win every award going. When an engineer meets a writer, sparks fly in . . .' Pari paused for dramatic effect, '*Sarah and James – A Love Story*.'

Finally, it was time for the groom's speech. Sarah knew James had been nervous about it, as public speaking wasn't his forte. To Sarah's surprise, a screen was wheeled out.

'Before I met Sarah, I didn't believe in love at first sight,' began James. 'I thought that was something that only happened in the movies. But my wife' – he paused as the guests whooped and cheered – 'taught me that it *can* happen in real life.' He turned to Sarah and smiled, his eyes full of love. 'Sarah is the wordsmith, not me. So I thought I would *show* everyone how she makes me feel.'

James gestured to someone to dim the lights and a video began to play on the screen.

It was a montage of famous kisses from some of their favourite movies, from *Gone with the Wind* to *Breakfast at Tiffany's*. Tears rolled down Sarah's cheeks, smudging her wedding make-up, as it ended with Lady and Tramp's iconic smooch over a plate of spaghetti.

James raised a glass to his new wife. 'Sarah, we met at the movies and I will love you until the final credits roll.'

Everyone applauded and clinked their forks against their glasses. 'Kiss, Kiss!'

Sarah was happy to oblige.

'How was that?' James whispered nervously as they took to the dance floor for their first dance. They had chosen the theme song from the classic French musical *The Umbrellas of Cherbourg*.

'It's my new favourite movie,' said Sarah.

James waltzed Sarah around the dance floor, cheek to cheek. Soon, everyone else was dancing, to a mix of songs they'd chosen from movie soundtracks.

'May I have this dance?' asked James's dad, who looked very smart in his suit.

'Of course.' Sarah took his hand and her newly minted father-in-law twirled her around the dance floor.

'I had no idea you could dance like this, Sean.'

'Mary loved to dance. Back in Dublin when we were courting, we'd often go out dancing,' he reminisced nostalgically.

'I wish I'd got to meet her,' said Sarah. From what James had told her, his mother had been kind, generous and cheerful – all qualities she had passed to her son.

'She would have loved you,' said Sean. 'Because you make James so happy.'

'He makes me happy too.'

When the song finished, Sean took a small box out of the breast pocket of his suit. 'I have a wedding gift for you.'

'Oh, but you already gave us a gift,' said Sarah. He'd given them a framed poster of *Diamonds are Forever,* signed by Sean Connery.

'This one is just for you.'

Sarah opened the box. It was a gold necklace with an emerald pendant.

'It's beautiful,' said Sarah, allowing her father-in-law to fasten it around her neck.

'It was my Mary's – the green of the stone matched her eyes.'

After thanking Sean and giving him a kiss on the cheek, Sarah joined Pari and a group of her girlfriends, who were dancing to 'Night Fever' with exaggerated disco moves. Then Chuck Berry's 'You Never Can Tell' began to play.

Laughing, Pari and Sarah recreated the dance contest between Uma Thurman and John Travolta from *Pulp Fiction* – or at least tried to. Sarah slipped off her flats and did the twist, as Pari held her nose and pretended to swim. Everyone gathered around them in a circle and clapped when they finished.

Sometime during the course of the evening, Meg and her mum had reappeared. Geraldine had thrown herself into the dancing, and was pogoing so energetically to 'I've Had the Time of My Life' that her fascinator had flown off her head. Her mascara was smudged from crying, giving her panda circles under her eyes.

'How are you doing, Mum?' asked Sarah.

'This is a traditional Masai dance,' shouted Geraldine over the music as she bounced up and down. 'Warriors do it at weddings.'

'Maybe you should take a break—'

'Nonsense!' said Geraldine, hopping off. 'I'm having the TIME OF MY LIFE.' She laughed hysterically.

Sarah watched in horror as her mother leapt around the dance floor and crashed into her ex-husband, who was slow-dancing with his fiancée.

'Geraldine, you are embarrassing yourself,' hissed Charles. 'You've had too much to drink.'

'I'M EMBARRASSING MYSELF?' screamed Geraldine. 'YOU'RE THE ONE CARRYING ON WITH SOMEONE YOUNGER THAN YOUR DAUGHTERS!'

'I realise that you're jealous of my happiness,' said Charles. 'But please don't ruin Sarah's special day. Let's try to be civil.'

'Jealous?' Geraldine laughed bitterly. 'What do *I* have to be jealous about? While you've been babysitting your little girlfriend, I've been seeing the world on my Carmichael Fellowship. THE ONE YOU DIDN'T GET – HA!'

Charles's face turned red with anger. 'YOU CAN TAKE YOUR CARMICHAEL FELLOWSHIP AND SHOVE IT UP YOUR—'

'Mum! Dad!' pleaded Sarah.

'Please, Geraldine,' said Tiffany, placing her hand on Geraldine's arm. 'I'd like us to be friends again.'

'Friends?' Geraldine scoffed. 'Oh really? You'd like us to be friends . . .'

Uh-oh, thought Sarah as her mother lunged at her father's fiancée, clawing at her like a rabid animal.

'YOU STOLE MY HUSBAND!' screeched Geraldine.

'YOU DIDN'T DESERVE HIM!' yelled Tiffany, trying to push her off. 'You were more interested in your research than in him!'

Sarah stood, mortified, as the two women tussled on the dance floor. She felt frozen in place, unsure how to intervene.

Quick as a flash, James saved the day.

'Let's dance, Geraldine,' he said. Putting his strong arms around his mother-in-law, he steered her to the other side of the dance floor and stroked her back comfortingly as Geraldine wept on his shoulder.

'I think we'd better head home,' said Sarah's dad, giving her a kiss goodbye. 'It was a lovely day.'

Apart from the brawl, thought Sarah.

Soon, other guests began to say their goodbyes.

James handed Geraldine over to Meg, who took her mum up to her room.

'Want to get out of here?' James whispered in Sarah's ear.

'Yes, please.' She couldn't wait to be alone with her husband.

A few hours later, they were buckling their seat belts for their early-morning flight.

The captain made an announcement. 'Welcome aboard this British Airways flight to Los Angeles. We have some newly-weds on board – congratulations to Sarah and James O'Hara!'

Everyone on the plane applauded.

'How did they know?' asked Sarah, turning to James.

He grinned. 'A little birdie told them.'

Deciding where to go on honeymoon had been the easiest part of wedding planning: it had to be Hollywood.

'What should we watch?' asked Sarah, flicking through the in-flight magazine.

'The new Steven Spielberg movie is supposed to be good,' said James.

After take-off, they snuggled under their fleece blankets and watched *Catch Me If You Can* on tiny screens on the back of their seats. Sarah's head rested on James's shoulder as they watched the movie. It was about a young con man, played by Leonardo DiCaprio, who posed as an airplane pilot in the 1960s.

'Wow, flying was a lot more glamorous back in the old days, wasn't it?' said James, taking off his headphones when the movie was over.

'Poor guy. I felt sorry for him, even though he was stealing millions,' said Sarah.

'He was lonely,' remarked James. 'That's why he phoned the FBI every Christmas Eve. Because he missed his family.'

Being surrounded by their friends and family on their wedding day had made Sarah realise how lucky she and James were. Her parents weren't perfect, but they both loved her in their own way. And now, she and James were their own little family.

'Complimentary champagne, Mr and Mrs O'Hara,' said the flight attendant, bringing them two glasses of champagne from first class.

Sarah laughed. She still wasn't used to being called Mrs.

'What were you saying about travelling not being glamorous any more,' said Sarah, clinking glasses with her husband.

'To us,' said James. 'On our wedding day.'

'But it's not our wedding day any more,' replied Sarah.

James put the time on his watch back eight hours. 'It's still our wedding day in California – for another ten minutes.'

Sarah reached for her husband's hand and laced her fingers between his. 'My favourite part of our wedding day was just now – watching a movie, just the two of us.'

James pressed his lips to her hand. 'I look forward to watching many, many more movies with you, Mrs O'Hara, even when we're old and grey.'

Sarah gazed into his eyes, as blue as the sky outside the plane's window. 'James O'Hara, I take you to be my lawful wedded husband, to have and to hold from this day forward, for better or for worse, through comedies and dramas, through thrillers and musicals . . .'

'Through horror and romance . . .'

'Through science fiction and animation . . .'

'Til death do us part,' they said together. And then they sealed their vows with a kiss.

Chapter 3

Present Day

With its original flagstone floors, bright copper pans hanging from the ceiling and a dresser crammed full of colourful, mismatched mugs and crockery, the kitchen was Sarah's favourite room in the cottage. An Aga kept the room warm, despite the cold outside. But the kitchen's cheer wasn't doing much to lift Sarah's mood as she sipped her coffee and gazed gloomily out of the window, its sill covered in plants and pots of herbs. Outside, it was a grey, drizzly day, not that it had stopped James from disappearing on his usual long Saturday-morning cycle ride.

She poured herself another cup of coffee. She was going to need it, she hadn't slept well for the past few days, replaying Holly's hurtful words in her head.

'Just because you regret giving up on your dream doesn't mean I'm going to give up on mine!'

Holly's words rankled because Sarah knew that there was some truth in them. Ever since hanging up that movie poster – a reminder of what *could* have been, if she'd made different choices – Sarah had been wondering if she had given up on her writing too easily. Sure, there had been reasons: she'd been busy raising the kids and helping to run the cinema. She'd tried to make time – snatching moments here and there – but it hadn't been easy. So she'd given up, just like Holly had said.

She could hear her daughter singing along to the *Wicked* soundtrack in her bedroom. Guilt prickled Sarah's conscience as she listened to her daughter hit a high note. Had she stopped her from going to the audition because she was jealous of her talent – and the fact that she still had her whole life ahead of her?

No, thought Sarah, tightening the belt of her dressing gown. *I'd never do that.* She wanted her daughter to act, if that's what she wanted to do. Sarah would support Holly however she could. But she and James both wanted Holly to get the best education possible, as a strong foundation.

'What's wrong, Mum?' asked Nick.

Startled, Sarah turned around. She hadn't heard her son come into the kitchen, his slippers silent on the flagstones, and wondered how long he had been observing her. He was wearing pyjamas with his favourite manga character on them that she'd ordered from Japan last Christmas.

'I'm just feeling a bit down today,' admitted Sarah. There was no point lying to her son; Nick could read her every mood.

He came over and put his arms around her. Sarah relished the fact that her youngest was still happy to give her a cuddle.

'Thank you, my sweet, sweet boy,' she said, stroking his sandy hair still tousled from sleep.

Sarah got a big bowl out of the cupboard and started mixing together ingredients for pancakes. Nick sat down at the scuffed oak table, reading one of his manga magazines.

Butter sizzled on the skillet as Sarah poured batter into the frying pan. She dropped in blueberries to make a smiley face.

As intended, the delicious smell of pancakes cooking lured Holly down to the kitchen.

'Morning, Holly,' Sarah said. 'I made your favourite.'

Ignoring Sarah's peace offering, Holly went to the cupboard and got out a box of cereal.

Great, thought Sarah. *She's still giving me the silent treatment.*

'I'll have her pancake,' said Nick.

Sarah slid it onto his plate. Twelve-year-old boys had bottomless appetites. No sooner had she restocked the fridge than it was empty again.

Just as Sarah was about to sit down and eat her own breakfast, a ginger cat came into the kitchen and meowed.

'Ah,' she said. 'You want your breakfast too, Jonesy.' She poured cat biscuits into his bowl.

The cat, named for the ship's cat in *Alien*, nibbled his food.

'His litter tray needs cleaning too,' said Nick, his mouth full of pancake.

Ugh.

Sarah went into the tiny utility room and changed the cat litter. While she was in there, the washing machine beeped. She hung the damp clothes out on the old-fashioned wooden airing rack suspended from the ceiling. When they'd bought the cottage, she'd thought it was a charming period feature. That was before she'd dried hundreds of loads of laundry on the rickety device.

'Is my PE kit clean?' called Nick, just as she was raising the rack up again, to dangle overhead like a colourful chandelier of pants, T-shirts and socks.

'Did you put it in the hamper?' Sometimes Sarah suspected that the dirty socks and underwear spawned in the hamper – surely that was the only explanation for how there were always so many clothes to wash.

'No, it was in my bag. Oh, and my trainers are getting tight.'

Sarah sighed. It looked like she'd be doing another load of washing tomorrow and somehow find time to take

Nick shoe-shopping. How was it possible that he'd already outgrown the trainers she'd bought at the start of term?

By the time she sat down to eat her pancake, it had gone cold.

'You two need to give me your Christmas lists. And your birthday list, Holly.' Sarah knew better than to try to choose things herself for her teenaged daughter. She would only get it wrong. She hoped neither of the kids wanted anything big for Christmas. There wasn't a lot of spare money about this year, not with the cinema struggling.

'I just want money,' said Holly. 'So I can get professional headshots done.' She narrowed her eyes at her mother. 'Or are you going to stop me from doing that, too.'

Don't rise to the bait, Sarah told herself.

'I just want art stuff and a new LEGO kit,' said Nick.

'"*I just want art stuff,*"' mimicked Holly, in a perfect imitation of her brother. 'God, you're such a little goody two shoes. Aren't you too old to play with LEGO?'

'Ignore her, Nick,' said Sarah. 'You can build LEGO models as long as you like. Plenty of grown-ups love LEGO.'

'Holly just feels frustrated,' said Nick sagely.

'Shut up,' Holly told him. 'I don't need you telling me what I feel, you little weirdo.'

That was it – Sarah had had enough. It was one thing being horrible to her, but Holly didn't need to be mean to her brother as well. 'Holly – if you don't drop the bad attitude, the only thing you can expect in your stocking is a lump of coal.'

Holly gave her mother a look of pure contempt. 'I'm just trying to help. Can't he at least *try* to act normal? He sits by himself in the canteen at lunchtime. It's tragic.'

Nick bit his lip and Sarah knew he was trying not to cry.

'If you can't be civil, you can and go start on your chores,' Sarah told her.

'I'm afraid I've got far too much homework to do my chores,' said Holly, her voice dripping with sarcasm. 'I know how *important* my schoolwork is to you.' She smirked triumphantly and went upstairs.

Sarah closed her eyes and took a deep breath, willing herself not to scream in frustration. Had she been so disrespectful at Holly's age? No, Geraldine would never have stood for it. She knew she should force Holly to come back downstairs and clean the living room, but she didn't have the energy for another battle.

'I'll do the breakfast dishes,' said Nick.

'Thanks, sweetie.' Sarah tousled her son's hair affectionately.

Sarah dragged the vacuum cleaner into a room with exposed oak beams and a big fireplace. The living room was decorated with an eclectic mix of second-hand furniture from their friend Ian's antique shop, movie posters, prints that they'd picked up on their travels and artwork by local artists who had displayed their work in the cinema café. It was a wonderfully cosy room, but the downside to living in an old cottage was that it attracted dust and cobwebs.

Sarah hoovered up the cat hair, then dusted off the mantel, which was packed with framed photos, of Holly looking angelic in a primary school photo, her arms around her little brother protectively. How things had changed.

But Holly wasn't the only one who had changed. Sarah picked up a picture of her and James on holiday in Hong Kong, gazing lovingly into each other's eyes on top of Victoria Peak. When was the last time they had looked at each other that way?

There was a clatter of cycling shoes on the kitchen's flagstones and a moment later James came into the living room in his skintight cycling shorts and jersey. Sarah averted her eyes. It was *not* a good look, despite the fact that James was still lean and fit. Middle-aged men in spandex looked ridiculous.

'Still in your pyjamas,' said James cheerfully, leaving footprints on the carpet she'd just hoovered. 'I'm glad you had a lie-in.'

'I *didn't* have a lie-in,' snapped Sarah irritably. 'I just haven't had a chance to shower. I've been too busy.'

James crossed his arms over his chest as he watched her attack a cobweb in the corner of the room with unnecessary force. 'Are you annoyed that I went for a bike ride?'

It wasn't about the bike ride. She knew exercise was important for his mental health. But what about *her* mental health? Writing used to be her release. No wonder she'd been feeling so frustrated and angry. She had no outlet for her creativity. Unless you counted pancake art.

'No. It's just . . . everything,' said Sarah, exasperated. 'I never get any time to myself. And even if I did, I don't have the brain space to do anything – I'm too busy worrying about Mum and the kids. Holly was right – I haven't written a word in years.'

Maybe it was her own fault, for not *claiming* her space the way James had. Sarah had got so used to putting everyone else's needs first, she had almost forgotten she even had her own needs.

'It's nearly Christmas,' said James soothingly. 'We'll get a few days off soon. Maybe you can do some writing then?'

Sarah groaned. 'Christmas is just more work for me!' How could he not see that? So much stress went into making Christmas a magical day for the whole family. There were presents to be bought and wrapped. Cards to write. Food to prepare. It wasn't done by Santa's elves – it was done by her. 'I haven't done any Christmas shopping, or put up any decorations, and I haven't even planned the bloody film festival!'

'But you love the film festival.'

Sarah *did* love the festival, and picking the movies they showed. She wasn't normally so Scrooge-like.

'I just don't know if I can be bothered with it this year,' said Sarah. 'Can we really afford to run it?'

'I'm sure you don't really mean that,' said James. 'Everyone loves the film festival. They look forward to it all year. We wouldn't want to let them down.'

Great. Once again, what Sarah wanted was irrelevant. Sometimes it felt like her husband cared more about everyone else in Plumdale than he did about her.

Shaking her head in dismay, Sarah went upstairs to get ready for work.

Holly was in her room, but instead of doing her homework as she'd told Mum she was trying to figure out what to wear to work. That was *waaaay* more important.

A few weeks ago, she'd painted her bedroom walls deep purple, covering up the babyish floral wallpaper that had adorned her room since she was little. Mum had warned her that the colour was too dark, but Holly had gone ahead anyway. Now her room made her feel like she was trapped inside a plum, not that she was going to give her mother the satisfaction of admitting that.

Holly pulled on some jeans and a cropped, scoop-necked top. Then she took off the jeans and put on a denim mini-skirt. Did it look like she was trying too hard?

She wriggled out of the skirt and put her jeans back on. She studied herself in the mirror.

Yes, that was better.

She tuned out the sound of her parents squabbling downstairs as she did her make-up.

Copying something she'd seen on a make-up tutorial, she drew dramatic swooshes of kohl on her eyelids, making her blue eyes pop. Her drama teacher at school was always saying that eyes were the windows of the soul.

Standing in front of the mirror, Holly practised conveying different emotions with just her eyes. She lowered her lids in what she hoped made her look like a smouldering temptress.

'Holly!' Mum shouted up the stairs. 'Hurry up or we'll be late for Kids' Club!'

Now, the emotion in her eyes was unmistakeable – irritation. Kids' Club was a nightmare – some kids acted completely feral at the cinema and their parents didn't even tell them off.

'Holly!' called Mum again. 'Are you nearly ready?'

'Yes!' shouted Holly. Her mother was *soooo* annoying. Holly was sure her mum could have persuaded Dad to let her audition if she'd wanted to. But no, she'd stopped Holly from being involved in the only interesting thing ever to happen in Plumdale.

Did she really think pancakes could fix things? (That said, it had taken all of Holly's willpower not to have one.)

Downstairs, Mum was fussing over Nick. As usual. 'Are you sure you're going to be OK at home?'

'He's twelve,' said Holly. 'He's not a baby.' Holly's little brother didn't like noisy situations, and the Saturday morning Kids' Club was LOUD. He'd been relieved when his parents had started letting him stay at home. No such luck for her though.

Nick picked up the cat who was rubbing against his legs. 'Jonesy will keep me company.'

'Bye, squirt,' said Holly, even though Nick was rapidly catching up with her height. She felt bad about being mean to him earlier. He was actually a pretty cool kid, just . . . different.

Holly and her parents stepped out of the house into the cold, drizzly morning.

'I bet it's going to be busy today,' said Mum, unlocking the mud-splattered Volvo.

Rainy days were good for the cinema. Holly wasn't an idiot. She knew that the cinema was in trouble and they'd probably need a whole monsoon season to change its fortunes. But somehow she couldn't imagine them not having the Picture Palace in their lives — it was her second home. She'd even taken her first steps in the lobby.

Holly's parents were weirdly quiet in the car. They usually chatted and sang along to indie rock songs on the radio. But today, Mum just gazed out of the window, stony-faced. She was obviously still sulking about the fact that Holly hadn't eaten her pancakes.

Good, thought Holly. She deserved to be upset. But she couldn't help missing her parents' terrible singing. It was better than the silence.

Holly swiped through her notifications as they drove along. Her friend Riley had sent her a message, asking her if she wanted to go Christmas shopping at the outlet mall in Swindon.

Soz. Have 2 work 2day.

Then, her pulse racing with excitement, she checked film-boi06's profile. She scrolled through his feed, looking for new updates. Her heart leapt as she saw he had posted a picture from the night before. She enlarged the image, trying to work out if the girl he had his left arm around was just a mate, or his girlfriend. His right arm was around a male friend in a football jersey, so it was impossible to read anything into the picture. Holly studied the caption – *epic sesh* with a dancing girl emoji – trying to parse a deeper meaning from it. She didn't think he had a girlfriend, but there was no way to be sure without asking him – and she definitely wasn't going to do that!

She scrolled through older images, which she had practically memorised. She sighed at the adorable throwback image of him as a little boy with wild curls, cradling a puppy.

Filmboi06 was Aaron, who worked at the cinema. She'd gleaned the following information about him from his socials:

1. He REALLY liked movies
2. He had a pet dog named Molly (presumably the one from the picture)
3. His grandparents lived in Jamaica – there were lots of photos of him on the beach, with his amazing abs on display
4. He played rugby (which explained the abs)
5. He had a great smile and perfect teeth, thanks to the braces he'd worn until the end of Year 11 (judging from older pictures on his profile)
6. He'd run a 10K to raise money for a cancer charity, in memory of his aunt
7. He liked grime music (Holly had tried listening to grime artists but couldn't really get into it. She was more *Bugsy Malone* than Bugzy Malone . . .)
8. His most-used emoji was the dancing lady, followed by the skull
9. He liked to bake and had made his mum a very impressive birthday cake

10. He had dressed up as T'Challa – aka Black Panther – for Halloween

Not that she was a stalker or anything . . .

Of course, she could have gathered this information by actually talking to Aaron. Unfortunately, every time they worked together, Holly got uncharacteristically tongue-tied and could barely string a sentence together.

Today, thought Holly. *Today you're going to talk to him about something more than refilling the popcorn machine or restocking the coffee cups.*

When they got to the cinema, Dad unlocked the doors and switched on all the lights. They had over an hour until the Saturday Morning Kids' Club screening of *Encanto.*

The lobby doors opened and Aaron came in. He looked gorgeous – as usual – in jeans, a long-sleeved T-shirt and some vintage-style Reeboks. Holly knew – courtesy of a recent Instagram post – he'd found them at a charity shop.

Uh, Say something! she commanded herself.

'Aaron Burr, sir,' she said, regretting the words the second they came out of her mouth.

He looked confused. 'Um, my surname is Armstrong?'

Holly laughed nervously. 'I know. It was a joke. There's, ah, a character in the musical *Hamilton* called Aaron Burr?'

'Oh,' said Aaron. 'I haven't seen it.'

'It's really good,' babbled Holly. 'Lin-Manuel Miranda's a genius. He, like, wrote the songs in *Encanto* too – which was why I was thinking about him.'

OK, you can stop talking now.

Mum went into the office and came out with a list. 'Holly – can you check the bathrooms. Aaron, I need your help decorating the lobby for Christmas.'

Holly glowered at her mother. Was she actively trying to ruin her life? OK, Mum didn't know Holly was secretly in love with Aaron. But still – bathroom duty was the worst.

She went over to the cleaning cupboard and got out rolls of toilet paper and an industrial-sized bottle of hand soap. She refilled all the cubicles and soap dispensers, and then sighed. After Kids' Club, it would be a complete mess in here – kids seemed incapable of aiming their wee *inside* the toilet bowl.

Holly checked her make-up in the mirror, then went back out into the lobby. A woman with a black bob approached, pushing a baby in a buggy. There were dark circles around her eyes, her coat was buttoned up wrong and it looked like she hadn't brushed her hair.

'Is Sarah here?' asked the woman.

'I'll get her,' said Holly. She went over to the office, where Mum was standing on a footstool, handing boxes of Christmas decorations down to Aaron. 'Some lady is asking for you, Mum.'

Her mum got down and they went out to the lobby.

'Oh, hi, Iris,' said Holly's mum. 'Is everything OK?'

'Henry left his favourite toy behind when we were at the Baby and Me screening the other day. I wonder if you found it?'

Mum went behind the counter and pulled out the lost-and-found box.

Iris rummaged through the collection and pulled out a rubber giraffe toy. 'Oh, thank goodness!' She handed it to her son. The baby kicked his legs gleefully and immediately began to gnaw on one of the giraffe's ears.

'Are you all right?' asked Mum. 'You look a bit tired.'

'Last night was rough,' admitted Iris. Tears glittered in her eyes. 'I feel so low.'

'Oh, honey.' Mum gave the lady a hug. 'It will get easier – I promise. I wish I could grab a coffee with you, but I've got to decorate the cinema or the Plumdale Beautification Society will tell me off.'

'I'll do it!' Holly seized the opportunity to be on her own with Aaron. 'I'll decorate.'

'Are you sure?' her mother asked suspiciously.

'Absolutely.' Holly smiled, hoping that her eyes were conveying innocence. 'I'm sorry I was such a brat earlier.' She waved her hands, shooing her mum and Iris away. 'Go hang out with your friend.'

'Oh, OK. . .' said her mum. 'Thanks.'

As Mum and her friend went over to the café area, Holly smoothed down her top, her hands trembling with anticipation. *Don't mess this up*, she told herself.

Holly went into the office and coughed nervously.

'Hey,' said Aaron, who was wrestling with the artificial Christmas tree. 'Can you grab the other end?'

She helped Aaron carry the tree out of the office and, working in silence, they set it up in its stand.

Say something, Holly told herself.

'So, um, have you put up a Christmas tree at home yet?'

'Not yet,' said Aaron. 'Sometimes we don't even bother. We usually go to Jamaica to visit my granny over Christmas.'

Holly nearly said 'I know' but remembered she only knew that from her online stalking. 'That's cool – I wouldn't mind Christmas on the beach.' Actually, though, she loved Christmas in the Cotswolds. Every shop in the village was beautifully decorated and all the houses twinkled with fairy lights.

'This year, we're staying home because I've got to work on my uni applications and study for my A levels.'

Uni applications sounded so grown-up. No wonder Aaron barely paid her any attention – she hadn't even done her GCSEs yet, and he was getting ready to go to university.

'What do you want to study?' she asked.

'Film Studies,' replied Aaron. 'I want to direct movies one day.'

'Cool,' said Holly. 'I want to be an actor. Maybe you can cast me in something – *ha ha ha.*' She laughed nervously.

Gah! Why am I acting like such a massive dork?

'Yeah, maybe,' said Aaron, adjusting some of the branches.

Once the tree was up, they went back into the office to fetch the boxes of decorations. There were star-shaped fairy lights and a collection of film-themed baubles – from boxes of popcorn to a shiny gold Oscar.

'Why is this stuff in here?' asked Aaron, holding up a reel of old 35mm film.

'Oh, we always use it as garland.'

'Cool,' said Aaron, starting to unspool the film.

Working together, they wound the film garland and fairy lights around the tree. Holly tried not to blush every time Aaron's fingers brushed against hers. Every cell in her body was acutely aware of how close they were.

'It must have been so cool growing up with your own movie cinema,' said Aaron. His T-shirt rode up as he reached up high to hang a gold star on top of the tree, and Holly caught sight of a sliver of his smooth, toned stomach. She gulped and then realised he was waiting for a response.

'Um, yeah, I guess . . .' It wasn't so cool when your mum and dad could never come to parents' evening together become one of them needed to be here. Or when they had to work all weekend, because that was the cinema's busiest time.

'You could go see any movie you wanted,' Aaron commented.

'Not *any* movie.' Holly corrected him. 'I sneaked my friends into a screening of *It* back in Year Five. Mum found us and I got in *biiiiig* trouble.'

'Probably for the best.' Aaron chuckled. 'That movie is terrifying.'

'Nothing is scarier than my mum when she's angry.'

'I'm actually doing my final project on horror movies,' said Aaron, hanging up an ornament shaped like a clapperboard. 'I'm focusing on contemporary directors like Jordan Peele.'

Holly made a mental note to watch every movie Jordan Peele had ever made before the next shift they had together so she could casually drop references to them into conversation.

When all the decorations were up, Aaron plugged in the lead. The fairy lights made the metallic baubles twinkle.

Before she could help herself, Holly sang the first line of 'It's Beginning to Look a Lot Like Christmas'.

She cringed inwardly, but Aaron smiled at her – showing off his perfect white teeth. Her aunt Meg would approve.

'Go us,' said Aaron, giving her a high five.

Us! Holly practically swooned.

There wasn't much time to admire their handiwork – or Aaron's smile – because customers began arriving with their children for the film. Holly sold tickets, while Aaron served popcorn and sweets. Kids chased each other around the lobby, shrieking with excitement. Her mum had been right – the rainy weather boosted ticket sales, with parents looking for a way to entertain their kids indoors.

The presentation started and soon, from inside the auditorium, came the sound of 'Surface Pressure.' Holly hummed along to the song as she wiped down the counter.

'I, um, saw you in the school play last year,' said Aaron. 'I'm not surprised you want to act professionally. You're definitely good enough.'

Holly looked at him in surprise, flattered that he'd recognised her. She'd played Penny Pingleton in *Hairspray*, her hair teased into a beehive. 'Thanks,' she said.

Suddenly, Holly became aware of a commotion. A dad holding a crying toddler came out of the auditorium.

'There isn't any sound,' he told them angrily.

Uh-oh.

Holly hurried into the auditorium. The picture was still running but no sound was coming out of the speakers. She ran upstairs to the projection booth and found her father desperately pressing buttons on the sound system.

'What's going on?' Holly asked him.

'One of the amps has broken,' Dad said, pulling out a cable. 'I'm going to rewire another amp to the speaker.'

'Well, how long is that going to take?' said Holly. Peering down at the auditorium from the projection booth, she could see that children had left their seats and were running amok in the aisles, flinging popcorn around. Some of their parents were standing up and putting their coats on.

'Go back down and apologise,' said Dad. 'Let the customers know I'm trying to sort it out and we'll give everyone a refund – and complimentary popcorn the next time they come.'

Holly hurried back down to the auditorium. She stood at the front and clapped her hands to get everyone's attention. 'Hi, everyone. Unfortunately, we're having some slight technical difficulties and we're trying to get it resolved as soon as possible. We're sorry about this and everyone will be getting a full refund.'

'Boo!' shouted a boy, throwing a piece of popcorn at her. The other kids in the audience laughed.

This was bad. Very bad. Holly needed to do something to distract them – and fast.

She glanced up at the screen behind her. 'How about we sing some of the songs from *Encanto* together – I'm sure you all know the words.'

She began to sing. For a few lines, she was singing solo, but, soon, all the kids in the audience were joining in with a rousing rendition of 'We Don't Talk About Bruno.' To Holly's huge relief, just as they reached the final chorus, the sound kicked back in.

'Yay!' The children cheered.

Phew, thought Holly.

As Holly hurried out of the auditorium, Aaron was standing at the back. He held the door open for her.

'Nice save,' he murmured.

Oh, God, thought Holly. Aaron probably thought she was a weirdo for knowing all the lyrics to some kids' movie. 'It's not like, my favourite movie or anything,' she babbled. 'It's just that I had to do *something* and I knew some of the songs—'

'It was cool – very, very cool.' His brown eyes held hers and Holly felt like he was seeing her – *really* seeing her – for the very first time.

10th October 2004

'Happy Birthday!' Sarah whispered, kissing James's strong, freckled shoulder. It was peeling slightly, from getting sunburnt on a beach in Thailand. They'd been travelling around Asia for the past three weeks. After roughing it at backpackers' hostels, living on noodles and banana fritters, they'd decided to splash out for the last stop on their trip – Hong Kong. They were spending James's thirtieth birthday in the iconic Peninsula Hotel, overlooking Hong Kong harbour.

James rolled over to face her and smiled sleepily. 'Good morning, beautiful.'

'How does it feel to be old?' she teased him. Her own thirtieth birthday was still two years off, though she'd found her first grey hair a few months ago in the work bathroom and freaked out.

'My mum went completely grey by the time she was thirty-five,' Pari had told her. 'Of course, having me as her kid was probably a contributing factor.'

Sarah stroked the side of her husband's face, his cheek rough with morning stubble. There were the beginnings of crinkles around his eyes when he smiled, but Sarah thought he was even more handsome now.

'Oh, there's plenty of life in the old dog yet,' James said, hooking his leg over her thigh to pull her close.

Afterwards, they ordered breakfast to the room and lounged in bed in their towelling robes, eating croissants and a plate of exotic fruit.

'So, how is your birthday going so far?' Sarah asked him.

'Five stars,' James said, popping a piece of pineapple in his mouth.

'I could get used to this,' sighed Sarah, sipping her cup of tea. She had never stayed anywhere so luxurious before.

James's phone beeped and he checked the message.

'Everything OK?' Sarah asked. She hoped it wasn't his work. Even though they were on holiday, James had taken several calls from his office. Ever since the company had floated on the stock market, he'd been busier than ever. The software company was under a lot of pressure to continue to innovate and deliver strong returns to their new shareholders.

'It's just Dad, wishing me a happy birthday.'

'So what do you want to do with the rest of the day?' Sarah asked, pouring him another cup of tea.

'Well, I wouldn't mind doing that again . . .' James tugged at the tie on her bathrobe.

'Later,' said Sarah, laughing. 'We have a whole city to explore and we only have three days before we head home.'

James groaned. 'Don't remind me. I wish I didn't have to go back to work'

Sarah didn't relish the thought of going back to work, either. Budget cuts and redundancies at the BBC meant that the script-editing team was severely overstretched. She still loved working with screenwriters and nurturing new talent, but she felt frustrated by the organisation's resistance to change. Rupert remained the head of drama commissioning and routinely blocked the programmes she championed – preferring to play it safe with crime serials and costume dramas. As much as Sarah adored Jane Austen, if she had to adapt another one of her novels, she thought she might scream. The BBC's licence payers deserved programming that was as diverse as Britain was, not just petticoats and posh people.

'We need stuff we can sell to the Yanks,' Rupert was always telling her. 'They can't get enough of our corsets.' He'd leered at Sarah, eyeing up her chest as he said it.

Pushing thoughts of work out of her mind, Sarah went over to the window and opened the blinds to an incredible view of skyscrapers. Far below, the Star Ferry chugged across Victoria Harbour.

'How about we take the cable car to the top of Victoria Peak?' suggested James.

'Sounds good to me. I'd like to visit a few temples, too,' said Sarah, flipping through the pages of their *Rough Guide*.

They took a long shower together, sampling all of the complimentary toiletries. James washed Sarah's long hair with divine-smelling jasmine-scented shampoo.

'Oh, that feels so good,' murmured Sarah, as her husband's fingers lovingly massaged her scalp.

Once they'd dressed, they set off to explore the city, crossing the harbour by ferry and taking the old-fashioned tram up to the top of Victoria Peak.

'This was considered a marvel of modern engineering when it was first built,' James read from the guidebook. 'All the equipment and construction materials had to be hauled up the mountain by workers. It used to be powered by steam.'

Sarah was more impressed with the view of the city beneath them than the cable car's inner workings as they climbed to the peak's leafy summit. They weren't the only people with the same idea; it was the Harvest Moon Festival, and families were enjoying the holiday together.

James used the camera on his new phone to take pictures of the view. 'It's so handy not to have to lug a camera around.'

Sarah shook her head affectionately. 'You and your gadgets.'

Rather than taking the cable car back down, they hiked to the base along a winding path. By the time they reached the bottom, the sky was growing overcast. They took the ferry back across the harbour, then wandered down Tung Choi Street, browsing through market stalls selling counterfeit DVDS, designer knock-offs, sunglasses, tourist souvenirs and jade trinkets.

Sarah bought replica designer bags for Pari and her sister, and a pale blue cheongsam for herself. She had no idea if it would fit, but she loved the silky fabric with its delicate flower print.

'These look so real,' said James, admiring a tray of fake Rolexes. He held one up to his ear to hear it ticking. 'And they actually work.'

'Let me get you one for your birthday,' said Sarah. The whole trip was James's birthday celebration, but she wanted to get him a present too. 'A successful thirty-year-old needs a fancy watch. Or at least a replica fancy watch . . .'

James strapped his new watch around his wrist and checked the time. 'It says it's time for lunch.'

'Oh, good,' said Sarah. 'I'm starving.'

'It's probably from all the exercise this morning.' James winked at her.

They sampled snacks from the market's food vendors, walking along, eating deliciously spicy fish balls and soy-braised cuttlefish off bamboo skewers. Food had been a highlight of their trip; they'd sought out local delicacies wherever they had gone.

'Ugh. What's that smell?' asked Sarah as she caught a whiff of something pungent.

A moment later, the odour's source revealed itself to be a stall selling the appropriately named stinky tofu.

'It's meant to be really tasty.' James ordered two squares of the fermented beancurd and held one out to her. 'Go on – I think you'll like it.'

Sarah took a cautious bite. The outside was crisp, but the inside was meltingly soft and creamy. 'Yum.' Despite its off-putting name, stinky tofu was delicious.

'It's even better with chilli sauce,' said the vendor, offering them a bottle.

Sarah squeezed a dollop on her tofu. The vendor was right – the spicy tang perfectly complemented the fried snack.

'Try some of this,' said James, ordering a round, bright orange delicacy from the next vendor.

'What is it?' asked Sarah suspiciously.

'Deep-fried pig's intestine.'

'Thanks, but I'll pass.' She liked to try new foods, but she drew the line at pig's intestine.

'All the more for me,' he said, enthusiastically taking a big bite. 'Mmm. Chewy.'

James was a much more adventurous eater than she was. It was as if he was making up for the years after his mum passed away when he and his dad had existed mostly on jacket potatoes and beans on toast.

'You'd be a shoo-in for that new show where celebrities go to the jungle and have to eat bugs and sheep's testicles.' Sarah laughed. One of her former colleagues from the BBC was working on the popular programme. Sarah had thought about leaving as well, to write her own scripts. But the thought of making that jump was scary.

For dessert, they joined a long queue to buy mooncakes at a bakery. The sweet cakes came with all different fillings – from red bean paste to duck's egg yolk – and had beautiful decorative patterns stamped on the top.

'They all look so good,' said Sarah when they got to the front of the line.

'Lotus seed is very nice,' suggested the man working behind the counter.

Munching their mooncakes, they wandered through Kowloon, through a walled park where children flew kites, old women practised tai chi and men played mahjong, their jade tiles clacking. At the edge of the park, nestled among ultra-modern tower blocks, they came across a little temple. Stone steps, flanked by dragons, led up to a pagoda with a green-tiled roof.

As James snapped photos of the dragons, Sarah wandered into the temple courtyard. There was a large bowl with sticks of incense burning. Two women were leaving offerings of fruit on an altar, around a statue of a rabbit.

'It's a tradition for Harvest Moon Festival. We are making offerings to the Moon Rabbit,' explained the smartly dressed younger woman, seeing the curious expression on Sarah's face. 'In Chinese mythology, he belongs to the Moon Goddess.'

'Brings good luck,' said the older woman, reaching into her bag and handing Sarah a melon. 'For you to make offering too.'

'Thank you,' said Sarah. She placed the fruit carefully on the table with the rest of the array.

'Now you will have a baby,' said the older woman, grinning at Sarah.

Sarah felt her cheeks flame. She and James hadn't discussed having kids yet.

'Stop, Ma,' scolded the younger woman. 'You are embarrassing her.'

'No, no, it's fine,' Sarah assured her. Having an embarrassing mother was a universal phenomenon. Post-divorce, Geraldine had thrown herself into dating and liked to overshare details of her sex life with Sarah and Meg. Her most recent fling had been with a bucket drummer she'd met at a climate-change protest. Her career was thriving too – she'd just been appointed Head of the Anthropology department at the University of Bristol.

'The Moon Rabbit symbolises fertility,' explained the younger woman.

Sarah wasn't worried about that – she was still in her twenties. But just to be on the safe side, she bought a packet of incense sticks inside the temple. She waved James over, then they lit the incense sticks and added them to the burner in front of a gold statue of Buddha. Watching the smoke drift upwards to the top of the temple, Sarah said, 'Apparently, this will bring us prosperity, fertility and good luck.'

'I'm already the luckiest man alive.' James pulled her close for a kiss.

Their luck ran out on the walk back to the hotel. The heavens opened and rain poured down in sheets, gushing down gutters in torrents.

'Come on,' said James, tugging Sarah under the awning of a convenience store to shelter from the downpour. Rain hammered at the fabric over their heads.

A taxi drove past and James tried to flag it down, but it didn't stop, just splashed them as it went through a puddle.

'I guess we'll just have to wait it out,' he said.

Pushing her sopping hair out of her face, Sarah glanced up at the sky. The rain didn't show any sign of abating. As her eyes travelled down again, they landed on the building across the street. There were Chinese characters above the doorway, and, next to them, in much smaller words, it said: *Lux Theatre*.

'Look, James!' Sarah said, pointing. 'There's a cinema. We can watch a movie until the rain stops.' She felt excited at the prospect of an afternoon at the movies. They hadn't seen a film since their flight over to Asia.

They darted across the street and ran into the lobby. It was like stepping back in time. There were ushers in smart red jackets, classic martial arts movies on the walls and an old-fashioned weighing machine.

James approached the ticket booth. 'Can we please have two tickets to whatever is showing next, please?'

'*2046* starts in twenty minutes,' said the man selling tickets. Hong Kong had been handed back to China a few years previously, but most people in the former British colony spoke excellent English.

The man had them pick their seats on a paper seating chart. He wrote out their tickets by hand, his black pen forming elegant characters on the paper, then directed them to the auditorium.

Sarah could feel her wet jeans sticking to her thighs and water from her hair running down her neck in rivulets. 'I feel like a drowned rat.'

'We'll soon dry off,' said James cheerfully, putting his arm around her shoulders.

Set in 1960s Hong Kong, the film wove together multiple meandering stories. One was about a science-fiction author writing a novel about a mysterious room 2046, where whoever was in it could revisit the past but never return to the present. Another followed a woman desperately in love with the writer. Every Christmas Eve, they met for dinner, but the writer never reciprocated her feelings.

When the lights came back on, Sarah sat in awed silence. 'That was amazing.' She'd loved the film, with its melancholy soundtrack, gorgeous period costumes and saturated colours.

'I thought it was confusing,' admitted James. 'Even with the subtitles.'

'It was like a strange dream,' said Sarah. 'Dreams don't always make sense.'

Outside the cinema, it had stopped raining and dark had fallen. The promenade at Tsim Sha Tsui waterfront was decorated with colourful lanterns for the autumn harvest festival. Families were out strolling, admiring the lights and the full moon shimmering over the harbour. Children held home-made lanterns on sticks and wore traditional outfits made of silky brocade. Sarah and James bought paper lanterns with the white Moon Rabbit on them from a vendor.

A little girl in a pink dress with a matching ribbon in her hair rode her bike towards them. She was going fast – her long black hair streaming out behind her. Her parents shouted after her in Cantonese. Although Sarah didn't understand the words, she could tell they were warning her to slow down. Too late. The tyres skidded on the wet pavement and the girl fell off her bicycle. She sprawled on the ground, crying.

Sarah gasped. 'Oh no.'

They dashed forward to help her up.

Sarah crouched down in front of the girl. Her knee was bleeding and there was a scrape on her chin. 'Does it hurt?'

The little girl nodded, her lip trembling. Sarah took out a tissue from her backpack and pressed it gently to her grazed knee.

'Would you like my lantern?' James held out his lantern to the little girl. 'Look – it's got a bunny on it.'

'What's your name, sweetie?' asked Sarah.

'Iris,' said the girl shyly, taking the lantern.

Eventually, the girls' parents caught up with them. Iris's mum gave her a hug, then, once she'd checked her wounds, scolded her in Cantonese. Turning to James and Sarah, the woman tried to give them back the lantern, but James insisted that Iris keep it.

'Thank you,' said Iris's mother.

Iris's dad picked her up, while her mother wheeled the bicycle along. Sarah smiled as the adorable little girl wrapped her arms around her dad's neck and waved at them over his shoulder. She turned to watch them go, the rabbit lantern bobbing along.

An image of her and James, each holding the hand of a little girl with curly brown hair and blue eyes, popped into her mind. Suddenly, Sarah was overcome with an intense longing – a *hunger* – to have a baby of her own.

'She was cute,' said James as they strolled along.

'Yes,' agreed Sarah. She glanced at him out of the corner of her eye, wondering if he was thinking the same thing.

Don't be ridiculous, she told herself. The woman at the temple must have put ideas into her head. They weren't ready to start a family. They lived in a small flat and worked crazy hours. Much as she loved living in trendy East London, Sarah couldn't imagine raising kids there, with sirens wailing at all hours and buses belching pollution into the air. Plus, she wanted to finish her screenplay before starting a family. She still hadn't completed *The Ghost Writer* because she was too busy editing other people's scripts. She'd thought about starting something new, but was so tired on the weekends she couldn't muster up the energy.

Further along the promenade, the pathway was embedded with plaques and handprints, honouring the greats of the Hong King film industry.

'It's like the Walk of Fame in Hollywood,' said James. On their honeymoon, they had visited Hollywood Boulevard, looking for their favourite actors' stars.

'Look, it's Wong Kar-wai,' said Sarah, pointing to the star commemorating the director of the film they'd just seen.

As they continued down the promenade, they also spotted stars for Maggie Cheung and Gong Li, who had acted in the movie.

Back at the hotel, Sarah kicked off her trainers. 'I'm exhausted.'

'Maybe we should lie down for a bit . . .' said James, sliding his hand under her still-damp T-shirt and nuzzling her neck. 'God, you always smell so good.'

'Like Christmas.' Sarah laughed, remembering what he'd told her the first time they'd made love.

After they'd made love, they lay entwined in a tangle of Egyptian cotton sheets. James stroked Sarah's belly. 'I keep thinking about what the lady said at the temple.'

'Me too,' she admitted.

James propped himself up on his elbow and smiled at her. 'I think we'd be good parents.'

Sarah knew that James would be an amazing father – she'd seen how gentle and kind he'd been with the little girl who'd fallen off her bike. Her sister's kids loved their uncle James. But even though she wanted kids too, Sarah was secretly scared she wouldn't be very good at it.

'I'm just not sure I'm ready yet,' she said, reaching up to push away the hair that had flopped in front of his face.

'There's no rush. And in the meantime, we'll just have to have fun practising . . .'

James bent down to kiss her, as Sarah arced her body to meet his.

Later, they changed into evening clothes. Sarah put on the silky dress that she'd bought at the market.

James whistled in appreciation as she twirled to show off her new outfit. 'Very glamorous.'

Holding hands, they took the lift to the cocktail bar at the top of the hotel. The harbour and the city's high-rises were ablaze with light.

'This holiday has been incredible,' Sarah said, sipping her martini. 'I wish we didn't have to go back to work.'

'It will be Christmas before you know it,' said James. 'We'll get a break then.'

Sarah and James would celebrate in Ealing with Sean. Geraldine would probably spend Christmas with Meg and her kids in Edinburgh, while Sarah's dad and Tiffany usually jetted off for a winter-sun break, so Tiffany could maintain her year-round tan.

Sarah sighed. 'I know. But work is just so all-consuming. After a day or two back at the BBC, I'll be stressed as ever. On the weekends, I'm too drained to write.'

James looked thoughtful, twiddling the cocktail stick in his drink.

'Penny for your thoughts,' said Sarah.

'Maybe it doesn't have to be like that.'

'What do you mean?'

James took a crumpled piece of paper out of his pocket. 'I've been carrying this around with me for weeks. Waiting for the right moment to show you.'

He handed over the piece of paper – an estate agent listing. The building in the photograph was one she'd seen before.

'Is this that the old cinema in the village where we got married?'

James nodded. 'I've been checking on the internet every so often, in the hope that it would come on the market. A few months ago, it finally did.'

Sarah looked at the asking price and gulped. 'That's a lot of money.'

'I know,' said James. 'But I think we could just about swing it.'

'How?'

'My shares have gone up in value since the stock market flotation. If I sold them while they're high, and we sold our flat – which has gone up in value – I think we'd have enough to put down a decent deposit on the cinema and to buy someplace to live as well.'

Sarah studied the pictures of the cinema's interior. 'It needs a lot of work.'

'It won't be easy, but Dad says he'll help restore it.' James's blue eyes sparkled with excitement. 'It still has a lot of its original features. Just think – we could show whatever we wanted to: old classics, arthouse movies and foreign films, like the one we saw today.'

'You've clearly given this a lot of thought,' Sarah said.

'I have,' admitted James. 'You know it's always been my dream.'

Sarah thought of Plumdale, the village they'd got married in. It was safe and green and picture perfect. The sort of place where you could raise a family . . .

As if he'd read her mind, James said, 'When we do eventually have kids, I don't want to be working crazy hours, always at the beck and call of the board of directors.'

Neither did she.

'If we were our own bosses,' continued James, 'it would be easier for you to find the time to write.'

Sarah picked up the cinema details again and studied them. She imagined it transformed into a beautiful place like the vintage cinema they'd visited today. She pictured herself writing, in a peaceful country cottage, with a view of rolling hills . . .

'What do you think?' James asked her.

At the temple, they'd made an offering to ensure good fortune. But what was the saying – fortune favours the brave. Instead of waiting around for things to change, perhaps it was time for them to make their own good luck. As long as they were in it together, what could possibly go wrong?

Looking up, she met James's eyes and smiled.

'Let's do it, birthday boy. Let's buy a cinema.'

Chapter 4

Present Day

Nick looked at the clock on the wall, willing the minute hand to move more quickly. There were still ten minutes left until the end of his maths class, and the end of the school day, but each second felt like an eternity. At the front of the classroom, Mr Wu was explaining about the properties of right angles.

It wasn't that Nick didn't like maths. Quite the opposite. But it was hard to concentrate on geometry when his senses were being assaulted by everything else in the classroom.

Nick's table was next to the ancient radiator, which was making a dull clanking noise – THUD, THUD, THUD – as it blasted out hot air. The room was stifling. He was acutely aware of his shirt sticking to his back under his itchy wool blazer. Mum had cut out the tag, but he could feel a bit she'd missed rubbing against the back of his neck. Nick squirmed in his chair uncomfortably.

Grace Maxwell, who was sitting next to him, gave him a contemptuous look. She seemed to have forgotten that they used to be friends in primary school, when they both liked playing with LEGO. Nick still did. He liked dreaming up amazing creations and inventing worlds. His bedroom was cluttered with space stations and castles that he'd built and couldn't bear to dismantle, despite what his sister said about it being babyish.

But Grace had left her LEGO days behind. She'd recently started wearing eye make-up and some sort of perfume that smelled like overly ripe strawberries. The sweet/rotten scent invaded Nick's nostrils and made him want to throw up.

Why didn't anyone else seem to notice these things?

'Can anyone tell me what the hypotenuse is?' asked Mr Wu.

Nobody put their hand up. Nick knew the answer but didn't want to call attention to himself.

'Anyone?' said Mr Wu. 'Nick?'

'Fifteen,' mumbled Nick.

'Correct,' said Mr Wu, writing on the board.

Damon Carter hissed, 'Hey, my name is Nick and I've got a tiny little prick.'

Everyone around him tittered. Nick's cheeks burnt with embarrassment. He stared down at his desk and willed himself not to cry.

The bell rang, signalling the end of the school day, and Nick's classmates were instantly jolted out of their lethargy. They rushed out of the classroom, jostling and yelling across the room.

Nick remained in his seat, holding his hands to his ears to drown out the cacophony. As eager as he was to get home, he knew that the longer he waited, the less likely he'd have to deal with bullies like Damon Carter in the hallway.

He felt a tap on his shoulder.

'Are you OK, Nick?' asked Mr Wu, with a kind smile. 'Remember, you can always go to the library if you need a time-out.'

'I'm fine,' Nick mumbled.

Mr Wu wasn't just his maths teacher, he was also his form tutor. Mum had spoken to him about how Nick was a HSP – highly sensitive person – and found certain situations overwhelming. Now, all of his teachers knew he was a freak. Nobody had told his classmates, but nobody had to. Other kids could sense that he was different. He might as well have the word 'loser' tattooed on his forehead.

It hadn't mattered so much in primary school. There were only twenty kids in his class and they'd accepted Nick, because they'd always known him. But things were completely different here at Severn Valley secondary school. The other kids from his primary school had quickly made new friends and moved on. Nick had never felt so alone. He wished things could go back to how they used to be, when everyone played cops and robbers together at lunchtime.

'You did really well on the last maths mini test, Nick,' said Mr Wu, sitting down at Nick's table. He was young-ish and wore a sweater vest. Nick knew that Grace and some of the other girls thought the teacher was good-looking – he'd heard them giggling about it. 'Full marks. Have you considered joining the maths club?'

Nick shrugged. 'Maybe.' He was good at maths, but art was his favourite class. He loved drawing manga-style cartoons. When he was doing that, he could block out everything else.

'It meets on Tuesday lunchtimes.'

Nick spent most lunchtimes in the toilets to avoid the chaos of the canteen and the glare of the fluorescent lights. The loo was nearly as bad, with its pungent disinfectant smell that did little to mask the other, even worse, odours. The younger boys roughhoused and chucked wet paper towels at each other, while the older boys vaped, puffing out cloyingly fruity scents that made him feel nauseous. But at least he could hide in a toilet stall.

'You know I'm new to the school?' said Mr Wu.

Nick nodded.

'I'll let you in on a secret. It's hard for teachers to settle in, too. If you ever need anyone to talk to, my door is always open.'

'Thanks,' Nick muttered. There was no way he'd ever take Mr Wu up on his offer. People already thought he was the teacher's pet.

'Right.' Mr Wu took out his phone and checked the time. His home screen was a chubby baby boy with a shock of black hair. 'Well, I should be getting home – and so should you.'

Taking a deep breath, Nick put on his noise-cancelling headphones and ventured out into the hallway. Luckily, by now the corridor had emptied. Nick retrieved some books from his locker and headed out to the bus stop.

He saw his sister holding court with a group of her friends. He wondered what it would be like to be one of the popular kids like Holly. They were all looking at something on Holly's phone.

'He's so cute!' squealed Holly's best friend, Riley.

'I can't believe a sixth-former said you were cool,' said Chloe.

Nick knew they had to be talking about Aaron, who worked at the cinema. It was obvious that his sister had a massive crush on him. Holly thought Nick was clueless, but he didn't miss much. He could always tell what people were feeling and couldn't understand why other people couldn't. It was as obvious to him as the colour of someone's hair.

'Oh, look, it's your little brother,' said Chloe.

'Hey, Nicky!' Riley waved at him in a mockingly friendly way. 'Want to sit with us?'

'Shut up,' said Holly, giving her friend a shove.

For the first week of secondary school, Mum had forced Holly to take the bus home with Nick. She'd grudgingly complied, but, after that first week was over, she'd stopped acknowledging his presence at school.

The bus, when it pulled up, was so crowded that Nick decided to walk home instead, even though it took nearly an hour. The sky, heavy with clouds, was the colour of the graphite pencils Nick used for sketching. Hopefully it would snow and school would be closed for days.

Nick took out his key and let himself into the cottage. Holly had made it home before him, judging from the Doc Martens and backpack strewn on the floor. Going into the kitchen, Nick fixed himself a hot chocolate and two slices of toast with peanut butter. He was always ravenous after school because he was usually too tense to choke down the packed lunch Mum made for him.

Meow.

Jonesy rubbed against his ankles, demanding attention.

'Did you miss me, Mr Fluffypants?' Nick murmured, picking him up. He stroked the cat's soft, tabby fur as he purred. That always made him feel better. Too bad he couldn't take Jonesy to school with him. He'd heard about some kids getting to take emotional support animals to school. But Jonesy had a mind of his own. If allowed to go to school, the cat would probably spend the whole school day hunting for mice, sleeping on the radiators and begging for scraps in the canteen. Or worse, cosying up to Grace Maxwell. Cats were fickle like that.

Still, giving Jonesy cuddles after school went a long way towards helping Nick relax. He scratched the cat behind his ears and Jonesy purred with satisfaction.

Once Jonesy had had enough, Nick went upstairs. He'd done all his homework at breaktime, so he got out his art things. It was Holly's birthday tomorrow and he was making her a birthday card. Not that she deserved one, given how moody she'd been lately, but she was still his sister. Besides, Nick liked having a project to work on.

He decided to draw her as a manga heroine, holding a sword as if she were a ninja warrior. As he sketched, he made up a story in his head, about a warrior who could defeat bullies with one lash of her magical sword of justice. He was so engrossed in his work, it took him a while to realise that his parents had come home. Voices floated up from the kitchen.

'. . . I know it's your night off, but one of us has to go – we need to have two people on duty. I've tried everyone else on the rota already. I'd go, but I promised Holly that I would help her study for her chemistry test tonight,' said Dad. 'You know how much she needs the help.'

'What if the sound system breaks again?' said Mum.

'I sorted out the wiring,' Dad replied. 'It should be fine for a bit.'

Mum groaned. 'Yes, but we both know it's going to break again. Last Saturday was a complete nightmare. Why can't you accept that it's broken, James? That some things CAN'T be fixed!'

Nick's stomach twisted with anxiety. He hated it when Mum and Dad argued. But it was almost worse when they didn't. Things had been weird between them for a few days, the air prickling with unresolved tension. Nick was like a human barometer; he could pick up on people's moods instantly. He'd know his mum had been upset for weeks. Maybe before she even realised it herself. When she smiled, her mouth moved but her eyes looked sad.

He tiptoed to Holly's bedroom and, ignoring the sign on the door that said KEEP OUT, went inside.

His sister was watching Netflix on her laptop.

'Ever heard of knocking?' Holly asked, taking off her headphones.

'What are you watching?' Nick asked her.

'Get out.'

Nick backed away. He should have known better than to try to speak to her.

'No, stupid,' said Holly. '*Get Out*. It's a horror movie.'

Nick didn't like horror movies. He hated the horrible feeling of waiting for bad things to happen. That's how he felt now – like something awful was going to happen to his family unless he found a way to stop it. In movies, a hero always saved the day.

But Nick was no hero.

'Mum and Dad are having another fight,' he told her.

'So what do you want me to do about it?' she said.

'Do you think they're going to get divorced?'

What if he had to choose which parent to live with? How could Nick possibly do that? He loved them both equally. There was no way he could choose between Mum and Dad.

Nick remembered when Grace's parents got divorced in primary school. She had cried and cried the day her dad had moved out of their house. Nick had felt so sad for her that he'd cried too.

'Why are you crying?' Grace had wanted to know. 'Your parents aren't getting divorced.'

Nick always felt things deeply. When people he cared about were hurt or sad, he felt it like a physical ache. And when they were happy, he shared their joy intensely. Mum had once told him that his empathy was a superpower, but Nick didn't agree. He thought it made him weak. It was why boys like Damon Carter picked on him – they knew he was vulnerable.

'You're such an idiot,' said Holly, rolling her eyes. 'Get out. And I'm not talking about the movie this time.'

When they were little, his big sister used to comfort Nick when he was upset. She'd let him sleep in her bed if he had a nightmare, singing him Disney songs and rubbing his back until he fell back asleep. She'd help him build his LEGO models and then act out funny stories with the mini figures.

Nick shut the door behind him, trying not to cry. He missed Holly, even though she was still there. Why did everything have to change?

James looked out of the kitchen window. The clouds outside were heavy and iron grey. The forecast was predicting a snowstorm later. But he'd already unleashed a storm inside the house, by telling Sarah one of them needed to go to the cinema on the only night they both had off this week.

'We just can't go on like this,' said Sarah. Her jaw was tense and she was gripping the handle of her mug so tightly, the whites of her knuckles showed. 'Something has to change.'

'Business will pick up again,' said James. 'I'm sure it will. There are some big movies out next year – event cinema. Then maybe we can hire some more staff.' He'd been telling himself this for the past few years. It was getting harder and harder to believe it himself. He'd hated having to ask Sarah to fill in, but nobody else was available.

Sarah shook her head. 'You need to face the facts, James. The cinema is failing. Last weekend was a total disaster. Thank God Holly saved the day.'

'But I managed to repair the sound.' Why wouldn't she give him any credit for that?

'It was a false economy,' replied Sarah. 'We lost all our takings in paying out refunds. We need a new sound system and we simply can't afford it.'

'I'll find the money,' said James desperately. Though he had no idea where. They had already sunk everything they had into the business. There was no way the bank would lend them more money to cover the cost of a new sound system. They were still paying back the government loans that had got them through Covid.

'I'm not just talking about the cinema,' said Sarah ominously. 'Didn't you listen to anything I said on Saturday?'

He *had* listened and felt terrible about the fact that his wife felt so unhappy and unfulfilled. He just felt powerless to do anything about it. The cinema was running him ragged. He'd love to be around more, but it just wasn't possible. Not if he was to keep the Picture Palace going.

'We'll get through this,' he said. 'We've gone through rough patches before and we've got through them together. Like when my dad passed away, or after Nick was born. We've always helped each out.'

'This feels too big to fix,' replied Sarah sadly. 'Maybe we should just cut our losses and walk away.'

James didn't know whether she was talking about the cinema or their marriage. And he was too scared to ask.

'You're catastrophising,' he said. 'I'm concerned about you, Sarah. You've not been yourself lately.'

'Exactly!' cried Sarah. 'That's what I've been trying to tell you. I've lost all sense of who I am. I feel . . . invisible.'

James stared at her in disbelief. How could she feel this way? It didn't make any sense. Of course she wasn't invisible. She was the very centre of their family. They all adored her.

'I think you should go to the doctor,' suggested James. 'You're not sleeping well and you seem angry all the time.'

Sarah laughed humourlessly. 'When would I even find the time to go to the doctor? I'm too busy ferrying Mum around to *her* doctor's appointments.'

'I'm worried that your anxiety is back,' said James.

Sarah slammed her mug down on the counter. 'How *dare* you psychoanalyse me!' she shouted. 'Or pretend that this is all just in my head?'

'Whoa! That's not what I meant!' protested James.

'I'm not the only one with a problem. This isn't about *me*, James. It's about *us*.'

'I'm just worried about you,' said James. 'The last time you were sick, I didn't realise until too late. I don't want to make that mistake again. I want to help.'

'Well, you have an interesting way of showing it,' said Sarah sarcastically. 'By creating even more work for me.'

James held up his hands in defeat. 'Look, if you really don't want to go to the cinema tonight, I'll go. It's just that I promised Holly I would help her with her homework.'

'No, of course I'll go. I'll do what's needed, just like I always do.' Sarah put on her coat, grabbed her bag and went out, slamming the door behind her.

Well, I made a complete mess of that, thought James despondently as he started to make dinner. Somehow he had only made things worse.

'Where's Mum?' Nick asked, coming into the kitchen a while later.

'She's had to go to the cinema,' explained James. 'Someone called in sick, so she's covering the evening shift.' He pointed to the carrots. 'Can you chop these for me, bud? I'm making shepherd's pie for dinner.'

Nick washed his hands and started cutting the carrots into neat discs.

'How was school today?' asked James.

Nick shrugged. 'I got a hundred per cent on my maths test. We're doing geometry.'

'That's brilliant.' James picked up one of the carrot discs. 'Have you learnt how to calculate the circumference of a circle yet?'

'Two times pi times the radius,' said Nick flatly without looking up.

James knew something was wrong. 'What's up, Nick? I can tell something's on your mind.'

'I heard you and Mum fighting,' said Nick.

James sighed and put down the peeler. 'I'm really sorry you had to hear that, Nick. Did it make you feel upset?'

Nick nodded, his eyes welling with tears.

James pulled Nick into a hug. 'You mustn't worry, OK? Everybody argues sometimes – even people who love each other very much.'

He knew he was trying to convince himself of that as much as Nick.

James took a deep breath, determined to be strong for his son. 'Let's talk about something more cheerful. Can you believe it's nearly December – almost time for the film festival.'

'Have you and Mum picked the movies yet?' asked Nick.

'Not yet,' said James. 'But we will.'

He was sure Sarah didn't mean what she said on the weekend about not going ahead with the festival. It was a family tradition. All four of them always watched the movies together and Nick was always allowed to stay up late, even on a school night.

James opened the back door and went outside to put the vegetable peelings into the compost pile. Fluffy white flakes were falling from the sky. 'Nick!' he called. 'Nick – come outside!'

The ground and tree branches were already covered in a light dusting of snow. Jonesy was scampering across the grass, vainly attempting to catch falling snowflakes in his paws. In the distance, their neighbours' cottages puffed smoke from their chimneys, their windows and Christmas lights glowing brightly in the dark night. The countryside looked magical as flakes swirled through the air, like a snow globe come to life.

'It's really coming down,' said James.

Laughing, Nick scooped up some snow and shaped it into a ball. He threw it at Holly's window, where it hit the glass with a soft thump.

A moment later, she opened her window and stuck her head out. White flakes landed on her dark hair and glowed in the dark night.

'It's snowing, Holly!' Nick called up to her.

'Yeah, I can see that,' she said. But a few minutes later she joined them outdoors. Soon, she and Nick were running around, laughing and flinging handfuls of snow at each other. James wished Sarah were there too.

'Make a wish!' he called to the kids. 'It's the first snowfall of the season.'

He closed his eyes and looked up to the heavens. Cold flakes landed on his cheeks and eyelids, like angel's kisses, as he made his wish.

Please let this be a good Christmas, he thought. *And let me find a way to make Sarah happy again.*

8th December 2006

James stood outside the cinema with his wife and father, looking up at the glowing marquee with *GRAND OPENING TONIGHT* written in black letters. The cream-coloured façade, which had been covered with ugly steel cladding when they'd purchased it, had been restored to its 1930s glamour. In the classic art deco style, two elegant wings curved in above the entrance, giving the building the feel of an ocean liner. And in a way, a cinema *was* like a boat, because a film could transport you to any time and place – from fantasy kingdoms populated by elves and distant planets ruled by aliens to a coliseum in ancient Rome.

'I can't believe it is finally happening,' said James. 'The Picture Palace is actually opening.'

Sarah gave him a hug. 'I never doubted it for a minute.'

'Oh, I did.' Sean chuckled. 'For instance, when we discovered that the roof had been completely corroded by damp and lichen.'

'Or when we found that all the walls were insulated with asbestos,' added James, wincing at the memory.

'Not forgetting when English Heritage rejected our plan to have a café,' said Sean.

The cinema, designed by the noted architect Reginald Dickson, was a Grade II listed building, which had added a further complication to what was already an extremely tricky renovation. English Heritage had had to approve their designs, to ensure that they were preserving the architectural heritage of the building, while also conforming to contemporary health-and-safety regulations.

'I couldn't have done it without the two of you,' admitted James.

The past two years had certainly been a wild rollercoaster ride, with twists and turns that had had James clinging on for dear life. There was a good reason the cinema had been derelict for so long – nobody had been crazy enough to take it on. Many people had warned him it was a fool's errand, that even if he managed to complete the restoration, a small community like Plumdale couldn't sustain a cinema. James was determined to prove them wrong. He'd ploughed all their assets into the cinema, so he didn't really have any other option but to make it a success.

Thank God for his dad. While working on the renovations, James's recently retired father had been living with them in their cottage on the outskirts of Plumdale, a short drive from the cinema. From his Pinewood experience, Sean knew how to manage a team of builders. He'd ensured that the workers adhered to their vision. Aware of their limited budget, he'd looked for ways to save money without cutting corners or compromising on quality.

Sarah had been instrumental, too. After the first year of renovation, they'd hit a major snag when they'd knocked down some walls to construct new bathrooms and discovered major structural defects. Water damage from the roof had caused the building's steel frame to corrode, which would have taken them thousands of pounds over budget to repair. When the bank had refused to lend the necessary funds to reinforce the frame, Sarah had stepped in. She'd launched a fundraising drive, calling in favours from actors she knew from her BBC days.

The local community had been amazing as well. The Plumdale Beautification Committee had rallied, determined to rid the village of a derelict eyesore and give it a working cinema again. Practically overnight, James and Sean had found themselves a whole crew of volunteers. In exchange for a lifetime membership that entitled them to discounted tickets, helpers had ripped up carpets, removed damaged plaster, painted walls and tiled the bathrooms. Neighbours who weren't handy had helped in other ways, bringing the workers tea and home-made biscuits.

James unlocked the cinema's doors and they stepped into the double-height foyer with its ceiling lights shaped like stars. It bore no resemblance to how it had looked the first time he'd gone inside. The stench had made him gag. The lobby had been filled with garbage and broken glass. The moth-eaten seats had been ripped out of the auditorium and were piled in a heap. Pigeons had been roosting in the balcony and a thick layer of guano had covered most surfaces. A leaking roof and corroding pipes had meant that stagnant water had puddled on the floor. Mice had nibbled through wires and insulation. The place had been such a mess, James had wondered if he'd made the biggest mistake of his life.

Then, moments after entering the auditorium, a pigeon had pooped on his head.

'That's a good omen,' Sarah had told him, laughing. 'It means good luck.'

The pigeon poo had proved prophetic. In addition to plenty of mishaps, they had enjoyed some good luck too. When the ugly brown 1960s carpet had been ripped up, they had discovered a pristine black-and-white marble floor underneath. The gilded framing around the proscenium arch had gleamed as good as new once the layer of bird droppings had been removed. Best of all, hidden under the floor at the front of the theatre, had been a magnificent organ. The instrument was housed within a console, made up of curving geometrical panes of green glass. It was a work of art, evoking the bygone days of silent movies.

James had taken great pains to ensure that the cinema closely matched its former appearance. He and Sarah had spent hours in the Plumdale library, where Pam Cusack, the librarian, had found them old photographs of the cinema's interior. From door handles to light switches, every choice had been carefully considered. They had retained the original features wherever possible, while modernising the plumbing, electrics and ventilation systems.

Now, the curved chrome counter gleamed. Rather than just selling tickets and the usual cinema snacks, they had installed an Italian coffee machine and had delicious cakes supplied by a local baker. They had added tables and chairs, creating a café area. There was a well-stocked bookcase with books about cinema, and the walls had been hung with paintings by local artists. A noticeboard announced upcoming events at the cinema, a carol concert, an amateur dramatic society's pantomime and a Christmas craft fair at the village hall. James's vision was that the cinema would be a hub for the whole community.

'I'm going to make a coffee,' said Sarah. 'I need all the practice I can get. That machine is more complicated to operate than the control deck of a spacecraft.'

James chuckled. 'It's worth it, though – it's the best coffee in the Cotswolds.'

'Let's go do one final check,' said Sean.

James and his father walked through the cinema. In the bathrooms, which they had decorated with black-and-white tiles, they checked the taps. James spotted a smudge on the chrome-framed mirror and polished it with his sleeve. He saw his father's reflection next to him – the facial resemblance between the two men was unmistakeable, with their blue eyes, strong noses and prominent cheekbones. Over the past two years, Sean's hair had turned white, the ageing process no doubt accelerated by the stress of the renovations.

'Sorry your retirement hasn't been very relaxing so far, Dad,' said James.

'I've enjoyed every second of it, son,' replied Sean.

Going into the auditorium, they admired the fruits of their labour. James gazed up at the ceiling, with its elegant geometric patterns. The cream-coloured walls undulated gently with stucco waves, and they had managed to restore the original scallop-shell-shaped lights. The ornate proscenium arch gleamed and red curtains covered the screen.

'Ah,' said Sean, sitting down and reclining back. 'These seats are so comfortable.'

The three hundred seats had been upholstered in plush red velvet. Some had small brass plaques on the armrests, bearing the name of a donor who had contributed to the fundraising campaign.

'I wish Mum was here to see this,' confessed James. His mum's favourite films had been musicals; she had always hummed show tunes while doing chores around the house.

'Oh, she's looking down on us and smiling,' said Sean. 'In fact, I'm convinced she had a word with the big man upstairs when things were looking bad for us.'

After his mother had died, James and his dad had struggled to talk about their feelings. Mary had been a chatterbox, and, after her passing, a pall of silence had fallen over the flat in Ealing. Each lost in their grief, James and his father had numbly haunted the rooms, as if they'd been ghosts themselves.

Things had changed when they had started to go to the cinema together every weekend. It didn't matter what was. For an hour or two, lost in the story showing on the screen, they could escape from their sadness together. Movies had given them something to talk about, to fill the silence. After watching a movie, they would discuss the film over a pub lunch. Cinema had been their comfort and salvation. Movies had helped them connect to each other during that dark time.

James's hair flopped in front of his eyes and he pushed it back. 'If Mum was here, she would tell me I need a haircut.'

Sean chuckled, which turned into a chesty cough. He braced himself on the armrests as he caught his breath.

'That doesn't sound good,' said James, patting his dad's back. 'You should get that checked out.'

Sean waved away his son's concerns. 'No need. It's probably just a cold – there's always one going around at this time of year.'

The auditorium door opened and Roger came in. 'Sarah sent me to fetch you. Coffee's ready.'

Roger, a small, dapper man in his early fifties, was the cinema's head projectionist. James sometimes wondered if Roger's arrival had also been the result of his mum's divine intervention. Roger had worked in cinemas for decades, progressing from ticket sales to projectionist. He knew everything there was to know about running a cinema.

They went back out to the lobby, where three coffees were waiting for them in the café. Sarah was sitting at one of the tables typing on her laptop. She had gone freelance after leaving the BBC and had had a steady stream of work editing scripts. Her freelance income was a blessing, as the cinema had run so far over budget. Once the cinema was up and running, the plan was that she would be able to devote more time to her own writing.

James took a sip of his coffee – Sarah had made his with extra milk, just the way he liked it. 'What are you working on?' he inquired.

'An episode of *The Vicarage Mysteries*.'

'Ooh, what's it about?' asked Roger, nursing his espresso. He and his partner, Omar, were both fans of the long-running programme.

'Someone donates a Fabergé egg to the parish jumble sale,' said Sarah. 'But it gets stolen.'

Roger chuckled. 'Of course it does. There's never a dull moment at St Julian's.'

After they finished their coffees, Sean took out a pack of cigarettes from his shirt pocket and tapped them on the table. Getting up, he headed out of the cinema's back door to have a smoke in the car park. James noticed that it was empty. The only vehicles were their car and Roger's. 'What if nobody comes?'

'They'll come,' said Sarah confidently. She went back to working on her laptop.

'Let's run the trailers,' suggested Roger. 'Just to check Groucho is working OK.'

They went upstairs to the tiny projection room. James took the reel of film from its metal cannister and, supervised by Roger, loaded it onto the top of the projector. One of the biggest surprises was how much physical strength it required. Roger's wiry arms were strong from years of loading heavy film cannisters onto projectors.

James threaded the 35mm film through various cylinders, fitting the holes running along the edge of the film into the moving sprockets that gripped it in place. It was a delicate operation, as the tension had to be exactly right.

Roger watched James's every move. 'Make sure the film isn't twisted.'

James tinkered with the amount of clearance, then twisted the framing knob and focus knob, making minute adjustments.

'Always remember to check – and then double-check,' said Roger patiently.

James opened the projector's lamp house and turned the motor on. The top reel spun anti-clockwise, feeding film through the projector, then onto the bottom reel, which spun clockwise. As if by magic, an image appeared on the cinema screen as the trailers played.

'Looks good to me,' said James.

Roger turned the focus knob a few millimetres, making a minute adjustment. Once satisfied, he prepared the feature presentation, making sure the cue marks were perfectly positioned to ensure a seamless changeover.

'We're ready,' he announced once he had finished.

James went back downstairs to change into smart clothes for the grand opening. In the office, he put on a suit for the first time since giving up his software job, while Sarah slipped into a dark green dress. It matched the emerald necklace Sean had given her as a wedding gift.

'I've never been so nervous,' said James, doing up his shirt buttons. 'Not even on our wedding day.'

Sarah laughed. 'Should I be offended by that?'

'Not at all. I knew I wasn't making a mistake marrying you,' said James. 'But I'm not so sure about the cinema. What if we've just spent two years of our lives, and our entire savings, on something that doesn't succeed.'

He was aware of everything Sarah had given up so that he could pursue his dream.

'It will be a success,' Sarah assured him, straightening his tie. She pushed the hair out of his eyes and then gave him a kiss. 'How could it not be when so many people have come together to help us?'

'Well, here goes,' said James. Taking Sarah's hand, he went into the lobby and flung open the cinema doors.

Ian Griffiths, who ran an antique shop a few doors down, was the first to arrive. A volunteer from the Plumdale Beautification Society, he'd helped with the renovations. Ian had hooked them up with an upholsterer and the skilled craftsman who had restored their stucco mouldings.

Next to turn up was Pam, the librarian who had helped them with their research. A short middle-aged woman, she was wearing a hand-knitted mohair jumper. She looked around the lobby admiringly. 'It's so good to be back in here. I took my kids to see movies here most Saturdays when they were little. I was so sad when this place shut down in 1976.'

'At least it didn't become a bingo hall,' said her best friend, Olwyn Powell, a teacher from the next village over. 'That's what happened to a lot of these old art deco cinemas.'

'Oh, I don't know,' said Vi, a trendy-looking local artist who had curated the display in the café. 'I don't mind a bit of bingo.'

'I had my first kiss here, in the back row of the stalls,' Ian told Sarah and James. 'During a screening of *Jaws*.'

'Who was the lucky lady?' asked Sarah.

Ian's eyes twinkled. 'A gentleman never tells.'

'Pari!' squealed Sarah, noticing her best friend come in. Pari had used her contacts in the comedy world to help the cinema. She'd organised a fundraising gig and got big-name comedians to donate.

James gave Pari a hug. 'It's good of you to come.'

'It worked out well,' said Pari. 'I have a gig in Oxford tomorrow. Besides, I know how much this means to you both.'

Pari still juggled working at the BBC with plugging away at her stand-up. James wasn't sure why she hadn't made it big yet – she was funnier than most people on TV.

'*Bonjour*,' said a dark-haired man in a suit. 'I was very happy to see that you will be showing some French films.' Roger's partner, Omar, a maths teacher at the local secondary school, was originally from Morocco. He spoke fluent French as well as his native Arabic.

James nodded enthusiastically. 'Sarah is going to run a weekly world-cinema club.'

There was a murmur as David Langdon, the local MP, came into the cinema with his teenaged daughter, Kath. The MP was a notorious womaniser, who featured regularly in gossip columns. Despite his questionable morals, he'd been extremely helpful when it came to navigating planning permissions and dealing with English Heritage.

'Thanks for all your help, David,' said James.

'My pleasure,' replied David, pumping his hand heartily. 'I'm always glad to see new jobs being created in my constituency.' He smiled proudly at his daughter. 'Plus, Kath loves going to the pictures. She can't wait to see the film.'

'Are you a Jude Law fan?' James asked her.

The teenaged girl blushed awkwardly. 'I prefer Cameron Diaz.'

'Let's get you some popcorn.' Sarah led the MP's daughter over to the café area.

James looked around the lobby, which was now full of guests drinking champagne that Roger and Omar had procured on a trip to their holiday home in Normandy. He was touched that so many friends, old and new, had turned up for their big night. It felt like the whole community was rooting for them to succeed.

'It's time,' said Sarah, coming over and slipping her arm around his waist.

They walked over to the auditorium doors. James cleared his throat. 'Thanks very much to all of you for coming, and for all of you who helped along the way. After thirty years, the magic of cinema finally returns to Plumdale tonight.'

Pari let out an enthusiastic whoop.

Sarah cut the red ribbon stretching across the auditorium doors. 'I declare the Plumdale Picture Palace open!' she announced.

As the audience filed into the cinema, Olwyn played a medley of show tunes from movie musicals on the Wurlitzer organ.

'Come on,' said Sarah, nudging James. 'We don't want to miss the trailers.'

They took their seats in the circle with Sean. James looked down at the packed stalls below, filling with people. His heart swelled with pride.

'We did it,' whispered Sarah, squeezing his hand.

The feature presentation was a new Christmas film called *The Holiday*. It was about two heartbroken women who swap houses – one in Los Angeles, the other in a village not unlike Plumdale – after bad break-ups, and both fall in love in the process. James still didn't love romcoms as much as his wife, but this one seemed like it might stand the test of time.

Halfway through the movie, Sarah stood up and slipped out of the auditorium.

'Everything OK?' James whispered when she returned.

'I just got my period,' Sarah said quietly.

James put his arm around her and pulled her close. He knew that despite the happiness of the day, his wife's heart was breaking. The cinema was their baby – but they wanted a real baby, too. Despite doing everything they could to conceive, Sarah's period had arrived like clockwork every month.

Dr Curtis had assured them that there was nothing to worry about. 'You're young and healthy,' he'd said, sounding unconcerned. 'Come back once you've been trying for over a year.'

It had been ten months now. James knew how badly Sarah longed to be a mother, how difficult she found it when yet another friend announced her pregnancy, or she saw a cute baby in a pram.

James wanted children, too, but as long as he had Sarah, he felt complete. But just as Sarah hadn't given up on his dream of owning a cinema, even when things got tough, he wouldn't give up on their dream of having a baby.

'We'll just have to keep trying,' he whispered, kissing the side of her head.

Sarah's emerald necklace, that had once belonged to his mother, glinted in the light from the projector. James hoped that if his mum was looking down on them, she might help them out yet again.

Chapter 5

Present Day

Sarah drove to the cinema, replaying her argument with James over and over in her head. She was still fuming. How *dare* he suggest she was losing her mind again! James was the one with delusions. Why wouldn't he admit how unsustainable their situation was? The cinema was haemorrhaging money; Saturday's refunds had been the last thing they needed. Luckily, Holly had been amazing in a crisis; she'd had the audience eating out of the palm of her hand.

I should have let her go to the audition, thought Sarah. She'd always known her daughter was talented, but seeing her in action had made her realise how much she'd matured as a performer. As she'd watched her belting out Disney songs, Sarah had seen how much her daughter loved entertaining. How *alive* she was when she was on stage.

As she drove through the countryside, past quaint country pubs advertising Christmas dinners and pretty stone cottages decked out with fairy lights and wreaths, Sarah started to calm down. James's concern had made her fly off the handle because he'd triggered her deepest fear – that she was getting ill again. That it wasn't just the cinema and family worries and creative frustration causing her low mood.

I can't go crazy again, thought Sarah. *Too many people rely on me.*

A few flakes of snow drifted through the air as Sarah pulled into the car park at the back of the cinema.

Tonight's World Film Club screening was *Fanny and Alexander*, Ingmar Bergman's semi-autobiographical master-piece. But would anyone venture out into the cold to watch a long and challenging Swedish movie?

Aaron was slumped behind the concession stand, scrolling through his phone. He quickly put it in his back pocket as Sarah came in. But he wasn't able to hide the look of disappointment on his face that it was Sarah, rather than Holly, covering the night shift.

Sarah knew that her daughter had a crush on Aaron too. And she could see why – he was cute. But Holly was far too young – and ambitious – to get tied down to a local boy, even one as nice as Aaron.

'Have we sold any tickets?' Sarah asked him.

'A few,' he said.

Just then, the doors opened, sending an icy blast of air into the lobby.

'You're brave,' said Sarah as Iris came into the lobby, brushing a few snowflakes off her black bob.

'Oh, I'm excited about the snow,' said Iris, pulling off her gloves. 'I've never seen it before – except for in movies.'

'No, I meant because *Fanny and Alexander* is three hours long,' teased Sarah.

'I just had to get out of the house. Henry has a cold, poor little guy. I've been cooped up with him at home all day. When my husband came home from school, I practi-cally ran out of the door.' She handed Sarah her credit card. 'I should probably get a coffee to stay awake, not that it stopped me from dozing off last time.'

'Wait a minute,' said Sarah, something suddenly dawning on her as she looked at the name on Iris's card. 'Your husband is a teacher?'

'Yes, he teaches maths at Severn Valley secondary.'

Sarah laughed as she began to make Iris's latte. 'Your husband is my son's teacher. What a small world.'

Lowering her voice so that Aaron wouldn't hear, Iris said, 'By the way, I took your advice and went to the doctor. He diagnosed postnatal anxiety and recommended a local therapist.'

Sarah nodded sympathetically. She'd suspected as much. After having Nick, she'd suffered from severe postnatal anxiety, so she'd recognised the signs. She shuddered involuntarily, remembering those awful months.

James had been incredibly supportive once he'd realised she was unwell. Sarah felt a pang of guilt over their argument earlier. She probably shouldn't have jumped down his throat when he suggested seeing the doctor.

'It takes time to get better,' she said, pouring milk over the espresso before handing it to Iris.

Iris added a packet of sugar to her coffee and gave it a stir. 'I just feel ashamed that I'm struggling when everyone says that this first year with my baby should be magical.'

'Your hormones are completely out of whack and you've just experienced two major life changes — having a baby and moving to a foreign country,' said Sarah. 'There's no shame in seeking help. You need to stay healthy for Henry's sake, and your own.'

Pot . . . kettle . . . black . . . thought Sarah. As Iris went into the auditorium, she resolved to make an appointment with her own GP.

Sarah helped Aaron tidy up the concession stand, then slipped into the back of the cinema to watch the movie. As the Swedish family on screen celebrated Christmas with a lavish feast and games, Sarah felt a spark of Christmas spirit flicker inside her. Perhaps she'd been wrong to consider not going ahead with the film festival. Christmas movies *did* bring a lot of joy.

Hours later, as the credits began to roll, Sarah got up and went into the lobby. During the film, a thick covering of snow had covered the village like icing on a Christmas cake. It looked beautiful, but the country lanes would be impassable until they'd been cleared by a snowplough.

Customers straggled out of the auditorium, blinking as they entered the light.

Sarah sent James a text message. *Not safe to drive – staying at the cinema tonight.* There was a sofa and blankets in the office, and she kept a toothbrush and a few other toiletries in a desk drawer. It wouldn't be the first time she'd been stuck there overnight. Perhaps it wasn't such a bad thing – after their argument, they both needed space to cool down.

'Why don't you head home,' she told Aaron, who lived in the village. 'I can close up on my own.'

'Thanks,' said Aaron. As he was about to go out of the door, he called over his shoulder, 'Oh, and wish Holly a happy birthday from me tomorrow.'

'I will,' Sarah called back.

She had already wrapped her daughter's present but would have to bake the cake when she got home. Hopefully Holly wouldn't refuse to eat it just to spite her.

Sarah checked the auditorium, collecting any rubbish that had been left behind. When she returned to the lobby, one customer remained there. A man in an expensive-looking sheepskin coat, biker boots and a beanie hat pulled down low was jabbing at his phone.

'Excuse me,' he said in an Australian accent. 'I'm trying to order an Uber back to my hotel, but I'm not having any luck.'

'Uber doesn't operate around here,' explained Sarah. She went over to the noticeboard in the café area and unpinned a business card for Cotswold Cars. She handed it to the man. 'You can try this.'

'Thanks.' The man dialled the number. 'Bugger!' he said, scratching his salt-and-pepper stubble. 'No one's picking up.'

Kevin Williams, who was the owner and sole employee of Cotswold Cars (the 's' in cars being somewhat misleading), also played bass in a hard rock cover band called Zed Leppelin that performed in local pubs. He was probably currently strumming the 'Stairway to Heaven' guitar solo right around now.

'How did you get here this evening?' Sarah asked her stranded customer.

'My assistant drove me,' he replied. 'I told her I'd make my own way back to Merricourt Manor.' He opened the cinema door, letting a flurry of snowflakes blow into the lobby. 'Maybe I could walk?'

'Not a good idea. Merricourt Manor is a few miles away,' said Sarah. 'It wouldn't be safe on a night like this.' It was snowing very heavily and there was no pavement once you left the village.

Defeated, the man shut the door.

Sarah thought for a moment. 'There might be rooms at the Rose and Crown. Shall I give them a call?'

'If you wouldn't mind.'

Sarah made a quick phone call. 'No luck, I'm afraid. They've got a wedding party staying there, so all the rooms are occupied.'

'No room at the inn, eh?' The man gave her a wry smile.

Sarah knew she couldn't turf him out into the cold. He'd freeze to death.

'Look, I can't get home either,' said Sarah. 'You're welcome to stay here too. The roads should be clear by morning.' She just had to hope that the Bergman fan wasn't a psycho killer.

'Well, thank you for your hospitality,' said the man. 'I was about to start building an igloo out in the village square.'

Laughing, Sarah went behind the concession stand. 'It's not as comfortable here as at Merricourt Manor, but it's warm, we have plenty of snacks, and we can always watch another movie. Can I get you a drink?'

'I'd love a flat white,' said the man, setting down his leather satchel and shrugging off his coat. Underneath it he was wearing black jeans, a chunky watch with a thick leather strap and a grey cashmere sweater that clung to his muscled physique. Even without the foreign accent, his outfit would have given away the fact that he wasn't a local. You couldn't buy clothes like that in Plumdale's only gentleman's apparel shop, Country Pursuits. Sarah suspected that his ensemble cost more than she spent on her whole family's wardrobe.

Over the hiss of the coffee machine, Sarah introduced herself. 'As we're spending the night together, we should probably get acquainted. I'm Sarah.'

'Noa,' he replied. He pulled off his beanie, releasing an impressive mane of wavy dark hair streaked with grey.

Sarah stifled a gasp of recognition as she realised who she was speaking to. It was Noa Drakos, the Academy-Award winning director.

'Is this your cinema?' he asked.

She nodded. 'Mine and my husband's.'

'It's beautiful. I grew up in a little town outside Cairns. It was devastated by a cyclone in 1918 and rebuilt in the art deco style. Your cinema reminds me of the Roxy, where I used to watch films growing up.' Noa stretched his legs out, resting the heel of his right boot on the toe of his left.

Sarah carried the flat white, and a herbal tea for herself, over to the table he was sitting at.

'Thanks,' he said, gesturing for her to sit down opposite. He picked up the coffee and inhaled deeply. 'This smells amazing.'

'By the way, I loved *ANZAC*.' Sarah decided not to be coy and pretend that she didn't know who he was.

'Thanks, Sarah. I'm flattered.' He looked into her eyes intently. His eyes were such a dark brown, Sarah could hardly make out their pupils. 'I can tell you have good taste, or you wouldn't be screening *Fanny and Alexander* – it's one of my favourite movies.'

'Oh, me too!' said Sarah. 'I've always thought it was about the magic of storytelling.' Bergman's film was like a love letter to stories and cinema.

'The character of Alexander is based on Bergman himself. Like the boy in the movie, he received a magic lantern from an aunt when he was ten. It was what made him want to make movies.' Noa took a sip of his coffee.

'What made *you* want to make movies?' asked Sarah. She had so many questions for him – where he got his inspiration, which actors he'd enjoyed working with most – and which he'd found difficult. She'd met a few directors in her BBC days, but nobody of Noa's stature.

'I got a Super Eight camera for Christmas when I was a kid. From that point onwards, I saw life through a lens.' He formed a circle with his thumb and forefinger, and, holding it up to his right eye, trained his gaze on Sarah.

Sarah squirmed under his scrutiny. She wasn't used to being studied like this; most of the time she felt invisible.

'Was it hard to get your first film made?' she asked, trying to deflect his attention.

It didn't work.

'Have you ever acted, Sarah?' asked Noa, lowering his hand. 'The camera would love those golden eyes of yours.'

Noa was acting like *she* was the interesting one, not him. *Is he flirting with me?*

Sarah dismissed the thought immediately. Judging from the red-carpet photos she'd seen in magazines, Noa only dated stunning actresses – usually ones who appeared in his movies.

'No, but my daughter, Holly, wants to act,' said Sarah. 'It's a shame she's not here tonight, I know she'd love to meet you. And James – my husband – too. He's a big fan of your work.'

'Tell me about him,' said Noa. 'This husband of yours. Are you happily married like the Ekdahls in the movie?'

Sarah thought about his question. How could you sum up three decades of marriage? 'Well, yes . . . most of the time. I mean, he's a great dad, he works hard—'

'Oh, dear . . .' said Noa, wincing. 'That doesn't sound like a glowing endorsement.'

'Marriage is just . . . complicated.' Sarah looked down at her wedding ring, thinking about the argument she and James had had earlier that evening. He was right – they *had* helped each other through some very tough times. They'd had plenty of good times, too. But somehow, recently, they'd stopped having *fun* together. There was just no time for it.

'I'll have to take your word for it.' Noa didn't sound convinced. 'I've never been brave enough to make it down the aisle.' He smiled at Sarah. 'Your husband's a lucky guy.'

Remembering her argument with James, Sarah hardly felt like a poster child for wedded bliss. Feeling self-conscious, she stood up and put their empty cups in the bin. 'Do you want another drink?'

He came over and leant against the counter. Sarah could smell his aftershave – a woody, musky scent. 'I don't suppose you have anything a bit stronger back there . . .'

'We don't have a licence to serve alcohol,' said Sarah.

'Shame,' said Noa. He rubbed his temples, then dragged his hands down his artfully stubbled cheeks. He had chunky silver rings on several fingers. 'I've had a complete nightmare of a day.'

Sarah held up her finger. 'Hang on a minute. I've just remembered something.'

She went into the office and found a bottle of whisky in a filing cabinet. It had been a gift from one of the regulars who attended the Golden Oldies screenings, who'd been grateful to James for programming her Fitbit.

Sarah returned to the lobby, waving it in the air. 'Look what I found.'

Noa rubbed his hands together.

Sarah poured them each a generous measure. She wasn't normally a whisky drinker, but nothing about this night was normal. 'Cheers.' She touched her glass to Noa's. The whisky burnt as it slid down Sarah's throat. 'So tell me why your day was such a nightmare.'

'How long do you have . . .' He sighed.

'All night,' said Sarah, smiling.

'I'm shooting a movie at Merricourt Manor,' the director explained. 'We decided to film on location here in the UK because of the tax breaks.'

'But it's winter,' said Sarah. She remembered from her BBC days that location shoots – even on films set in winter – usually occurred in the summer, when the days were longer and the weather better.

'You're right,' said Noa, nodding. 'That *is* unusual. But Merricourt Manor is fully booked with weddings in the spring and summer. We liked the location so much we decided to wait until December. Plus, the film is set at Christmas, and the village is already decorated, so we won't have to do much set-dressing.'

'Makes sense,' remarked Sarah. Ian and the Plumdale Beautification Committee made the village look picture-perfect at Christmastime.

'Well, it *did*, but the council has just withdrawn permission for us to park our crew vehicles on the grounds. Something to do with a badger sett? There was a big protest. Turns out badgers are protected. So we need a new location base – and fast – or we won't be able to wrap the shoot before Christmas.' Noa ran his hand through his thick hair, looking thoroughly exasperated.

'Oh, dear.'

'But that's not all.' He leant forward and lowered his voice conspiratorially, even though they were all alone. 'Between you and me, the script stinks. It might as well have been written by AI.'

Sarah winced. She had been following the recent Hollywood writers' strike with interest and was glad that screenwriters protected their profession against artificial intelligence. You couldn't replace human creativity with computers.

'What's it about?'

Noa grimaced. 'It's so cheesy. It's about two exes, who haven't seen each other in years. She's left an inn by an elderly relation, and he's the hotel handyman. The deal is that they have to spend one Christmas there together before she can sell it. The working title is *Ex-mas Eve*.'

'Let me guess,' said Sarah. 'She's called Eve . . . and they fall in love again by the end and she decides not to sell the inn.'

'Bingo.'

'Why are you making it? I've got to say, it doesn't sound like your sort of thing.' Sarah secretly loved the heart-warming holiday fare churned out by streamers every year. She and Holly had watched loads of them together. But Noa Drakos was an auteur. His last film, shot in black and white, had flopped at the box office but had been adored by the critics.

Noa let out a frustrated sigh. 'I need the money. I can finance a passion project with the money I'm making from directing this drivel.'

'Oh, it can't be that bad, I'm sure,' said Sarah.

'Want to bet?' Noa pulled open his satchel and took out a script. He slapped it onto the table.

Sarah's fingers itched to pull it towards herself. It had been so long since she'd read a script. *Should I ask?* Sarah wondered, trying to work up the courage.

Noa riffled through the pages, shaking his head in dismay.

Sarah poured herself another shot for Dutch courage. She gulped some down, then cleared her throat. 'Er . . . would you mind if I take a look?' she asked hesitantly. 'I, um, used to be a script editor at the BBC.'

Noa stared at her in surprise. 'Seriously?'

'Yes – I worked in the drama department, and then as a freelancer. I used to write my own stuff too. I've got an unfinished screenplay in the bottom drawer of my desk.'

Noa laughed in disbelief. 'Surely this is the sort of thing that only happens in a romcom. I'm snowed in all night with a gorgeous woman . . . and she just happens to be a script editor.'

Sarah blushed at Noa's compliment. Maybe he *was* flirting with her. Some guys just couldn't help themselves – they flirted with *everyone*. Noa was obviously one of those.

'You really want to read it?' he asked.

'Well, it's not like I have anything else to do.' Actually, there were plenty of things Sarah could do. Sleep. Get started on her online Christmas shopping. Plan the Christmas film festival. But it had been ages since she had worked on a script. Her pulse was racing with excitement at the thought of doing something creative again. Could she still do it?

She drained the rest of her whisky, willing him to say yes.

'Go right ahead.' Noa slid the screenplay over to her. 'I'd love to know what you think.'

Sarah picked up the script with trembling fingers.

'If it's OK with you, I might try to get some sleep,' said Noa, yawning.

'You can use the sofa in my office.'

'Cheers,' said Noa.

She led him into her office and got out a blanket and pillow from the cupboard. Then Noa kicked off his boots and lay down on the sofa.

Going back into the café, Sarah made herself another coffee, then sat down at the table and read the script from beginning to end. When she was done, she re-read it, this time scribbling notes in the margins. She worked feverishly through the night, fuelled by caffeine and adrenaline. Her mind was buzzing with ideas. Yes, the script was flawed. But she knew how to make it better.

At around five in the morning, when the sky was still dark, she heard a snowplough trundling through the village. The noise woke Noa up and he came out of the office. He stretched and Sarah caught a glimpse of his taut, gym-honed stomach.

'So, what did you think?' asked Noa, as Sarah made him a coffee.

'Well, the dialogue is wooden, but that can be fixed. The bigger problem is that the characters feel two-dimensional. To root for them getting back together, we need to understand who they are.' Sarah's ideas poured out of her in a rush. 'Maybe you could show some flashbacks to their previous relationship, so we get a better sense of their emotional conflicts?'

'OK . . .' said Noa.

'And the ending needs work,' continued Sarah. 'It relies too much on coincidence – even for a romcom. But I've got some ideas for how you could resolve the story in a more satisfactory way.'

Noa stared at her, frowning.

Uh-oh, thought Sarah. She'd been too honest. She should have tempered her criticism with some praise. After all, what did she know? This guy had an Oscar on his mantelpiece, not her. She'd let the whisky, and the strange situation, go to her head.

'So when can you get me a new draft?'

'Excuse me?'

'I want to hire you to do a rewrite of the script,' said Noa. 'I can offer you twenty thousand.'

'Y-you want me to work on your movie?' stammered Sarah. She wasn't sure what surprised her more – the job offer or the figure he'd just named. It was enough to buy a new sound system for the cinema.

'Yes, but I need it to be done quickly – we start shooting in two weeks.'

'Give me a minute,' said Sarah, her head spinning. 'I need to think.'

She went into the bathroom.

This is crazy. I haven't written anything for years. There was so much going on at home and at work, and Christmas was right around the corner. She'd just been telling James that she had too much to do — so why was she even considering it?

Because it was a golden opportunity. The chance of a lifetime.

When Sarah came out of the toilet stall, she stared at her reflection. Her eyes were sparkling and her cheeks were flushed.

Pulling her phone out of her pocket, she fired off a quick text message to Pari.

I just spent the night with Noa Drakos.

Pari replied instantly. *WTF?*

As a stand-up comedian, her friend had been a nocturnal creature throughout her twenties and thirties. Now she woke up at the crack of dawn to go to gym classes with terrifying names like Bootie Boot Camp and Body Blitz Insanity.

We got snowed in together at the cinema.

Sarah added the snowflake emoji and then the laughing face emoji.

Ask him if he's happy with his current representation.

Sarah laughed. Pari's law degree, combined with the skills she'd honed as a stand-up, had made her an incredibly successful agent. She had the hide of a rhinoceros and never stopped negotiating the best deals for her clients.

He asked me to work on a script.

As Sarah typed it, her heart raced with excitement. Her eyes weren't sparkling just because a handsome film director had been flirting with her all evening. Or because of the whisky she'd drunk. It was because tonight, for the first time in ages, she was working with words. Doing the thing she loved. A long-dormant part of her was beginning to wake up again. And, oh, how much she had missed it.

Of course he did. You're the best. You should do it.

That was all the encouragement she needed. Sarah washed her hands and splashed some water on her face. Then she returned to the lobby. She thought about waiting until she'd spoken to James, but how could he possibly object? This job would mean they could replace the sound system, which he would surely be delighted about. It was the answer to their prayers.

'I'll do it,' she said. 'I'll rewrite the script for you.' She couldn't wait to get started, to take a script in hand and make it sing.

'Great!' Noa clapped his hands together. 'I have a good feeling about this. And to think it was Ingmar Bergman who brought us together.'

He smiled at her and Sarah basked in the warmth of his gaze. Noa saw her as a fellow creative. Nobody had looked at her that way in a very long time.

Sarah went to the door and peered out. The street lights were still on, though the sun was just beginning to rise. The road was clear and it had stopped snowing.

'Shall I drop you off at Merricourt Manor on my way home?' said Sarah.

'That would be amazing,' Noa replied.

Sarah switched off the lights in the office and lobby, then led Noa to the back door, leading out to the car park. Hers was the only car in the lot, swaddled by a thick blanket of snow.

'Do you own the car park too?' Noa asked.

'Yes,' said Sarah, trudging through the snow.

'Interesting . . .' said Noa, looking around. 'You've got a lot of space out back here.'

Sarah brushed snow off the windscreen and unlocked the car. Driving carefully down the freshly salted country lanes, she dropped Noa off at Merricourt Manor. The hotel looked stunning, the dawn sunlight casting a rosy glow over the grounds. No wonder he had chosen it as his film's location.

'I can't wait to crawl into bed,' said Noa, yawning. 'I can probably get a few more hours before my first meeting.' Pausing before getting out of the car, he touched her arm. 'Thanks for an unforgettable night, Sarah. My people will be in touch soon with your contract and an NDA.'

Sarah watched him go into the hotel, then set off for home. She hadn't slept at all, but she was used to feeling tired. Sleep could wait. She'd have just enough time to bake Holly a birthday cake before she woke up.

How was it possible that Holly was sixteen? It felt like only yesterday that she'd been in her belly. Having a teenaged daughter – especially one as beautiful as Holly – had been making her feel old lately. But maybe she'd been looking at things the wrong way. Sarah's life might be half over, but she still had half a lifetime ahead of her and it was time to start making every day count. She was finally going to do the things she had always meant to do.

She'd been handed a second chance and she wasn't going to waste it!

30th November 2007

'Come on out, baby,' Sarah said, running her hands over her stomach. The baby kicked in response to her voice, a tiny heel protruding from her huge belly. Sarah laughed. As much as she longed to hold her baby, she would miss having him – or her – all to herself.

After her initial joy at discovering she was finally pregnant, Sarah had passed an anxious first trimester. She'd sobbed with relief at her first scan, so convinced was she that something would go wrong.

'Oh, honey,' the midwife had said. 'Welcome to motherhood. My youngest is twenty-seven and I still worry about him.'

Once she'd heard the heartbeat, and seen the scan, Sarah had relaxed – a bit. She had relished everything about her pregnancy, from morning sickness and stretch marks, to back pain and heartburn, because she had wanted it for so long. Every kick, every jab of a tiny elbow, convinced her that everything was still OK.

'I can't wait to meet you, little one,' she said to her bump.

She and James had decided not to find out the gender. Meg thought it was a boy, because she was carrying so low, but Sarah didn't mind either way – she just wanted the baby to be healthy.

Sarah looked around the nursery, with the cot James had assembled and lemon-yellow walls they had painted together. A mobile with sea creatures hung over the cot. The changing table was stocked with nappies and wipes, the dresser filled with tiny onesies and sleep suits. Her bag for the hospital was packed, with her birth plan, healthy snacks and an iPod loaded with relaxing music. Everything was ready – or as ready as it was possible to be before such a life-changing event.

Sarah opened the baby gate at the top of the stairs and waddled downstairs. In the kitchen, she struggled with the child lock on the cupboard door. When she finally managed to get it open, she opened a tin of pineapple and ate the sweet chunks straight from the tin.

Sarah had told James that their baby wouldn't be crawling for several months, but he'd wanted to be prepared, baby-proofing the whole cottage. Meanwhile, Sarah had bought every baby and pregnancy book she could get her hands on from the Stowford bookshop. Nora, the shop's owner, had joked that Sarah was single-handedly keeping the shop in business.

Despite all her cramming, Sarah still felt unprepared. She kept having a dream that she was sitting an exam and hadn't studied enough. Only this was real life, and the exam was a baby.

She drank the juice straight from the tin, then threw it in the recycling bin and rang her mother.

'Has the baby come?' Geraldine said, answering after only one ring.

'Not yet,' replied Sarah, sighing. 'I'm so impatient. I hate waiting.'

She was nearly two weeks past her due date.

'You and your sister were both late as well. In your sister's case, that never changed.'

Sarah laughed. She pitied the patients at her sister's dental practice, who were invariably kept waiting because Meg was so chatty. 'I hope I don't have to be induced like her.' She wanted a natural birth, with minimal medical intervention.

'I've just been reading a fascinating book about birthing traditions in Native American tribes,' said Geraldine. She was on a work trip to Washington, doing research at the Smithsonian Institute. 'When a Cherokee baby was due to be born, they would try to frighten it out of the womb – by telling it that something scary was coming and they had to get out.'

'You want me to scare my baby into the world?' The world was a terrifying enough place already. Sometimes Sarah wondered if she and James were being irresponsible, bringing a new human being into such turbulent times. Civil wars were raging in several countries. Global warming was melting the polar ice caps at an alarming rate. World financial markets were in freefall.

'They also drank a tea made of wild cherry bark to speed labour along.'

Sarah looked at her selection of herbal teas. She plucked out a cherry-and-cinnamon tea bag and boiled the kettle – maybe that would work.

'And Cherokee women didn't eat raccoon meat after the birth,' continued Geraldine. 'They believed it would make the baby ill.'

'The thought of eating raccoon makes *me* feel ill,' said Sarah.

'Have you chosen names yet?'

'We're waiting to meet the baby,' Sarah told her mother.

'If it's a boy, you should name him Barack, and if it's a girl you can call her Michelle.' Geraldine was a big fan of the handsome young Democrat, who was poised to become the US's first Black president, and his lawyer wife.

Neither of those names were on Sarah's shortlist.

'I'm scared, Mum.'

'Oh, childbirth is not as bad as everyone makes it out to be,' said Geraldine breezily. 'If it was, people wouldn't have more than one, would they?'

'Not just about the birth . . . about being a good mum.'

There was a long pause, broken only by the crackle of static. For a moment, Sarah wondered if they had been disconnected.

'Well, I'm hardly an authority on the subject,' came Geraldine's voice down the line. 'But I do know that the main thing a child needs is love – and you and James already love that baby with all your hearts.'

Sarah looked down at her bump. It was true. She would gladly sacrifice her own life for this baby that she'd never even met, whose diurnal rhythms she already knew as intimately as her own heartbeat, whose nocturnal gymnastics kept her company late at night, when she lay awake worrying. That connection would never be severed, not even once the umbilical cord had been cut.

Geraldine cleared her throat. 'I know I wasn't a perfect mother,' she admitted. 'But I hope I'll make it up to you by being an excellent grandmother.'

For all her mother's faults, Sarah had never doubted that Geraldine loved her and Meg. Even now, in her mid-thirties, Sarah turned to her mum for reassurance. It was true what the midwife had said – a mother's job was never over.

'Thanks, Mum.' Geraldine was happier sharing arcane facts about remote tribes than sharing her feelings, so Sarah appreciated that she'd made the effort.

'Now, if you want to get that baby out,' Geraldine said briskly. 'I'll tell you what worked for me – having sex. Your father and I made love the day you were born, and my waters broke right after I climaxed. I found being pregnant deeply erotic . . .'

Oh, God. That made Sarah feel more ill than the thought of eating raccoon.

Fortunately, just then James came home brandishing a takeaway bag triumphantly.

'Um, I've got to go, Mum. James just brought dinner home.' With a quick goodbye, she ended the call.

'I got chicken tikka masala, sag aloo and pilau rice,' announced James, unpacking foil containers.

'Yum,' said Sarah, setting the table. Curry was another thing that supposedly induced labour. They'd had curry for dinner every night this week. So far all it had induced was wind.

'Who were you on the phone with?' James asked.

'My mum. She was extolling the joys of pregnancy sex . . .'

'Well, she's right.' James came up behind her, wrapping his arms under her bump and kissing her neck. 'It *has* been pretty great.'

They'd made love throughout Sarah's pregnancy. After their difficulties getting pregnant, it had been a welcome return to sex for recreation, rather than procreation.

When they finished eating the curry, Sarah started to clear the table.

'I'll do that – you put your feet up,' said James, taking her plate.

'I've been putting my feet up for weeks now. It's getting a bit boring.' She had been on maternity leave for almost a month. She'd tried to use the time off to do some writing before the baby came, but after just a few lines she usually needed a nap. Growing another human being was exhausting!

'If you feel up to it, why don't you come to the cinema with me tonight,' suggested James. 'Roger is going to see the school play with Omar, so I said I'd operate the projector.'

'What's on?' The thought of going to see a movie was very tempting, although there was a very good chance that she'd fall asleep in the middle of it.

'We're kicking off the festive season with *Home Alone*.'

That sealed the deal. 'Oooh,' said Sarah. 'I love that film.'

'Sarah!' cried Roger, when they arrived at the cinema. He gave her a hug. 'You are positively glowing.'

It was lovely to be back at the Picture Palace, where

the lobby had been decorated for Christmas. She'd missed the place, and her colleagues, more than she'd expected. 'What's new, Roger?'

'Well, my friend over at the Bristol Odeon told me that they are going digital, just like the Regal in Cheltenham.' He shook his head dolefully.

'I suppose they want to be ready for *Avatar* when it finally comes out,' said James.

The whole industry was eagerly awaiting James Cameron's new film. The *Titanic* director had used cutting-edge digital animation and the studio was pressuring cinemas to convert to digital ahead of its release.

'The big cinema chains just want to save money,' grumbled Roger. 'If they go digital, they don't need to employ projectionists any more. They can just press a button.'

James chuckled. 'Don't worry, Rog. Have you seen how much digital systems cost? We won't be installing one any time soon. Not with a baby on the way.'

'Well, I'd best be going,' said Roger. He looked even more than dapper than usual, in a silk paisley waistcoat and a tweed jacket. 'The curtain on Severn Valley secondary school's production of *Little Shop of Horrors* goes up at eight p.m.' He gave Sarah a hug. 'Let us know when the bambino – or bambina – arrives.'

Sarah went over to the concession stand. 'Hi, Harry.' Sarah greeted the ginger-haired teenaged boy working behind it. He was studying creative writing at university and was back for the Christmas holidays. 'Can I have a box of popcorn, please?' Sarah looked at the array of cinema snacks. 'And some Maltesers too.'

'I guess you're eating for two?' joked Harry, scooping up the popcorn.

'Right,' said Sarah, rubbing her aching back.

All the pregnancy books said eating for two was a myth. But she was always hungry. Hopefully her snacking wouldn't turn her baby into a junk-food addict.

'We have no idea what we're doing. We won't mean to, but we'll probably mess you up,' Sarah murmured, caressing her belly.

Oops. That wasn't what her mum had meant about scaring the baby out. Her little one was more likely to want to stay in her cosy womb for ever!

'Are you OK, Mrs O'Hara?' Harry held out the box of popcorn with a concerned look on his face.

'Oh, I'm fine,' said Sarah. 'Just talking to the baby . . . all the books say to do that. She walked towards the auditorium. 'Don't be scared, baby,' she whispered. 'We love you. And we can't wait to meet you.'

'*Don't be scared, baby,' she whispered. 'We love you. And we can't wait to meet you.'*

Sarah went into the auditorium, waved up at James in the projection booth and settled into a seat. She opened the bag of Maltesers and poured them into the box of popcorn. She munched her sweet-and-savoury snack as the trailers played. She wondered if she'd get to see any of the coming attractions. She hoped to breastfeed, so it might be a while before she could go out. The books all warned about 'bottle confusion'. It was weird to think that she might not be able to watch a movie here, until she could leave the baby with James or a sitter. Of course she could always watch DVDs, but it just wasn't the same as seeing a film on the big screen.

Maybe we could start doing special screenings for parents and babies, thought Sarah. They could do a matinee once a week, when it was usually pretty quiet anyway. She made a mental note to share her idea with James later that evening.

Watching the movie, Sarah chuckled as little Kevin McCallister – accidentally left behind when his family went away for Christmas – rigged up the house with booby traps to stop two burglars from invading. She suddenly felt something wet on her seat. Had she peed her pants from laughing too hard?

No – her waters had just broken.

Grabbing the seat in front of her, she stood up awkwardly, knocking her popcorn and Maltesers all over the floor.

'It's happening!' she shouted over the sound of the film. 'James! The baby is coming.'

Someone in the next row leapt up and helped her out of the auditorium.

James met her in the lobby. 'Let's get you to the hospital,' he said, helping her into her coat. He fumbled in his pocket, searching for his car keys.

'Good luck,' said Harry, holding the back door open for them. 'I'll lock everything up tonight.'

Once they were in the car, James began driving slowly to the hospital.

'If you drive any slower, I'll have the baby in the car,' muttered Sarah, shifting uncomfortably in her seat. Water was still leaking out of her.

'I'm just nervous,' said James.

'You're not the one about to push a baby out of your vagina,' replied Sarah. That made her realise something – she didn't have her birth plan. 'Oh, no. I don't have my hospital bag!'

'Should we swing home and get it?' asked James.

Sarah's stomach went taut and a terrible cramp clenched her middle. Groaning, she gripped the dashboard and tried to take deep breaths, as the books said to do. Unfortunately, the stupid books had neglected to describe quite how painful a contraction felt. It was like a period pain times a hundred.

No, make that times a million. After what felt like an hour of agony – but was only a minute – she slumped back in her seat.

'No – just drive!' She moaned.

By the time they reached the hospital, Sarah's contractions were coming every five minutes.

'Am I ready to push?' she asked the midwife, a no-nonsense woman named Angelica.

'You're only four centimetres dilated,' said Angelica, after examining her.

Sarah spent the early hours of the morning pacing the maternity ward's corridors. Every time a contraction came, she stopped and clutched James's arm until it passed.

'You're doing brilliantly,' he said.

'If I knew it was going to take this long, I would have stayed to watch the end of the movie.'

Long after the sun had risen, Sarah was fully dilated. It was time to push, but the baby was in no rush to make an appearance.

'Are you sure you don't want an epidural?' the midwife asked, after Sarah had been pushing for several hours.

Sarah shook her head, sucking down another lungful of gas and air.

When the baby still failed to make an appearance, Angelica called in a doctor. They listened to the baby's heartbeat on the monitor and frowned.

'Is something wrong?' asked James.

'The heart rate is too low,' said the doctor. 'Your baby is in distress – we need to move things along.'

'Oh, God,' whimpered Sarah. Fear gripped her more tightly than any contraction. 'Please help my baby.'

'Sarah, we're going to use forceps,' Angelica explained calmly. 'Hopefully, this will help get baby out. If that doesn't work, we'll perform an emergency caesarean.'

Sarah nodded, her eyes wide with fear. She saw James's lips moving silently and knew he was praying.

'Push, Sarah,' said the midwife when her next contraction started. 'Push as hard as you can.'

Exhausted though she was, Sarah bore down with all her might. Then, she felt a searing pain, as if she had been sliced right open.

'It hurts,' she wailed.

'Good girl,' said the midwife. 'You're crowning – I just need you to give me one more big push.'

'I can't,' cried Sarah.

'You can,' said James, pushing sweaty hair off her face.

Another contraction seized her. Sarah gripped her husband's hand and pushed as hard as she could. Then came the most wonderful sound she had ever heard – the reedy cry of a newborn.

'Congratulations, Mum,' said Angelica, smiling. 'You have a little girl.'

James cut the umbilical cord, then the midwife whisked the baby off to an examining table to check her over.

'Is she OK?' asked Sarah, watching woozily. The baby's eyes were scrunched shut, her face was red, and she was covered in white goo; she was so beautiful, it made Sarah feel light-headed. Her husband and midwife undulated before her in hazy waves. None of the books had mentioned this . . .

'She's absolutely perfect,' said Angelica, beaming. She wrapped the baby in a blanket. 'Nine pounds, three ounces – no wonder you had such a job getting her out.'

The midwife handed James the baby and checked on Sarah again. Suddenly, her smiling face became serious. She pressed an alarm bell.

'What's wrong?' asked James, cradling the baby.

'Sarah is losing a lot of blood,' said Angelica.

They sounded miles away. Sarah tried to tell James she was fine but couldn't seem to make her mouth work. She felt like she was floating.

A doctor came running in and helped Angelica set up an IV drip.

'What are you doing?' asked James.

'It's oxytocin,' explained the midwife as she massaged Sarah's uterus. 'It will help the uterus contract and stop the postpartum haemorrhaging.'

The last thing Sarah remembered, before she passed out, was someone putting an oxygen mask over her face.

When Sarah opened her eyes a few hours later, she found herself in a sunny hospital room.

James stood by Sarah's side, cradling a little bundle in his arms. 'Your mummy's awake,' he crooned to the baby.

'I thought we were going to lose her,' said Sarah, reaching for her daughter.

'I thought we were going to lose *you*,' James said, placing their baby in her arms. 'You both gave me quite a scare.'

The baby let out a cry and flailed her little fists. There was a plastic bracelet around one of them which read *Daughter of Sarah O'Hara, 1/12/07*.

'I think she's telling us that she's a fighter.' James smiled at Sarah. 'Just like her mama.'

Sarah stroked her daughter's soft cheek and the baby's blue eyes blinked at her. 'Hello, little stranger,' she whispered to the tiny bundle in her arms.

Sarah placed her daughter on her breast. The baby rooted around, until her tiny rosebud mouth clamped instinctively around her nipple, and she began to drink her first precious drops of milk.

'She's got your eyes,' Sarah said, stroking the baby's dark tufts. She could not stop staring in amazement at her perfect daughter. 'And your nose.'

James perched gently on the edge of the bed. He stroked the baby's tiny nose. 'Hey, give me my nose back.'

Angelica, the midwife, came in to check on them. 'How are you feeling, Mum?'

Sarah felt sore all over, her hair was matted and sweaty from the exertions of labour, her swollen stomach still looked pregnant, and she was on a drip.

'So, so happy,' she said.

The baby stopped feeding, so Sarah placed her gently over her shoulder and rubbed her back until the baby let out a tiny burp.

James gazed at his wife in admiration. 'You're a superhero.'

'No, I'm just a mum,' said Sarah.

Mum. She loved how that sounded.

'Same difference,' said the midwife, smiling at them. 'I'll go and make you a cup of tea and a snack.'

The baby opened her blue eyes and gazed up at her mother in wonder. Sarah held out her finger and the baby gripped onto it.

That's right, little one, thought Sarah. *I'm here for you – and always will be.*

Chapter 6

Present Day

'Meow!' A ginger paw batted Holly on the head.

'Stop it, Jonesy,' groaned Holly, pulling the duvet over her head. 'It's my birthday – I want a lie-in.'

Determined to get some affection, the cat changed tactics. He strutted along the length of Holly's body and pounced on her toes.

'OK, OK,' Holly grumbled, throwing off the duvet and giving the cat a cuddle. Jonesy was more effective than any alarm clock. Holly needed to get up anyway – she and her mum always spent her birthday in London, shopping and going for a fancy afternoon tea.

Dazzling light streamed in from the window, as early-morning sunshine reflected off the freshly fallen snow.

I hope the trains are OK . . .

Although Mum was still in her bad books, Holly was looking forward to their day out. She liked having her mother's full attention for a change, without her fusspot brother kicking off about something or other. They were seeing Auntie Pari, too. Holly's godmother never treated her like a kid. She usually bought Holly a new outfit, too, from somewhere cool, like Urban Outfitters or Brandy Melville. There weren't any good clothes shops in Plumdale, unless you liked waxed jackets, flat caps and wellies.

A delicious scent was wafting out of the kitchen as Holly descended the stairs in her pyjamas. Nick was already at the table, doodling in a sketchbook. Mum was humming as she spread icing on a freshly baked chocolate cake. She seemed suspiciously cheerful given the early hour.

'Happy birthday, sweetheart.' Mum came over to give her a hug, but Holly ducked away.

She looked critically at her mum's clothes. God, she really had stopped making an effort. 'Didn't you wear that yesterday?'

'I stayed at the cinema last night because of the snow,' explained Mum. 'But I hurried home in time to make your cake.'

'You didn't need to do that,' said Holly. 'I'm not a kid any more.' At sixteen, she was old enough to get a full-time job, drive a moped, order a glass of wine at the pub (as long as she also ordered a meal) and get married (with her parents' permission). Not that she particularly wanted to do any of those things. But the point was she *could*, if she wanted to.

'We always have birthday cake for breakfast,' said Mum, looking hurt. The birthday-cake-for-breakfast tradition had only come about because one or other of her parents often had to work at the cinema in the evening. They celebrated birthdays in the morning, with cake and presents, so everyone could be there.

'Yeah, that's the tradition,' added Nick, looking up from his sketchbook. 'That's how we *always* celebrate birthdays.'

Holly wasn't planning to spend her birthdays in Plumdale for ever, no matter how delicious her mum's cakes were. (She always put a bit of coffee in the batter, to enhance the chocolate flavour.) In two years, she'd be out of here. Hopefully at drama school, but even if she didn't get accepted, she'd work as a waitress and go to auditions.

'By the way,' said Mum. 'Aaron asked me to wish you a happy birthday.'

'Oh,' said Holly, trying to sound unbothered as she poured herself a cup of tea from the pot on the table. 'That's nice.' Inside, her heart was doing star jumps in her chest. She hadn't told him it was her birthday, so the only way he would know was if he had been looking at her socials.

Or unless her mum had mentioned it at work . . . Holly sipped her tea. Out of the kitchen window, she saw her dad shovelling the garden path. She pulled out her phone and, ignoring all the birthday messages from friends, checked whether the trains were running.

Phew! They were.

Mum carried the cake over to the table. She'd piped SWEET SIXTEEN in white icing. 'Ta-da.'

Holly's mouth watered as she inhaled the delicious scent of Belgian milk chocolate – Mum always used the good stuff for their birthday cakes. The top layer was slightly wonky but Holly knew it would taste amazing. She took a photo and added it to her Instagram story. Her heart soared when – straight away – Aaron liked it. She grinned. So he *had* been checking out her socials.

'Here,' said Nick, handing her an envelope. Holly opened it and took out a handmade card with a manga-style illustration of a dark-haired girl with bunches holding a sword.

'Is that supposed to be me?' asked Holly.

Nick nodded.

'That's really good.' She propped the card up on the table and gave her brother a hug.

'Get off!' protested Nick. But he had a smile on his face.

Dad opened the front door and stood at the entrance. 'Boy, is it cold out there.' He shut the door, then peeled off his jacket and gloves.

'Have some tea to warm up,' said Mum, pouring him a steaming mug.

'Thanks,' said Dad.

The family sat around the kitchen table and Dad stuck sixteen candles around the cake's edge.

'Dad and I got you this.' Mum handed Holly a small turquoise-blue box, wrapped with a ribbon.

Holly untied the ribbon and gasped when she saw Tiffany & Co written on the box. She opened it and took out a silver necklace with a heart-shaped pendant.

'It's beautiful,' she said, letting Mum fasten it around her neck. 'But it must have been expensive.'

Dad smiled. 'It isn't every day that our only daughter turns sixteen.'

Mum nodded. 'We wanted to get you something special. It seemed fitting, because we named you after the main character in *Breakfast at Tiffany's*.'

Holly loved being named after Holly Golightly. She had dressed up as her namesake for a fancy-dress party – a little black dress accessorised with pearls, long gloves and an even longer cigarette holder – but none of her friends had got the reference.

I bet Aaron would get it, she thought.

'I love it,' said Holly, touching the pendant. She hugged her parents. Mum looked ridiculously pleased and Holly felt bad she'd been so mean to her. *I'm going to be nicer from now on,* she resolved.

'Can we have cake now?' begged Nick, swiping a bit of icing from the side of the cake.

Holly batted him away. 'Hands off – I get the first piece.'

Dad lit the candles and they all sang 'Happy Birthday'.

'Make a wish,' said Mum.

Holly closed her eyes. *I wish for Aaron to kiss me,* she thought, blowing out the candles.

'I bet I know what you wished for,' crowed Nick as Mum handed out slices of cake.

Holly's face flamed. Was her crush that obvious?

'You wished to become a famous movie star,' guessed Nick, shovelling a bite of cake into his mouth.

'Speaking about movies . . .' said Mum, looking like she was about to burst. 'I have some big news. Last night I met Noa Drakos!'

'The director?' said Dad.

Mum's eyes sparkled with excitement. 'We both had to spend the night at the cinema because of the snow—'

'Hang on a minute,' said Dad. 'He was there with you all night?'

'Yes,' replied Mum. 'There was no way for him to get back to his hotel. So, anyhow, we got talking – first about Bergman, and then about other stuff – and . . .'

Holly's heart began to pound. Maybe Mum had told him about her and the director wanted to give her a part in the movie.

OMG . . . OMG . . . OMG . . .

'. . . He let me read his script,' continued Mum. 'I suggested some revisions and he loved my ideas. In fact' – she paused for dramatic effect – 'he's asked me to do a rewrite on the movie he's shooting here!'

Everyone looked at Mum in silence, trying to process her unexpected news.

Nick was the first to speak.

'Congratulations, Mum,' he said, giving her a hug.

'Wow . . .' said Dad. 'That's . . . amazing.'

'I know, right? But you haven't heard the best bit yet,' said Mum, grinning.

Here we go, thought Holly. *This* was where her mum was going to make this her best birthday ever.

'I'm getting twenty grand,' said Mum. 'That's enough to replace the sound system!'

Who cared about the stupid sound system!

'What about me?' demanded Holly. 'Did you tell him about me?'

'Yes, I mentioned I had a daughter.'

'And . . .'

Mum looked confused. There was a bit of chocolate icing on her lip. 'And . . . what?'

'Did you ask him if I could be in the movie?' asked Holly impatiently. *Why was Mum acting so stupid?*

'Well . . . no,' said Mum. 'That didn't seem appropriate.'

Holly glared at her mother. This was *unbelievable. She* had spent *hours* on her own with an Oscar-winning director and hadn't asked him if Holly could be an extra? *What the actual hell?*

'You hypocrite,' said Holly.

'Holly,' warned Dad. 'Don't speak to your mother that way.'

'But it's true! She stopped me from auditioning for the movie, but the second there was a chance for her to be involved, she grabbed it. It's not fair!'

'The two things are totally unrelated,' said Mum.

Holly snorted. 'Yeah, right.'

'It was a joint decision,' Dad reminded her.

But Holly wasn't listening. 'I can't believe you'd do this to me.'

'You're being ridiculous, Holly,' said Mum. 'None of this was planned. And I certainly didn't mean to upset you.'

'I'm going to ask Auntie Pari what she thinks,' threatened Holly. 'I bet she'll think you're really selfish for not getting me a part.'

'About that . . .' said Mum, looking uncomfortable. 'Holly, I'm sorry but we'll have to postpone our trip to London. It's a really tight deadline. I need to get started on the script right away. There's more snow forecast for tonight, so I was going to suggest postponing anyway – in case the trains home get cancelled.'

Oh, wow. Another betrayal. Holly instantly revoked her decision to be nicer to her mother. 'That's fine. It's not like it's an important birthday or anything,' she said, her voice dripping with sarcasm. 'Just my sixteenth.'

'I'm really sorry, honey,' said Mum, her eyes pleading with Holly for understanding. 'But this is a big opportunity for me, and the pay is excellent. The money is a lifeline for the cinema. I'll make it up to you – I promise.'

'But it's my birthday TODAY!' shouted Holly. She knew she was acting like a baby, and she didn't care. She wanted to pick up the rest of the cake and fling it against the wall. 'I've been looking forward to this trip for ages!'

'I'll go to London with you,' suggested Dad. 'As long as you apologise to your mother.'

Holly turned to her father, frowning. 'But you hate shopping.'

'I'll do my own thing. You can go off to Topshop or wherever, and have tea with Pari.'

Holly rolled her eyes. 'Topshop doesn't exist any more, Dad. I want to go to Carnaby Street and Covent Garden.'

'Well, we're not going anywhere until you apologise,' said Dad.

Holly turned to her mother and forced her facial features into an expression of contrition, her eyes filled with remorse. *Oh, I'm good,* thought Holly. No wonder her drama teacher had predicted that she'd get top marks in her GCSE.

'Sorry, Mum,' Holly cooed sweetly. 'I'm really happy for you.' She didn't mean it. Not one little bit. But there was no way she was missing out on a trip to London.

'Show me what you got,' said Auntie Pari, pointing to the shopping bag by Holly's feet. They were sitting on a squishy chintz sofa in the old-fashioned tea room of Brown's Hotel in Mayfair, which had been decorated with decadent swags of pine and holly. There was a three-tiered silver cake stand on the table in front of them, laden with equally decadent finger sandwiches, scones and cakes. It was the fanciest place Holly had ever been – she'd felt like a movie star as the host showed them to their table.

Holly held up the minidress she'd bought. It had spaghetti straps, a corset-style bodice and an asymmetrical hem.

'Ooh, very sexy,' said Pari approvingly. She leant forward. 'By the way, *are* you having sex with anyone?'

'No!' said Holly, blushing with embarrassment. (That was another thing you could do legally when you were sixteen. Not that she wanted to discuss her non-existent sex life with her godmother.)

'But there's someone you like?'

'Maybe . . .' replied Holly.

'Well, he . . . or she . . . isn't going to be able to resist you in that.'

'He,' said Holly shyly.

'Well, just remember,' said Pari, adding a drop of milk to her cup of tea, 'if you *are* going to have sex, be sure to use protection. And never let anyone pressure you into doing anything you don't want to do.'

Holly's cheeks burnt brighter than the strawberry jam on the table. Maybe it was a good idea her mum hadn't come along. And as for Dad, he'd probably spontaneously combust at the thought of her even kissing a boy.

'More cake?' asked a tuxedoed waiter holding a silver tray. There were slices of chocolate Yule log, little ginger-bread men and mini mince pies, in a nod to the festive season.

Holly pointed to the chocolate log, while Auntie Pari shook her head.

Using silver tongs, the waiter placed the cake on Holly's plate. She took a bite, the sweet cream inside oozing out.

'Oh, to have the metabolism of a sixteen-year-old again.' Auntie Pari sighed wistfully.

'Being sixteen sucks,' said Holly. 'My parents still treat me like a child.'

'Well, I hate to point out the obvious, but you *are* still a child,' said Pari, sipping her tea.

'It's so annoying – Mum decides she's going to be a screenwriter again, just in time to ruin my life,' moaned Holly, stabbing her cake in frustration. 'This could have been my big break.'

'She did the right thing,' Pari said, to Holly's disappointment. She'd been expecting Pari to be on her side. 'You're too young. Go to drama school, learn your craft and *then* you'll be ready to work professionally.'

'Natalie Portman was already a major film star when she was sixteen,' Holly pointed out, adding a dollop of jam to her scone. 'So was Saoirse Ronan. And Keira Knightley.'

'They're the lucky ones. The list of talented teenaged stars who burnt out is much, much longer, darling.' Pari looked enviously at the scone Holly was eating and shrugged. 'What the hell.' She popped a pink macaron into her mouth. 'YOLO – isn't that what you kids say?'

'Don't you think I'm talented enough to make it?' Her aunt had come to see her in *Hairspray* and said she had star quality.

'You're definitely talented enough,' said Pari, brushing crumbs off her fingers. 'But that's no guarantee. The entertainment industry is brutal. So many incredibly talented people don't succeed, and sometimes less talented ones do – just because they are in the right place at the right time. That's why I never take on clients your age. You need to have the resilience to deal with constant rejection – and that only comes with maturity.'

Holly groaned. 'Ugh, when did you get so boring, Auntie Pari? You sound just like Mum.'

'Your mum isn't boring,' said Pari. 'She's brave.'

'Ha!' Holly snorted. 'Yeah, right. Name one brave thing she's ever done.'

Pari sipped her tea thoughtfully. 'When I used to be a stand-up, I got a lot of abuse from hecklers – really nasty stuff. One time, at the Edinburgh Festival, a heckler called out something very offensive. Your mum stood up and challenged him. He was drunk and threw a bottle of beer at her head. She had to go to hospital to get stitches.' She tapped her forehead. 'She still has a faint scar right here.'

Holly had never asked how her mum had got that scar. She'd always assumed it was from some childhood injury. She had to grudgingly admit it would have taken a lot of courage for Mum to stick up for Pari like that.

'And she's one of the most creative people I've ever met. I always thought it was a shame she stopped writing. I'm so glad she's got a chance to go back to it.'

'I don't understand why she didn't stay at the BBC,' said Holly. 'It sounds like such an interesting job.' Growing up in London would have been so cool. Not just because of the trendy shops and fancy restaurants. There were loads of theatres with discounted tickets for young people, where you could see famous actors on stage. The Plumdale Players' annual pantomime in the church hall – usually starring her parents' friend Ian – didn't really compare.

'Because she loved your dad more than her job,' said Pari. 'She wanted to raise her family somewhere safe and be there for you and Nick.'

'Oh, so it's all my fault.'

Pari set down her teacup and gave Holly a stern look. 'That's not what I meant. When Sarah called me after giving birth to you and asked me to be your godmother, she told me she had never been so happy. So maybe stop giving her such a hard time, OK? You and Nick mean the world to her.'

Holly looked down at her heart necklace, chastened. Deep down, she knew how much her mum loved her. She showed it every day, in all the little things she did for her and Nick. Now, Holly felt guilty about how she'd acted this morning. Her mum deserved to be happy.

She got out her phone and typed out a message.

Thanks for my necklace. I love you. Xxx

'Good girl,' said Pari, smiling. 'Now how about we get you a pair of new shoes to match that cute little dress of yours.'

James was waiting for Holly on the concourse at Paddington. He checked his watch – she was a few minutes late. His mind started to race – was she lost? Had she been hit by a bus? Had she got mugged?

She's sixteen, he told himself. *She can look after herself.* When he'd been sixteen, he'd been taking the Tube to school, sneaking into pubs and hanging out at Camden Market on the weekends. But Holly hadn't grown up in the city like him. He couldn't help worrying about his daughter – Holly would always be his little girl. He'd sworn to protect her on the day she'd come into this world, and that would never change, no matter how old she was.

'Sorry I'm late,' she said, hurrying over to him laden with shopping bags.

James felt his shoulders relax. 'That's OK. Did you have a nice day?'

Holly nodded. 'Where did you go?'

'I went to Ealing,' said James. 'Where I grew up.'

While Holly had been shopping and having tea with Pari, he'd visited his parents' graves. He'd placed a wreath of holly and ivy on their shared headstone, which was decorated with a simple cross. 'Sorry I haven't been here for a while,' he'd said to them. 'I wish you could see the kids. Holly is nearly grown-up now. She wants to be an actor and is so talented – I'm not sure where she gets it from. Maybe you, Mum?'

James's mother had loved to sing and dance.

'And Nick is an amazing artist,' James told his dad. 'He and I love building models together, the way you and I did, Dad.'

He shoved his hands into his pockets. The skies were a dull grey, the wind biting. It looked like it might snow. He looked at the names and dates carved on his parents' headstone. They were united in death, as they had been in life. His parents never had the privilege of growing old together; illness robbed them of the chance to enjoy their retirements. James hoped that he and Sarah would be luckier. He still loved Sarah with all his heart and couldn't imagine a future without her. But he'd been so preoccupied with the cinema that he'd neglected their relationship, and her needs. He needed to put things right and just hoped it wasn't too late.

An announcement blared on the loudspeaker. 'Great Western Railway is sorry to announce that all further trains are cancelled this evening, due to poor weather conditions.'

'What are we going to do?' asked Holly, looking panicky.

'Don't worry,' James reassured her. 'I'll sort it out.' He rang Pari and explained the situation. When he got off the phone, he told Holly, 'Pari is out at the theatre tonight – one of her clients has a premiere – but she told me where to find her spare key.'

Much as he liked his wife's best friend, he was secretly pleased that it would be just him and Holly tonight – she was usually too busy with school and friends to hang out with her dad.

They decided to walk to Pari's house in Notting Hill. Festive lights twinkled in the dark. The pavements bustled with Christmas shoppers and a man in a Santa suit clanged a bell, collecting for charity.

'I feel like I'm in a Christmas movie,' said Holly, as snowflakes dusted her hair. 'I keep expecting Hugh Grant to step out of one of these houses.'

James smiled, making a mental note to propose *Love, Actually* as one of the film-festival movies. Sarah loved a Richard Curtis romcom.

They turned onto Pari's road. She lived in a row of brightly coloured houses – hers was pastel pink. James located a key, hidden in a plant pot, and opened the door.

The kitchen was like something out of a luxury interiors magazine. With its marble island, sleek cupboards and special tap that dispensed boiling water, it couldn't have been more different to the cosy but rustic kitchen at home.

'I'm going to live in a house like this one day when I'm a rich and famous actor,' announced Holly, dropping her shopping bags on the granite floor.

James chuckled. 'You should have seen the house Pari and your mum shared in their twenties. Mice, mould and pants drying on the radiators . . .'

He opened the massive fridge. It was empty apart from a bottle of Prosecco, a shrivelled lemon, a lump of cheese and a half-eaten container of takeout sushi. Some things hadn't changed . . .

'Let's order in some food for dinner,' he suggested, scrolling through a delivery app on his phone.

When their noodles arrived, they settled down in Pari's living room, which had an orange velvet sofa and wallpaper with parrots on it.

'Oh, my God – is this Mum?' said Holly, spotting a framed picture on the bookcase.

In the photo, Sarah's arm was slung around Pari's shoulder in a crowded field. She was wearing a short slip dress, Doc Martens and sunglasses, and holding a pint glass.

'OMG. She had a nose ring,' said Holly, peering at the photo. 'And purple hair.'

'I took that photo. We went to a music festival shortly after they both started working at the BBC – that was actually the first time I met Pari.'

'They look so young,' commented Holly.

It was Sarah's smile that struck James, more than her youthful appearance. He'd seen that smile again this morning, when she'd told him about her new gig. She was so happy, she'd been practically glowing. Seeing her fizzing with excitement had made him realise how much she needed this. The film director's sudden appearance in their lives did truly feel like a Christmas miracle.

Though, if he was being honest, he hadn't loved the fact that she'd spent all night alone with him. The Aussie director had a reputation as a ladies' man. It had been bothering him all day, even though he knew his reaction was ridiculous – Sarah had never given him any reason not to trust her. He supposed he was just feeling a bit jealous because a stranger had found the solution to the cinema's problems, instead of him.

'Let's watch a Christmas movie,' said Holly, slurping up some noodles.

James switched on the television and browsed through the streaming services. 'They've got *Home Alone*. That's what your mum was watching the night she went into labour with you.'

'Really? You guys never told me that.'

James didn't like talking about it because it had been the most scared he'd ever been. But Holly was sixteen now. She was old enough to hear the story. Old enough to know what her mum had gone through to bring her into the world. 'When Mum was in labour, I thought we were going to lose you. And her.'

Holly put down her chopsticks and stared at him. 'What happened?'

'You didn't want to come out. That should have been our first clue that you were going to be stubborn.'

'Ha ha.'

'And then when they finally got you out, your mum suffered a post-partum haemorrhage.' James could still remember every detail of that horrible moment as if it were yesterday – the heart-rate monitor beeping, doctors rushing in, blood gushing.

'What's that?' Holly asked. Her face looked so innocent, it was hard to believe she was nearly grown-up.

'Bleeding after giving birth,' he explained. 'Luckily, the doctors managed to get it under control, but it was touch-and-go for a while. Your mother was such a trooper – all she cared about was whether you were OK.'

Holly's blue eyes welled with tears. 'Poor Mum.'

'Hey,' said James, giving her a hug. 'She was fine in the end. And it was all worth it because we got you.'

Holly snuggled up next to James and he put on the movie. He'd have been happy to watch anything – he just felt lucky to share this precious moment with Holly. It impossible to imagine a world without his daughter in it.

When *Home Alone* was over, Holly switched off the telly. 'That movie is so funny.'

'Apparently it only took John Hughes nine days to write the first draft of the screenplay,' said James. 'And speaking of screenplays – I'm going to call Mum and find out how she's getting on.'

Kissing Holly goodnight, he rang his wife.

'How's it going?' he asked when she answered.

'Great!' said Sarah. She sounded wide awake, despite the late hour. 'I'm nearly done reworking the opening scenes. I just hope it's OK; it's been such a long time since I've done this . . .'

'I'm sure it's fantastic.' He was determined to be supportive. He could tell how much she needed this – and not just because of the money.

'What have you two been up to?'

'We just watched *Home Alone*,' said James. 'I was thinking maybe that should be one of the Twelve Films of Christmas. And maybe *Love, Actually* too.'

'About that . . .' said Sarah, worry creeping into her voice. 'As much as I want to do it, I just don't see how I'm going to have time to plan the festival this year. Not with this deadline.'

Here was the perfect opportunity to step up, to give Sarah the space she was craving and let her shine. To show her that he wanted to help.

'Leave it to me,' James volunteered quickly. 'I'll manage the film festival. We've left it a bit late, but I'm sure I can sort it out.'

And hopefully, in doing so, he could also sort out their marriage . . .

30th November 2009

'Come in,' said Sarah, opening the door to let their friends Nora and Simon Walden inside the cottage.

Nora handed her an apple tart, still warm from the oven.

'Oh, this looks delicious,' said Sarah. 'Thanks so much.'

The couple owned a bookshop in Stowford. Fellow film buffs, Nora and Simon had been thrilled to have a cinema in the area again. Their bookshop always posted the week's cinema listings on their noticeboard and when a film based on a book came out, the cinema promoted the book on behalf of the bookshop. As parents of an eight-year-old daughter, Nora and Simon had also been an invaluable source of parenting advice.

James came downstairs holding Holly, whose second birthday it was tomorrow. Sarah felt a rush of love as she saw her daughter in her Winnie-the-Pooh pyjamas, chubby cheeks flushed pink and dark brown curls damp from the bath.

'Someone doesn't want to go to bed yet,' said James.

'Da da,' said Holly, looking pleased with herself – and wide awake.

'Oh, I remember those days,' said Nora, smiling fondly.

'To be honest, bedtime doesn't get much easier,' remarked Simon. 'Charlotte wants us to read at least two chapters of *Harry Potter and the Deathly Hallows* every night.'

'We brought something for the birthday girl,' said Nora, reaching into her bag. She handed Holly a copy of *The Gruffalo* and a chocolate advent calendar.

'Thank you so much,' said Sarah.

'Charlotte loved that book when she was little,' explained Simon.

'Let me get you a drink.' James passed Holly to Sarah.

Holly wrapped her little arms around her mother's neck. Sarah delighted in the squidgy solidity of her daughter and her intoxicating baby smell – better than any perfume. Caring for a headstrong toddler was exhausting, but Sarah loved every minute of it. She couldn't believe Holly was two already. Every day, more of her personality revealed itself. Their little girl was lively, strong-willed and quick to laugh. She loved any sort of music, bobbing her head to anything with a beat. It was exciting to watch her become a little person, but Sarah already felt nostalgic for the baby days.

Maybe we should start trying for another one . . .

She and James hadn't discussed having another baby yet. They were both frightened of another difficult birth. But Holly was such a delight that it hadn't put Sarah off her desire to have another child. She wanted Holly to have a sibling. Growing up, Meg had been Sarah's constant companion. Being an only child had to have been lonely for James.

They went into the living room, where Pari was sitting on the sofa, chatting to Roger and Omar. Ian from the antiques shop was there too. Pari had come for the weekend, to celebrate her god-daughter's birthday with a trip to the Cotswolds wildlife park. Sarah hoped her best friend wouldn't find the gathering too provincial, or too couple-y.

Ian was studying their framed poster of *Diamonds are Forever*. 'Is this signed by Sean Connery?' he asked.

'Yes,' replied James, opening a bottle of wine.

'Oh, I love Sean Connery,' enthused Roger. 'Now *he's* what I call a film star.'

'I thought Daniel Craig was your favourite Bond, *mon amour*,' said Omar.

'It would fetch a few bob, if you ever want to sell it,' said Ian.

Sarah shook her head. 'We could never sell it. James's father gave it to us as a wedding present.'

Sean split his time between Ealing and the Cotswolds, helping out at the cinema and babysitting Holly, who adored her doting grandfather. He'd recently been diagnosed with COPD – a lung condition caused by years of smoking and wood-dust inhalation. He was on medication and had finally – on doctor's orders – quit smoking.

As James handed out drinks, Sarah introduced Nora and Simon to everyone.

'You look really familiar,' said Simon, shaking Pari's hand.

'I don't think we've met before,' said Pari.

Sarah set Holly down on the floor. She toddled over to the coffee table and stuffed a crisp in her mouth.

Simon snapped his fingers. 'I've got it! We saw you perform at the Edinburgh Festival.' He turned to his wife. 'Remember, honey – when we went up for the book festival and went to a comedy show at the Pleasance.'

'Of course,' said Nora. 'You were hilarious. You did a whole bit on what to write in office birthday cards.'

'And there was a bit where you described taking a boyfriend home to meet your parents.' Simon smiled. 'Are you still together?'

'Oh, he was entirely fictional.' Pari took the crisp Holly

was holding out to her and popped it in her mouth. 'I'm single as a Pringle.'

'You didn't tell me your best friend was a famous comedian,' Nora said.

'I'm hardly famous,' said Pari.

'So when can we see you perform again?' asked Simon.

'Well . . . never,' replied Pari.

Sarah stared at her friend. 'What are you talking about?'

'I'm giving up comedy.'

Sarah was shocked. Comedy had been Pari's dream for as long as she'd known her. She was the funniest person Sarah had ever met – bar none. 'But why?'

'There's lots of reasons. I'm tired of being on the road,' said Pari. 'And I've got to be realistic – if I haven't hit the big time by now, it's probably never going to happen.'

A lot of her male contemporaries, who had been playing the same tiny venues as Pari ten years ago, were now regulars on comedy quiz show panels. Some even had their own shows. They were less talented but had something she didn't have – a penis.

'I guess this will make it easier to focus on your work at the BBC,' said James. Pari was on the production team of a popular sitcom.

'Actually . . . I've resigned.'

Sarah couldn't help feeling a bit hurt. How did she not know any of this? Pari had made all these huge decisions – and she hadn't discussed any of them with her. 'What are you going to do instead?'

'I'm going to be an agent,' announced Pari. 'I have loads of contacts in the industry, from the Beeb and from the comedy circuit. I've been on both sides of the fence – I know what it feels like to be the talent, but I also understand the business side of things.'

'How exciting,' said Simon.

'I've already signed a few clients,' continued Pari, helping herself to another crisp. 'Some up-and-coming comedians, and a few actors I've met through work. I'm excited to help them build their careers.'

James raised his wine glass in a toast. 'Here's to new beginnings.'

'New beginnings,' mumbled Sarah. She was still trying to process Pari's revelations. Her initial hurt was beginning to turn to guilt. She'd been so consumed with helping at the cinema and dealing with toddler tantrums, she hadn't kept track of what was going on in her best friend's life. The long phone calls they used to share had been replaced with text messages and quick chats while Holly napped.

Nora laughed, catching sight of Holly's face. 'Oh my goodness! What have you done, sweet pea?'

Chocolate was smeared all over Holly's face – and her pyjamas. While the adults had been chatting, she'd managed to break into the chocolate advent calendar and had crammed several days' worth of chocolate into her mouth.

'Come on, you little rascal,' said James, picking Holly up. 'Let's get you cleaned up and into bed.'

A timer went off and Sarah hurried into the kitchen to check on the lasagne. The cheesy top layer was browned to perfection and the filling was bubbling away. She pulled the dish out of the oven and set it on the table with a big green salad and homemade garlic bread. She lit a few candles, then went back to the living room. 'Dinner's ready.'

Everyone gathered around the wooden table. James refilled wine glasses, while Sarah served up the lasagne.

Ian rubbed his hands in anticipation. 'This looks delicious.'

'It's my mum's recipe,' said Sarah. Geraldine's lasagne had always been the hit of any faculty pot-luck supper.

'What's she up to these days?' asked Pari, breaking off a piece of garlic bread.

'Mum's working on a new book.' Geraldine was as busy as ever with her academic research but was a devoted grandmother. She visited regularly, telling Holly stories from world mythology and bearing age-inappropriate gifts – the latest being a doll from South America with an intricately beaded dress.

'I think I'll put this aside until she's a bit older,' Sarah had said, spiriting the doll away. It was a full-blown choking hazard.

They didn't see much of Sarah's dad. His second marriage to Tiffany had ended in divorce. He'd taken early retirement and moved to Spain, where he spent his days golfing. 'I knew it wouldn't last,' Geraldine had crowed when she'd heard the news. 'His child bride didn't want to spend the rest of her life with a boring old git.'

'It's so nice to have a home-cooked meal for a change,' said Pari. 'Instead of a ready meal for one.'

Ian patted his belly. 'I love to cook, but the problem with living on my own is that I eat it all up myself. I need someone to cook for.'

Sarah suddenly had a horrifying thought – did Ian and Pari think she was trying to set them up? The president of the Plumdale Beautification Society was a lovely guy but not really Pari's type.

'Where's your agency going to be based?' Sarah asked.

'I've rented a small office in Soho,' said Pari.

'If you need any furniture, I can sort you out. I'm in the antiques business.' Ian slid his business card across the table to Pari.

It seemed that Ian was mostly interested in Pari as a potential customer.

Pari slipped Ian's business card into her pocket. 'Did you hear about Jack?' she asked Sarah. 'He's leaving the BBC too. He sold a script to a small indie studio.'

Feeling a pang of envy at her former colleague's success, Sarah took a big sip of her wine. She hadn't written much since Holly's arrival. She tried to work on *The Ghost Writer* while Holly was napping, but after she'd tidied up the mess she created while awake, there was hardly any time left.

'I'm going to reach out and see if there's a part for one of my actor clients,' said Pari, helping herself to more salad.

'How's business at the bookshop?' Ian asked Nora and Simon.

'Slow,' admitted Nora.

Stock markets had crashed around the world and even here in the Cotswolds, unemployment was at a record high.

'Am I crazy to be setting up an agency in the middle of a global recession?' asked Pari.

'Oh, I don't know,' said Roger. 'People always want entertainment, especially when times are tough. During the Great Depression, cinema boomed. Movies helped give people hope.'

James and Sarah exchanged glances. Hollywood might have been recession-proof in the 1930s, but not today. Their ticket sales were down. These days, people were less likely to buy cinema tickets when they could watch a DVD at home for less money. Plus, over the past year, more and more cinemas had converted to digital projection systems. It was hard not to worry that their traditional projector was soon going to be obsolete.

'We're lucky because we own the bookshop outright,' said Nora. 'But lots of other businesses in Stowford have closed down because they can't afford the rent.'

'It's the same in Plumdale,' agreed James.

'One of our customers told me he lost his job at the BMW factory last month,' said Simon. The car factory outside of Oxford had recently laid off over a thousand people.

'At school, we've noticed an increase in children receiving free school meals,' added Omar.

Sarah felt sad that so many local people were struggling. Although relative newcomers to the village, she and James felt like part of the community. The other local business owners had been incredibly supportive.

After having Nora's delicious apple pie for dessert, they returned to the living room with coffees and a box of chocolates.

'We showed Charlotte *The Muppet Christmas Carol* for the first time last night,' said Nora, stirring her coffee.

'Oh, that's such a great Christmas movie,' replied Sarah. She couldn't wait to share classic Christmas films with Holly when she was older.

'My favourite Christmas film is *Die Hard*,' said Simon.

'That's not a Christmas movie,' scoffed Sarah.

'That's what I always tell him,' remarked Nora. 'See, Simon – Sarah agrees with me.'

'I'm with Simon. *Die Hard* is set at Christmastime,' said James. 'It's about a man trying to get his family back. Isn't that what Christmas is all about – family?'

They had a lively debate about what constituted a Christmas movie – and what the best one was.

'I like all the oldies,' said Roger. '*Holiday Inn* and *White Christmas*.'

'For me, the perfect Christmas film is *It's a Wonderful Life*,' said Sarah.

'Is it terrible that I've never seen it?' asked Pari.

Roger gasped in mock outrage.

Pari popped a chocolate in her mouth. 'What's it even about?'

'It's about a guy named George Bailey,' explained James, 'who wants to go travelling and become an architect. But he has to take over his family's bank instead.'

'My heart bleeds for him,' said Pari sarcastically.

'At beginning of the movie he's planning to commit suicide,' continued Sarah.

Pari pulled a face. 'It sounds super depressing.'

'Oh, but it isn't,' Omar assured her. 'An angel comes down and helps George see how his small acts of kindness to friends and family have made a huge difference in people's lives.'

'For instance, during the Great Depression, he loans customers his own money so they can keep their houses,' Roger elaborated.

Ian snorted. 'They definitely don't make bankers like that any more. I can't tell you how many house foreclosures I've been to lately. It's great for my shop – I can pick up cheap furniture – but sad that so many people can't afford to pay their mortgages.'

Sarah suddenly had an idea. If George Bailey could do something to help his community during tough economic times, perhaps they could too . . .

'James, what if we showed free Christmas movies for local residents this year,' she mused. 'It sounds like a lot of local people could use a bit of a pick-me-up.'

A movie couldn't solve anyone's problems, but it could provide a few hours of escapism, a much-needed break from troubles and worries.

'That's a great idea,' said James.

Sarah's gaze landed on the chocolate advent calendar that Holly had ravaged. 'Maybe we could do it like an advent calendar.'

'How do you mean?' asked Roger.

'We won't say what movie we're screening before-hand. It will be a surprise – like opening a door to an advent calendar.'

'That's brilliant!' said James.

Roger frowned. 'I hate to be a spoilsport, but how can you show twenty-four movies for free? You're going to have to pay the distributors and you won't be making any profit.'

'True,' concurred James.

The room fell silent for a moment as they tried to think of a solution.

'Maybe we could just show twelve movies,' said Sarah. 'And call it the Twelve Films of Christmas?'

'And we can ask people to make a donation if they can afford it,' suggested James. 'Everything left after covering our costs we can donate to charity.'

Sarah nodded, getting more and more excited about the idea.

'I love it!' said Nora. 'We can help promote it to our customers.'

'What movie will you show first?' asked Roger.

Sarah and James's eyes met across the table. She smiled at her husband. He reached over to squeeze her hand. *It's a Wonderful Life,*' they said at the same time.

After the other guests had left, James went upstairs to check on Holly.

Pari insisted on helping Sarah with the dishes. 'That was fun,' she said, loading plates into the dishwasher.

Sarah scraped off the burnt bits from the bottom of the lasagne pan. 'I've been a bad friend.'

'Because you were trying to set me up with Ian?' teased Pari.

'I wasn't trying to set you up!' protested Sarah. 'He's just a bit lonely.'

'I'm kidding,' said Pari.

'I mean because I had no idea that you were grappling with all these big life decisions. I'm sorry I haven't been there for you.'

'Don't be silly. You have a lot going on too,' said Pari. 'By the way, I think my god-daughter might be the cutest – and smartest – kid that ever lived.'

'Still,' insisted Sarah. 'I'm your best friend. I want to know what's going on with you. Are you sure you aren't going to miss comedy?'

'I'll miss some things about it,' replied Pari. 'But I'm ready for a change. I'm tired of the comedy circuit – gross venues with sticky floors, staying in Premier Inns right on the motorway, and eating service-station crap for dinner. And most of all the constant sexual harassment.'

Sarah handed Pari the lasagne dish to dry.

'I want to make sure new performers have an easier time than I did – especially other women. Things are changing, but not quickly enough.'

Sarah nodded. She'd witnessed the abuse her friend had faced on stage. Being a stand-up comedian meant making yourself incredibly vulnerable – it was just you and a microphone; there was no place to hide from the audience. Pari had shrugged off the heckling, just as she'd shrugged off the unwanted advances from fellow comedians and sleazy venue owners. But it had clearly taken its toll.

'I'm going to do everything I can to make entertainment more diverse and inclusive,' explained Pari, putting the pan on the drying rack. 'And hopefully make pots of money while I'm at it.'

Pari was tough and determined – both excellent qualities in an agent. She was also incredibly loyal. Sarah knew she would fight tooth and nail for anyone she believed in.

'You're going to be an amazing agent.' Sarah hugged her friend, even though her hands were sudsy.

After showing Pari to the guest bedroom, Sarah went into her own room. To her surprise, the bed was empty. She went into Holly's room and, in the soft glow of the nightlight, saw that James had dozed off in the rocking chair with Holly asleep on his shoulder.

Sarah's heart swelled as she watched the two people she loved most in the world sleeping soundly. Her perfect little family. She wouldn't trade this for anything – not even a film deal. Sarah's dreams had changed, same as Pari's. Maybe that was what it meant to grow up – accepting that life didn't always work out the way you thought it would. Her writing career had stalled, but hopefully she could go back to it later. Holly was healthy and happy, and that was all that really mattered.

It truly was a wonderful life.

Chapter 7

Present Day

'Out of the way, loser,' said Damon Carter, barging into Nick and sending him sprawling on the ground. The contents of Nick's backpack spilled out across the corridor. As his cronies egged him on, Damon kicked Nick's pencil case across the floor. Nick's charcoal drawing pencils scattered everywhere.

'He shoots, he scores!' cheered Damon.

Laughing, he and his mates from the football team continued down the corridor to the gym. Cheeks burning with shame, Nick scrabbled about on the floor, gathering up his belongings. He shoved his drawing pencils back into his pencil case. Luckily, only a few had broken. At least Holly hadn't witnessed his latest humiliation. She would have told his parents and Mum would have marched down to the school, demanding to talk to the headteacher.

As if that would solve anything.

Nick picked up a pear that had spilled out of his backpack. It was too squashed to eat now. *I wish it was a Clear-Clear fruit,* thought Nick. In his favourite manga series, *One Piece,* the characters could eat magical fruits that gave them supernatural powers. There was one special fruit – the Clear-Clear fruit – that allowed you to become invisible.

Sighing, Nick dropped the squashed non-magical pear into the bin.

Normally, he avoided the corridors when they were so busy, but he'd been in a rush to get to the library. Mrs Holmes, the school librarian, always put out new books on a Wednesday. Last week, she'd promised Nick that she had ordered the latest volume of *One Piece*. Entering the library, Nick headed straight to the display of new books. He reached for his favourite manga, but he wasn't fast enough. Someone else got there before him.

'Sorry,' said Mr Wu, turning around. 'Are you a *One Piece* fan too?'

'Yeah.' Nick loved the long-running manga series about a crew of pirates on a quest to find a mythical treasure. There were epic battles and adventures, with loads of funny bits too. Eiichiro Oda's illustrations featured bright, colourful panels, energetic action scenes and unusual perspectives. Nick was obsessed with trying to copy his style.

'Who's your favourite character?' asked Mr Wu.

'I like Nami best,' Nick mumbled. Nami was the pirates' navigator. What she lacked in fighting prowess, she made up for with her smarts.

'She's my wife's favourite character as well,' said Mr Wu. 'I'm getting this out for her – she loves manga. She's been feeling down lately. I thought it might cheer her up.' He held the book out to Nick. 'But here, I can take something else for her instead.'

Nick shook his head. 'No, that's OK.' It sounded like Mr Wu's wife needed cheering up, and nothing was better for that than losing yourself in a pirate adventure.

'Are you sure?' asked his teacher.

Nick reached for a volume of *Dragon Ball*. 'I'll take this out instead.' Mr Wu was one of the few things he liked about school, so Nick was happy to wait for the new *One Piece*.

'Thank you,' said Mr Wu, taking the manga volume over to the circulation desk. 'I'll bring this back to school as soon as my wife has read it.'

Nick went to sit on a beanbag. Unlike the rest of the school, the library was quiet and calm. There were a few kids doing homework at tables, and one or two others browsing the shelves. It was the only place in the whole building where Nick felt he could relax.

'You're staying late, Nick,' remarked Mrs Holmes. The school librarian was decorating a Christmas tree with hand-made paper baubles. On each one, she'd written a suggestion for a book to read.

As much as he hated school, Nick just didn't feel like going home today. Ever since he'd heard his parents arguing, he'd felt anxious. He couldn't stop worrying about his mum and dad, and what would happen if they split up.

When he finished the book, he took out his sketchpad and started to draw. He was working on an idea for a new manga character called Kanjo who had the power to change people's feelings. He could strike fear into a baddie's heart, just as easily as he could turn tears into smiles. Nick was trying to teach himself Japanese using YouTube tutorials and Duolingo. Kanjo was the Japanese word for emotion.

Before Nick heard the girl's voice, he smelled her minty chewing gum – even though chewing gum wasn't allowed at school.

'Hey, that's really good.'

A girl with long, jet-black hair was standing over him, a book tucked under her arm. She was in Year Seven too – they were in the same geography class but had never spoken before.

'I'm Julia,' she said, plopping herself down on the beanbag next to him. 'Mind if I sit here?'

Nick shook his head, even though he felt anxious about having to talk to someone new. Luckily, Julia didn't seem to notice his awkwardness, or if she did she didn't mind.

'My twin brother, Adam, has football practice after school, and I have to wait until he's done to get the bus home to Stowford,' she explained.

Nick knew who her brother was. Adam was on the Year Seven football team with Damon Carter. He wasn't one of the boys who was there when Damon had knocked him over earlier, but Nick was wary of all the sporty kids.

'My dad is super over-protective.' Julia shifted on the beanbag until she got comfortable, tucking one leg underneath her bum. 'Probably because he's a single parent.'

'Are your parents divorced?' asked Nick.

'My mum left when me and Adam were tiny.'

'I'm sorry.' Nick felt a rush of sympathy for Julia and her brother. He couldn't imagine growing up without a mum.

'Don't be,' said Julia. 'I don't even remember her, and my dad's great.'

As Julia read her book, Nick went back to his drawing. He shaded dark shadows under Kanjo's eyes. Nick was so engrossed in his drawing that he didn't notice Julia watching him until she spoke again.

'Why does the boy look so sad?'

'He's an empath,' explained Nick. 'He can suck out someone's sadness and make them happy again. But he has to carry those feelings around with him.'

'Poor guy,' said Julia sympathetically.

Nick looked at her more closely. Her hair wasn't really black – she'd dyed it. There was an inch of blonde roots growing out of her scalp. Her eyes were ringed with black liner (which was also against school rules), she had chipped black nail polish on her fingers, and there was a ladder in her black school tights. But despite her slightly gothic appearance, she had a friendly face.

Nick tore the sheet out of his sketchbook. 'You can have it if you want.'

Julia grinned. 'Are you sure?'

Nick shrugged. 'It's no big deal. He's just a character that I'm working on.'

'Thanks,' said Julia, unzipping her backpack and putting the drawing carefully inside. 'How did you learn to draw like that?'

'Mostly just reading lots of manga and watching YouTube videos.'

'Do you like anime too? Like *Spirited Away?* Or *My Neighbour Totoro?*'

Nick nodded enthusiastically. 'I've seen all the Studio Ghibli movies.' Nick hadn't met many other kids who were fans of the Japanese animation studio. 'How did you get into anime?'

'My dad used to take me and my brother to the Saturday morning Kids' Club at Plumdale Picture Palace. They show all sorts of cool movies. Ever been there?'

Nick nodded and gave her a shy smile. 'Yeah, I actually know it pretty well.'

Julia dragged her beanbag closer to Nick's. Now he could smell her shampoo — it was the same coconut one his sister used. 'So what's that character for?'

'I'm trying to create my own manga, but I haven't really worked out the story yet.'

'Maybe I could help you,' offered Julia. 'I'm no good at drawing, but I like writing stories.'

'That would be cool,' said Nick, trying not to sound too excited. It seemed like she might actually want to be friends.

Mrs Holmes, the librarian, shushed them good-naturedly, so Nick went back to his drawing and Julia to her book. Nick could smell Julia's minty gum and hear the rhythmic sound of her chewing, but it didn't bother him.

Just before five, Julia stood and shoved her book in her bag. 'I'd better go. Football training will be over now. See you around, Nick.'

'Bye.' Nick watched Julia lope out of the library, with her backpack slung across her back. He knew he should head home, too.

Nick quickly gathered up his things, but before he left school, he checked the sports noticeboard to see what days the Year Seven football team practised – Monday and Wednesday. Maybe Julia would be in the library again after school on Monday. Although next time, he'd wait until the coast was clear to avoid another run-in with Damon.

When he got home, Nick could hear his mother's voice drifting out of the living room. Peeping in, he saw his auntie Pari's face on his mother's laptop screen. His mum's back was to him; she hadn't heard him come in.

'It feels amazing to be writing again,' Mum said. 'I sent Noa the first act and he was really happy with it. I feel like we have a real connection, you know?'

'I'm sure the fact that he's easy on the eye doesn't have anything to do with that,' teased Auntie Pari.

'He's even better looking in person than he is in photos,' gushed Mum.

Pari chuckled. 'I think someone's got a crush.'

'Stop!' Mum giggled. 'Our relationship is purely professional.'

Nick frowned. Mum sounded giddy – like Holly and her friends when they were talking about the boys they liked. He knew he shouldn't eavesdrop but couldn't force himself to move.

'Seriously, Noa has been so encouraging about my writing. He says he wants to read *The Ghost Writer*. If I ever get around to finishing it.'

'Well, I'm thrilled you're working on the script,' said Pari. 'One of my clients — Mateo Ajose — is playing the lead. We need it to be a hit.'

'Noa needs it to be a hit, too,' shared Mum. 'His last movie didn't do very well at the box office.'

'I still don't understand why he parted ways with his usual studio,' remarked Pari. 'There were some rumours that he's difficult to work with.'

'I find that hard to believe. He's been absolutely lovely to me. Noa says he's working with a streamer so he can finance a passion project,' said Mum.

Noa says, Noa says . . . thought Nick. He didn't like how this movie had taken over his mother's life. It was like Noa Drakos had put her under a magic spell.

'Sounds like you might be his next "passion project".' Pari chuckled.

Anxiety gnawed at Nick's stomach. Was Mum having an affair with a famous film director? What if she left them, the way Julia's mother had . . .

'Oh, please, Pari.' Mum scoffed. 'The man has dated pop stars. As if he's going to be interested in me. And in any case, my libido has been non-existent.'

What does that mean?

'Ah, the joys of being a middle-aged woman,' said Pari, sighing. 'I'm not even interested in my rabbit any more.'

When did Pari get a pet? wondered Nick.

'I went to see the doctor this week,' said Mum. 'They did some blood tests to check my hormone levels and wrote me a prescription for HRT. Hopefully it will improve the anxiety and brain fog.'

Nick felt a jolt of fear. Was Mum ill? Did she have a brain tumour? Was that why she had been acting so sad these past few months? A terrifying thought occurred to Nick – was Mum DYING?

'I hope it helps,' said Pari.

'I'd better go,' said Mum. 'Noa wants to see a new draft of the second act by tomorrow morning.'

Nick darted out of the corridor and sprinted up to his bedroom as Mum ended her call. He had so many questions, but he couldn't ask Mum – he was too scared of what she might say.

Nick sat down on his bed and wrapped his weighted blanket over his shoulders to try to calm himself down. Jonesy came crawling out from under the bed and jumped onto his lap. As Nick stroked the cat's back, Jonesy purred and kneaded his lap.

'Grown-ups are so confusing,' he confided in the cat. He wasn't sure if Mum was madly in love with a famous film director or seriously ill.

Either way, there was something worrying going on. And Nick didn't know what to do.

Frowning, Sarah deleted the line she'd just written and wrote it again. 'You have the bed, I'll sleep on the floor,' she said as she typed.

Yes, that was much better. She was working on the scene where the two main characters discovered that they had to share a bedroom in the inn because it was fully booked for Christmas.

Sitting at the kitchen table, Sarah was so engrossed in her work, she nearly jumped out of her skin when someone tapped her on the shoulder. She turned around and saw Holly, wearing the dress she'd bought in London and her Tiffany necklace.

'You nearly gave me a heart attack,' she said with a gasp.

Holly gave an impatient huff. 'I've been standing here saying your name for like a minute.'

'Sorry, I was completely caught up in the script.' Sarah smiled at her daughter. Things between them had mercifully improved since Holly's birthday. She was just giving Sarah a normal level of teenaged attitude, rather than full-blown hatred. 'You look nice. Are you going out?'

Holly gave her a withering look. 'Duh? It's the first film of the festival? What time are we leaving for the cinema?'

'Oh, crap!' Sarah had completely lost track of time. If she didn't get a move on, they'd be late.

Saving her work, she dashed into the bathroom to shower. After drying herself off, she rubbed oestrogen gel on her belly. The hormone replacement therapy had already improved her sleep. She hadn't had a hot flash in days, either.

Her period was still as regular as clockwork, so it hadn't occurred to her that she was in perimenopause. But the GP had explained that her mood swings and anxiety were both classic symptoms of the change. It was a relief to finally find out what was wrong with her. As her brain fog lifted and her mood improved, she was beginning to feel like her old self again.

Sarah swung by Valley Vistas to pick up her mother. Geraldine was waiting for her outside. Nick jumped out of the back and helped his grandmother into the passenger seat.

'It's OK, I can manage,' said Geraldine. 'No need to fuss.' But Sarah noticed how she clung to Nick's arm as she lowered herself into the car. *Age catches up with all of us,* thought Sarah. Even her mother, who had travelled the world on her own doing anthropological research. She'd been doing so well until Long Covid had slowed her down, sapping her energy. It just went to show that you had to live your life to the fullest while you could. Even HRT couldn't turn the clock back.

'Sorry I'm a bit late, Mum,' Sarah said. 'I was working on the screenplay.'

'That's quite all right,' said Geraldine cheerfully. 'I'm glad to see you using your brain again.'

Sarah bristled at her mother's implied criticism. 'Yeah, yeah, I know you think I've been wasting my life here in Plumdale,' she said defensively. She knew she sounded as snippy as Holly. Did all grown women revert back into a stroppy teenager when talking to their mum?

'I didn't say that,' Geraldine scolded her. 'You're putting words in my mouth. I'm just glad you're writing again because I know it makes you happy. It always has – you loved writing stories as a little girl.'

Mollified, Sarah started to drive to the cinema. Geraldine took something out of her bag – some sort of poster.

'What's that?' asked Sarah.

'I've decided to organise a lecture and discussion series at Valley Vistas. I'm giving the first talk – it's on the role of grandparents in different cultures. I was hoping I could hang the schedule up on the cinema noticeboard.'

'Of course you can,' said Sarah. 'I think that's wonderful.'

'It was Roger from the cinema who suggested it,' said Geraldine. 'After the Golden Oldies screening, Pam insisted that I join them. They seem to have appointed her as my unofficial welcoming committee.'

Sarah was delighted that Roger and Pam had succeeded where she had failed. She had been suggesting for weeks that Geraldine engage with the local community. 'I'm glad you're making friends.'

'Well, I wouldn't go that far.' Geraldine sniffed. 'But I suppose it's better than sitting around on my own doing crossword puzzles.'

Sarah rolled her eyes.

When they arrived at the cinema, the lobby was packed with people.

'You made it!' exclaimed James, sounding relieved. He kissed her on the cheek.

'Of course,' said Sarah. She'd never missed a Christmas film-festival screening.

James took his mother-in-law by the arm. 'Let's find you a seat, Geraldine.'

'Sarah!' called a woman in her mid-fifties, waving madly. She had long, wavy auburn hair streaked with grey and wore a vintage-style dress.

'Hello, Nora,' said Sarah, giving her old friend a hug.

'I hear you're working on the movie that our friend Mateo is starring in,' said Nora.

'Word travels fast,' commented Sarah.

The American actor had worked in a pub in Stowford before he became famous. He and his wife, Sam, were good friends of the Waldens. They were how Pari had ended up representing him – they'd put in a good word when Mateo's old agent retired.

'Sam is delighted that he's filming locally over the holidays,' said Nora. 'So he can spend more time with her and the little ones.'

'Be sure to tell her about our Baby and Me screenings,' said Sarah.

'I will,' promised Nora.

Simon came over holding two steaming cups of hot

chocolate. He handed one to Nora. 'I can't believe the film festival is still going strong. How many years has it been?'

'Fourteen,' said Sarah. She pulled Nick, who was standing around awkwardly, over to her and tousled his hair. 'It's been around longer than this guy.'

Nora smiled warmly at Nick. 'We've had to make the manga section even bigger, Nick. It's so popular these days.'

Nora and Simon had added a manga section to their bookshop after Nick had told them how much he loved Japanese graphic novels. Now he visited the shop regularly to get his fix of manga and books about drawing.

'I want a hot chocolate too,' said Nick.

Sarah watched him go over to the concession stand, where Holly was helping Aaron serve festive refreshments. Aaron handed Holly a Santa hat, like the one he was wearing. Holly put it on, then giggled as Aaron adjusted it for her, tucking a stray lock of hair under the hat's furry white band.

So that's why she didn't want to be late, thought Sarah. *And why she's wearing her new dress.*

She went over to the table where her mum and James were sitting. Geraldine was watching Holly and Aaron too.

'It's so interesting how universal flirting is.' Geraldine looked amused. 'I've studied tribes all over the world and the behaviours are the same everywhere.'

'What do you mean?' asked James.

Sarah looked at her mother and they both shook their heads. *How could someone so intelligent be so clueless?*

Geraldine patted his arm. 'Your daughter is clearly crazy about that boy. And he's completely smitten with her.'

'Really?' James turned to Sarah for confirmation.

She nodded. 'Really.'

Sarah watched as Holly took a sip of her hot chocolate. Some whipped cream got on her nose and Aaron wiped it off with his finger. Holly giggled and toyed with her necklace.

'Well, well, well,' said James. 'I guess Holly really is growing up.'

'You're OK with this?' asked Sarah.

James shrugged. 'He's a nice kid – polite, hard-working, bright. She could do a lot worse.'

'She's too young,' said Sarah.

'Oh, please. That didn't stop you,' said Geraldine. 'I came home from work and caught you snogging Neil Butler on the sofa when you were only fourteen.'

'Neil Butler, eh?' teased James, raising his eyebrow.

'Don't worry. He had a mullet and rather unfortunate acne,' said Geraldine.

Sarah wasn't sure why she felt so uncomfortable about Holly having a boyfriend, if indeed that's what Aaron was. James was right – he was a lovely boy. She just didn't want her to get hurt when Aaron went off to uni. And she certainly didn't want her daughter to sacrifice her dreams for the sake of a boy.

Stop making this about you, said a voice in her head.

'Come on,' said James, rounding up the family. 'It's time for the film.'

They settled into their seats. Sarah felt a shiver of anticipation as the curtains drew back. It was fun not to know what movie she was about to see, to experience the surprise along with the rest of the audience for a change.

Sleigh bells rang out and a black-and-white image of a storybook filled the screen.

Aaahhh! Sarah smiled knowingly before the title even appeared. *It's a Wonderful Life* had a special place in her heart, not just because the Frank Capra classic was a masterpiece – which of course it was – but also because it was what they had chosen to launch their very first film festival.

It was a movie about thwarted ambitions and the weight of family obligations. It took a visit from an angel to show the main character, played by Jimmy Stewart, that those sacrifices were worthwhile.

As always, the film wove its heart-warming spell over her. It made her want to go ice skating and carol singing, to bake cookies and drink hot cocoa. Sarah hoped that the words she was writing would have the same effect on audiences. *Ex-mas Eve* probably wouldn't be a master-piece – even with Noa at the helm and a starry cast – but hopefully it would fill viewers with a sense of warmth and wellbeing. At least, that's what she was aiming for. And so far, Noa seemed happy with her work.

Noa was *her* Christmas angel. It felt like he'd been heaven-sent to give her a second chance at making some-thing of her life. To finally revive her long-lost ambitions.

'Did you enjoy that?' asked James after the closing credits played and the house lights came back on.

'Oh, yes,' said Sarah, her eyes glowing with pleasure. 'It was . . . *wonderful.*'

14th February 2011

'Happy Valentine's Day, beautiful,' James said, handing Sarah a card he'd bought at the corner shop that morning when he'd gone out to buy milk. The selection had been pretty poor; he'd chosen one with two grey teddy bears hugging, surrounded by pink hearts.

'Oh, honey, I can't believe you remembered, what with everything else happening today.' She opened the card, propped it up on the kitchen counter and gave him a kiss.

'I know I usually get you flowers too,' he said. 'But that seemed unnecessary, given the circumstances.'

Every available surface held a flower arrangement. It was like the Chelsea Flower Show in his father's tiny flat.

Sean had passed away three weeks previously. He'd been receiving treatment for COPD, but a bout of pneumonia over the winter had finished him off. His weakened lungs hadn't been able to cope with the infection. After several weeks in hospital, he had passed away, with James and Sarah at his bedside. He'd received last rites from Father Anthony and had been at peace, unlike James. He was furious that his father had been taken from him so soon.

Sarah unscrewed the lid on a jar of mayonnaise and started making sandwiches for the funeral. Nothing had changed in the kitchen of the former council flat since James had grown up there – the smoke-stained floral wallpaper, the speckled linoleum countertop, the dark wooden cupboards all remained as they'd been when it had been his mother making sandwiches for his packed lunches.

The doorbell rang and James went downstairs to answer it. *Flowers or casserole?* he wondered. A steady stream of neighbours had been dropping off bouquets and meals since Sean's passing.

It was Mrs Gilligan from two doors down. She thrust a casserole dish at him. 'I've made you a spicy tuna bake. It's my own recipe.'

'Thanks, Mrs Gilligan.'

'Sure your da was a very nice man. We'll miss him.'

Me too, thought James.

'Are you waking him at home?' she asked, peering around the door.

'No,' said James. 'There will be a reception after the mass in the church hall. You're welcome to join us.'

'I'll be there,' promised Mrs Gilligan, patting his arm. 'You're all in my prayers.'

James put the tuna bake in the fridge. He appreciated the neighbours' kindness, but most of their offerings had gone uneaten. Neither of them had much of an appetite – even for Mrs Khan from downstairs' delicious chicken curry.

No sooner had James shut the fridge door than the front bell went again.

'I'll get it,' said Sarah.

This time, it was a stunning bouquet of lilies. James took the card out of the envelope. It read: *Our deepest condolences, Roger and Omar. x*

The couple had also made a generous donation to the British Lung Foundation in Sean's memory.

Roger had been holding down the fort at the cinema, as James had been staying in Ealing since Sean had been hospitalised.

Sarah found a space for the flowers. 'Well, I suppose we should get dressed.'

James went to his childhood bedroom, where the model airplanes he'd built with his dad still hung from the ceiling. Tape marks remained on the walls where he'd once displayed posters of Demi Moore, Michelle Pfeiffer and other 1980s film stars he'd fancied. He couldn't bring himself to sleep in what had been his parents' bedroom, so he and Sarah had been squeezing into the single bed together. At least it no longer had a *Return of the Jedi* duvet cover. James slept with his arms wrapped tightly around Sarah, like a shipwrecked sailor clinging to a piece of driftwood. Sarah had been his rock these past few weeks. He wouldn't have been able to bear it without her tireless support.

'I miss Holly,' said James. He longed to give his little girl a cuddle, to hear her squeal with delight when he swung her in the air.

'Me too,' admitted Sarah. 'But Mum says they're having fun.'

Geraldine was looking after their daughter for a few days, while they were in London for the funeral. They had debated whether Holly should come, and ultimately decided she was too young. Although they had tried to explain to their daughter that Sean had gone to heaven, Holly kept asking for Granda. Sean had doted on Holly, taking her on walks, singing her Irish lullabies and buying her a toy workbench with little wooden tools. It felt so unfair that they had been cheated of more time together, that Sean wouldn't see his granddaughter grow up. James vowed to keep Sean's memory alive, so that Holly didn't forget him.

'She took Holly on an outing to Peppa Pig World today.'

'Bet she loved that,' said James. Three-year-old Holly was a big fan of Peppa and her little brother, George. Recently, she'd started asking for her own little brother. That was another thing that was hard to explain to her – how badly they wanted to give her a sibling too.

James put on the black suit Sarah had bought him for the funeral, as he'd been too busy with death admin to go out and look for anything.

'I'm dreading this,' said James, tucking his shirt into his trousers. The trousers felt loose around the waist, as he'd barely been eating.

Sarah put her arms around his shoulders. 'It's OK to cry if you need to, James. I know you're trying to stay strong, but you've got to let it out at some point.'

He hadn't shed a tear for his father, not even on the day they'd lost him. It wasn't that he was trying not to cry, it was that he *couldn't*. There was a constant tightness in his chest, an accumulation of unshed tears building up inside him. He just hoped that the dam wouldn't burst in the middle of his eulogy.

James wrapped his arms around his wife's waist and buried his face on her shoulder, inhaling her comfortingly familiar scent of citrus and spice. They stood like that for ages, with Sarah stroking his back reassuringly.

Eventually, the undertakers arrived to drive them to the church. They drove past the cinema where he and his dad had gone every weekend to watch movies. It had recently shut down, which felt like another blow. It wasn't surprising, though. Their own cinema was thriving, but the running costs were higher than James had ever anticipated.

At the church, the pews were full of neighbours, cousins, Sean's former colleagues from Pinewood, and a few of James's oldest friends and their parents. For such a quiet, unassuming man, Sean had made his mark on everyone he'd met. James had received cards and messages from so many people who shared stories of Sean's kindness. Knowing how loved his father was brought James some small comfort, but didn't alleviate the tightness in his chest.

As the organist began to play 'An Irish Blessing', James and the other pallbearers carried Sean's coffin down the aisle. James stared straight ahead stoically as he listened to his father's favourite hymn. A lump was lodged in his throat and his chest felt so tight, it hurt to take a breath, but the dam held.

James's cousin Sinead did the first reading. As they listened to the words chosen to bring comfort, Sarah began to cry. James put his arm around her shoulder and handed her the handkerchief in his pocket. They weren't just mourning Sean, they were also grieving for the baby they'd lost last year. Their joy over Sarah's pregnancy had turned to sorrow at their twelve-week scan, when no heartbeat could be detected.

'Don't lose faith, my boy.' Sean had comforted James after hearing the news. 'It's all part of God's plan.'

James envied his father's faith. Intellectually, he knew there was no scientific proof for the existence of a higher power, or the afterlife. Yet, he had to hope that his father's spirit, and that of their unborn child, were with God. Even if heaven did not exist as a place where angels strummed on harps, James believed that his father's spirit was alive, somewhere in the cosmos. Energy could not be created or destroyed, it just changed form.

'Good luck,' whispered Sarah, her eyes bright from tears, as James stood to give the eulogy. James had agonised over the speech, knowing it was impossible to put into words how much his dad had meant to him. How he would always strive to live up to the values his dad had instilled in him.

Here goes, thought James. He cleared his throat and began to speak, hoping he would do his father justice.

'As most of you know, my dad worked for years at Pinewood Studios. I was named after James Bond, because Dad loved those films and was proud to have worked on them. I may have been named after a movie hero, but my dad was one of life's true unsung heroes. He was a kind and decent man – a loyal husband, a loving father, a hard-working colleague and a caring friend.' James's voice cracked with emotion as he read the words he'd written. 'He always went out of his way to help other people and never expected a thing in return.'

Pausing to compose himself, James looked up and saw many people in the congregation nodding in agreement. He went on to tell them how much his father had adored his mother. How he'd always encouraged James's academic interests. The happy holidays they'd had visiting family in Ireland.

He concluded by saying, 'Some of my happiest memories of Dad were watching films together, and, later, working side by side as we restored a cinema in the Cotswolds. He was an excellent craftsman, but an even better father and grandfather. Dad, the final credits have rolled, but you will never be forgotten.'

'Well done,' Sarah whispered, squeezing his hand when he sank back into his seat, weak with relief that he'd got through the eulogy without breaking down.

After the mass was over, Sean's coffin began its final journey to the strains of 'Ave Maria'. In the churchyard, Sean was lowered into the ground. His name had already been added to the cross marking his wife's grave: Sean Nicolas O'Hara and Mary Eileen O'Hara. It gave James some small comfort to know that his parents were reunited at last.

Sarah sobbed quietly as the priest said one last prayer. But James's eyes remained as dry as the soil that would cover his father's grave.

Afterwards, there was a wake in the church hall, with the sandwiches Sarah had made, and cakes provided by various neighbours and parishioners. Sean's former colleagues laughed as they traded anecdotes over cups of tea.

'Remember when Sean pretended to have sawn off his finger on the set of *Interview with a Vampire*,' said one colleague, reminiscing.

'Oh, yes,' said another, chuckling. 'There was fake blood spurting everywhere.'

A bald man in a smart suit and sunglasses approached James. 'It was a lovely service. You did your father proud,' he said in a thick Scottish accent.

'Mr Connery,' James stammered. 'Thank you so much for coming.' He'd met the famous actor once before as a boy. His dad had taken him to visit the set during the filming of *Never Say Never Again*, the actor's last appearance as Bond.

'Sean was a fine man,' said the film star, shaking James's hand. 'Everyone always used to joke that *he* was the most important Sean at Pinewood.'

James laughed. His dad would have loved that.

'He was very proud of you,' added the star. He patted James on the shoulder, then his bodyguard escorted him out of the reception.

Sarah appeared at James's side. 'Was that . . .'

'Yup,' said James. '007 himself.'

His dad would have been delighted that Sean Connery attended his funeral, but no more so than any of the other people there – Mrs Gilligan, cousin Sinead and the chippies from Pinewood. Sean had treated everyone with equal respect and had encouraged his son to do the same.

When the crusts on the remaining sandwiches had begun to curl, and the tea urn had run dry, people started to say goodbye. As lovely as it had been to hear their stories and receive their condolences, James couldn't wait for the funeral to be over. Once the final stragglers had left, James and Sarah returned to the flat, which reeked of lilies. It was preferable to the smell of smoke, which was imbued in the walls and carpet.

In the living room, James stood in front of the cabinet that housed his dad's most prized movie memorabilia. There was a copy of every movie he'd worked on, and props from various film sets he'd built – a James Bond pen that was secretly a recording device, a light sabre, a mask from Kubrick's *Eyes Wide Shut*.

'What am I going to do with all his stuff?' wondered James. 'Maybe we can display some of it at the cinema.'

'We don't have to decide now,' said Sarah soothingly. 'Let's just relax – it's been a long day.'

'I'm actually a bit hungry,' admitted James. 'I didn't eat anything at the wake.'

Sarah microwaved two portions of Mrs Gilligan's spicy tuna pasta bake and poured them each a glass of wine.

'Interesting,' he said, taking a bite. 'I've never had tuna with jalapenos before.'

'It's . . . tangy,' said Sarah.

'Are you tired?' asked James, as they washed up.

Sarah handed him a dish to dry. 'Not really.'

'Let's watch a movie,' said James. There could be no better way of honouring his dad. 'Maybe a romcom, as it's Valentine's Day.'

Sarah browsed through Sean's collection of films that he'd worked on at Pinewood. 'Aha!' she cried, pulling out a DVD of *Love, Actually*. 'Perfect!'

They settled back down on the sofa with their wine to watch the Richard Curtis romcom, which wove together the stories of eight couples over Christmastime, at different points in their relationships – from first love through to marriage breakdown and . . . grief.

As James watched Liam Neeson give a moving speech at his wife's funeral on screen, the dam inside him finally burst. James began to sob and sob.

'Oh, God,' Sarah said, lunging for the remote control to stop the movie. 'I'm so sorry. I completely forgot about this scene.' She held him tight, as tears poured out. 'It's

OK,' she murmured, stroking his back soothingly. 'Let it all out.'

When he'd finished crying, James felt a million times lighter. The tears had been cathartic. He reached for the remote to turn the movie back on.

'We can watch something else,' said Sarah.

'It's OK,' said James. 'Let's stick with this one.'

He lay down on the sofa, resting his head on Sarah's lap. As she gently stroked his hair, he let himself escape into the movie. For 135 blissful minutes, he could forget about his own sadness. It was how he and his dad had coped with his mother's passing, using films to temporarily relieve the pain.

As the final credits rolled, James searched for his father's name in tiny letters. 'Christmas will be weird without him,' he said, sitting up with a lump in his throat. His dad always spent Christmas with them.

'Maybe we should go away this year,' suggested Sarah. 'We could visit Meg in Edinburgh, or my dad in Spain.'

As James pondered her proposal, Sarah suddenly clutched her stomach.

'What's wrong?' James asked.

'I don't feel so good . . .' Lurching up from the sofa, she ran to the bathroom. A moment later, James heard the sound of retching.

'Oh, no,' said James, when she emerged from the bath-room. 'Mrs Gilligan's spicy tuna bake was a mistake.'

'I don't think it's that,' she said.

'Did the egg mayo sandwiches go bad?' James hoped they hadn't given Sir Sean Connery and all the other funeral guests food poisoning.

Sarah sat down next to him and smiled. 'I think I'm pregnant, James. I'll have to take a test to be one hundred per cent sure, but I'm nearly a week late. With everything that's been going on, I didn't even notice.' She pressed a hand to her chest and winced. 'My boobs are sore, which is always one of the first signs.'

He stared at her in astonishment. 'That's incredible.'

'It's early days,' Sarah said nervously. 'Lots of things could still go wrong. I won't be able to relax until we know everything's OK.'

James knew that they would both worry constantly until they saw a heartbeat on an ultrasound. But his own heart was already racing with excitement and hope – something that he would never have thought possible on such a sad day.

Please, Dad, if you're up there somewhere, can you keep an eye on this little one . . .

James could feel tears welling up inside him again – a poignant mixture of grief and joy. He'd thought there were none left, but he was wrong. 'It makes me sad that Dad won't get to meet the new baby. He would have been so happy for us.'

'He'll be with us in spirit,' said Sarah. 'And we'll make sure to tell the baby all about him.'

James nodded, blinking back his tears.

'If it's a boy, we can call him after your dad,' suggested Sarah. 'Sean Nicolas.'

'Or maybe Nicolas Sean,' said James. The baby would be his own person and deserved his own name.

James put his hand on Sarah's belly and gently caressed it. There wasn't a bump yet, but a baby was growing inside her. Just as one life had ended, a new life was taking its place. Perhaps it was just magical thinking, but James felt as if his dad was still looking out for him, letting him know that life would go on without him.

'I can't wait to meet you, little one,' he whispered, his heart full of love.

Chapter 8

Present Day

Sitting in the cinema's office, James looked at the list of films in his hand. Like Santa Claus, he'd made his list and was checking it twice.

1. ~~It's a Wonderful Life~~
2. ~~2046~~
3. ~~The Holiday~~
4. *Love, Actually*
5. *The Polar Express*
6. *Home Alone*
7. *Catch Me If You Can*
8. *Elf*
9. *Little Women*
10. *Tokyo Godfathers*
11. *An Affair to Remember*
12. *While You Were Sleeping*

It wasn't just a list of this year's Twelve Films of Christmas, it was a love letter to his wife. James had selected each movie to remind Sarah of a special moment in their lives. They'd been together for so long that it had been difficult to whittle it down to just twelve movies, but he wanted Sarah to remember all the wonderful times that they had shared together.

Tonight's movie was *Love, Actually.*

James hadn't picked it because Sarah loved Richard Curtis romcoms. At least, not *just* because of that. They'd watched the movie together the night of his father's funeral.

He remembered the psalm that had been read on that bittersweet day: 'Sorrow and suffering will pass, but joy continues in spite of hardship.'

It had proven to be true. He and Sarah had had their share of difficult times, too, like any long-term relationship. But they'd got through them together, snatching moments of joy and laughter wherever they could.

A knock on the office door summoned James back to the present.

'Hey, Dad,' said Nick. He was still wearing his school uniform.

'Good day at school?' asked James.

Nick shrugged. 'It was OK.'

James was happy to hear it. OK was progress – a few weeks ago the answer had consistently been 'bad' – and sometimes 'terrible'.

Nick picked up the list of movies from the desk. 'Are these the Twelve Films of Christmas?'

'Yes,' said James, taking the list back and sticking it in his pocket. 'But you weren't supposed to see that. They're supposed to be a surprise. Promise you won't tell anyone – especially Mum.'

'I won't. But can you tell me what day you're showing *Tokyo Godfathers.*'

Tokyo Godfathers was a heart-warming anime movie about three homeless people in Tokyo who find a baby in the snow at Christmas.

James checked his calendar. 'The sixteenth of December. Why?'

'I might invite someone from school who likes anime.' Nick was trying to play it cool, but James heard the undercurrent of excitement in his voice.

James grinned, thrilled that his son had made a friend. 'That's great, mate. What's his name?'

'*Her* name,' said Nick. 'Julia.'

James raised an eyebrow.

'But I don't know if I should invite her. She might not say yes.'

'You'll never know unless you ask her,' said James.

'But what if she says no?' Nick pulled off his tie and shoved it into his schoolbag.

'Then it's her loss,' replied James. 'I remember how nervous I was before I asked your mother out – I thought she was way out of my league.'

'Ew,' said Nick. 'I don't want Julia to be my girlfriend. I just want her to be my friend.'

'Same thing applies – if you want to get to know her better, you need to be brave and take a chance, even if it is a bit scary.'

'Maybe I will.' Settling down on the sofa, Nick took out a manga from his schoolbag and began to read.

James went into the auditorium and checked the wiring on the speakers.

'Don't die on me tonight,' he bargained with the equipment. 'Not with a full house.'

They had placed an order for a new sound system, using the first instalment of Sarah's screenwriting fee as a down payment. However, it was just a matter of time until something else went wrong. The projector had been overheating with alarming regularity and those cost even more than sound systems. Sarah had been right – the cinema wasn't sustainable. It was operating at a loss.

James looked around the crowded lobby, trying to spot his wife. The kids had both come straight from school, so Sarah could work in peace at home. Holly was chatting with Aaron behind the concession stand.

'I dare you to sing tonight,' James heard Aaron say.

'No, I couldn't,' demurred Holly, giggling

He saw Geraldine, sitting with Pam, Vi, Olwyn and Roger, and went over to say hello.

'What are you making?' James asked Pam, who was knitting something with burgundy-coloured wool.

Pam held up her creation. 'It's a scarf for the refugee charity in Calais that Roger volunteers at.'

'It gets very cold there in winter,' explained Roger. 'Most of the people there have risked their lives to try to get to safety, and they only have the clothes on their back.'

'It's a shame they're not always welcome when they arrive,' said Vi.

'My parents were refugees,' said Pam, returning to her knitting. 'They fled Poland at the beginning of World War II.'

'Omar sought asylum Paris in his twenties because it's illegal to be gay in Morocco,' explained Roger. 'He hated leaving his family, but it wasn't safe for him there.'

James knew how important the charity in Calais was to Roger. They always supported it on Christmas Eve, the final night of the film festival, when they usually raised hundreds for the cause. It had always seemed fitting. After all – Mary and Joseph were refugees, too, when they fled to Bethlehem to escape Herod.

'I can't knit,' said Geraldine. 'But maybe we could hold a coffee morning at Valley Vistas to support the charity?'

'Oh, that's a wonderful idea.' Roger beamed gratefully.

James smiled to himself. His mother-in-law would be in her element, organising her new friends. He suddenly remembered why he'd come over in the first place.

'Did Sarah drive you here?' he asked his mother-in-law.

'No, we all got a lift in the Valley Vistas minibus,' said Geraldine.

James hoped Sarah hadn't forgotten about the screening. His grand romantic gesture would be futile if she didn't see all the movies.

Fortunately, just before the film started, Sarah hurried into the auditorium. 'Sorry I'm late,' she whispered, sitting down next to James in the seat he'd saved for her. 'I was reworking a tricky scene.'

When Hugh Grant's voiceover began over the opening scene of *Love, Actually*, Sarah gave a little squeal of delight. James smiled in the dark, gratified that he'd pleased her.

After the movie finished, people milled around the lobby drinking hot chocolate and chatting about the film and their plans for the holidays. Aaron and Holly passed through the crowd, wearing Santa hats and holding charity donation buckets for tonight's charity, which provided respite care to families with very sick children.

James spotted Ian talking animatedly to Hermione from the candle shop. He and Sarah went over to join them.

'I know it's a bit dated,' Hermione was saying to Ian, 'but I do love that movie. It's so romantic. It almost made me believe in love again.'

'It's a bit silly, though,' said Ian. 'And are we supposed to believe that Italian gal falls in love with Colin Firth even though he can't speak a word of Italian?'

'Well . . .' said Sarah and Hermione at the same time. And then they both burst out laughing.

'I mean, it's Colin Firth,' said Sarah. 'Mr Darcy himself.'

Ian caught James' eye and they both shook their heads in despair as the wosmen giggled.

'Anyway, did the movie help you find your Christmas spirit?' Ian asked Hermione.

Hermione pursed her lips. 'Well, I suppose I'm starting to feel a *bit* Christmassy . . .'

'Let me get you a glass of mulled wine,' said Ian. 'That should do the trick.'

Putting his arm around her, Ian steered Hermione through the crowd over to the refreshment stand.

James nudged Sarah. 'I think love might be in the air,' he murmured. Listening to Ian and Hermione talk about the movie reminded him of the first time he and Sarah had met. Sparks had flown as they'd discussed the film they'd just seen. By the end of that night, he'd been head over heels in love. So maybe *Love, Actually* wasn't so silly after all.

As he watched Ian hand Hermione a glass of mulled wine, James remembered that exhilarating first flush of love. The heady passion he and Sarah had felt back then. What they had now was a different sort of love – more worn in, like a comfortable pair of jeans.

A very frayed pair of jeans, with more than a few holes in the fabric.

Just then, Aaron whistled to get everyone's attention. 'Tonight we're raising money for a really important cause. If everyone digs deep and donates as much as they can afford, Holly says she'll sing for us.'

Holly blushed, but she looked pleased as people came forward to put money in her bucket.

'Go, Holly!' called Ian, raising his glass of mulled wine.

'Holly! Holly!' chanted the crowd.

Holly held up her hand for silence and a hush fell over the lobby. Taking a deep breath, she launched into a solo rendition of 'All I Want for Christmas is You', which had featured in the movie they'd just watched. As her powerful voice rang out across the lobby, James got goosebumps.

'That's our girl,' Sarah whispered in James's ear as Holly hit the final high notes.

'Bravo!' cried a man in a cashmere coat, clapping his hands. He took out his wallet and stuffed a wad of bills into the donation bucket.

'Noa!' exclaimed Sarah. 'What are you doing here?'

'I'm guessing this talented young lady is your daughter,' said the director. He was accompanied by his assistant, a young woman with trendy retro-style glasses and a very short fringe.

'Yes, that's Holly,' said Sarah. 'And this is my husband.'

The director gave James a dazzlingly white smile. If he hadn't opted for a life behind the camera, Noa Drakos could have easily worked in front of it – he was ridiculously handsome.

James extended his hand to the director. 'Nice to meet you.'

'Hi, Jim.' Noa shook James's hand with a firm grip. 'I've heard a lot about you.'

Jim? Clearly Noa hadn't heard *that* much about him. Nobody ever called him Jim.

'Your wife is incredible,' said Noa. His hand rested on Sarah's back.

'Yes, I know,' replied James.

'She's been working miracles on my script.'

'Oh, I've barely done anything.' Sarah brushed away the compliment, but she was glowing at his praise. 'Just made what was already there better.'

'Stop being so modest,' said Noa, his hand still on her back. 'I'd be lost without you, darling.'

Darling. James suddenly had a horrifying thought. Was Sarah cheating on him with Noa Drakos? Who would blame her if she *was* having an affair with the director? He was rich, successful and charming – and, more importantly, *new*. Everything James wasn't.

Stop being so insecure! James told himself sternly. Sarah would never betray him.

'Were you at the screening just now?' asked Sarah.

'Oh, no, I'm too busy for that,' said Noa. 'I've got a business proposal for you. We'd like to hire the cinema as our location base while we shoot at Merricourt Manor and around Plumdale.'

Sarah and James exchanged confused glances.

'Why here?' asked James.

'We'd like to use the café as our warm area,' continued Noa. 'But mostly we're interested in using your car park and the side alleyway, where we can park our trailers and electricity generator.'

'We would need to get permission from the local council, of course,' said the assistant.

'Our local MP might be able to help,' said Sarah. 'She's a big supporter of independent businesses.'

Noa snapped his fingers and his assistant handed James a contract.

James scanned the document. The production company were offering a substantial sum to use the car park and lobby for two weeks, while they filmed in and around the village.

He passed the contract to Sarah. Her eyes widened as she read it.

'Can we think about it for a bit?' James wanted a chance to mull the offer over. It seemed too good to be true.

'I'm afraid we need a decision tonight,' said Noa. 'We're also looking at the polo club as a possible location – but of course we'd prefer to use the cinema. Sarah mentioned it's been struggling.'

James didn't like being pressurised like this. And he also didn't like being made to feel like a charity case.

'Please say yes, Dad,' begged Holly.

Noa smiled at her. 'Your mum says you're an actor?'

Holly nodded.

'Would you like to be in the film?' asked Noa. He looked at his assistant. 'Surely we can find something for her to do – maybe she can be a carol singer?'

'If she's under eighteen she'll need a chaperone at all times,' said his assistant.

'That's fine. Sarah will be there,' replied Noa. 'I need her on set in case we need any last-minute rewrites.'

James felt his hackles rising. He didn't like how Noa seemed to be staking a claim on his whole family.

'The cinema needs to stay open,' insisted James. 'We've got our customers to think about. We can't just shut in the middle of our film festival.'

It wasn't just for the customers' sake – he needed it to go ahead so that Sarah could see all of the films. So she could see how important their relationship was to him.

'We'll be sure to keep disruption to a minimum, and to repair any damage,' said Noa. 'We'll be out of your hair well before Christmas.'

Everyone was looking at James now. He knew what they wanted him to say. This was clearly the answer to their prayers. So why was he hesitating?

Sarah turned to James. 'It sounds good to me. We can plough the money back into the cinema and pay back some of the loans.'

James pushed his misgivings away. Sarah was right – they needed the money to keep the cinema going. 'All right,' he said. 'Let's do it. As long as it doesn't interfere with the festival.'

'Of course, of course,' said Noa breezily. 'We can add in a clause about that.'

'And can I be in the movie?' asked Holly, turning to her parents with pleading eyes.

'Yes,' said Sarah. 'As long as you make up the schoolwork.'

Holly let out an ear-piercing shriek. 'Oh my God! This is so cool!'

James stared at his wife in surprise. When Holly had asked to go to the open casting call, they'd *both* agreed that she shouldn't miss school. Why hadn't Sarah even consulted with him before saying yes? Come to think of it, she hadn't asked him before accepting the scriptwriting job either. Obviously, he would have told her to go for it. But it would be nice to be asked. They were supposed to be a team.

It's because you're irrelevant, thought James. That was how he felt right now. It was Noa who was turning his family's fortunes around, not him.

Holly squealed and threw her arms around her mother's neck. 'Thanks so much, Mum.' She hugged James. 'And Dad.'

Aaron stepped forward nervously. 'Um, hi, I'm Aaron. I just wanted to say what a fan I am.' He shook Noa's hand. '*ANZAC* is, like, a total masterpiece. We watched it in my film studies class. I want to be the sort of director you are – an auteur.'

'How would you like to do work experience on the film?' said Noa. 'We can always use an extra runner.'

Aaron's eyes lit up. 'Seriously?'

'Naturally,' said Noa. 'We film-makers of colour need to support each other.'

Aaron looked at James and Sarah anxiously. 'Is that OK?'

James forced himself to smile. 'Why not.' It would have been churlish not to let Aaron take up Noa's offer, even though it was going to make things difficult for himself. With Sarah chaperoning Holly, and Aaron working on the movie too, James would be running the cinema single-handedly.

It's only for a few weeks, James reminded himself. Maybe he could persuade Roger to come out of retirement and do a few shifts.

Everyone crowded around Noa as he regaled them with anecdotes about filming *ANZAC*.

Nick came over to stand next to James. 'Mum looks happy,' he said quietly.

'Mmm,' murmured James, putting his arm around his son. 'She does.'

They watched Sarah laughing as Noa described how seasick several members of the cast had been. She *did* look happy. James just wished that he'd been the one to put that smile on her face.

'What a brilliant night,' said Sarah as she smoothed night cream on her cheeks.

James sat on the edge of the bed, taking off his socks. 'Glad you enjoyed it.'

'So what did you think of Noa?'

'He's very . . .' James tried to find a neutral word. 'Charming.'

Sarah laughed as she brushed her hair. 'You didn't like him.'

'I didn't say that.'

'You didn't have to. I could tell you and Nick weren't keen. But Noa's been very good to me.'

'I was just surprised you agreed to Holly being in the movie,' said James, throwing his socks in the hamper. 'We never discussed it.'

Sarah set her brush down and turned to face him. 'Oh, I'm sorry. I was kind of put on the spot. But I actually think we made a mistake by not letting Holly audition in the first place. She's so talented. We shouldn't stop her from doing the thing she loves. I don't want to hold her back.'

As they got into bed, Sarah surprised him again by reaching for him under the duvet. 'Hello, you,' she whispered, slipping her hand under the waistband of his boxers.

James instantly forgot his grievance as their bodies found each other and moved together in a familiar rhythm. They both came quickly.

'Sorry,' said James, when he'd caught his breath. 'It's been a while.'

For months, his attempts to initiate sex had failed. Sarah never seemed to be in the mood.

'That was great,' said Sarah, rolling off him. 'My libido is coming out of hibernation – the HRT must be starting to work.'

'That's good. I've missed this.' He kissed her shoulder. 'I've missed *you*.'

Sarah sighed. 'I don't know why – I don't feel very desirable these days.' There was an audible pop of her knee as she shifted under the duvet. 'See what I mean – my body is falling apart.'

James propped himself up on his elbow. 'Sarah, your body is just as attractive to me now as it was when we were young.'

Sarah snorted dismissively. 'You're just saying that to make me feel better.'

'No, I'm not. It's true.' He tenderly caressed her belly that had carried Holly and Nick, tracing her C-section scar up to her navel. His hand skimmed over her breasts that had nourished two babies. Sliding up her long neck,

214

his thumb stroked her beautiful lips, the lines at each side evidence of her ready smile.

His own body had changed plenty, too. Despite his long cycles, he could no longer fit into his old jeans with a twenty-eight-inch waist. His spine ached in the morning until he did a few stretches and the backs of his hands were dappled with sun spots. But their bodies could still give each other pleasure – and that was something to celebrate.

'Anyway, the part of you I find sexiest hasn't changed a bit.'

'Oh, yeah. What's that?' asked Sarah.

He kissed her forehead. 'Your mind.'

Soon, Sarah was snoring gently on her side of the bed. But James couldn't get to sleep. A troubling thought had crossed *his* mind. Was it the HRT that had revived Sarah's libido? Or the attentions of a handsome Australian film director? Had Sarah been thinking about Noa when they made love tonight?

12th November 2011

The baby would not stop crying. Sarah checked his nappy – dry. She tried feeding him – again – but he spat her nipple out, as if it offended him. She put him on her shoulder to wind him, but he either didn't need to burp or refused to. She tried rocking him, swaddling him, bathing him, singing to him, cuddling him, bouncing him on her lap, jiggling him on her hip. Nothing worked. On and on he cried.

She felt like she was losing her mind.

'What's wrong, Nicky?' she begged, on the brink of tears herself. 'How can I make it better?'

Nick just wailed, his whole body going stiff with a rage that turned his face red.

Holly had been an easy, placid baby. She'd been happy lying on a blanket, kicking her chubby legs under a baby gym as Sarah cooed and sang nursery rhymes. By four months, she was sleeping through the night. That first year had been an idyllic time as Sarah bonded with her daughter, who grew more adorable and affectionate every day.

Nothing about Nick had been easy – not even his conception. 'Unexplained secondary infertility', the doctor had called it. Once she'd finally got pregnant, Sarah had suffered from severe morning sickness that had carried on well into her third trimester. She'd spent the whole pregnancy worrying that she would miscarry again. She'd been monitored carefully because of her previous complications, but, as her due date drew closer, she was convinced that something would go wrong like last time. And in the end, it had.

Nick had been breech and they couldn't get him to flip. After several hours of painful labour, Sarah had been rushed to the operating theatre for an emergency C-section. Six weeks later, the incision on her abdomen was still sore.

And she was so, so tired.

Nick didn't distinguish between night and day. He'd be wide awake at three in the morning, when Sarah could barely keep her eyes open. James had tried to help with the night feeds, but Nick refused to take a bottle. In any case, James was working extra long hours at the cinema while Sarah was on maternity leave. They'd decided not to take on extra staff, to save money.

When Nick finally fell asleep, Sarah lay awake, unable to sleep because of the worries swirling through her head. She was gripped by the fear that something bad was going to happen to her baby. That she would accidentally hurt him somehow. She knew it was irrational. She knew she needed to sleep. But she just couldn't seem to turn her brain off.

Her mum friends, like Nora, had assured her that this stage would pass. But Sarah hadn't told them how bad she was feeling. It was humiliating to admit that after trying for a baby for so long, she was miserable. Having a second baby should have been easy, as she'd done it before. Meg had continued running her dental practice with three kids and had somehow made it look effortless. Sarah could barely find the energy to get dressed in the morning and get Holly to school before the bell. James did the school run whenever he could, but he was usually needed at the cinema.

She thought about calling James now, just to hear his voice, but checking her watch realised he was probably busy selling tickets for the early-afternoon matinee. In desperation, Sarah rang her mother instead. 'Mum, Nick won't stop crying. I don't know what to do.'

'Is it nappy rash?' asked Geraldine.

'No.'

'Is he teething?'

'He's only six weeks old.'

'Did you try the *rebozo* I sent you?'

Geraldine had given her a shawl from Guatemala that was meant to wrap the baby to its mother's chest. 'Yes, but Nick didn't like it.'

That was an understatement. He'd squirmed and squalled so much it felt like having a writhing octopus pinned to her chest.

Geraldine sighed down the phone. 'You were a colicky baby, too. Maybe have a drink tonight – that always worked when I wanted to get you and your sister off to sleep.'

Tempting though it was to down a bottle of wine and knock herself out, Sarah was too scared to risk it. What if she dozed off holding Nick and accidentally rolled on top of him and crushed him to death?

'He still hasn't smiled,' said Sarah. 'Holly smiled when she was six weeks old. I don't think Nick likes me.'

'Don't be ridiculous,' replied Geraldine. 'Why wouldn't he like you – you're his mum. Anyhow, it's best not to compare them. Every child does things at their own pace.'

Despite her mother's reassurance, Sarah suspected that was the problem – there was something wrong with her and the baby knew it. Maybe there wasn't enough love in her heart for two children. With Holly, she'd felt an instant rush of love as soon as she'd been placed in her arms. This time round, she'd hadn't felt any joy – only intense worry.

'Anyway, I've got to go, darling – I have a department meeting. I'll check in with you later.'

As Nick continued to howl, Sarah scrolled through her phone, desperately seeking solutions on all the parenting forums. Was Nick lactose intolerant? Maybe her milk was making him sick. Should she change her diet? She usually only managed to swallow a few bites before Nick started fussing.

Some of the mothers on the forum extolled the virtues of cranial osteopaths, saying they worked miracles. Others recommended baby massage, or taking herbal supplements. There were lengthy debates about dummies, with some people saying they were lifesavers and others warning that it would cause more problems in the long run.

'Oh, no,' said Sarah, noticing the time on her phone. She was late to pick up Holly from school. Again. Where had the whole day gone? There was a load of laundry in the machine, still waiting to be hung out to dry. The breakfast dishes were piled in the sink. There was hardly any food in the fridge, since she hadn't been to the supermarket. Last time she'd gone, she'd worn Nick in the sling and he'd cried the whole time. It had been so stressful she'd abandoned her trolley in the dairy aisle, in tears herself.

'Let's go get your sister,' she said, bundling Nick into his pram. She checked the straps over and over again, for fear that he'd go flying out. Mercifully, Nick dozed off in the pram, lulled to sleep at last by the motion. The tension between Sarah's temples eased slightly. She could hear herself think for a change.

Unfortunately, the thoughts whirling through her mind were all worries about the things that could go wrong. That she'd lose her grip on the buggy and it would roll into traffic. That the blanket she'd tucked around Nick might ride up and smother him. She reached down and adjusted the blanket, even though it was nowhere near his face.

At school, Holly was waiting in the empty playground with Miss Varma, her reception teacher.

'Sorry I'm late, honey,' Sarah said, crouching to give Holly a hug.

'Why are you still wearing your pyjamas?' asked Holly.

Sarah looked down and was mortified to see that she was indeed still wearing her tartan pyjama bottoms. There was a stain of dried egg yolk on the right thigh, where Holly had wiped her fingers on them after breakfast.

'Silly me,' said Sarah with forced joviality. 'Mummy forgot to get dressed today.'

'Look what I made.' Holly handed Sarah a painting with three figures – a mum, a dad and a little girl.

'Where's Nick?' asked Sarah.

'He's a naughty, noisy baby.' Holly pouted, crossing her arms over her chest. 'I want him to go away.'

'Holly!' said Sarah. 'You can't say that. Remember how much you wanted a baby brother?' She felt like a hypocrite, as there were times she wished that Nick would go away, too. Just for a few hours, so she could get some sleep.

'Sibling rivalry is perfectly normal,' said Miss Varma, laughing. 'By the way, there's a letter in Holly's schoolbag about our class nativity. You'll need to make a costume – Holly's going to be a sheep.'

Oh, God, thought Sarah. How on earth was she going to find time to do that?

'Baaaaaa!' Holly bleated, wiggling her bottom as if she had a tail.

'I've noticed when we've been practising our carols that she's got a lovely singing voice,' said Miss Varma.

It was true – her daughter loved to sing. Holly's singing was one of the few things that soothed the baby.

'Can we go to the library, Mummy?' asked Holly, tugging on her hand. 'I want to get a book about sheeps so I can be a good little lamb.'

'Sure, honey.' Anything to avoid going back to the chaos at home.

They walked to the library, with Holly singing the Christmas carols she'd learnt at school. Located at the end of Plumdale high street, the library was a small golden stone building with a peaked roof. Inside was a wonderful children's section.

As Holly ran off to look through the picture books, Pam Cusack, the librarian, came over to admire the baby. 'Oh, isn't he precious. What a little angel.'

Sarah burst into tears.

'Oh, dear,' said Pam, hurrying to get her a tissue. 'Someone's got a touch of the baby blues.'

'I'm sorry,' said Sarah. 'I don't know what's wrong with me. He *is* perfect. But I can't seem to stop worrying that something's wrong.'

'Those first few months are so hard,' said Pam. 'Why don't you rest here for a minute.' She led Sarah over to an oversized beanbag chair. 'I'll help Holly choose some books.'

Nick was still sleeping in the pram. Sarah curled up on the beanbag.

I'll just shut my eyes for a minute . . .

'Wake up, Mummy,' said Holly, shaking her arm.

Sarah sat up and peered into the pram. It was empty. Nick was gone. Someone had kidnapped her baby. 'Nick!' she shouted, staggering to her feet. Sarah's heart raced. She couldn't breathe. Cold sweat drenched her whole body. 'Someone's taken my baby!'

'It's OK, Mummy.' Holly pointed across the library to where Pam was gently bouncing Nick in her arms. 'Nick woke up but we let you have a nap.'

Dizzy with relief, Sarah collapsed back onto the beanbag. Her breath came in ragged gasps and her heart felt like it was going to explode.

Oh, God, she thought. *I'm having a heart attack. I'm dying. My poor children are going to be motherless.*

Coming over, Pam put Nick gently back in his pram. She crouched down next to Sarah, stroking her back. 'Try to take deep breaths.'

Sarah tried to do as she'd been told, but it felt like there was a tight band around her chest, making it hard to get air in her lungs.

'Count to five on the exhale,' coaxed Pam.

Eventually, when her heart rate had slowed and Sarah could breathe normally, she said, 'Thank you.'

'I think you had a panic attack,' said Pam, handing her a glass of water. 'Shall I fetch James from the cinema?'

Sarah's hand shook as she took a sip of water. 'No!' She didn't want James to know what a bad mother she was.

'It's nothing to be ashamed of, Sarah,' said Pam. 'We have a lot of books about anxiety in our non-fiction section, if you'd like me to show you.'

'I'm fine,' she insisted. 'Just tired.'

Pull yourself together, thought Sarah. If people thought she was losing her mind, they might take Nick and Holly away from her.

The library was closing, so Sarah checked out some picture books for Holly – including one about sheep – and stowed them under the pram.

'Look after yourself, Sarah,' said Pam, handing her back the library card. She smiled at Holly. 'And be sure to help your mummy.'

As soon as they got home, Nick began to fuss so Sarah fed him. Then, holding him over her shoulder, she hung damp Babygros and school uniforms on the rickety wooden clothes airer, while Holly sang to herself and crawled around the floor, pretending to be a sheep. When the washing was all hung, she put Nick in his baby bouncer and started on dinner.

As she chopped vegetables for pasta sauce, the sharp blade flashed. Suddenly, a terrible thought popped into her head. What if the knife flew out of her hand and stabbed one of the children?

Sarah set down the knife, trying unsuccessfully to banish the intrusive thought.

'I'm hungry,' whined Holly.

Nick started to grizzle in the bouncer.

The witching hour had begun.

Sarah quickly sautéed the vegetables, dumped in a tin of chopped tomatoes and sprinkled in some seasoning. Her stomach growled, reminding her that she hadn't eaten anything since breakfast.

'Let's read my new book.' Holly came over holding the book about sheep.

'I can't right now. Mummy needs to finish making dinner.' She gave the bubbling tomato sauce a stir. 'Why don't you do some colouring.'

'No!' shouted Holly. She threw the book on the ground.

'Pick that up,' said Sarah.

Holly threw herself on the ground and beat her fists against the floor, howling. People had said to expect a bit of regression once the baby arrived. This was a full-on toddler tantrum – and Sarah simply couldn't cope with it. Not on less than two hours of sleep.

'Stop that right now!' shouted Sarah. 'You are not a baby, you're a big girl. Didn't you hear what Pam said about being Mummy's helper.'

Nick began to wail too. Taking him out of the bouncer, she saw that poo was seeping up the back of his nappy, staining his Babygro.

Sarah wearily took him upstairs to change his nappy. She stripped off his stained onesie and cleaned him off. The soft spot on his nearly bald head pulsed as he squirmed on the changing mat. It was a terrifying reminder of her baby's fragility.

What if I accidentally drop him?

She couldn't get the image out of her head.

It was suspiciously quiet downstairs. 'Are you OK down there, Holly?' she called, as she wrestled Nick into clean clothes.

'I'm being a good girl, Mummy,' Holly called back.

The smell of sauce wafted up the stairs. Sarah's stomach rumbled again.

'Listen, little guy . . .' She tickled the baby's tummy. 'Can I finish making dinner before you kick off again?'

He stared up at her with big blue eyes, as if searching her face for clues. Sometimes Sarah got the uncanny feeling that he could sense her mood.

Sarah carried him downstairs and into the kitchen. Her eyes widened in alarm as she saw that Holly had pushed a chair over to the stove. She was holding a wooden spoon and leaning dangerously over the boiling pot.

'Look, Mama,' she said, grinning. 'I'm helping make dinner.'

'No!' shouted Sarah.

Holding Nick with one arm, she crossed the kitchen in two bounds and scooped Holly up, yanking her away from the heat. As she did so, her elbow knocked over the pot, spilling sauce all over the floor and wall.

Holly began to wail and that set Nick off too.

'Are you OK?' asked Sarah frantically. 'Did the sauce burn you?'

Once she'd checked Holly over, Sarah sank to the floor in relief, clutching both of her babies close.

That was how James found them – all three of them sobbing, the floor covered in red sauce like a blood-splattered murder scene.

'Oh, my God.' He stared at the carnage in alarm. 'What happened here?'

'Daddy!' cried Holly, running over to him and throwing her arms around his legs. 'I was just trying to help Mummy!'

'Pam phoned me and said she was worried about you,' James said, taking Nick off Sarah. 'So I asked Roger to cover for me tonight.'

Sarah went into the living room and lay on the sofa, staring at the ceiling as her thoughts spiralled out of control. *I'm a bad mother. Holly and Nick are going to be taken away from me.*

She was dimly aware of James making Holly's dinner, then taking both children upstairs for a bath. Once he'd put them to bed, he came downstairs and cleaned the kitchen. When he finally joined her in the living room, Sarah braced herself for what he was about to say.

'James, I—'

He held up his hand. 'We'll talk later.'

He made her cheesy scrambled eggs, buttered toast and a cup of tea. She was ravenous and devoured it quickly, so James made her another round of toast. It tasted so good.

While she was eating, he ran her a bath with lavender-scented bubbles. After a long soak, she changed into the pyjamas he'd left warming on the radiator and felt almost human again.

She went into their bedroom, where Nick was sleeping in his Moses basket. She gazed at her son and silently promised him that she'd do better.

'Come here,' said James, throwing back the covers and inviting her into bed.

She got in and curled up next to him.

James stroked her hair. 'I'm sorry I didn't realise how much you were struggling.'

'It's not your fault,' she whispered. 'I didn't want anyone to know. I was ashamed.' If James hadn't come home early tonight, she might have been able to clean everything up before he got back. But it was no use pretending any more. 'I can't stop worrying. About the baby. About everything. These terrible thoughts are going round and round my head. I feel like I'm going mad.'

'Why didn't you tell me sooner?'

'You're so busy with the cinema. I didn't want to burden you.'

James squeezed her hand. 'You and the kids are more important than the cinema.'

'I'm a terrible mother, James. Nick hates me. And you probably hate me too, now that you've seen what a mess I am.'

'I could never hate you,' promised James. 'But I *am* worried about you.'

'I'm scared, James,' Sarah whispered.

He put his arm around her and hugged her tight. 'You're going to be OK,' he said, stroking her damp hair. 'We'll get through this together. I promise.'

Six weeks later, Geraldine arrived with an overnight case.

'There's plenty of breast milk in the freezer,' said Sarah. 'The GP's number is by the phone in the kitchen. Remember to make sure Holly goes to the toilet before bed. She gets three stories at bedtime, but will try to get to you to read more. Nick needs to sleep on his back—'

'Go,' said Geraldine, shooing her out of the door. 'Or you'll miss your train.'

Sarah and James were going to London for the night. They were staying in Pari's new house in Notting Hill while she was away in Los Angeles, visiting one of her clients on set. Her agency was thriving. She had a staff of ten and represented several up-and-coming stars. One of her actors had landed a main part in a superhero franchise, earning her an enormous commission and making her the hottest agent in town.

Pari had recently taken on an agent to represent screenwriters. 'When you finish your screenplay, we can represent you,' she'd told Sarah.

At the moment, the only stories Sarah was telling were of the bedtime variety.

Once on the train, Sarah checked her bag to make sure she'd packed her medication. James had taken her to the GP the day after her meltdown and the doctor had diagnosed post-partum anxiety. Apparently, it was more common among women, such as Sarah, who had experienced miscarriages and traumatic births.

The medication had already helped enormously, but so had the army of friends James had rallied to provide support. Ian had brought them casseroles for dinner. Pari and Meg called every day to see how Sarah was doing. Roger agreed to do extra shifts at the cinema to ease the burden on James. And Nora and Simon had come over to babysit so Sarah could nap.

'It feels so weird,' said Sarah. 'To be out and about without any little ones in tow.'

'I'm glad to have you all to myself,' said James, taking her hand.

Sarah rested her head on her husband's shoulder and dozed for most of the journey, waking up just as they were pulling into Paddington.

'I still can't believe Pari lives in such a posh house,' said Sarah when they arrived at the house Pari had nicknamed the 'Pink Palace'. As a stand-up comedian, Pari had been so broke that she used to steal tea bags and toilet paper from the BBC.

They found a bottle of champagne chilling on the kitchen counter and a note from Pari.

Make yourselves at home – and have fun! xxx

James removed the foil and popped the cork. He poured two glasses.

Sarah took a sip, relishing the taste of the fizzy wine. She didn't need to worry about her milk for two whole days.

'Here's to your health.' said James, touching his glass to hers.

Sarah took a big gulp of her champagne. She had never been so grateful to have her health back. 'Thanks for making me go to the doctor,' she said. 'I'm sorry I was such a basket case.'

James set his glass down and pulled her close. 'You never need to apologise for being ill, Sarah,' he said. 'For better, for worse, in sickness and in health — that's what we promised each other on our wedding day.'

Over the past decade, their marriage vows had been tested by the strain of opening a cinema, becoming parents and losing a loved one. But Sarah adored her husband even more than she had as a bride. The stresses they'd faced together had made their love grow stronger.

James went over to the window and looked out. They were a stone's throw away from Portobello Market and all of Notting Hill's trendy cafés and restaurants. 'The world's our oyster — what do you fancy doing today?'

Sarah considered all their options. They could go to a gallery. Or go Christmas shopping. They could have cocktails in a fancy bar or take a long walk along the river. 'You know what I'd really like to do . . . is see a movie.' Despite owning a cinema, she hadn't been to see a film in months.

James grinned at her. 'And that is why you are the perfect woman.' He took out his phone and looked up the film times.

They decided to see a Japanese film called *Tokyo Godfathers* at the Prince Charles.

Afterwards, for old times' sake, they went out for Chinese food at Wong Kei. London had changed a lot since they'd left for the Cotswolds — people whizzing around on Boris Bikes and construction for the Olympics in full swing — but some things remained the same. The restaurant's portions were still enormous and the servers reassuringly grumpy.

And just as they had on their first date, they talked about the movie they had just seen — an animated story about a motley trio who rescued a baby girl from the trash on a cold December night.

'It's so sad to think anyone would do that to a baby,' said James.

'I felt sorry for her,' admitted Sarah.

'The baby?' asked James.

'No,' said Sarah. 'The woman.' In the film, the baby had been snatched – and then abandoned – by a woman crazed with grief after a stillbirth. Sarah remembered how distraught she'd been after her miscarriage. She also knew all too well how hormones could mess with your mind.

She'd felt sorry for the baby's mother too, desperately worried about her missing child.

She was no longer plagued by irrational anxiety, but the fear of losing a child would never go away. It was every parent's worst nightmare.

Thinking of her own baby at home, she pulled out her phone to check for any messages from her mum.

All fine here. Hope you and James are having fun.

'All good?' asked James.

Sarah nodded.

Her mother would no doubt ignore all the instructions Sarah had provided, but that was a grandparent's prerogative.

'What should we do next?' James asked, as they left the restaurant and walked through Soho hand in hand. 'Go to the pub? See a late movie?'

'Go to bed,' replied Sarah.

'Sure,' said James. 'It's late, and I know you're tired.'

'That's not what I meant,' said Sarah, her voice husky.

Her husband looked at her, understanding registering in his blue eyes.

'Oh . . .' He grinned with delight, then he quickly flagged down a passing black cab.

★

The next morning, they had a long lie-in, then went for a roast dinner at a pub.

'This is the life,' said Sarah, sitting by the roaring fire.

'Do you miss living in London?' James asked her.

Sarah thought about it as she sipped her cider. 'Seeing how well Pari has done for herself does make me wonder what our lives might be like if we'd stayed here,' she mused.

'I wonder about that sometimes as well,' said James.

'How about you?' she asked her husband, stealing one of his roast potatoes in exchange for her Yorkshire pudding. 'Do you miss it here?' Unlike her, James was a native Londoner.

'I do miss being able to come up and visit Dad.'

'Did you want to pop over to Ealing?' she asked. 'To see the flat one last time?'

They were close to closing on the sale of James's father's flat. It had taken a long time, as a previous buyer had been stuck in a chain and pulled out at the last minute.

'No, that's OK,' he answered, surprising her. 'It doesn't feel like home any more.' They had removed all the contents and repainted the flat, in an effort to sell it. Sean's film memorabilia was displayed in the cinema's lobby.

Then James surprised her again.

'I was thinking that we could use some of the money to pay for a digital projection system.'

'But you've always been such a staunch advocate for 35mm film.'

'I don't think we can hold out any longer,' he explained. 'Some film companies aren't even making 35mm prints any more. If we don't update, we won't be able to show new releases.'

'What about Roger?' The projectionist was a good friend as well as their employee.

'Omar is taking early retirement at the end of this year and Roger has decided to retire as well. They're buying a house in Normandy and planning to spend half of the year in France.'

'Oh, that's wonderful.'

'Anyone can operate a digital projector, so it would mean I can be around more for you and the kids. I don't want to miss out on Holly and Nick's childhood. The whole point of running our own business was to escape the rat race and have a decent work/life balance.' James put his hand on her knee. 'How does that sound?'

'Really good,' said Sarah. If a projector meant more time with her husband, she was all for it.

They had just enough time to take a walk to see the Christmas lights before heading back to the station. As lovely as it had been to visit London, she couldn't wait to go back home to her babies.

'Mummy!' cried Holly as they came through the door. She launched herself at her mum, clinging to her like a limpet. 'Did you get me a present?'

'Maybe,' said James. He held out the Paddington toy they'd bought at the station.

'Mummy's back,' Geraldine announced, handing the baby to Sarah.

Nick's wispy blonde hair stuck straight up, making him look like he had a quiff. His serious blue eyes searched Sarah's face as she cradled him close.

Inhaling the delicious scent of her freshly bathed son, Sarah felt her breasts tingle and her milk let down, leaving damp circles on her shirt. 'I missed you, little guy,' she whispered, smiling down at him.

Nick blinked his blue eyes, and then, for the first time ever, he smiled back.

Chapter 9

Present Day

On Wednesday after school, Nick and Julia were huddled together at a table in the library. Julia was writing in a notebook, while Nick shaded in a drawing of a cruel half-lizard, half-alien villain who bore a striking resemblance to Damon Carter.

He and Julia had been meeting in the library twice a week after school, on the days her brother's football training was on. They had nearly finished planning out the first volume of their manga. Together, they had invented a character named Kayda who could transform into a fire-breathing dragon.

'So, I was thinking,' said Julia, looking up from her notebook. 'The goodies can escape by finding a portal to another dimension. But time stands still in the real world, so the baddie's still waiting for them when they come back.'

Nick quickly sketched out a scene, showing Kayda tearing open a portal into another realm with her dragon claws.

'Give her longer fangs.' Julia offered Nick a Haribo sweet from a bag hidden in her blazer pocket. (Snacks were strictly forbidden in the library.)

'Maybe they should stay in the other dimension, where they're safe,' said Nick, erasing the dragon's fangs.

Julia chewed on a fizzy cola bottle as she thought. 'No – they've got to go back and fight, of course.'

'Hey, that's really good.' Nick turned around and saw his maths teacher standing behind them. Mr Wu must have been on library duty. 'May I?'

Nick handed Mr Wu the sketchpad as Julia quickly hid the sweets.

The teacher studied their work. 'This is very impressive. Maybe the two of you should set up a manga club. My wife's an illustrator. She used to work on manga – I'm sure she'd be happy to give you some tips.'

Nick and Julia exchanged grins.

'That would be cool, Mr Wu,' said Julia.

Nick and Julia returned to the new dimension they were creating. They were so in the flow that they didn't notice how quickly the time had passed.

'There you are!' exclaimed Adam, coming into the library, wearing his muddy football kit. It wasn't obvious that he and Julia were twins, because her fair hair had been dyed black. If you looked closely, though, you could see that they had the same wide blue eyes, button noses and pale skin. 'I've been looking everywhere for you.'

'Sorry,' said Julia. 'I lost track of time.'

Nick's heart sank when he saw that Julia's brother was with Damon Carter and a few other boys from the football team.

Damon's eyes gleamed with malice as he sauntered over to their table. He was eating a bag of crisps and when he finished, he threw the packet at Nick. 'Well, well, well. Isn't this sweet? Two little freaks having a play date.'

Nick sat frozen with dread.

Damon snatched Nick's drawing. 'Look at this!' he crowed, waving it around. 'He's drawing CARTOONS! What a baby.'

'Give that back,' said Nick, trying to grab the drawing.

'Make me!' taunted Damon. He held the paper higher, laughing as Nick jumped up and tried to get it back. It was no use – the other boy was much bigger than him.

'Give it back to him,' demanded Julia, her voice even.

'I will if you ask me nicely,' said Damon.

'Please can I have it back,' pleaded Nick, willing himself not to cry.

'I didn't mean you, loser, I meant her,' said Damon. 'Goth Girl.'

Julia stood up and scowled at Damon. 'Give it back, dickhead!'

'OK, then. Have it your way.' Slowly, deliberately, Damon tore Nick's sketch up into tiny pieces and sprinkled them over Nick's head. 'Oh, look.' He sniggered. 'It's snowing. Or is that Nick's dandruff.'

Julia slammed her Doc Martens down on Damon's foot.

'Ow!' Damon wailed. He hopped around, clutching his foot. Then, his eyes narrowing, he lunged at Julia.

With courage that he didn't know he possessed, Nick jumped in front of his friend, to shield her from Damon. 'Don't hurt her!'

'Get out of my way, freak,' hissed Damon. Nick could smell cheese-and-onion crisps on his breath. 'I'm going to teach your girlfriend some manners.'

Nick stood his ground, refusing to budge.

'Don't you dare lay a finger on my sister!' shouted Adam, pulling Damon back. 'Or her friend.'

The commotion brought Mr Wu hurrying over. 'All of you – out! This is no way to behave in the library. I'm giving you all a detention.'

'But if I get another detention I'm off the football team for the rest of the season,' whined Damon.

'You should have thought about that before you tore up

Nick's drawing.' Mr Wu reprimanded him. 'This school has a zero-tolerance policy about bullying.'

Nick hastily shoved his belongings into his backpack.

Outside of school, Damon and his football friends hurried off, muttering darkly. But Adam stayed behind with Julia and Nick.

'Your friend is a jerk,' said Julia.

'He's not my friend,' replied Adam. 'We're just on the same football team.'

'Thanks for sticking up for me,' said Nick.

'That's OK. Any friend of my sister's is a friend of mine.' Adam held out his hand to Nick. 'I'm Adam, by the way. Julia showed me the drawing you gave her – it's really good.'

Nick had been brave once today. He decided to be brave again.

'Do you guys want to come and see an anime Christmas movie with me on Saturday night?' he asked them.

'Where?' asked Julia.

'The Plumdale Picture Palace,' said Nick. 'You don't need to pay – my parents own the cinema.'

'That's awesome, man.' Adam fist-bumped Nick. 'We love it there.'

'No wonder you know so much about movies,' remarked Julia. 'Of course we'll come.'

Nick grinned as the twins waved goodbye and headed home to Stowford. He'd never got a detention before, but it had been worth it. His tally of new friends had just doubled – from one to two.

Nick stood at the bus stop. He didn't want to go home, as his mum would be working on the script. That's all she seemed to do these days. He didn't want to go to the cinema, either, as the film crew had already started moving in. This stupid movie was ruining everything. He wished he had dragon claws like his manga character so he could rip a portal to a new dimension and hide there until the filming was over. But short of that, his gran's flat would do.

There was something he wanted to talk to her about.

He got off the bus and walked to Valley Vistas. The lobby had paintings on the walls, comfy-looking sofas and a lift, which he rode up to the second floor. As he knocked on the door to his grandmother's flat, he could hear noise coming from within. It sounded like she was having a party.

'Oh, hello, Nick, dear,' said Grandma, opening the door. He went inside and found her flat packed full of people and smelling deliciously of cinnamon and ginger. 'What a pleasant surprise.'

The living room and kitchen were open plan. Nick could see Roger in there, as well as a few of the ladies who went to the Golden Oldies screenings. Everyone seemed to be baking and there was a rack of homemade gingerbread biscuits cooling on the table. Roger was mixing up ingredients in a bowl, while Olwyn pressed out shapes and Vi slid a tray into the oven. His grandmother, who had never baked anything in her life as far as Nick knew, seemed to be bossing everyone about.

'Why, hello, Nicolas,' said Pam, looking up from the dough she was kneading. She used to work at the Plumdale library and had introduced Nick to manga. 'Do you want to take over for a bit – this is hard on my arthritis.'

'Sure.' Nick rolled up his sleeves and washed his hands. 'What are you all doing?'

'We're making treats for a coffee morning tomorrow,' explained Nick's grandma. 'It's for charity.'

Nick's mouth watered as he kneaded the dough. The biscuits looked – and smelled – amazing. And it had been a long time since lunch.

'Show Vi your drawings, Nick,' urged Grandma. 'She's a painter.'

Wiping his hands off on a tea towel, Nick obediently took his sketchbook out of his schoolbag and showed it to the pink-haired old lady.

'Your characters are so expressive,' said Vi appreciatively, turning the pages. 'And your line work is very sophisticated – is this charcoal pencil?'

Nick nodded.

'I usually work in oils,' said Vi. 'I run a life-drawing course in the recreation room once a month.'

'Vi's trying to convince me to be one of her life models,' said Nick's grandmother. 'She says I have excellent bone structure.'

'You're very welcome to come along too,' Vi told Nick.

'Um, maybe,' said Nick. Hell would freeze over before he'd draw his grandmother naked.

'As you're here, you can do me a favour,' said Grandma. She led Nick into her bedroom. 'Can you get that box on the top shelf,' she asked, opening up her walk-in wardrobe. 'It's too high for me to reach.'

Nick dragged a chair over, stood on it and got the box down. It was full of Christmas decorations.

'I wasn't going to decorate for Christmas, but my friends insisted,' she said.

Nick was glad that his grandmother had made some new friends, like him. He was excited to hang out with Julia and Adam outside of school.

'We haven't put our tree up at home yet either,' he said. Picking out a tree was one of his favourite holiday traditions. When they were little, he and Holly used to play hide-and-seek among the rows of trees. He wondered if his parents had forgotten, as nobody had even mentioned it.

'Well, your mum has been busy,' said Grandma.

'I hate that stupid movie,' complained Nick. 'It's taking over everything.' He especially hated Noa – what a smarmy show-off. Why couldn't Mum see that his smiles were fake?

That reminded Nick of why he had come. He had questions, and he could always rely on his grandmother to tell him the truth.

'Grandma . . . what's a libido?'

'It's your sex drive,' Grandma replied. 'It is perfectly normal to have sexual feelings during adolescence. You mustn't be ashamed of it.'

What? This wasn't about him. It was about Mum. Actually, that was worse. Now he knew that when she was talking to Pari, it had been about sex. *Gross.*

'I've always thought it was a shame that our culture doesn't celebrate the onset of puberty the way others do.' Nick's grandmother sat down on her bed, in a way that suggested she was about to go off on one of her lectures. 'In many societies, young men go through rites of passage at the onset of adolescence – the Apaches take ice baths, indigenous Australians go on walkabouts in the bush—'

Nick interrupted before his grandmother forced him to take a freezing cold bath.

'Is Mum ill?'

Grandma looked at him sharply. 'Why do you ask that?'

Nick sat down next to his grandmother. 'I heard her telling Auntie Pari that she went to the doctor. And she's been acting weird and unhappy.' Admittedly, his mum seemed more cheerful now that she'd thrown herself into working on the movie script. But Nick hadn't forgotten the months leading up to it, when her smile hadn't reached her eyes.

'I wonder if her anxiety is back,' said his grandmother. 'It was bad right after she had you. It's not that unusual – a woman's hormones can go haywire after giving birth.'

What? This was news to Nick. He didn't know that he'd made Mum sick. What if he'd made her sick again? He knew she worried about him.

Noticing the horrified look on Nick's face, his grandmother patted his knee. 'Don't worry, Nick. I'm sure she's fine. She would have mentioned it to me if anything was wrong.'

Nick carried his grandmother's decorations into the living room. He set up her little tree in the corner and wound fairy lights around it. Then her friends helped to decorate it.

'I got this ornament in Peru,' his grandmother explained, adding a little llama to the tree. 'And this jade bauble is from my time in China.'

'You really have been everywhere, Geraldine.' Pam smiled at Nick. 'Do you want to travel the world like your grandmother, Nick?'

'Nope. I like Plumdale.' Nick thought it was the perfect place to live. At least, it used to be, before stupid Noa Drakos and his film crew moved in.

'This one is my favourite.' Grandma showed Nick a lumpy angel made of dough. 'You mum made it when she was in primary school.'

'So you *do* have a sentimental side after all, Geraldine,' teased Roger.

By the time the last batch of biscuits had come out of the oven, the tree was fully decorated.

'Many hands make light work,' said Olwyn. 'Now, I'd better get back home – I need to finish reading *The Kyoto Magical Cat Café* before my book club tomorrow.'

'I'd better get home too,' said Nick.

His grandmother offered him the plate. 'Take a biscuit to tide you over.'

As he walked home, Nick took a bite of the star-shaped biscuit, but it felt like clay in his mouth – he was too worried to enjoy it. He'd hoped to get answers from his grandmother, but he was no closer to solving the Mum mystery.

It felt like his family, who mattered more to him than anything else, was falling apart.

As James cycled to the cinema, he noticed more traffic on the road than usual. Sarah had taken the car earlier that morning so she could cover the Baby and Me screening.

'I really don't mind,' she'd said. 'I have a meeting with Noa to discuss the final draft.'

There was a blast of a horn and James swerved out of the way, narrowly avoiding being run over by a huge lorry.

'Hey, watch it!' he shouted.

As it sped past, he noticed the writing on the vehicle's side – *Star Lights: Film Equipment*. It was no doubt heading to the same place he was.

Preparations for filming were in full swing in Plumdale, transforming it from a sleepy village to a Hollywood backlot. Trucks and movie trailers were parked all along the road leading into the village, with more arriving in a steady convoy.

Not wanting to take his chances, James got off his bike and walked, irritation growing with every step. Crew in fluorescent yellow vests spoke into walkie-talkies, while others unloaded equipment.

'Mind your back!' shouted someone, carrying a huge white reflector past.

James ducked out of the way, only to narrowly avoid being hit by a cart filled with black cases of lenses and rolls of gaffer tape in every hue. There was an enormous generator parked in the alley at the side of the cinema, like a giant carbuncle.

What an eyesore, James thought. The Plumdale Beautification Society wouldn't be too happy about that. Although, at the last film-festival screening, Ian had mentioned that he was going to be an extra in the movie, so perhaps he didn't mind.

A reporter with platinum-blonde hair and an American accent stood on the pavement in front of the cinema, being filmed by a cameraman. 'This is Goldie Johnson, reporting live from Plumdale, where Noa Drakos will be filming his comeback movie, *Ex-mas Eve.* The film stars heart-throb Mateo Ajose and up-and-coming starlet Mia Winslow. Will this be the hit the award-winning film-maker needs to get his career back on track?'

Not wanting to get in the shot, James wheeled his bike down the side alley to go in through the back entrance. It was even busier in the car park. There were trailers parked there, a row of portable toilets, and some gazebos had been set up as well for the costume and make-up teams. James locked his bike up, then headed for the back door.

A burly man holding a clipboard was blocking the way. 'Name,' he barked.

'James O'Hara.'

The man checked his clipboard and shook his head. 'Sorry, film crew and authorised personnel only.'

'I *own* the cinema,' snapped James impatiently. He checked his watch. Delays to his journey meant he was running late, and he'd promised Sarah he'd get here by the time the Baby and Me screening was over.

'Nice try – I haven't heard that one before. Look, everyone in town is hoping to meet the stars,' said the security guard. 'But you need to move on now.'

James had met Mateo Ajose a few times through their mutual friends, Simon and Nora, but he wasn't going to bother telling that to the security guard. 'Let me in!'

The man spoke into his walkie-talkie, never taking his eyes off James. 'We have a problem, sir. A fellow is causing a disturbance. Says he owns the cinema.' The guard laughed dismissively.

A moment later, Noa appeared at the back entrance. He looked as cool as ever in jeans and a black T-shirt that showed off his muscular arms. It was as if he was so tough the cold didn't affect him. James felt like a wimp in his thick winter parka.

'So sorry about that, Jim.' Noa apologised smoothly. 'Our security team is overzealous.'

'He wasn't on the list,' said the security guard, still eyeing James suspiciously.

'Please, do come in.' Noa magnanimously stepped aside to let James in, as if *he* owned the bloody place.

Fuming, James made his way into the cinema. The lobby teemed with film crew and film equipment littered the ground. He stepped over some thick black cables that snaked across the lobby on the way to the concession stand.

'Oh, good, you're here.' Sarah came out from behind the counter and gave James a peck on the cheek. 'You can take over now. Is it OK if Noa and I use the office? We need a quiet place to read through the final scene.'

'Why don't you ask him?' muttered James sourly. 'He's acting like he owns the place.'

But Sarah didn't hear – she was already halfway to the office.

Just then, the Baby and Me screening finished. Parents came out of the auditorium with their infants. The sound of children crying only added to the din.

Sarah's new friend, Iris, was struggling to get her buggy over the cables. She was with an attractive lady with long dark hair wearing a baby girl in a baby carrier.

'Here, let me help you.' James lifted the front wheels up to manoeuvre the buggy over the obstruction. 'I'm sorry about the disruption – it's complete chaos in here today.'

'That's pretty normal for a movie set,' said the woman with the baby carrier, smiling.

Suddenly, James recognised her – she was Mateo Ajose's wife.

'Nice to see you, Sam,' he said. 'Have you met Iris?'

She nodded. 'We met earlier. Iris helped me out when Priya here had an exploding nappy situation. She loaned me a spare Babygro in the ladies' room.'

'Speaking of that,' said Iris. 'There's no toilet paper left in there.'

Bloody hell, thought James. The film crew were supposed to be using the portaloos outside, but he'd noticed them going in and out of the much-nicer cinema toilets. At this rate, they'd be spending all the money they were getting on toilet roll.

As the two mums headed off, James went to restock the bathroom. Then he got out his laptop and updated the film times on the cinema's website. They were showing *Elf* – the eighth film of Christmas – as a special sensory-friendly matinee. He'd had to change the start time to accommodate the film crew.

So much for keeping disruption to a minimum . . .

As he was finishing, Kath Langdon, their local MP, appeared.

'Hi, Kath,' James said. 'How's your dad?'' Kath's father, David, had been their MP for years. Kath had stood for the seat when he'd retired.

'Dad's fine. And I've got good news – I was able to fast-track the permits,' she said. 'I just need a few signatures.'

All the café tables were occupied by film crew, so Kath took a thick stack of papers out of her briefcase and spread them out on the ticket counter.

'Thanks so much for your help,' said James, signing the paperwork. 'I know how busy you are.'

'No worries,' said the MP. 'The film will be excellent for the local economy. If the movie is a success, it should drive visitors to the area – fans will want to visit locations.' She grinned. 'I'm a big Mia Winslow fan myself.'

'Hopefully tourists will come and see a movie here while they're at it,' said James. That was the point of all this disruption – to save the cinema.

He went to file copies of the paperwork in the office, before remembering that Sarah was in there. The door to the office was open a crack, and he could see her and Noa sitting on the sofa, their heads practically touching.

'We shouldn't do this,' murmured Sarah. 'Not here. Not now.'

'No, I've waited too long to tell you how I feel,' said Noa. 'I've tried to fight my feelings, but it's no use. I can't stop thinking about you. I'm in love with you.'

'I love you, too,' said Sarah.

'Then we owe it to ourselves to give this thing between us another chance. Before it's too late—'

James grimaced. He knew they were just reading the script, but he hated hearing his wife declaring her love to another man. Who had she been thinking about when she'd written those words?

'That's working really well now,' said Noa.

'It was a team effort,' replied Sarah.

'By the way, I read *The Ghost Writer* last night. Your script has got such potential. You really should finish it so I can direct it.'

Sarah laughed. 'I've been trying to finish it for years. Somehow life always gets in the way.'

'That's why I've never had a family,' remarked Noa. 'It's hard to be an artist with the distraction of family life.'

Is that what I am, thought James, feeling a stab of guilt. *A distraction?*

'That's why I usually only get involved with other people in the industry,' continued Noa. 'They're the only ones who get it. Who understand that you need to be a bit selfish in order to make art.'

'I'm starting to see that,' said Sarah quietly.

'You should come and work for me in LA,' urged Noa. 'I want you to edit the script for my passion project. You're wasted here in this little nothing town.'

James felt like he'd just been sucker punched.

There was a long pause on the other side of the door.

'Oh, that's very flattering,' said Sarah.

'It's not flattery,' replied Noa. 'You're very good at this.'

'I . . . I'd need to think about it.'

'Don't sell yourself short, Sarah,' said Noa. 'You deserve more than this. You shouldn't be stuck here in this cinema, showing other people's movies. You should be writing your own.'

Reeling from what he had just overheard, James staggered outside to get some air. The worst thing about what the director had said was that it was right – Sarah did deserve more than this. More than him.

Looking out at the film set being constructed in the village square, James rued the day Noa Drakos had ever set foot in the cinema. What had seemed like a blessing was starting to feel like a curse.

8th August 2017

James rode his bicycle over slick cobblestones on the way back from the nearest bakery, keeping the bag of croissants and *pains au chocolat* under his windbreaker to stop the pastries from getting wet. Despite the raindrops pelting his face, there was something exhilarating about being on a bike again – for the first time since he was a kid.

Maybe I'll get a bike of my own to cycle to the cinema, he thought.

He turned down a path leading to a half-timbered cottage with a thatched roof. The cottage garden bloomed with an abundance of roses, foxgloves and sunflowers – evidence of its owners' green fingers. James had no idea how sunflowers thrived here, since they hadn't seen the sun emerge from behind the clouds since driving out of the tunnel at Calais.

He leant the bike against the cottage and went inside.

'I'm back!' James called, setting the pastries on the table. He took off his wet jacket and hung it on a hook beside the door.

'I made coffee,' said Sarah, who was working on her laptop at the kitchen table.

'Thanks.' James kissed her on the cheek then he poured himself a cup of coffee from the silver press. It smelled like heaven. 'Did you get much done?' he asked her. Sarah was trying to use this holiday to get back to *The Ghost Writer*, the screenplay she'd been writing off and on for years.

'Not really,' replied Sarah. 'It's slow-going – I'm so out of the habit of writing.'

They were staying in Roger and Omar's cottage just outside Honfleur. With its cobbled streets, picturesque harbour and access to sandy beaches, it was easy to see why Impressionist painters had fallen in love with the pretty port. Monet had painted it in all different lights. Unfortunately, they had only seen it in one light – grey. It had rained every single day they'd been here.

The children came down the steps from the loft, where they slept in twin beds. Nick was still in his Pokémon pyjamas with the label cut out of them because he hated the feel of anything scratchy against his skin. Holly, ever the optimist, was wearing shorts over her neon-pink-and-green bathing suit and loudly singing 'Let it Go' from *Frozen*.

'I had a dream that I was best friends with a mermaid,' announced Nick, yawning. 'She took me to her underwater kingdom.'

'Come have breakfast.' Sarah spread apricot jam on a croissant. She took a big bite and sighed happily.

'I'm sick of croissants,' whined Holly. 'I want Frosties.'

'Have a *pain au chocolat* then,' said Sarah. 'Daddy went out in the rain specially to get breakfast.'

Holly picked up a pastry and took an unenthusiastic bite.

'So what should we do today?' asked James, sipping his coffee.

'We could visit the cathedral in Rouen,' suggested Sarah. 'That's only about an hour's drive.'

'I want to go swimming,' said Nick. 'I might meet a mermaid.'

'You said we could go to the beach on this holiday,' said Holly mutinously. Only nine and a half, she was already showing the early signs of adolescent moodiness. God help them when she was an actual teenager.

The children rarely agreed on anything. Four years was a big age gap and they had very different personalities – Nick quiet and sensitive; Holly a born performer. Occasionally, Nick agreed to play a supporting role in one of Holly's plays (she was always lead actor, director, costume designer and choreographer of the productions she staged in the living room). Likewise, Holly sometimes helped Nick with his LEGO creations, acting out stories with the minifigures. So it was annoying that they couldn't capitalise on this rare moment of unity.

'It's raining again today,' explained Sarah. 'We just have to hope the sun comes out before we go back to England.'

They had gone for walks on the beach in the rain, to collect shells and look for crabs in the rock pools. They'd all had fun, despite the weather, until Nick had slipped on a seaweed-covered rock and skinned his knee. He had howled and howled. In the end, James had had to carry him back to the cottage.

Somehow, Nick always seemed to feel pain more intensely than others. No, scrap that, he felt *everything* more intensely. James worried that life was going to be difficult for his son unless he toughened up a bit.

Nick's first few years of primary school had been challenging. Not in terms of the academics – Nick was a very clever child, reading way above his age level. He was also a gifted mathematician, easily grasping concepts such as fractions when most kids his age could barely cope with subtraction. Socially, though, he had struggled. When Holly had been Nick's age, their weekends had been dominated by play dates and birthday parties. Nick wasn't invited to many parties and when he was, James or Sarah usually had to collect him early because he was crying. Nick just seemed to find everything overwhelming.

'We could go to a museum,' said Sarah, flipping through a guidebook. 'There's a lace-making museum in—'

'No!' shouted Nick, Holly and James. They had been to more than their fair share of museums this week.

The holiday had started promisingly on Monday, with a trip to the aquarium in St Malo. They'd all enjoyed that. Holly had loved the sharks, and Nick had been transfixed by the jellyfish, their amorphous, translucent shapes floating in their tank, delicate tentacles streaming behind them. When James had finally told him they had to move on, he'd realised that his son had been crying.

'What's wrong, buddy?' he'd asked.

'The jellyfish are so beautiful,' Nick said, his eyes shining with wonder.

On Tuesday, they visited the Bayeux Tapestry. The museum was packed with tourists, all trying to escape from the rain. Nick hated crowds, and fussed so much that they left without seeing the famous scene of the arrow piercing King Harold's eye. By that point, James had such a bad headache, it felt like an arrow was piercing *his* eye.

On the way home, they stopped at a winery.

'I think we're going to need this,' Sarah muttered, as they loaded a case of pinot gris into the boot of the car.

On Wednesday, they on a tour of a goat farm. Holly enjoyed petting the goats. Nick, however, hated the smell. To avoid another scene, they left before the cheese tasting. Later, they gone to dinner at a brasserie on the harbour.

'It's too noisy!' Nick said, covering his ears in distress.

'What do you mean?' James asked. There was some background noise – the clatter and clank of cutlery on china, the burble of conversation, the popping of corks – but nothing too loud.

In the end, they had to leave before they finished their

steak frites.

'You said I could have chocolate mousse for dessert,' Holly complained.

To appease her, went for ice cream and ate their cones watching the sun set over the harbour.

'Nick ruins everything.' Holly fumed, licking her salted-caramel-flavoured cone.

To his shame, James shared her frustration. His son was adorable, affectionate, creative and bright, but he was also incredibly awkward. James didn't love him any less because of it. Sometimes, though, he wished they could go on outings like normal families without triggering a meltdown.

Thursday's visit to the war museum in Caen was the worst. The exhibition on D-Day and the Battle of Normandy was too much for Nick. He found the photographs of the battle scenes distressing and began to sob. Neither Sarah nor James could console him.

'Why did those people have to die?' he wailed.

'I guess he's just too young for this,' Sarah said, stroking her son's back.

James wasn't so sure. There were plenty of other young children at the museum. None were reacting the way Nick was.

'James!' said Sarah, in a tone that suggested it wasn't the first time she'd called his name. 'I said – what do you want to do today?'

'Sorry,' he said, shaking his head. 'I was miles away. How about doing a jigsaw?'

Holly groaned. 'We've done all the puzzles. Most of them are missing pieces.'

'What about playing some board games, then?' James suggested.

'Nick is too little,' said Holly. 'He can only play

Candyland and Snakes and Ladders and babyish games.'

'I'm not a baby!' said Nick.

'Are too!' retorted Holly. 'You're always crying like a big baby. Wah! Wah! Wah!' She pretended to cry.

Tears began to well in Nick's eyes. His lower lip trembled.

'See!' shouted Holly.

James acted fast to avert another meltdown. 'Let's do some colouring!' He picked Nick up and set him down at the kitchen table with paper and crayons.

'I need more coffee,' muttered Sarah. She shut her laptop down and poured them both another cup. 'Looks like today is going to be another washout.'

'How long before holidays are actually relaxing again?' James wondered aloud, thinking back to the exciting holidays he and Sarah had taken before they'd had kids – to far-flung places like Los Angeles and Hong Kong. When they could read books and sunbathe by the pool, instead of staying vigilant when the kids were paddling. When they could dine on local delicacies, instead of choosing restaurants with chicken nuggets and fries on the children's menu. When they could browse through souvenir shops, without fear that someone was going to break something valuable.

'You know what they say – a chance is as good as a rest,' remarked Sarah half-heartedly.

They had been grateful to Roger and Omar for the cottage, which was comfortable, tastefully decorated and, above all, free. But so far, the holiday had been much more stressful than staying at home. Nick wasn't coping well with the change of routine.

James glanced over at his son, completely absorbed in his drawing of an underwater scene, with tropical fish, mermaids and a castle. He obviously found it easier to exist in imaginary worlds than the real one.

'What should we do today?' James whispered to Sarah. 'I'm running out of ideas here.'

She sighed in defeat. 'Well . . . we could always see a movie?'

A few hours later, they bought tickets to a screening of *Spider-Man: Homecoming*. The Cinéma Henri Jeanson showed an eclectic programme of French cinema and arthouse classics alongside subtitled Hollywood blockbusters.

A plaque commemorated the cinema's namesake.

'What does it say?' asked James, who had forgotten most of his rudimentary secondary-school French.

Sarah translated. 'Henri Jeanson was imprisoned in World War Two for being a pacifist. He was a journalist and screenwriter.'

'Oh, like you,' said James.

'Hardly,' replied Sarah, shaking her head. 'Not sure I can call myself a screenwriter any more. I can't seem to finish anything.'

'You will,' he reassured her. Just as one day their holidays would return to being more relaxing, it would get easier for Sarah to write once the kids were older.

'Look at this,' said Sarah, pointing to the flyer on the noticeboard. 'They run special screenings for senior citizens.'

'What a great idea,' said James. 'We could do something like that at the Picture Palace – there are lots of retired people in the area.'

'Daddy!' cried Holly, rushing ahead to the concession stand. 'Please can we get popcorn?'

'Popcorn!' clamoured Nick, jumping up and down.

James bought snacks, then they made their way into the auditorium.

'Fingers crossed this wasn't a terrible idea,' said Sarah,

as they took their seats.

The film's rating was a 12, but it seemed worth the risk. They had some old Spider-Man comics at home from when James was a boy and Nick loved to look at the pictures.

At first, Nick seemed to be enjoying the film until a bomb blew up the Washington Monument on screen . . .

'I don't like it!' Nick cried.

'It's OK,' whispered Sarah. 'It's not real. It's just a movie.'

Moments later, another explosion in the film ripped a ferry in half.

Nick promptly began to howl. He wriggled off Sarah's lap, spilling a box of popcorn, and began to have a tantrum, thrashing around on the cinema floor.

'*Tais-toi*!' hissed someone in the row behind. James could feel angry eyes burning into his back as he stood up.

The whole family exited the cinema as quickly as if Spider-Man's nemesis, the Green Goblin, was chasing them.

'The big baby spoils yet another thing,' grumbled Holly in the lobby.

'I can take Nick back to the cottage if you and Holly want to watch the rest of the film,' said Sarah.

'No,' said James. 'This is our family holiday. We should stick together.'

He glanced over at Nick, who had squatted down to befriend a stray cat. His son laughed when the cat rolled around on the ground. Nick seemed fine at the moment, but it was hard to relax knowing the slightest thing could trigger a meltdown. James sighed, hoping they could get through the rest of the day without another tantrum.

They picked up some seabass at the fish market, then walked back to the cottage. By then, the rain had petered out. Nick returned to his drawing of the underwater kingdom, while Holly played games on the family iPad.

They usually restricted her screen time – but desperate times called for desperate measures: unlimited Roblox.

James opened one of the remaining bottles of wine and poured himself and Sarah each a large glass. He wiped down the garden furniture and they took their wine outside.

'To this holiday almost being over,' he said.

They touched glasses and sipped their wine, savouring the rich, fruity notes – and the peace and quiet.

'This is delicious,' said Sarah.

'At least one thing about today isn't a complete disaster,' remarked James. 'I guess Nick was too young for that movie.'

Sarah set her wine glass down. 'It's not about his age, James, and you know it. We can't go on ignoring what we've known ever since Nick was a baby. That he's different.'

'There's nothing wrong with being different,' replied James.

'I didn't say there was. But I think we should have him tested, like the school suggested. My mum knows an educational psychologist at the university who can do it for us.'

Before school had broken up, Nick's teacher had suggested that they might want to consider having him tested for autism, or some other form of sensory processing disorder. James had been avoiding this conversation, shutting it down every time Sarah brought it up. He was annoyed that she'd got her mum involved – Geraldine had a way of taking charge.

'No way,' said James, shaking his head vigorously.

'What are you so afraid of, honey?' Sarah asked. 'You know we'll love him just the same, no matter what the results are.'

'I don't want him to be labelled,' said James. He knew first-hand how horrible boys could be to other boys, how any sign of difference or weakness could get you bullied in the playground. He'd cried a few times at school after his mother's death and been mocked relentlessly for it. He wanted to spare Nick that torment.

'Labels don't have to be negative,' said Sarah. 'They can be empowering.'

'Whatever this is, he might just grow out of it.' James knew he was trying to convince himself as much as he was trying to convince his wife.

'Maybe,' replied Sarah doubtfully. 'But if there's something wrong, a diagnosis will help us know how to support him. When I was suffering from anxiety, finding out what was wrong was the first step in me getting better. You encouraged me to get a diagnosis.'

'Look what I found in the wardrobe upstairs,' called Holly, coming into the garden holding a cardboard box of DVDs. 'We can watch one of these.'

James was grateful for the interruption, though he knew Sarah wouldn't let it drop. He rooted through the French films and classic movies, looking for something suitable for the kids.

'What about this?' asked Holly, holding up a copy of *Last Tango in Paris*. 'I love dancing.'

'Nope!' James quickly took the DVD off her. 'It's too, ah—'

'French,' supplied Sarah, coming to his rescue.

'Here we go!' said James, discovering a copy of *Elf*. 'This is the perfect thing. It's about a human raised by elves in Santa's workshop.'

'But it's not Christmas,' said Holly.

'Doesn't matter,' replied James. 'It's a great movie.'

And, unlike *Last Tango in Paris*, it wasn't an erotic drama! They went inside and he loaded the disc into the machine, hoping it still worked. To his relief, the movie began to play.

Sprawled on the living-room sofa next to Sarah and

Holly, with Nick snuggled up on his lap, James let the film transport him to Manhattan at Christmastime.

'Come on, everyone,' Holly urged them, as Buddy the elf encouraged everyone to sing loudly to spread Christmas cheer. 'Sing!'

They all sang along and cheered as Santa's sled rose into the sky.

Nick clapped his hands when the movie finished. 'I love Buddy the elf! Daddy, can we have spaghetti with maple syrup for dinner?'

'No,' said James, laughing.

'Why not?' said Nick. 'That's Buddy's favourite meal.'

'Because we have some lovely fish to grill,' said Sarah.

James went outside to fire up the barbecue.

'Oh, my goodness,' said Sarah, coming out to join him and lifting her face to the sky. 'Is that the sun? I hardly recognise it.'

The sun was indeed peeking out from behind the clouds.

'Tag – you're it!' squealed Holly, running across the wet grass in bare feet as her little brother chased after her, giggling.

As James grilled the seabass, he thought about the film they'd just seen. Buddy the elf stayed true to himself and eventually saved the day.

James watched his sweet, sensitive, artistic son playing with his sister. Why should Nick have to change to fit in? Or hide his true self?

He took a deep breath. 'OK,' he said, turning to Sarah. 'Let's get Nick assessed.'

'Really?' she said, her face lighting up. 'What made you change your mind?'

James laughed. 'Believe it or not, the movie. It made me realise that I need to stop being scared of the fact that Nick is different. He is who he is – and always has been.'

Sarah put her arms around him. 'Whatever the outcome of the assessment, we'll make sure Nick knows it's OK to be different. That he can be himself.'

James nodded. 'You're right. He'll be fine. Because we love him no matter what.'

They stood with their arms around each other, watching the sun begin to set as the children laughed and played together on the lawn.

Thanks, Buddy, thought James. For bringing a little Christmas magic to their summer holiday.

Chapter 10

Present Day

Holly was brushing her teeth when someone pounded on the bathroom door. 'I'll be out in a minute,' she garbled through a mouthful of toothpaste.

Ignoring her, Nick burst into the bathroom in his school uniform. 'I need to talk to you.'

Holly glared at her brother. It was impossible to get any privacy in this house.

'It's important,' said Nick. 'It's about Mum.'

Holly was not in the mood for her brother's drama. He was bound to be making a big deal out of nothing. She spat out her toothpaste. 'I can't deal with this right now, Nick. This is a big day for me.'

Today was her first day on a movie set. She was just an extra, but lots of famous stars had got their starts working as background artists – Brad Pitt, Leonardo DiCaprio, Kristen Stewart, Renée Zellweger. Who knew what it might lead to. Best of all, Aaron would be there, too. Ever since the *Encanto* disaster, they'd been chatting at work and messaging outside of it. Holly liked him even more now that she was actually getting to know him instead of just stalking his socials. But they were just friends – Aaron hadn't asked her out or even tried to kiss her.

'But, Holly, she might be sick—'

'Nick!' bellowed Mum from downstairs. 'You're going to miss the bus if you don't leave now.'

'She sounds fine to me,' said Holly.

Sighing in defeat, Nick left the bathroom. A moment later, Holly heard the front door slam.

'Morning!' said Mum when Holly went downstairs. She pressed two tablets out of a foil packet and swallowed them down with a gulp of her coffee.

Holly suddenly felt a wrench of concern. Was Nick right – was there something wrong with Mum? 'Are you sick?'

'What?' Mum looked down at the pill packet in her hand. 'Oh, this? It's HRT. It helps with my menopause symptoms – mood swings, hot flashes, night sweats—'

'Eww,' said Holly, holding up her hand. 'Too. Much. Information.'

'It's important to talk about this stuff,' said Mum. 'You'll go through it one day too.'

'Great,' said Holly sarcastically. 'I can hardly wait.'

When the toast popped up, Mum spread peanut butter on both pieces and handed one to her.

Holly shook her head. 'I'm too nervous to eat.'

'Just a few bites,' urged Mum. 'It's going to be a long day.'

Jonesy rubbed his sleek ginger body against her legs, purring, as Holly nibbled her toast.

'Hey, Fluffyface.' Holly scooped the cat up and gave him one of her crusts.

'Don't feed the cat,' grumped Dad, coming into the kitchen. 'He's already had his breakfast.'

He got a mug down from the shelf, banging it noisily on the counter as he made himself a cup of tea. His hair was a mess, as if he'd been tossing and turning all night.

'Did you do the work school set for you?' he asked her.

'I'm going to do it over the weekend.' Holly licked peanut butter off her finger. She was going to have to brush her teeth again, she didn't want Aaron to think she had peanut-butter breath.

'Well, make sure you do,' said Dad. 'That was what we *agreed*. Not that agreements seem to count for anything around here . . .'

Taking his mug of tea, he stomped up the stairs.

Holly and her mum exchanged looks.

'Someone's in a bad mood,' said Mum.

'Maybe he's going through menopause too,' joked Holly.

They both laughed. She and Mum had been getting along better since her birthday.

'And get a move on,' Dad shouted down the stairs. 'We need to leave early. Traffic's been a complete nightmare.'

When they arrived at the cinema, Holly's heart raced with excitement as she saw crew wheeling equipment around and speaking into walkie-talkies. Everyone looked like they were doing something important. *This is really happening*, she thought, her heart thudding with excitement. *I'm actually in a movie.*

'Look at that.' Dad tutted, pointing to the cables snaking across the lobby floor. 'We've got a Golden Oldies screening today. Our elderly customers are going to trip over those. I asked the crew to move them after the Baby and Me screening, but they've ignored me.'

'I'll mention it to Noa,' said Mum.

Roger was behind the ticket counter. He'd agreed to come out of retirement to help Dad run the cinema while Mum and Aaron were working on the movie. Dad went to join him while Holly and Mum went out into the car park. Extras were standing around sipping hot drinks and squeezing instant hand warmers to ward off the winter chill. Holly looked around for Aaron, but couldn't see him anywhere.

Following the smell of sizzling bacon, Holly and Mum went over to craft services. The trestle tables heaved with a tempting array of food, from fruit and nuts to cookies and crisps. You could even get a hot breakfast!

Holly recognised several of the other extras from around the village – Hermione de la Mere from the candle shop and her parents' friend Ian Griffiths were sipping cups of coffee.

Mum went over to them. 'I didn't know you had the acting bug too, Hermione.'

'I've never done anything like this before,' admitted Hermione. 'Ian talked me into it.'

'We're a couple,' said Ian, taking a big bite of a blueberry muffin.

'Congratulations,' said Mum. 'I'm so happy for you.'

'No, in the movie,' clarified Ian. 'We're playing a couple having breakfast at the B&B.'

Hermione giggled. 'Well, we'd better practise so we're convincing.' She brushed muffin crumbs off his chest. 'There, that's better, dear.'

Holly exchanged knowing glances with her mother. Hermione and Ian would actually make a pretty cute couple in real life. Ian was a nice guy and Hermione was properly hot for someone old like Mum. To be fair, her mum was quite nice-looking. For once, she'd actually made a bit of an effort with her appearance today and was wearing a skirt, although in Holly's opinion it could do with being several inches shorter. She remembered the picture she'd seen at Pari's – Mum's fashion sense hadn't always been so tragic.

'Wardrobe?' said Mum.

For a second, Holly thought Mum had read her mind and knew she'd been silently criticising her outfit. Then she pointed to a tent that someone had just wheeled a rail of clothes inside.

They went inside the wardrobe tent together. A woman with a pincushion around her wrist checked a list when Holly gave her name, then headed over to a clothes rail and returned with an apron.

'I think there's been a misunderstanding,' said Holly. 'I'm not on the catering crew, I'm an extra.'

'That's your costume,' replied the wardrobe lady. 'You're playing a waitress. The girl who was supposed to do it slipped on some ice and broke her leg yesterday.'

'I guess you could say this is my lucky break then,' joked Holly. The wardrobe lady didn't laugh.

Holly put the apron on over the black skirt and white shirt she'd been told to wear. It was embroidered with a Christmas tree and the words *Pine Tree Inn*.

'That's the name of the inn in the movie,' explained Mum.

Costume sorted, Holly was dispatched to the hair and make-up team.

A young woman with a shaved head beckoned her over. She wore all black and had a belt around her waist, containing brushes and styling tools, like a make-up ninja. She reminded Holly of one of her brother's manga characters.

'Hey, I'm Zoe,' she said as Holly sat down in the chair in front of her. She tied a cape around Holly to protect her costume. Using a tiny spatula, Zoe expertly blended a few different shades of foundation on a mixing palette and began painting them on Holly's face. 'You've got lovely skin.'

'Thanks. I bet Mia Winslow does too,' said Holly. The up-and-coming film star had just been named the face of a big cosmetics brand.

Zoe brushed setting powder over the foundation. 'I wouldn't know. The stars get their hair and make-up done in their trailers. They don't mix with nobodies like us.'

'Oh.' Holly sighed, disappointed that she wouldn't be meeting the stars.

'Anyway, I'm glad I don't have to do Mia's make-up,' whispered Zoe as she applied Holly's mascara. 'It's been a complete nightmare on this shoot – she keeps crying and having to have her make-up redone.'

Holly had practised crying on cue in case she ever needed to do any sad scenes. Her drama teacher had told her to think about something really sad, so Holly thought about losing her grandpa. She'd only been little when he died, but she could still remember him. He used to sing her lullabies and take her to feed the ducks. She still had a little wooden duck he'd carved for her.

Zoe put Holly's hair up in a bun, leaving some tendrils softly framing her face.

'All background artists are needed at Location 1 now,' said a production assistant, speaking through a megaphone.

'You'd better go,' said Zoe, taking off Holly's make-up cape.

Coaches were lined up at the kerb outside the cinema, waiting to take crew and background artists to the location. Holly's heart leapt as she boarded the bus – there was Aaron, with a cardboard tray of hot drinks balancing on his lap. Best of all, there was a free seat next to him.

'Is it OK if I sit here?' she asked him.

'Course,' said Aaron.

Mum went to the back to sit with Ian and Hermione.

Holly slid in next to Aaron. She was conscious that their thighs were practically touching.

'I almost didn't recognise you,' he said. 'Your hair, um, looks nice up like that.'

'Thanks.' Holly touched her bun self-consciously.

They sat in awkward silence for a few minutes, as the coach set off.

'So, what does a runner do, exactly?' Holly asked. Aaron had been working on the film for a few days already.

'Well, stuff like this.' Aaron gestured to the hot drinks. 'Fetching things for the crew. I've mostly been helping out Kirsty, the second assistant director.'

'*Second* assistant director? How many assistant directors are there?'

'Three. The first assistant director organises the shoot schedule and liaises with the producers, and the second assistant director supervises the actual filming.' Aaron grinned. 'I haven't figured out what the third one does yet.'

'So what does Noa do?' asked Holly.

'The whole thing is his vision. He, ah, definitely knows what he wants . . .'

Before Holly could ask Aaron to elaborate, the coach went round a sharp bend. 'Whoa!' She started to slide off the seat.

As Aaron put his arm around Holly to steady her, one of the drinks on his lap pitched forward, spilling onto the floor. Luckily, it missed Holly's costume.

'Oh, crap!' Aaron said as green liquid pooled by their feet. 'That matcha was for Noa.'

'It was an accident,' said Holly. 'I'm sure he'll understand.'

She leant her head against Aaron's arm, which he hadn't removed. Holly closed her eyes and inhaled the smell of him – the fresh, clean scent of washing powder and Lynx deodorant, undercut by the slightest hint of sweat. He smelled of . . . boy.

She wished the journey would last for ever, but soon they were pulling up the long drive to Merricourt Manor. The extras were herded into the dining room of 'Pine Tree

Inn', which would rival Santa's workshop for festive vibes. It had been festooned with pine garland and poinsettias. Fairy lights twinkled around the windows looking out onto the frosty garden. It looked beautiful – no wonder Noa had chosen this for the movie's location.

'Dad and I got married here, you know,' said Mum.

'Sarah!' called Noa, beckoning Mum over to him. 'Can you please have a look at tomorrow's pages – I still don't think they're working.'

Mum took the script he was brandishing. 'Will you be OK if I work in the hotel lobby where it's quieter?' she asked Holly.

'Of course,' said Holly, rolling her eyes. When would Mum stop thinking of her as a kid?

They were filming the scene when Eve first arrives at the inn after a long absence. Most of the extras were instructed to sit around tables set for breakfast, with flowery china teacups and silver toast racks. A props person handed Holly a tray and a notepad.

'Extras playing inn guests, pretend to be talking to each other,' instructed a petite woman wearing a headset. That was Kirsty, the second director, Holly guessed.

Holding her notepad as if she were poised to take a breakfast order, she hovered by the table where Ian and Hermione were sitting. They weren't pretending to talk – they were deep in conversation.

'My ex virtually lived in hotels because he had to travel so much for work,' said Hermione.

'That must have been lonely for you,' said Ian sympathetically.

'Yes, it was,' confided Hermione. 'He never wanted me to come with him, and I now know it's because he was having affairs.'

'Well, he was obviously a fool,' remarked Ian, placing his hand over hers. 'And you're better off without him.'

The sound of Noa shouting drowned out Hermione's response.

'Where the hell's my matcha!'

'I'm really sorry, Noa,' said Aaron, stepping forward nervously. 'It spilled on the bus.'

'Are you serious?' Noa looked annoyed. 'I thought you wanted to make it in this industry, kid?'

'I-I do,' stammered Aaron, looking terrified. 'More than anything.'

'Well, that's never going to happen if you keep screwing up,' snarled Noa. 'Go back to base and get me another. Now!'

Holly felt terrible. It was her fault Aaron had been reprimanded. The only reason Noa's drink had spilled was that Aaron had been trying to keep her safe.

Holly tried to catch Aaron's eye as he hurried off, but his head was lowered in shame. She hoped he wouldn't hold it against her – on the minibus they had been vibing.

After a flurry of last-minute make-up and lighting adjustments, they were ready to start shooting. There was an excited murmur when Mia Winslow appeared in the dining room, holding a suitcase. The actress was tall and willowy, with honey-blonde hair – and, yes, perfect skin.

'Right, everybody,' said Kirsty once everyone was in position. 'DON'T LOOK AT THE CAMERAS. Pretend they aren't there.'

'And . . . action!' called the cameraman.

As she'd been directed, Holly pretended to write down a breakfast order on her notepad. Mia – playing Eve – came into the dining room, holding her suitcase, and gazed around the room, eyes shining with emotion. 'It's good to be home for Christmas,' she said, setting her suitcase down on the ground.

They did the scene several times, trying different camera angles. Holly thought Mia was giving a great performance, but Noa wasn't satisfied.

'You're not giving me anything,' he complained to Mia. 'Your character hasn't been back at the inn since splitting up with her ex. Her grandmother has just died. She should be overwhelmed with emotion.'

'I'm trying,' Mia said.

'Well, try harder.'

During a break in shooting, Aaron returned with a new cup of matcha. Noa took it without a word of thanks. He had a sip and pulled a face. 'It's cold.' He handed it to his assistant, who whisked it away.

Rude, thought Holly. But maybe that was just how things worked on film sets. Everyone on the crew seemed really busy – perhaps there wasn't time to be polite.

'Take twenty-two,' called Kirsty.

Mia started the scene again. 'It's good to be—'

'CUT!' shouted Noa, before she'd even got all of her line out. 'Do it again,' he told Mia. 'And this time, you might want to try acting for a change.'

'I *am* acting,' she said, biting her lower lip. 'I just can't figure out what you're looking for.'

Noa gave a huff of irritation. 'You know, there were hundreds of other actors I could have cast for this part. And it's not too late for me to change my mind.'

Mia's eyes filled with tears. A make-up artist hurried over and touched up her make-up.

In the next take, the actress's eyes shone and her voice cracked with emotion as she surveyed the inn's dining room.

'That's more like it!' said Noa, finally satisfied with his leading lady's performance.

Maybe that's why Noa is being so tough on her, thought Holly as the crew started setting up for the next scene. Maybe that's how you won Oscars.

Or maybe he was just a dick . . .

After filming a few more scenes, the background artists and crew were dismissed. Holly grabbed an empty seat on the coach. She was hoping Aaron would sit next to her, but instead Mum slid into the seat.

'Did you have fun?' Mum asked.

'Yes,' said Holly. 'But I'm tired.'

'You and Aaron looked very cosy on the coach earlier. You really like him, don't you?'

Holly stiffened. God, was it really that obvious?

'He clearly likes you too,' continued Mum. 'But I don't think you should get involved with an older boy.'

'Who said I'm involved with him?'

'I'm not an idiot, Holly,' said Mum. 'I can see what's going on.'

Holly felt her cheeks start to burn. 'It's none of your business. I don't want to have this conversation.'

'Well, I do,' said Mum. 'Aaron is a nice guy, but I don't think you should rush into a relationship at such a young age. He'll be off to uni next year and you need to focus on your GCSEs.'

Holly narrowed her eyes at her mother. Her parents had been annoyed with each other for months. Poor Nick was worried sick about it. And judging from Dad's mood this morning, they still hadn't sorted out whatever was wrong between them. Holly knew what was really going on here – her parents' marriage was in trouble and Mum couldn't bear for anyone else to be happy. 'What makes you think I'd take relationship advice from *you*?'

You idiot, thought Sarah, staring gloomily out of the coach's window. She and Holly had been getting along better, but now she'd gone and blown it. She should have kept her big mouth shut. Holly had refused to speak to her for the rest of the journey back to the cinema. Worst of all, Sarah knew her daughter was right – she was in no position to be dispensing relationship advice.

She still hadn't told James about Noa's offer.

Because you know he won't like it . . .

Being back at Merricourt Manor had stirred up all sorts of emotions. She and James had been so happy as newlyweds. Sure that nothing would ever change their love for each other. Back then, they didn't keep secrets from each other.

As Sarah stepped off the coach, a short, dark-haired woman in a tailored trouser suit and high-heeled ankle boots was getting out of a taxi.

'If you want him to commit to another season, you're going to have to improve the fee,' the woman said into her mobile. 'There's a lot of buzz around him since his BAFTA nomination, so he's not exactly short of offers.'

'Pari!' Sarah exclaimed when her friend finished her call. 'What are you doing here?'

'I thought I'd pay one of my biggest clients a visit on set.' Pari winked at Sarah. 'All part of the service – gotta earn that fifteen per cent commission. Plus, it was a good excuse to see you.'

Sarah hugged her best friend. 'Do you want to stay with us? I can make the kids double up.'

'Don't worry, I've booked into a spa hotel in Stowford. I haven't taken any holiday for months, so I might stay in the Cotswolds through Christmas. I desperately need to recharge my batteries.'

'That's amazing,' said Sarah. 'You can spend Christmas with us.' Her best friend was so busy, they rarely got a chance to hang out. She'd been gutted to miss their meet-up on Holly's birthday.

'Now, where are the trailers?' asked Pari. 'I need to find Mateo.'

Sarah led the way to the car park.

'Wow – the film crew have completely taken over,' said Pari, looking round at all the trailers and tents. 'I feel like I'm on a Hollywood lot.' Approaching the door of Mateo's trailer, Pari knocked on it. 'Yoo-hoo! It's the toughest negotiator in Tinseltown.' She grinned at Sarah over her shoulder. 'That's an actual quote from *Variety*.'

'Come in,' called a voice with an American accent.

Mateo Ajose was even more handsome in person than he was on screen. He had green eyes and dark curls flecked with gold. He'd won the genetic lottery, thanks to his Italian–American mother and Nigerian father.

'Well, well, well,' said Pari. 'If it isn't my favourite client.'

'That's what you say to all your clients,' quipped Mateo, giving his agent a kiss on each cheek. 'Hi Sarah,' he said, welcoming her inside.

Sarah was impressed that he remembered her name as they'd only met a few times. That had been before he'd done *Highgate*, the massively popular period drama that had sent his career stratospheric.

The actor wasn't alone in the trailer. His wife, Sam, was in there too, sitting on the sofa. And next to her, to Sarah's surprise, was Iris. Baby Henry was sitting on a blanket on the floor shaking a rattle. Trying to grab it off him was an adorable baby girl with her dad's dark curls. The two mums laughed when the little girl finally succeeded.

'Have this instead, Henry,' said Iris, handing her baby his toy giraffe.

'Fancy meeting you here,' said Sarah.

'Iris and I met at a Baby and Me screening,' explained Sam. 'I told her to pop by the set so Henry and Priya could have a play date.'

Henry bopped Priya on the head with his giraffe and the little girl started to cry.

'There, there,' said Mateo, picking up his baby girl and giving her a cuddle. 'Daddy's got you.' He pulled a funny face and the baby tried to grab his nose.

Sarah was glad to see that Iris had made a fellow mum friend, someone to share the trials and tribulations of motherhood with. Looking after a baby was a lonely business, even more so if you were struggling with anxiety. That's why she'd set up the Baby and Me screenings after having Holly – to build a supportive community of fellow parents. Even though their kids were now teenagers, Sarah was still good friends with some of the other mums she'd met at those very first Baby and Me screenings. She was proud that all those years later, the cinema was still connecting local parents.

'I hear you've set up a manga club at the high school,' she said to Iris. 'Nick was telling me all about it.'

'It's lovely to be doing something creative again,' said Iris. 'I was getting a bit bored at home.'

'Tell me about it,' agreed Sam. 'I used to always travel with Mateo when he was shooting on location, but I can't anymore because our eldest daughter is in primary school now. That's why I was so thrilled that *Ex-Mas Eve* was filming close to home.'

Sarah had seen pictures of their gorgeous converted farmhouse outside Stowford in magazines.

'How's the shoot going?' asked Pari. 'Is it a happy set?'

Priya started to fuss, so Mateo rocked her soothingly. 'I can see why Noa has got his reputation for being demanding. I haven't really bonded with Mia — she spends most of her time holed up in her trailer.'

Pari frowned. 'That's not good.' She turned to Sarah. 'What are your impressions?'

'Noa's definitely a perfectionist,' said Sarah. He'd had her reworking lines for tomorrow's scenes most of the day, so she hadn't seen much of the filming.

'We're way behind schedule,' said Mateo. 'Apparently we're not going to wrap until Christmas Eve.'

'That's a bummer,' said Sam. 'We'll miss the annual party at the Stowford bookshop.'

Oh dear, thought Sarah. James wasn't going to be happy when he found out that filming had been extended.

There was a knock on the door — an assistant summoning Mateo to the set.

'I should go too,' said Iris. 'Henry needs a nap.'

'So does Priya.' Sam kissed her husband on the cheek. 'See you back home, hon.'

'Is it OK if Sarah and I hang out in here for a bit?' Pari asked Mateo.

'Make yourselves at home,' said the star.

When they were alone, Pari kicked off her ankle boots and lay down on the sofa. 'I'm exhausted. I flew in on the red-eye from LA.'

Pari's job sent her back and forth across the pond several times a year. She had recently opened an LA office of her agency. Ironically, if Sarah took the job for Noa, she might actually get to see more of her best friend.

'Noa offered me a job,' Sarah confided in Pari. 'In LA.'

Pari swung her legs off the sofa and sat upright again,

suddenly wide awake. 'Oh, wow – that's incredible. He must be really impressed with you.'

Sarah helped herself to a grape from an enormous fruit basket on the coffee table. 'He wants me to work on the script for his next movie.' His passion project was about a classical musician who could see the future when he played the piano, and had to stop the world from impending disaster. The working title was *Fugue State*. 'And he's interested in *The Ghost Writer* too.'

Pari leant forward in anticipation. 'What did you say?'

'That I needed to think about it.'

Sarah had been thinking about it nonstop. She could picture herself writing in a Spanish-tiled house with a swimming pool in the back garden, and taking long walks along the Pacific coast. She and James had visited LA on their honeymoon. She'd loved the warm weather and relaxed vibe.

'What did James say?' asked Pari.

'I haven't told him yet.'

Pari quirked her eyebrow. 'What's up with that? You guys are so tight – you normally tell each other everything.'

'I just haven't found the right moment. And anyway, what's the point? It's not like I could accept the offer.'

'Why not?' demanded Pari.

'We've got the cinema, the kids are still at school, and there's my mum . . .' Sarah could think of a million reasons why it wasn't possible.

'Those aren't insurmountable problems, Sarah,' said Pari. 'They do have schools in California, you know.'

Holly would probably jump at the chance to move to Los Angeles. But Nick hated change. And James would never abandon the cinema. It was like a shrine to his father.

'Promise me this,' insisted Pari. 'Whatever you decide, make sure it's what's best for *you* for a change.'

Sarah nodded.

Pari shook her finger at her scoldingly. 'And if you ever finish your own script, don't sell it to Noa without consulting me first. You need an agent to get you the best deal.' Then she let out a big yawn and lay back down on the sofa.

'I'll let you nap in peace.'

Sarah went inside the cinema and found James frowning at his laptop.

'Where have you been?' he asked crossly. 'Holly's been back ages.'

'I was catching up with Pari,' she explained. 'She came to check on Mateo. What's up?' She already knew it wasn't anything good because a muscle in his cheek was twitching – a sure tell. Her husband could never be a poker player.

'That bloody generator surged and caused a power cut this morning,' moaned James. 'It blew out the whole cinema and completely messed up our software system. I had to cancel Golden Oldies and I've only just finished resetting it.'

'Oh, dear,' said Sarah. 'That's so annoying. I'm sorry I wasn't around to help.'

'Well, at least they'll be gone soon,' said James. 'And not a second too soon.'

Sarah didn't want to be the one to break the news, but he was going to find out sooner or later. She took a deep breath. 'The shoot is running behind. Mateo says they're going to be shooting here right up until Christmas Eve,' she said.

James stared at her incredulously. 'You cannot be serious.'

'But hey – they'll have to pay us more money,' said Sarah, trying to put a positive spin on it. 'So that's good.'

James slammed the lid of his laptop down in anger. 'That is out of order. That's not what we agreed.'

'I know it's really inconvenient, but just think of the money,' said Sarah. 'I'll speak to Noa. Hopefully the problem with the power won't happen again.'

'Yes, you speak to Noa,' said James. The twitch in his cheek was going wild. 'I know the two of you make a *great team*.'

'What's that supposed to mean?' asked Sarah warily.

'You know what I mean.' His blue eyes stared at her accusingly. 'When were you going to tell me that he asked you to go to LA?'

How did he know about that? She and Noa had been alone when they'd had that conversation. Sarah studied her husband suspiciously. 'Were you spying on me?'

James looked insulted. 'Is that how little you think of me? No, I overheard you talking to him in my office. Which Noa has taken over, just like he's taken over the rest of the cinema. It would appear he's also trying to take over my wife.'

Sarah didn't like what he was implying. Sure, Noa was a flirt. But she'd never given him any encouragement in that area.

'Firstly, it's *our* office,' she said, her tone icy. 'Secondly, he's paying us handsomely for the privilege. And thirdly, he's been good to me, James. Noa actually believes in my writing.'

James gave a dismissive laugh. 'Are you sure he's not just trying to get into your pants?'

Sarah inhaled sharply. Did James really think that was the only reason Noa was interested in her? That it had nothing to do with her talent?

'Why are you doing this?' she said, her voice trembling. 'Why are you trying to ruin the best thing that's happened to me in for ever?'

'I'm not,' said James. 'I'm just trying to look after the cinema.'

'That's right,' said Sarah bitterly. 'The cinema always comes first with you.' She shook her head sadly. 'For years, I've had to put my dream on hold because of this place. I thought the problem was the cinema. But maybe the real problem is . . . you.'

5th November 2020

Holly and her family were gathered in the living room in front of the television watching the evening news. The reporter wore a plastic visor and was standing in front of a hospital. Behind her, an ambulance pulled up, sirens wailing, and paramedics in protective suits unloaded a stretcher. The patient on the stretcher had a breathing mask covering their face.

'As Covid-19 cases continue to rise across the nation, England today enters a second lockdown until the second of December,' intoned the reporter solemnly. 'The prime minister is announcing new measures to tackle the spread of this new variant.'

The broadcast cut to the prime minister, his blonde hair looking characteristically dishevelled. 'To protect the vulnerable, everyone must stay at home, except for education and essential travel.'

'Well, here we go again,' said Mum, sighing wearily. 'Another lockdown.'

Holly's dad took off his glasses and rubbed his eyes, which had dark circles underneath them.

The Picture Palace had been shut from March to August. Audience numbers had been low since reopening. Even with socially distanced seating and masks, people felt nervous about sitting together in a confined space and had largely stayed home. Now the cinema was being forced to shut again.

'This sucks,' moaned Holly. She had been overjoyed to go back to school in September, after being stuck at home with her family all spring and summer. At first, it had been fun not to have to go to school. They had baked banana bread, played cards, taken long walks in the countryside and watched classic movies together. Once the novelty had worn off, though, it had just been boring. Holly was a social butterfly. She missed chatting to her friends at lunch and on the bus. There was nothing to gossip about because everyone was stuck at home.

Jonesy butted his head against Holly's hand, demanding that she scratch behind his ears. Holly obliged him and was rewarded by a rumbling purr.

That was one good thing about the first lockdown – they'd got a pet, after years of her and Nick begging for one. Dad had found a litter of kittens abandoned in the cinema car park. They'd adopted the runt of the litter, a tiny ginger ball of fluff, and rehomed the rest. Dad had named their kitten Jonesy, after the cat in some science-fiction movie. (Holly had wanted to call him Alexander Hamilton, but had been overruled).

'I know, sweetie, it's very frustrating,' said Mum. 'Just when we thought things were finally getting back to normal.'

'Maybe this *is* the new normal,' said Dad.

Holly stared at him in horror. Was she going to spend her teenaged years doing jigsaw puzzles and playing games with her parents and little brother?

'At least schools are staying open this time,' said Mum.

Holly groaned. 'It's so unfair. We have to do all the boring parts of school and none of the fun things.' She had been looking forward to auditioning for the school musical, but the production had been cancelled. All clubs and sports had been cancelled too.

'I liked it when the schools were shut.' Nick snapped a wheel onto his latest LEGO creation.

Nick had found home-schooling less stressful than going to school. Holly's little brother was annoyingly clever – he'd finish his primary school assignments quickly, then spend the rest of the day drawing, reading and building models. *Nice for some.* Holly had struggled to keep up with her schoolwork without proper lessons.

'I know it's difficult,' said Dad. 'But we'll get through this lockdown, so long as we stay positive.'

'Look, it's Auntie Pari!' exclaimed Nick, pointing at the television screen.

Holly's godmother was standing outside a West End theatre with one of her clients, a handsome actor called Mateo Ajose. Underneath Pari's picture, it said, *Pari Johal, CEO of Shakti Talent.* Once, Holly had asked her what the name meant, and she'd explained that *shakti* meant power in Punjabi.

'You were due to star in a production of *A Midsummer Night's Dream.*' The reporter addressed the actor. 'How do you feel about the fact that the show can't open as planned?'

'Very disappointed, obviously,' said Mateo. 'But the most important thing is saving lives.'

'Things are very tough for the entertainment community right now,' added Pari. 'It isn't just the actors who are out of work – it's the crew, the hair and make-up people, the musicians . . . They're mostly self-employed, so they haven't been furloughed. And even when they're not operating, theatres have bills to pay.'

'Cinemas too,' muttered Mum.

The people who worked at the cinema got money from the government during lockdown. But because Holly's parents owned the cinema, they didn't get anything themselves. They'd had to take out loans, as they'd had no income for months. She'd heard them having whispered conversations about money through her bedroom wall.

'The government has recently set up a rescue fund to help cultural organisations survive the pandemic,' said the reporter on television. 'But many theatres, museums and cinemas fear they won't be able to survive another lockdown.'

'Have we heard back from the Culture Recovery Fund yet?' asked Dad.

'Not yet,' replied Mum. 'It's such a shame, because people could really do with a bit of escapism.'

Holly's parents had applied for a grant so that they could host outdoor screenings while the cinema was shut. Holly hoped they got it, as drive-in movies sounded fun. She was desperate for somewhere to go – anywhere but home would do.

'I had really hoped we could go ahead with the Twelve Films of Christmas, so we could spread some festive cheer,' said Dad.

Something suddenly occurred to Holly. 'We can still go to London and see Auntie Pari on my birthday weekend, right?' Her thirteenth birthday was only a few weeks away. Last year, Pari had taken her to see *Hamilton*.

'Only if the lockdown has been lifted by then,' said Mum. 'It wouldn't count as "essential" travel.'

It's essential for me, thought Holly.

'But I can still have a birthday party, right?' She had been planning an epic birthday sleepover party. They were going to eat pizza, give each other manicures and watch *Little Women*, her favourite movie.

'Not if we're still in lockdown,' said Dad.

'But that's so stupid,' ranted Holly. 'My friends and I all sit together in the same classroom at school. What does it matter if we get together outside of school?'

'We've got to follow the rules,' said Mum.

The rules didn't make any sense. Wear a mask, don't wear a mask . . . Avoid restaurants, support restaurants . . . Take a Covid test, there are no tests . . .

It was the same at home – her parents were always setting stupid rules. They were super strict about her phone and wouldn't let her go on social media.

'We've all got to do our bit to protect those who are more vulnerable, like Grandma,' said Mum.

Geraldine had given a guest lecture at a university in Wuhan last November. She'd fallen ill as soon as she'd returned from her trip and had ended up in the hospital for several months on a ventilator, one of the UK's first Covid cases – although they hadn't known what it was at first. Since her illness, Holly's grandma had suffered with breathing problems and fatigue. She was still working at Bristol Uni, but Holly knew her mum was worried about her getting the virus again now that her immune system was weakened.

'Don't get your hopes up, Hol,' cautioned Dad. 'The virus spreads faster in winter, so I wouldn't be surprised if the restrictions get extended.'

'But it's my thirteenth birthday . . .' Holly said in a small voice, tears prickling her eyes. She knew she shouldn't be acting like a baby. Plenty of people had it far worse than her. Some kids at school had lost family members to Covid. Her parents' friend, Roger, couldn't attend Omar's chemotherapy appointments with him.

'We'll make it a special day,' promised Mum. 'No matter what.'

Yeah, right.

'Happy Birthday, Holly,' said Nick, jumping on her bed. He deposited a present tied with a ribbon on the duvet. 'Does it feel different being a teenager?'

'No,' said Holly, sitting up.

It hardly mattered that it was her birthday – it wasn't like she could do anything to celebrate. The national lockdown had been replaced with a new system of tiers. According to the newest set of rules, the cinema had to remain shut. Indoor gatherings were prohibited.

So that meant no party. No theatre trip to London. Nothing.

Well, there *was* chocolate cake – she could smell it baking downstairs.

'Open your gift, Holly,' said Nick. 'I made it for you.'

Jonesy padded into Holly's bedroom and jumped on the bed, not wanting to be left out.

Holly unwrapped her present. Nick had made her a room sign spelling out her name in purple LEGO bricks.

'That's really cool, Nick.' She put it on her bedside table and gave her brother a hug.

She played with Jonesy for a bit, dangling the ribbon from her present. Then Holly got out of bed and went to the bathroom. She looked in the mirror, wondering if she looked more grown-up. She turned to the side. *Nope.* Her boobs hadn't magically appeared overnight. Mum had bought her a training bra, but she didn't really have anything to fill it with. Holly hadn't got her period yet either, even though Riley had had hers for over a year *and* wore lacy 34C bras.

'Everyone develops at their own pace,' Mum had told her. But Holly hated feeling that she was being left behind.

The acne on her chin was the only sign of any hormonal activity. The pimples seemed to have multiplied overnight, like Gremlins who'd got wet. (That was one of the old movies Dad had showed her and Nick during lockdown.)

When she went downstairs for her birthday breakfast, the chocolate cake was on the table, as well as a small pile of presents and a huge badge Nick had made that read *13 TODAY*.

'Aren't you going to put your badge on?' asked Nick after everyone had sung 'Happy Birthday' to her.

'No,' said Holly. She was too old for birthday badges.

She took her phone off the charger and checked her messages. None of her friends had bothered to wish her a happy birthday.

Oh, well, thought Holly. It was still early. Maybe they were all still asleep.

They had cake for breakfast, then Holly opened her presents. Mum had got her a make-up palette and a set of brushes.

'Now that you're thirteen, you can wear a bit of make-up,' said Mum, smiling.

'Thanks,' said Holly. (Mum didn't need to know she already applied mascara and lipgloss in the bathroom at school.)

Dad gave her a gold Claddagh ring – two hands holding a heart topped with a crown. 'It was my mother's. The heart represents love, the crown loyalty and the hands friendship.'

Holly slipped it on her ring finger. It fit perfectly. 'It's beautiful.'

Auntie Meg had sent her a gift voucher. Nora and Simon had, as usual, given her a book. It was called *Hamilton: The Revolution* and was all about the musical.

'This one is from Grandma,' announced Mum, handing her the last present. 'She said to give you a hug from her as well.' Last year, her grandmother had been in hospital on Holly's birthday.

Holly opened the box and took out a new pair of red high-top Converse trainers – the exact ones she'd wanted for months. She eagerly put them on and took a photo. She was about to share it with her friends, but when she opened her messages there were still no birthday wishes from her friends.

She started to cry, tears plopping on her phone screen.

'What's wrong?' asked Mum. 'Don't you like your trainers? I thought those were the ones you wanted.'

'They are. But I don't have anywhere to wear them,' sobbed Holly. 'And all my so-called friends forgot about my birthday.'

Nick started to cry too.

'Why are *you* crying?' demanded Holly, glaring at him. 'Your birthday hasn't been ruined.'

'I'm crying because you're sad,' said Nick, sniffing. He put his arms around Holly, getting chocolate fingerprints on her favourite top.

When her brother was little, her parents had thought he might be autistic. But it turned out that he was just a HSP – a highly sensitive person. His nervous system was more sensitive than most people's. Dad had explained osmosis to her when she'd been learning about it in science. He'd got the sponge from the kitchen sink and demonstrated how it absorbed water. Well, that was Nick – he sucked up people's emotions.

Normally, Holly tried to be understanding of her brother. Today, however, she was not in the mood for his overreaction.

'Get over yourself, Nick,' she snapped, pushing him away in annoyance.

'Look, I know this isn't the day you wanted, Holly,' said Mum. 'But let's try to make the best of it, OK.'

Holly spent the day curled up on the sofa reading her new book. Mum made macaroni cheese – her favourite – for lunch. Auntie Pari called to wish her a happy birthday and promised to take her to see a musical as soon as theatres reopened.

But there were still no messages from her friends.

'Let's get takeaway pizza for dinner,' suggested Dad as the sun began to set.

'Good idea,' said Mum. 'We can all go collect it.'

'Why?' asked Holly. All she wanted to do was lie on the sofa and mope.

Dad jingled his car keys. 'It'll do you good to get out of the house.'

Sighing dramatically, Holly put on her new trainers and got into the car. They drove into the village and collected the pizza from the Rose and Crown; the local pub had started doing takeaway pizzas during lockdown. Across the road, the cinema looked cold and empty with all its lights off.

'Why are we going this way?' Holly asked Dad as they drove home. They were heading into the countryside instead of back home.

'I must have taken a wrong turning,' said Dad. 'I'll turn around up here.'

'The pizzas will get cold,' grumbled Holly.

Dad turned up the path to a farm. Ian Griffiths, wearing a high-vis vest, was directing a steady flow of incoming traffic.

Holly peered out of the window. 'What's going on? Why are there so many people here?'

Nick giggled, then covered his mouth.

Dad turned into the field, which was filled with cars parked in neat rows. There was a big inflatable screen at the other end of the field.

'Surprise!' shouted Mum, Dad and Nick.

Dad drove right to the front row. Everyone in the field tooted their car horns as they went past, a cacophony of beeps ringing out across the countryside.

'I don't understand . . .' said Holly.

'It's your birthday party!' squealed Nick.

'Our grant application was approved,' explained Dad, parking the car. 'We rented an outdoor screen, so we can do the Twelve Films of Christmas as a drive-in festival this year.'

'But today is just for you and your friends,' said Mum, smiling. 'You can't have a sleepover — but you can still have pizza and watch a movie.'

'I knew!' said Nick, bouncing excitedly on the back seat next to Holly. 'But I had to keep it a secret.'

Mum and Dad had invited all their family and friends, and everyone in Holly's year.

'Happy Birthday, Holly!' shouted Riley, leaning out of her mum's car. 'You didn't think we'd actually forget your birthday, did you?'

Nora and Simon were there, with their daughter, Charlotte, who used to babysit Holly and Nick.

'Thank you for the book,' called Holly, waving to them.

Roger and Omar had come too. Omar looked gaunt, following months of chemotherapy, and had lost all his hair. '*Joyeux Anniversaire*,' he wished her through his face mask.

Holly's face lit up as she spotted her grandmother's little red Toyota. 'Thanks for the trainers, Grandma,' she shouted, holding up one of her feet so Geraldine could see them through the car window. 'They fit perfectly.'

Grandma blew her a kiss.

Holly wished she could give her grandmother a hug, but they had to be very careful not to make her ill again.

An announcement instructed the audience to tune their car radios to a specific station and then *Little Women* began to play. Holly hurried back into the car to eat her pizza and watch Greta Gerwig's adaptation of Louisa May Alcott's classic novel, snuggled under one of the fleece blankets her mum had packed. It starred Florence Pugh and Saoirse Ronan, two of her favourite actors.

'Hot chocolate?' Mum asked, handing out steaming cups of cocoa she'd poured from a Thermos flask.

'I love happy endings,' said Nick, as the girls' father returned home from the Civil War, to be reunited with his family for Christmas.

Holly nodded. 'Me too.' Her heart was filled with love for her own family. They might be annoying sometimes, but they were also the best family in the entire world. She still couldn't believe they had done all this, just for her.

As the credits rolled, everyone tooted their car horns again in a final birthday salute.

'That made me feel really Christmassy,' remarked Mum as they drove home.

'It was nice when the Little Women gave up their Christmas breakfast for the poor family,' said Nick. 'But I'm glad we didn't have to give up Holly's cake this morning. Can I have another piece for dessert when we get home?'

'Of course,' said Mum.

'It feels good to do nice things for other people,' said Dad. 'That's why we run the Christmas film festival.'

Later that night, Mum came upstairs to say goodnight to Holly. She sat on the edge of the bed and tucked the duvet around her, the way she used to do when Holly was little. 'Who is your favourite March sister, Hols?'

'Jo,' Holly answered without hesitation.

'Mine too,' agreed Mum. 'She's part of the reason I wanted to be a writer.'

'You *are* a writer,' said Holly.

Mum sighed. 'I suppose so. I thought I would be able to work on my screenplay during lockdown, when the cinema was shut. But home-schooling and Grandma being so ill made that tricky.'

'I'm glad she's better now,' said Holly.

'Me too,' said Mum.

Holly glanced at the birthday badge Nick had made for her. He was really good at art. Lockdown had been so boring, she'd written a few plays for her and Nick to stage in the living room. Nick had spent hours designing the programmes, even though the audience was only Mum and Dad (and Jonesy of course – although he normally wandered off before the curtain call).

'I liked how in the movie Jo wrote plays for her sisters to perform,' said Holly. 'Like me and Nick.'

Mum stroked Holly's hair. 'My star in waiting.'

'What if the theatres never open again?' Holly wanted to be an actor. It was the only job she could imagine herself doing when she grew up.

'Theatres were shut for years during Shakespeare's life, because of the plague. You just need to be patient – the world will open again eventually,' Mum assured her.

Holly sighed in frustration. She was sick of life being on hold. Of waiting for things to happen to her.

'Oh, honey, I feel for you,' said Mum. 'I was thirteen too, once, believe it or not. I remember how hard being a teenaged girl is – and you're having to go through it during a global crisis.'

'It's scary,' admitted Holly.

'Remember, I'm always here for you, Holly. You can talk to me about anything.'

'Thanks, Mum,' said Holly, sitting up to give her a hug. 'I love you.'

'I love you too,' said Mum, squeezing her tightly. 'So did your birthday have a happy ending after all?'

Holly grinned. 'Best. Birthday. Ever!'

Chapter 11

Present Day

On the morning of Christmas Eve, James's legs pumped up and down as he cycled down the country lane, his breath clouding in the cold air. The fields and branches overhead were covered with a thick hoar frost. Things at home were even frostier. He and Sarah had barely spoken since their big argument. At least she'd come to the penultimate film festival screening of *An Affair to Remember*. He'd chosen it to remind her of the day he proposed.

She probably regretted saying yes.

I messed up . . . I messed up . . . I messed up, he chanted in his head as he pushed himself to go faster, the pain in his thigh muscles like a punishment for his churlish behaviour.

He'd let his irritation with the film crew and jealousy of Noa get the best of him. And he'd been hurt that Sarah hadn't told him about the offer. Instead of asking her about it calmly, he'd lashed out, belittling her talent. He would do anything to take back what he said. Her resentful words had been playing in a loop in his mind: *The cinema always comes first with you.*

He was horrified that Sarah believed that. Nothing could be further from the truth. Yes, he loved the cinema. It was a community, a family, where people came together to enjoy stories from all over the world. But nothing was more important than his *actual* family. He'd been so busy trying to keep the cinema afloat that he hadn't even noticed how frustrated and resentful she was.

He'd thought they were happy here in Plumdale, but owning a cinema had been *his* dream; Sarah had gone along with it because she loved him. Somewhere along the way, her own ambitions, of being a writer, had been sacrificed to family life. It clearly wasn't enough for her any more.

James knew what he had to do. If Sarah wanted to go to Los Angeles, he would go with her. Or let her go on her own. They could sell the cinema to the Valley Vista people. *That* was the grand romantic gesture he needed to make – not showing her old movies as a trip down memory lane. They needed to look to the future, not the past. He'd had his shot – Sarah was long overdue hers. And he wasn't going to stand in her way.

Whatever she wants to do, I'll support her.

James's legs pumped the pedals vigorously, his conviction growing with every turn of the wheels. Sure, he'd miss the cinema, but he'd find something else to do. He was still young (ish) and healthy. He wasn't ready to retire, nor could he afford to. Perhaps he could go back to engineering – he still had some contacts in the business. Alternatively, he could retrain to become a teacher; Holly always said he was good at explaining science.

James cycled hard towards home, filled with resolve. He was going to show Sarah that she came first in his heart, no matter what, no matter where. He'd go along with whatever she wanted to do. He wasn't sure where the road ahead would take him, but as long as she was by his side he knew it would be fine.

When James came into the kitchen, Nick was at the table wrapping presents in shiny red paper. Jonesy was playing with a piece of gold ribbon that had fallen on the floor, rolling around with his 'prey' in his paws.

'Don't peek!' said Nick, shielding the item he was wrapping.

James covered his eyes obediently.

'OK, you can look now,' Nick said a moment later.

It was just the two of them – and Jonesy – at home. Sarah and Holly were at the cinema, as there was a big outdoor scene filming in the village square today. The film crew had promised to be finished by eight, so the last film-festival screening could go ahead at nine. It was the only movie being shown today, so James had had the day off. He decided to get a head start on tomorrow's dinner so they could have a lie-in on Christmas morning – they all needed it after the past month.

Putting on an apron, he peeled potatoes, parsnips and carrots, and left them soaking in pans of cold water. Then he fried sausage meat, onions, breadcrumbs and sage, and other seasonings, using his mother's recipe. The herby aroma of the sizzling stuffing took him straight back to childhood. His mum would sing along to festive songs on the radio and sip a glass of sherry as she cooked their Christmas dinner.

Emotion overcame him as he remembered his parents. They'd both been gone for years, but he still missed them – especially around the holidays.

'What's wrong, Dad?' asked Nick, looking up from his wrapping. His worried expression, with the crease between his eyes, reminded James of Sarah.

James wiped his eyes with the bottom of the apron. 'Oh, it's just the onions making my eyes water.'

'Tell me the truth, Dad,' said Nick. 'Are you upset because Mum is sick?'

James looked at his son in surprise. 'No . . . Whatever gave you that idea?'

'So she's not going to die?'

'Well, she will, some day. Hopefully not for a very long time.' James gave the stuffing another stir. 'I was thinking of my own mum and dad – I always miss them at Christmastime.'

Nick came over and gave him a tight hug.

James kissed the top of his boy's head, which nearly reached his shoulder. Nick was growing like a weed and would soon be as tall as him. James hoped his son would never lose his sweetness and emotional intelligence.

Nick went over to the table and fetched one of the presents he'd just wrapped. 'Open it.'

'But it's not Christmas yet.'

'It will be soon,' said Nick. 'I can't wait for you to see it.'

James wiped his hands on a tea towel and opened the gift. Inside was a manga book. *Kayda's Quest* by Nick O'Hara and Julia Daniels, it said on the cover, with an illustration of a girl transforming into a dragon.

'You made this?' asked James, turning the pages in awe. His son's colourful illustrations were full of movement and emotion; just a few pen strokes managed to convey a huge range of expressions.

'Iris – Mr Wu's wife – helped us get it printed,' said Nick. 'Julia helped me with the words.'

'This is incredible,' James marvelled, turning the book over to read the back cover. 'You're only twelve and you're already a published author.'

Nick grinned. 'It's about a girl named Kayda who's scared of lots of things, but has to be really brave and fight a powerful baddie.'

'Does she win?' asked James.

'You have to read it and find out.' Nick helped himself to one of the carrots James had just peeled and bit into it with a loud crunch.

'It must have taken you ages to do all this,' said James.

Nick shrugged. 'Drawing makes me happy. I forget about everything else when I'm doing it. Plus, it was really fun to work on it with Julia.'

A lump came into James's throat as conflicting emotions fought inside him. He was bursting with pride over his son's artistic achievement. It was wonderful that Nick got such satisfaction and joy from his art. But it made James sad that Sarah had been unable to use her creativity for so long. No wonder she'd been so frustrated.

'I made one for Mum too,' said Nick.

'She's going to love it.' James was getting teary again.

Pull yourself together, he admonished himself.

He cleared his throat and forced himself to sound cheerful. 'Don't forget to hang up your stocking by the fireplace tonight.'

'What I want for Christmas doesn't fit in a stocking,' replied Nick.

'Oh?' said James. 'What's that?'

'I want you and Mum to get along again,' said Nick earnestly. 'For things to go back to how they used to be.'

'Believe me, son, I want that more than anything too.' James's voice choked with emotion.

As Nick tidied up the wrapping things, James took the stuffing off the heat.

'Can Julia and Adam come to the cinema tonight?' asked Nick. 'They want to watch the movie being filmed.'

James had met the twins when they'd come along to the screening of *Tokyo Godfathers*. They seemed like nice kids. He was so pleased that Nick had made some new

293

friends. They no longer needed to plead with him to go to school in the morning.

'Of course they can come,' said James.

'Great! I'll go and text them and let them know.'

Alone in the kitchen, James leafed through his son's manga story, stopping to admire a picture of Kayda brandishing a Samurai sword. It was time for him to be brave too. Fetching his laptop, James typed a quick email to the Valley Vistas managing director:

Our circumstances have changed. We would be interested in exploring your offer.

***

A snowflake fell on Sarah's hand and slowly dissolved on her woollen mitten – a gift from Pam – leaving a slightly chemical odour behind. The snow wasn't coming from the sky – it was coming from cannon-like machines pointed at the market square, where wooden stalls selling gingerbread, ornaments and mulled wine had been erected by the crew. It looked like an adorable Christmas market – apart from the boom mikes dangling overheard and the camera mounted on a dolly track.

Holly and some of the other extras, including Ian and Hermione, were playing carollers in a choir. Wearing Christmas jumpers, woolly scarves and Santa hats, they stood in front of a big Christmas tree waiting for their cue. They'd been waiting there for hours . . .

First, there had been a problem with the snow machine. Then Noa had decided that the Christmas tree didn't have enough decorations on it, sending Aaron scurrying off to find more. And when they were finally ready to shoot, Mia had refused to come out of her trailer. Mateo had been dispatched to try to coax the leading lady out.

Sarah stamped her feet to warm them up, wishing she'd thought to wear snow boots instead of trainers. She'd been hanging out with Iris and Sam while waiting for the filming to start. The two young mums were sipping mulled wine, making the most of their kid-free night out.

'I'm celebrating,' said Iris. 'Henry slept through till six this morning. No night-time feeds!'

'Woohoo!' Sam clinked her glass against Iris's.

Sarah smiled too, remembering how massive that milestone felt when Holly and Nick were babies. Now, she had to practically drag them out of bed!

'Hey,' said a voice behind her. James had just arrived with Nick and the twins in tow. The kids were throwing handfuls of fake snow at each other. 'How's it going?'

'Slowly,' said Sarah. At this rate, they'd still be here on Christmas morning!

James checked his watched and frowned. 'But the movie starts at nine.'

'Here they come now.' Sarah pointed to the stars approaching the set. Mia, as the elegant city girl, looked chic in a cashmere coat and furry hat, while Mateo, playing the inn's handyman, looked ruggedly handsome in a tartan lumberjack jacket and jeans. Make-up artists swarmed around the actors, adjusting their hair and touching up their make-up.

'Finally!' snapped Noa, leaping out of his canvas director's chair. 'Let's get going. Time is money, people.'

'Too right,' muttered a crew member. Sarah remembered from her BBC days that night shoots were more expensive than day shoots – and this one was massively overrunning.

A props person handed Mia a handbag and a cup of hot chocolate, and an assistant steered her to her mark, right by the choir.

'Quiet on set,' called Noa through a megaphone.

'Take one,' announced Kirsty, the second assistant director. 'Scene twenty-five.' She snapped the clapperboard. Then the cameras began to roll and the choir started to sing.

'This is the big romantic scene near the end of the movie,' Sarah whispered to the kids. 'It's when Ben – that's Mateo – finally tells Eve that he loves her.'

'Ooh!' said Julia. 'I love romantic movies.'

Nick and Adam groaned.

'Eve!' called Mateo, running across the market square. 'Eve! I need to talk to you!'

'It's too late,' said Mia, stepping away from the choir. 'I'm going back to the city.'

'No, I've waited too long to tell you how I feel,' said Mateo. 'I've tried to fight my feelings, but it's no use. I'm hopelessly in love with you.'

Sarah got goosebumps listening to the actors say the words she'd written.

'I love you too,' said Mia.

Sarah silently mouthed the next line along with Mateo: 'Then we owe it to ourselves to give this another chance.'

Dropping her shopping bag on the ground, Mia stood on her tiptoes to kiss Mateo. Snow began to drift down from the snow machines and the choir started to sing again.

'Ahhh!' sighed Julia.

Nick and Adam rolled their eyes.

'And . . . cut!' called Noa.

The two actors pulled apart, laughing as they broke character. The watching crowd applauded. Only Noa looked unhappy.

'We need to go again,' he said. 'Mia, can you try to actually look like you want to kiss Mateo this time?'

Sarah frowned. She thought both actors had played the scene beautifully.

Mia looked upset by the director's criticism but nodded.

'Is it hard to watch Mateo kiss someone else?' Iris asked Sam.

'I've got used to it,' replied Sam, taking a sip of her wine. 'It's just part of the job.'

Aaron and the other runners helped the crew set up the scene again, brushing away fake snow and resetting props. The camera wheeled back along its track. Reflectors were repositioned.

'What have we missed,' said Geraldine, coming over with Roger, Pam, Vi and Olwyn to join Sarah and the others.

'Not much,' Sarah assured her mum.

'We came in the Valley Vistas minibus,' Geraldine said. 'It felt like being on a school trip.'

'Except with booze,' added Pam, taking her silver flask out of her bag. She took a swig, then passed it to Vi.

'Take two,' called Kirsty, her voice weary. It had been a long day – and night.

The actors did the scene again. Still, Noa wasn't satisfied.

'Come on!' he shouted at the actors. 'This is supposed to be a *happy* scene. For God's sake, ACT HAPPY.'

Sarah winced at the director's harsh tone, feeling sorry for Mateo and Mia.

'It would probably be easier to do that if he wasn't keeping the cast and crew away from their families on Christmas Eve,' muttered Sam.

They did the scene a third time. It was going well, until right in the middle of Mateo's big declaration of love, there was a loud beeping noise.

'CUT!' bellowed Noa. 'Where the hell is that noise coming from?'

The insistent beeping was coming from right near Sarah.

'Whoopsie! I am sorry,' said Pam, fumbling in her handbag. 'That's me. I set an alarm on my phone to remind me to take my blood-pressure medication.' She jabbed at the screen of her phone, but the alarm continued beeping.

'TURN THAT FUCKING THING OFF!' Noa screamed at her.

'Oh, deary me . . .' Pam got more and more flustered, pressing buttons to no avail.

'Here, let me help,' said James. He quickly turned the alarm off.

Noah's assistant attempted to pacify him, but he just swore and pushed her away.

Sarah frowned. Over the past few weeks she'd seen that Noa was a control freak, and that he could be extremely demanding. She'd accepted it as part of the creative process that had won him many awards. But this behaviour was completely out of line. He couldn't treat people like this.

'What a rude man,' said Vi disapprovingly.

'He should wash his mouth out with soap,' agreed Olwyn.

'Thank you so much,' said Pam, as James handed her back the phone – now switched to silent. 'I don't know what we'll do when the cinema is gone, James, and we can't come to your repair shop after Golden Oldies.'

'What do you mean?' asked Sarah.

'When we organised the minibus this evening, the director of Valley Vistas mentioned you were thinking of selling the cinema.'

Sarah slowly turned to face her husband. 'What is she talking about?'

'Oh, dear,' said Pam. 'Have I put my foot in it?'

'It was just an enquiry,' James told Sarah. 'I thought it would be good to consider our options. In light of our . . . er . . . situation.'

Sarah's heart started to pound. She felt like she was going to be sick. Sure, things had been bad between her and James. They'd both said some terrible things when they'd argued. She had been sulking since then, but she'd assumed they would make up eventually. That things would get better when the film crew moved out and life went back to normal. Did James really think their relationship was over? Was their love not worth fighting for?

'W-why would you do that?' Tears clouded Sarah's vision. 'Don't I have a say in the matter?'

'Well, we both know it's not working—'

Sarah couldn't bear it any more; her heart was breaking. She ran into the cinema before she broke down in front of nearly everyone in Plumdale.

The lobby was mercifully empty, as the cast and crew were all filming outside. Sarah went into the office and threw herself onto the sofa — and then the tears came.

It was over. James had given up on them. Thirty years of marriage down the drain.

'Oh, Sarah,' said her mother, coming into the office and sitting down beside her. Geraldine gathered Sarah into her arms and let her weep. 'I know,' she said soothingly, stroking her daughter's back. 'I remember how tough it was being your age. It gets easier, I promise. You've been pushing yourself too hard.'

'It's not that.' Sarah sobbed into her mother's shoulder. 'It's me and James. Things have fallen apart.'

'I'm sure it's nothing you can't fix.' Geraldine handed Sarah a tissue.

'James has obviously given up on us.' She wiped her nose and sniffed. 'You'll probably be happy if we split up. You've never approved of my marriage anyway.'

'Sarah,' said Geraldine, shaking her head. 'How can you say that? True, I'm no fan of the institution of marriage. But I'm a fan of James because he *adores* you – anyone can see that.'

'Then why is he trying to sell the cinema behind my back?' wailed Sarah.

'I don't know,' replied Geraldine, taking her hand. 'But I think you should give him a chance to explain.'

28th October 2022

Nick sat at a table with his classmates Ollie, Abby and Grace. Their Year Six class was drawing pictures of the things they'd gathered earlier in the week on a nature walk – deep crimson maple leaves, golden beech leaves, glossy brown chestnuts and a silvery blue feather.

'Psst!' said Grace.

Nick looked up from his drawing.

'I'm having a Halloween party and you're all invited,' whispered Grace. 'We're going to play games and bob for apples, and I'm going to make spooky snacks.'

'Cool,' said Ollie.

Abby giggled excitedly. 'I can't wait!'

Nick smiled, masking his apprehension. When he was little, he had hated parties. His mum usually had to come and pick him up early. It wouldn't take much – just a balloon popping, loud music or a strange smell – to set him off. Now that he was eleven he was better at dealing with those situations. He still found new environments stressful, but Mum had taught him different coping strategies – like taking a time-out if he started to feel overwhelmed. He would take deep breaths and focus on three objects, three sounds and move three body parts. That usually calmed him down. When he got home, he would spend time alone in his room stroking Jonesy. It helped him relax. Mum said that Nick was like a mobile phone – his social battery needed recharging when he ran out of juice.

'My mum said we can watch a horror movie,' said Grace.

Nick felt his stomach twist. He *hated* horror movies. He didn't like watching anything with blood and guts. Even though he knew movies weren't real, violence on screen made him upset.

'My big brother showed me an old movie called *The Exorcist*. It was about a girl who gets possessed by a demon. Her head spins around!' Ollie rolled his eyes and moved his head around comically, making the others giggle. 'I wasn't even scared a bit,' he boasted.

'I might not stay for the movie,' said Nick. He hoped his friends wouldn't think he was a wimp.

'That's OK,' said Grace. 'I bet you'll have the best Halloween costume.'

Nick loved making things. The Viking ship he'd made last year was still on display in his teacher's classroom. When his Year Six class had dressed up for World War Two day, Nick had painstakingly created a gas-mask box for his evacuee costume.

'What are you going to be?' asked Ollie.

'I haven't decided yet.' Nick had lots of ideas – he just wasn't sure which one to go for.

Last year for Halloween, he and Dad had dressed up as Ghostbusters for a special screening at the cinema. Dad had helped him make a costume, using an old vacuum cleaner as a proton pack. Even though *Ghostbusters* was quite scary (there were some parts Nick had to close his eyes for, and cover his ears), it was also very funny.

'I'm going to be a vampire cheerleader,' said Abby.

'I'm being a zombie,' said Ollie. He stuck his arms out in front of him and moaned like a zombie.

Everyone at the table giggled.

'Is there something you'd like to share with the class, Ollie?' asked their teacher, Miss Pearce.

'No, Miss,' said Ollie. He bent his head and resumed colouring.

The break-time bell rang. Raindrops pattered against the window of the classroom and puddles had formed on the playing field. Rivulets of water streamed down the slide in the playground.

'We're not going out today, children,' said Miss Pearce.

'Aww!' chorused Nick's classmates in disappointment.

Yes! thought Nick.

'I wanted to go outside and play football' grumbled Ollie.

'Me too,' said Grace.

Nick liked wet play because everyone had to talk in indoor voices, so it wasn't as noisy as being out in the playground. Best of all, this year he was a wet-play monitor.

'See you after break.' Nick waved goodbye to his friends and hurried down the corridor to the infants' wing.

Only the most responsible and well-behaved Year Sixes were chosen to be wet-play monitors. Whenever the weather was too bad to go outside, they helped supervise the younger kids. Nick was assigned to Miss Varma's reception class. The bright and cheerful classroom hadn't changed much since he was in Reception. Colourful finger paintings hung from a string that stretched across the classroom. An alphabet decorated with animals and a behaviour ladder with gold stars hung on the wall. Plastic trays held reading books and there was a strong, but not unpleasant, smell of glue.

'Ah, here's Nick,' said Miss Varma, smiling at him as he entered the room. 'You know the rules for wet play – no running and use your indoor voices.'

It had been a rainy autumn so he'd helped out a few times already. The kids were happy to see him again.

'Nick! Nick!' called some children, waving him over to the home corner. 'Come to our café.'

The home corner had a pretend kitchen, with an oven and a sink, and baskets of wooden food. Nick sat down at the little table, feeling like a giant on the tiny chair.

'Hold my baby,' said a little girl, thrusting a doll in his arms.

'What's for dinner?' Nick asked.

A boy wearing an apron and a chef's hat was pretending to fry something in a pan. A girl with her hair in bunches set down a plate with a plastic banana on it in front of Nick.

'Oh, this looks good.' Nick pretended to nibble the banana. Then he offered some to the baby doll.

The little girl giggled.

Nearby, there was a sand table. Two boys were enthusiastically digging a tunnel for their toy truck, sending sand flying everywhere.

Nick jumped up to intervene before the classroom was engulfed by a sandstorm. 'Try to keep the sand inside the table.' He swept up the sand that had fallen on the floor and went to put it in the bin by Miss Varma's desk.

As he did, Nick noticed a little boy playing by himself with a wooden train set. He had brown hair and wore headphones over his ears. He'd noticed the kid before – always playing with the trains. Always by himself . . .

'Elliot is autistic,' Miss Varma told him quietly. 'He's very bright but is finding school a bit overwhelming.'

'Is he listening to music?'

'No, the headphones block out background noise,' explained Miss Varma. 'It helps him stay calm.'

Nick remembered how noisy and chaotic he'd found the classroom when he'd first started school. He'd dreaded school dinners in the hall, the smells making him queasy and the clattering cutlery giving him a headache. The playground was even worse, with kids rushing about shouting.

'Elliot hasn't made any friends yet,' confided Miss Varma.

That made Nick feel sad. It was lonely being the odd one out.

He went over to Elliot and crouched down to speak to him.

'Hi, Elliot,' he said softly. He wasn't sure if the boy would be able to hear him with the headphones on.

'Hello,' said Elliot, never taking his eyes off the train he was playing with.

'Is that a locomotive?' asked Nick.

'No,' replied Elliot, not meeting his eye. 'It is a shunter. It takes the engine off the train.' He picked up a different train. 'This is the hopper. It can carry over one hundred tonnes of freight.'

'Wow,' said Nick.

Elliot ran the train along the wooden tracks. He pointed to each of the train carriages in turn and told Nick what type it was and exactly what function it had. The little boy was a walking encyclopaedia of train facts.

'This is a diesel train,' said Elliot. 'It only goes two hundred kilometres per hour. The fastest train in the world went 574.8 kilometres per hour on the third of April 2007.'

'You know a lot about trains,' said Nick. 'Have you ever seen the movie *The Polar Express*?'

The animated movie was based on a children's book that Nora and Simon had given him for Christmas when he was little.

Elliot shook his head.

'I bet you'd really like it,' said Nick. 'It's about a boy named Billy who goes on a magical train ride to the North Pole and gets to meet Santa Claus. Santa gives him a bell you can only hear if you believe in Santa.'

Some people in Nick's class said that Santa Claus wasn't real and that people who believed in him were babyish. Ollie said that he'd caught his mum putting presents under the tree last Christmas Eve. Nick had asked Dad if Santa Claus was real, unsure if he wanted to know the truth. Dad had thought for a while before replying. 'Well, Saint Nicholas was a real person. He lived in Turkey during the Roman Empire.'

Nick frowned, not satisfied with Dad's answer. A lot of things about Santa just didn't add up. Nick had seen reindeer at the Cotswold Wildlife Park, and he just couldn't understand how they could carry a sleigh loaded with enough toys for the whole world – even if there were eight of them.

'But how can Santa Claus possibly travel all over the world in just one night?' He'd looked up how long it would take for a plane to fly around the globe – forty-four hours, and that was without any stops.

'You're right,' Dad said. 'Nobody can prove that.'

'So you *don't* believe in Santa?'

'On the contrary,' Dad replied. 'I *do* believe in Santa. But I think Santa is an idea, rather than a person. Every time you do something kind for someone – and don't expect anything back – Santa is real. You know that lovely feeling you get inside when you do something nice for someone else?'

Nick nodded.

'*That*'s the real Christmas magic,' Dad said. 'That's Santa Claus at work.'

That explanation was good enough for Nick.

Elliot attached a carriage to the back of the locomotive. 'I don't like going to the cinema. Movies are too noisy. They make my head hurt.'

'I used to feel that way too,' admitted Nick. He still did sometimes. Even though he was a kid himself, he despised the Saturday morning Kids' Club screenings at the cinema.

The bell rang. Not Santa's Christmas bell – but the end of playtime bell.

'You'd better get back to class, Nick,' said Miss Varma.

As he went back to his classroom, Nick thought how sad it was that Elliot didn't like going to the cinema. The little boy could watch *The Polar Express* on television, but that wasn't the same as watching a movie on a big screen. Dad always said that it was only in a cinema that you saw a movie the way that the director wanted it to be seen.

But, most of all, seeing a movie in a cinema was a shared experience. Nick responded to stories intensely. He liked knowing that other people sitting there in the dark were feeling the same things as him. Elliot shouldn't miss out on that experience, just because of his sensory-processing issues.

A few days later, Nick tried on his Halloween costume in his bedroom. He had decided to go to the party as Luffy, a character from the *One Piece* manga series. He was wearing Mum's straw hat, a red waistcoat from the back of Dad's wardrobe and a pair of old jeans he'd cut off at the knee. He added Holly's yellow scarf as a sash around his waist. Perfect – he looked just like the captain of the Straw Hat Pirates.

Nick had become obsessed with manga after Pam, the local librarian, had suggested he might like it. Most of his classmates had never heard of *One Piece*. But Nick was OK with being different.

Luckily, Nick's family never made him feel like he had to change or follow the herd. Holly teased him sometimes, but Nick knew his big sister loved him and always had his back. When he'd been in Reception, and was struggling to make friends like Elliot, Holly had made sure nobody picked on him in the playground.

'If you mess with my little brother, I'll mess with you,' she'd warned the other kids fiercely.

'Come on, Nick,' called Mum. 'We need to go and collect Grandma from the station.'

Nick quickly changed out of his costume and hurried downstairs. He was excited to see his grandmother, because she always told interesting stories about her travels around the world. She hadn't travelled anywhere since the pandemic, though, because of her health problems.

The countryside was ablaze with autumn colour as they drove to the station. The leaves on the trees made Nick think of crayon colours – Antique Brass, Raw Sienna, Brick Red and Burnt Orange. As they drove along, Holly sang the songs from *Hairspray*. She was playing one of the lead parts, so everyone had to listen to her practising all the time. It made a welcome change from the *Hamilton* soundtrack.

Mum lowered her window a bit. The wind whistling through the gap made Nick's ears hurt. He couldn't tune out the sound. 'Can you put the window back up?' said Nick.

'Yeah,' said Holly. 'It's cold.'

'That's odd. I'm absolutely boiling.' Mum put the window back up and wriggled out of her jacket.

'Maybe you're coming down with something.' Dad gave Mum a worried look as she flapped her top around to create a breeze.

Mum groaned. 'I hope not. I've booked a tour of Valley Vistas for this afternoon.'

'Does Geraldine know that?' asked Dad.

'No,' replied Mum. 'But I'm sure she'll love it. Pam and Vi say it's a great place to live and designed for accessibility.'

'Hmm,' said Dad. 'I can't see Geraldine agreeing to a care home – she's so independent.'

'It's *not* a care home,' Mum corrected him. 'It's a retirement village. She can still be totally independent. I'd just feel a lot better if she was living nearby.'

Nick could feel the worry in his mother's voice. When Grandma had been ill with Covid, he'd been scared that she would die.

'I'll come with you,' said Holly. 'I bet I can help persuade Grandma. I'll tell her that if she moves to Plumdale, she can see more of her favourite grandchild.' She put her hands under her chin and struck a pose, fluttering her eyelashes.

'You mean me,' said Nick.

'In your dreams,' teased Holly.

'I think your cousin Marcus might be her favourite,' said Mum, as Dad pulled into the station car park. 'He's doing a degree in anthropology.' Their older cousin and his siblings lived in Edinburgh, so they didn't see much of them.

As they waited on the platform for the train from Bristol, an express train whooshed past on the other side of the tracks. Nick suddenly thought of Elliot, the boy in Reception who loved trains. And then he had a brilliant idea . . .

'There's a little kid in Reception who has autism,' Nick told the others. 'He says he doesn't like going to the cinema because it's scary.'

'That was like you when you were little,' said Holly. 'Remember when you freaked out when we saw *Spider-Man* in France – that was totally embarrassing.'

Nick didn't remember that time, but there had been lots of other movies that had upset him when he was little.

'Could we maybe do special screenings at the cinema for people like Elliot and me?' Nick asked his parents.

Dad looked puzzled. 'How do you mean?'

'Well . . . we could keep the lights on low during the movie,' suggested Nick. 'And make sure the volume is quieter than usual.'

Dad stroked the stubble on his jaw thoughtfully. 'That would be easy enough to arrange . . .'

'And people could get up and leave if they need to,' said Nick, getting more and more excited about his idea.

'People can do that anyway,' Mum pointed out.

Nick thought about all the times he'd had to take a time-out. He always felt self-conscious when he got up and left. 'Yeah, but at special sensory-friendly screenings people wouldn't have to feel embarrassed about disturbing everyone else in the audience.'

'True,' agreed Mum.

'And we would only show *nice* movies,' added Nick. 'Nothing that will upset people.'

Holly frowned. 'Different people get upset by different things. I hate spiders, but you don't mind them.'

Whenever there was a spider in Holly's room or in the bathtub, she made Nick get rid of it. He would trap it under a cup and let it out in the garden.

'Maybe we can provide content warnings,' said Mum. 'So people know in advance what to expect.'

'So can we do all that?' asked Nick hopefully.

Mum and Dad looked at each other and then nodded.

'It's a wonderful idea,' said Dad. 'Cinema should be for everyone.'

Mum gave Nick a hug. 'I'm so proud of you, sweetheart. I wish we'd thought of this ourselves when you were little.'

'Yeah, it's a really good idea, Nick.' Holly tousled her brother's hair affectionately.

'Did you have any ideas about what movies we should show?' asked Mum.

Nick grinned. He knew exactly what the first movie should be. '*The Polar Express.*'

He couldn't wait to tell Elliot about the sensory-friendly screening the next time he saw him at school. And perhaps he was imagining it, but Nick thought he could hear Santa's bell ringing in the distance.

Chapter 12

Present Day

The church bells rang out over the village square at eight o'clock. James had had enough. He could feel the muscle in his cheek twitching. He ducked under the yellow tape that had been erected to keep the onlookers off the set.

'Hey,' said an assistant in a hi-vis jacket. 'Only cast and crew are allowed on set.'

Ignoring him, James marched over to Noa. 'It's eight o'clock. You need to wrap things up here. Our film festival screening begins at nine.'

'We're done when I say we're done,' said Noa, not looking away from the footage he was reviewing on a monitor. 'I'm filming a major motion picture here, OK? People can watch an old movie any time.'

'No,' said James, fighting to keep his voice even. 'I'm afraid that's not OK. We had an agreement and you have violated it. You and your crew need to leave.'

He couldn't stop Noa from luring his wife to Hollywood. It was no competition – hands down Noa could offer her more than James ever could. Nor could James stop the director from being mean to nice old ladies, or being a jerk to his cast and crew. But he could sure as heck kick him off his property.

'I think you should show me a bit more gratitude, Jim.' There was a warning in Noa's voice, despite the phony smile on his face. He gestured at the choir. 'I let your wannabe daughter be in the film – but I can just as easily cut her out. I threw your wife a lifeline and rescued her failed career – but I can make sure she never works in this industry again.' Noa took a step closer so he and James were practically nose to nose. 'And I saved your pathetic little cinema from going bust. So I'll keep filming here for as long as I damn please. NOW GET OFF MY SET.' The threat in the director's voice was no longer veiled.

'No,' stated James calmly. He gestured at the crowd of spectators. 'These people have come to see a movie and I'm not going to let them down.'

Noa laughed mirthlessly. 'I have two Golden Globes. I'm not going to let a loser from a nothing little town tell me what to do.'

James stood his ground, ignoring Noa's insult. He had something far more important than any award: friends.

'He is not a loser,' said Geraldine, coming out of the city followed by Sarah. 'And this isn't a nothing little town. It's a community.' She ripped the yellow tape down and marched forward onto the set.

'Get off my set, you old bat!' shouted Noa.

'We don't have Golden Globes, but we're the Golden Oldies,' said Roger, joining Geraldine in solidarity with James. 'And we love the Picture Palace.'

Linking arms, Pam, Vi and Olwyn stepped forward as well.

'Come on, everybody!' shouted Geraldine, turning to the rest of the onlookers. 'Are you going to let this Hollywood big shot push us around?'

'Let's go!' said Nick, pulling the twins onto the set.

Iris and Sam downed their glasses of mulled wine and crossed the barrier too.

'Get those idiots out of here!' Noa shrieked at his crew.

'That's your *audience*,' said James. 'Or have you forgotten who you make movies for?'

'I don't make movies!' said Noa. 'I make ART.'

'Well, you're going to have to make art elsewhere,' said James. Then he walked over to the generator and pulled out the plug. Suddenly, all the lights on the film set went out.

Noa let out a bellow of fury. 'I'm going to kill you!' He charged at James, his perfect white teeth bared in a furious grimace.

'Dad!' shouted Holly.

'James!' he heard Sarah cry.

Out of the corner of his eye, James could see his son running towards him. 'No, Nick!' he called out. He didn't want his son to get hurt.

Noa drew back his arm to punch James, but before he could land a blow the director suddenly pitched forward and face-planted onto the pavement, right at James's feet.

'Oops,' said Nick, holding up the end of the cable he'd just tripped Noa up with.

'I told him those were a trip hazard,' said James, winking at his son.

Noa staggered to his feet, blood streaming from his nose. One of his front teeth had chipped in the fall. His perfect smile was gone.

'Get my car brought round!' he screamed at Aaron.

'Get it yourself,' Aaron fired back. 'Holly is no wannabe – she's going to be a star.'

Noa sneered. 'You ingrate. If you'd played your cards right, I might have hired you one day.'

'I don't want to work for you,' said Aaron. 'You're a bully. I'm going to tell the whole world how badly you treat your cast and crew.'

'You wouldn't dare,' said Noa, wiping blood off his face with the back of his hand. 'I will destroy you.'

'It would be worth it,' replied Aaron, coming over to stand by James.

Mia Winslow stepped forward. 'I'll speak out too,' she said. 'I'll tell people how you forced me to take my top off at my audition. And how you've been harassing me ever since we started filming all because I refused to sleep with you.'

Mateo went over to his co-star. 'I'm sorry, Mia. I had no idea that was going on.' He looked at the director with contempt. 'People like you give this industry a bad name.'

'Might I remind you that every single person on this set has signed an NDA,' said Noa. 'I have a team of lawyers on retainer and will sue anyone who speaks out.'

'I didn't sign anything,' said Pam. 'And silly old me – I seem to have been accidentally filming this the whole time.' She held up her phone. 'Now, as you saw earlier, I'm not very good with technology, but James is. I'm sure he can show me how to send my little movie to journalists who might be interested in how you treat your cast and crew.'

Noa went to grab the phone, but Pam's friends formed a protective circle around her.

The director spun around to glare at his leading actors. 'I'll be in touch with your agents – don't think you're going to get away with this.'

'Pari will look forward your call,' said Mateo.

James knew Pari, more than most, would relish taking down a bully. She'd certainly encountered plenty of them during her comedy career.

'Without me, there's no movie,' said Noa threateningly.

'Don't be so sure about that,' called Kirsty from behind a camera. 'I'm sure I can finish making *Ex-mas Eve*. I've been doing most of the hard work anyway.'

'You can't do this!' howled Noa, as more blood trickled out of his nose. 'I have an Oscar!'

'Yes, that's true,' said James. 'But it would appear that you no longer have a cast or crew.'

Looking increasingly desperate, Noa tried a different tack. 'OK, I get it,' he wheedled. 'I know I've been tough on everyone. To show you what a good guy I am, I'll give you all a Christmas bonus if you carry on working. Who's with me?' He looked around expectantly.

Nobody stepped forward.

Noa let out a scream of frustration. 'You're all making a huge mistake!'

Everyone cheered as he stormed off the set.

Holly ran over to Aaron. 'That. Was. Epic.'

James smiled as his daughter threw her arms around Aaron's neck and kissed him.

'That's a wrap, folks,' called Kirsty as everyone cheered.

'Come on inside.' James beckoned everyone into the cinema. 'It's time for the movie.'

Laughing and talking, everyone with tickets for the screening started making their way into the cinema as the crew began packing up their equipment.

James started to follow the crowd inside, when someone tugged lightly on his arm.

'Can we talk?' Sarah asked him.

The cinema was packed with people, so James and Sarah went up to the projection room to get some privacy. There wasn't much in the tiny room apart from the projector and the new sound system, which had been installed days before.

'That was so brave of you,' said Sarah.

'You're not upset about what I did?' asked James.

'Not at all.' Sarah shook her head. 'I only wish I had seen through Noa's charm sooner and called out his bad behaviour myself. I let myself be swept away by the excitement of writing again.'

Sarah had met plenty of people like Noa at the Beeb, who abused their power just because they could. It was depressing that that sort of behaviour was still going on in the entertainment business.

'I'm sorry it took me so long to notice how much you missed writing,' said James. 'I didn't realise because I've been so wrapped up in the cinema. I didn't want it to be a failure because you put all your faith in me. I was desperate for it to be a success.'

'It *is* a success,' insisted Sarah, taking his hand. 'People love this place – you heard them tonight.'

James looked down at the audience filing into the auditorium. 'Yes, but it hasn't been worth it if it's been making *you* unhappy.'

'I *was* unhappy,' admitted Sarah. 'I'd been feeling lost, what with menopause and the kids growing up. I wasn't sure of my place in the world any more, and felt my life and dreams slipping away from me. But one thing has never changed: I've never stopped loving you, James.'

'I thought I'd lost you,' said James. 'I thought you were going to leave me and go live in LA with Noa in some massive mansion with a swimming pool and a private chef to make you both kale smoothies and quinoa salads on demand.'

'You know I hate kale.'

James laughed. He stroked the back of Sarah's hand with his thumb. 'I would understand if you wanted to take the job, you know. He's a jerk, but he can open doors for you.'

'Are you kidding? I don't want to work with Noa,' said Sarah. 'Even before tonight, I'd already decided that.'

She placed her hand tenderly on her husband's cheek and stroked it. 'I love writing movies – but I want to tell my own stories, not somebody else's.'

'That's why I was considering selling the cinema,' said James. 'To make that possible. To free you – *us* – from the burden of running it.'

'You're not the only one who loves this place, James,' said Sarah, the golden flecks in her eyes glittering with emotion. 'Plumdale needs the Picture Palace, and so do we.'

Owning a cinema was hard work. Over the years, they'd had to use all their ingenuity to find ways to keep it going. There had been plenty of tough times, but they were greatly outweighed by the good times.

A bit like their marriage.

'But the cinema's held you back all these years,' said James.

'I don't think it has, actually,' said Sarah. She'd been reflecting on this a lot over the past few weeks, as she worked on the script and watched the film-festival movies. She might have believed that in the past, but not any more. 'All those films we've shown here over the years – even the terrible ones – have taught me so much about cinema, and the craft of storytelling. The reason I struggled to finish anything before was that I wasn't ready. Now I am.'

She was going to rework *The Ghost Writer* and had already started. Instead of making the heroine a girl in her twenties, she was going to make her a middle-aged woman, like herself. Someone who had been through a lot in life – but still believed in the healing power of love. And once she was finished with that, she'd write another screenplay. Her mind was fizzing with the stories she wanted to tell. Stories about ordinary people, inspired by her friends in Plumdale. Every one of them was an everyday hero, whose story deserved to be shared.

James looked at her, his eyes shining with pride. 'I believe in you, Sarah. And I am so, so proud of you.'

How could she have ever doubted that he wanted the best for her?

Just then, the projector came to life. The cinema's curtains drew open with a swoosh and the advertisements began to play.

'You've been telling a story too,' said Sarah, smiling at him. 'The story of our life together. That's what the film festival has been all about, hasn't it? Celebrating all the special moments that we've shared.'

'I wasn't sure if you realised. . .' said James.

She had figured it out while watching *An Affair to Remember*. Suddenly, she'd understood why James had chosen all of those films. He'd curated a history of their love in movies, just for her. 'It was the nicest Christmas gift anyone has ever given me.'

'Oh, Sarah . . .' James reached for her.

She wrapped her arms around his neck and kissed him with as much passion as she'd felt the first time their lips had locked outside the Prince Charles cinema, on another Christmas Eve long ago. Cinemas had been the setting for their love story, and none was more special than the Picture Palace. Sarah would never want to give it up.

From their eyrie in the projection booth, Sarah looked down at the audience. Iris was sitting with Sam and Mateo, who was studiously ignoring all the sneaky selfies the other movie-goers were taking. She supposed he must be used to it.

'Oh, look, there's Kath,' said James.

Accompanied by her girlfriend and her dad, the politician was making her way to her seat, shaking hands with her constituents with one hand, while holding a bag of sweets with the other.

Sarah spotted Nick sitting with his new friends, laughing and throwing popcorn at each other.

It wasn't just the youngsters in high spirits – Geraldine and the other Golden Oldies were sitting together, surreptitiously passing Pam's flask around.

Ian and Hermione came into the auditorium holding hands, looking blissfully content.

'Looks like Holly and Aaron weren't the only couple to fall in love this Christmas,' said Sarah happily. There was no sign of her daughter and her new boyfriend, and Sarah decided not to think about where they were – or what they might be doing! Aaron had been incredibly heroic tonight and she'd seen how much he cared about Holly. Enough to stand up to a famous and powerful director. They had her blessing, not that they needed it. Holly was old enough to follow her own heart. Whatever the outcome of her romance, Sarah would be there for her – the way her mother had always been there for her.

Finally, it was time for the feature presentation. As romantic music played, the film opened on a shot of Chicago skyscrapers and a train squealing along an elevated track. Sandra Bullock and Bill Pullman's names appeared and then the title – *While You Were Sleeping*.

Of course, thought Sarah. It couldn't have been anything else but the film they'd seen the night they first found each other, two lonely singletons who loved movies. Her heart swelling with love, Sarah snuggled against James and thought how lucky they were to have found each other once again.

'Hark! The herald angels sing!' sang the audience as Olwyn accompanied them on the cinema organ. There was always a carol sing-along after the final Christmas movie. Olwyn brought her organ concert to a conclusion with a rousing rendition of 'We Wish You a Merry Christmas'.

Sarah and James had gone downstairs to join in the carols and indulge in some mulled wine and mince pies. Sarah knew how blessed she was to have her family – both real and found – with her tonight.

'The new sound system sounded amazing,' Roger remarked, jangling a collection bucket for the refugee charity in France. Sarah added some coins to the bucket.

'I see Holly and her young man have finally got together,' said Geraldine, peering at them through her red-framed glasses.

Sarah followed her mother's gaze to where Holly and Aaron were kissing under a sprig of mistletoe.

Nick pulled a face. 'Ugh! They should get a room.' Then he ran off with the twins to get more mince pies.

Geraldine nodded sagely. 'Indeed the Zulu people of South Africa build special courting huts so young couples can have a private place to be intimate.'

'They can use the garden shed to canoodle,' suggested James. 'Although my bike takes up a lot of the room in there.'

'I bet you wish you were going somewhere exotic for Christmas, Mum,' said Sarah. Geraldine was staying in Plumdale this year, because Meg's family had decided to visit her dad in Spain.

'Oh, I don't know,' said Geraldine. 'Plumdale is growing on me. I think I'm going to be very happy here.'

Sarah took her mother's hand. It was bony and covered in age spots, but her grip was strong – as was her love.

'Happy Christmas, Mum,' she said. 'I'm so glad you're here too.'

Eventually, the audience started to drift home, to fill stockings, leave mince pies out for Santa and put presents under the tree, which they'd finally put a few nights earlier. It had snowed while the film had been playing – *real* snow. It sparkled brightly under the neon light of the cinema marquee. Holly and Nick had walked ahead, their daughter's arm slung affectionately over her not-so-little brother's shoulder.

'What if you hadn't got the time wrong?' said Sarah as James locked up the cinema door. 'If you didn't end up seeing *While You Were Sleeping,* we never would have met that day.' She still had the ticket stub tucked into an old diary. She'd known even back then that it was a special night – that the cute film buff was going to play the leading man in her life.

'Oh, we would have met,' said James confidently. 'At some other movie. At some other cinema. On some other day.'

'How can you be so sure?' asked Sarah.

'Because we're soulmates,' replied James. Putting an arm around her shoulder, he gestured up at the stars twinkling in the night sky. 'It was written in the stars.'

If it had been a movie, violin music would have begun to swell. The camera would pan out over the snow-dusted village and the credits would begin to roll. But James and Sarah's love story wasn't a movie and it wasn't ending here. This was just one more scene in their story. Because sometimes, real life was even better than the movies.

Epilogue

Two Years Later

'This is Goldie Johnson for Entertainment News reporting from the Plumdale Picture Palace where the world premiere of *The Ghostwriter* is taking place tonight.' The reporter, wearing a sparkly gown, stood in the cinema lobby speaking into a microphone as a cameraman filmed. 'With me are screenwriter, Sarah O'Hara, and the film's director, Hollywood heartthrob, Mateo Ajose.'

I can't believe this is really happening, thought Sarah, smiling at the camera. She was wearing a slinky green silk dress with the white scarf her mother had given her as a wedding present draped around her shoulders.

Goldie turned to Mateo. 'Why did you chose *The Ghostwriter* for your directorial debut?' She held out her microphone to him.

'Firstly, because it's such a great script,' replied Mateo, smiling at Sarah. 'But also because it's set in the Cotswolds, which is my adopted home.'

Sarah glanced across the lobby, where Mateo's wife was standing with the Wus. Iris and Sam were both sporting large baby bumps – their due dates were within weeks of each other. For the past year, Iris had been teaching art at the high school and Sarah knew Nick would miss her while she was on maternity leave.

'We had such a lot of fun making this movie. It showcases the best of British independent cinema,' continued Mateo.

Most of the filming had taken place in and around Plumdale and Stowford. Sarah had visited the set several times and it couldn't have been more different to *Ex-mas Eve*. The film's budget had been much smaller, but, unlike Noa, Mateo had fostered a relaxed and collaborative atmosphere on set. The only tears shed were those required by the script.

'And I believe the two of you worked together once before, on *Ex-Mas Eve*,' said the reporter.

Sarah and Mateo exchanged knowing glances and nodded diplomatically.

Ex-mas Eve had been a modest box-office hit. Sarah and James had screened it as one of their film-festival movies last Christmas, and, although it wasn't likely to stand the test of time, Sarah had enjoyed it. As for Noa, his reputation had been tarnished so badly within the industry, that the only thing he'd directed recently was a soft-drink advertisement.

'So what's the movie about, Sarah?' asked Goldie.

'It's a ghost story that's also a love story,' explained Sarah. 'But mostly it's about the importance of finding your voice.'

Over the past two years, encouraged by her friends and family, Sarah had definitely found her own voice. In addition to *The Ghostwriter*, she'd finished two other screenplays – one of which had been optioned by a Hollywood production company. Nicole Kidman had even been mentioned as a potential star.

'And I hear there's another British director making their debut tonight,' said the reporter.

'That's right,' replied Sarah, nodding. 'We're showing a short film by a talented young filmmaker named Aaron Armstrong.'

Aaron, who was now studying film in London, had made the short as part of his course. He'd cast Holly as the lead, with Ian, Hermione and various other local residents playing supporting roles. He'd even convinced Geraldine to make her acting debut!

'One last question for Mateo – are the rumours you'll be the next James Bond true?' asked Goldie.

In his tux, Mateo certainly looked the part already.

He smiled mysteriously. 'You'd have to ask my agent.' Pari, who was standing just out of shot, winked at him.

When the interview was over, she came over and gave Sarah a hug. 'My favourite client – and this time I really mean it.'

'I couldn't have done it without you.' Sarah knew how lucky she was to have Pari in her corner. Her best friend had been encouraging her to write ever since they'd worked together at the BBC.

As Pari chatted with Mateo, Sarah headed across the lobby to find her family and friends, who were waiting for her in the café area.

"Hello, beautiful. You look like you should be starring in the movie," said James, handing her a glass of champagne.

Sarah adjusted his bowtie and gave him a kiss. 'You look very handsome too.'

'People are saying that the Cotswolds are the new Hollywood,' said James.

Sarah sipped her champagne and chuckled. 'I'm not sure I'd go that far.'

"Well, I don't want to alarm you, but there's a rumour going round that they're adding quinoa to the menu at the Fox and Hounds," teased James.

Sarah didn't want Plumdale to become like Hollywood – it was perfect just how it was. She'd flown out to LA with Pari to meet various producers, but had been happy to return home. This was where she belonged, surrounded by her loved ones.

Sarah gestured at the walls of the café where framed illustrations were on display. 'Nick's artwork looks wonderful.'

Under Iris's guidance, their son had experimented with new styles of illustration. Iris had encouraging him to think about applying to art college after finishing high school.

Nick, who was sneaking sips of champagne with Aaron and Julia, was now nearly as tall as his dad, with a hint of wispy facial hair above his lip. Nick and Julia had collaborated on several more volumes of their manga, which Nora and Simon stocked at their bookshop.

'We've sold out of your latest volume,' Simon told Nick.

'Our customers keep asking us when the next one will be out,' said Nora.

Nick held up his ink-stained fingers. 'We're working on it.' He and Julia were saving the money they earned in hopes of travelling to Japan together one day.

Geraldine came over to Sarah and kissed her on the cheek. 'Congratulations, darling. I always knew you had it in you – although you sure took your time.'

Sarah rolled her eyes. 'Thanks, Mum.'

At a nearby table, Holly was perched on Aaron's lap, chatting to her co-stars, Hermione and Ian. Holly had raided Sarah's wardrobe and was wearing the cheongsam she'd bought in Hong Kong years ago. Sarah didn't mind – it fit her daughter's willowy figure perfectly.

'I'm not the only one who deserves congratulations,' Sarah told her mother. 'Holly has some happy news too.'

'No!' cried Geraldine. 'You're only eighteen! That's far too young to get married, Holly. Have I told you about the Mosuo tribe—'

'Chill, Grandma.' Holly laughed. 'We're not getting married. I got offered a place at RADA.'

Everyone laughed as Geraldine gave an exaggerated sigh of relief, then went over to hug her granddaughter.

Sarah wouldn't be surprised if Holly and Aaron *did* end up getting married one day. Any qualms she'd had about her daughter's relationship had long been forgotten. Their love had lasted even after Aaron had gone to university, and having a boyfriend hadn't distracted Holly from pursuing her own dreams. She'd gone through several rounds of gruelling auditions to secure her drama-school place.

'Well, Holly might not be getting married . . .' said Hermione coyly, holding out her left hand, where a vintage diamond ring sparkled on her finger. 'But I am – Ian proposed!'

Everyone cheered and crowded around to congratulate the happy couple.

Sarah wasn't surprised; they'd been joined at the hip ever since filming *Ex-mas Eve* together. A few months earlier, they'd merged their shops and opened Cotswolds Interiors, selling antique furniture and home decor. It had been featured in the *Sunday Times* magazine, illustrated with a glamorous spread of Hermione lounging on a divan.

'We're getting married at Merricourt Manor in the spring,' announced Ian. 'And you're all invited.'

Sarah leaned her head against James's shoulder, remembering their own wedding day. 'That's where we got married.'

Geraldine groaned. 'Oh, God. Don't remind me – that was not my finest hour. I had too much to drink and started a fight on the dance floor.'

'I bet you won,' teased Olwyn.

Everyone chuckled.

'Plumdale is certainly a lot more fun now that you live here, Geraldine,' said Pam.

'Hear, hear,' agreed Vi.

Geraldine had thrived at Valley Vistas, just as Sarah had hoped she would. Her mum was always organising talks and excursions. She and her friends had just come back from a volunteering trip to Calais, to help out at the refugee centre. Afterwards, they'd all stayed at Roger's house in Honfleur, sampling local wines and visiting art galleries.

Roger, who now walked with a cane, was peering at the young woman opening the auditorium doors. 'Who's that,' he asked suspiciously.

'That's Annabelle,' explained James. 'She's our new assistant manager.'

They had hired Annabelle to help run the cinema and free up Sarah's time for writing.

'I'll be keeping a close eye on the picture,' warned Roger. 'I'll let you know if anything seems off.'

'I would expect nothing less,' said James, patting him on the shoulder.

As everyone started filing into the auditorium to watch the movies, Sarah hesitated.

'Aren't you coming?' asked James. 'This is your big night.'

'There's just one thing I need to—'

James took a box of Maltesers out of his tuxedo jacket and shook it, making the malted chocolate balls inside rattle. He grinned at Sarah. 'Don't worry – I came prepared.'

Sarah gave him a kiss. 'You are the best husband in the world.' She'd be willing to bet he also had a hankie in his pocket, for when she inevitably shed tears at *The Ghostwriter's* happy ending.

Together, they went inside their cinema and took their seats, flanked by Holly and Nick. As the lights dimmed and the curtains opened to reveal the screen, Sarah reached for James's hand. Because even after all the years they'd been together, there was still no one in the world she would rather watch a movie with than him.

Acknowledgements

This is a story about community and it wouldn't have been possible to write it without the support of my community. Thank you to my friends and family on both sides of the Atlantic, who encouraged me to keep going, especially when life wasn't like the movies. It will come as no surprise to readers that I am a massive film buff. Perhaps my biggest challenge in writing this story was deciding which movies to include! The Plumdale Picture Palace is fictional, but it is inspired by many independent cinemas I've frequented over the years. My current favourite is the Ealing Project, and I am extremely grateful to its manager, Lewis Neophytou, who took me behind the scenes and answered my questions about the day-to-day running of an independent cinema. Thank you also to my friend Samanthan Boffin for her insight into filming movies on location.

I am also grateful for my publishing community – and feel privileged to be working with the amazing team at Orion. Thank you to Sam Eades for giving me the opportunity to revisit the Cotswolds at Christmastime, and to my fabulous editor and fellow rom-com fan, Sanah Ahmed. Her insightful feedback helped me make this story as good as it could possibly be. I am also grateful to my wonderful agent and compatriot, Katie Greenstreet, for her belief in me. Many thanks are also due to my lovely colleagues at HCG, especially Megan Larkin, for holding down the fort while I was on sabbatical.

Finally, thank you to Robert Williams, for the hundreds of movies we have seen together, and to my daughters Eve and Rose, for giving me an excuse to rewatch my favourite ones with you.

If you loved *Christmas at the Movies*, don't miss Anne Marie Ryan's delightfully festive debut!

Happy ever after is only a page away . . .

It's almost Christmas and snow is falling the Cotswolds. Simon and Nora might be gearing up for the festive season – but their beloved bookshop is in trouble!

So Nora is delighted when a customer buys a book that's been gathering dust for years, even if it won't be enough to keep the bailiffs away.

Fuelled by mulled wine and mince pies, Nora and Simon hatch a plan to send six books to lonely villagers to rouse community spirit. The books change the recipients' lives, but is it too late to change the bookshop's fate?

RAISING READERS
Books Build Bright Futures

Dear Reader,

We'd love your attention for one more page to tell you about the crisis in children's reading, and what we can all do.

Studies have shown that reading for fun is the **single biggest predictor of a child's future life chances** – more than family circumstance, parents' educational background or income. It improves academic results, mental health, wealth, communication skills, ambition and happiness.[1]

The number of children reading for fun is in rapid decline. Young people have a lot of competition for their time. In 2024, 1 in 10 children and young people in the UK aged 5 to 18 did not own a single book at home.[2]

Hachette works extensively with schools, libraries and literacy charities, but here are some ways we can all raise more readers:

- Reading to children for just 10 minutes a day makes a difference
- Don't give up if children aren't regular readers – there will be books for them!
- Visit bookshops and libraries to get recommendations
- Encourage them to listen to audiobooks
- Support school libraries
- Give books as gifts

There's a lot more information about how to encourage children to read on our website: **www.RaisingReaders.co.uk**

Thank you for reading.

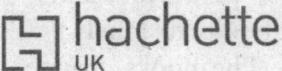

---

[1] National Literacy Trust, Book Ownership in 2024, November 2024
https://nlt.cdn.ngo/media/documents/Book_ownership_in_2024

[2] OECD. 2021. 21st-century readers: developing literacy skills in a digital world. Paris, France: OECD Publishing.
https://www.oecd.org/en/publications/21st-century-readers_a83d84cb-en.html

Credits

Anne Marie Ryan and Orion Fiction would like to thank everyone at Orion who worked on the publication of *Christmas at the Movies*

Editorial
Sanah Ahmed

Copy-Editor
Jade Craddock

Proofreader
Suzanne Clarke

Audio
Paul Stark
Louise Richardson

Contracts
Rachel Monte
Ellie Bowker

Design
Charlotte Abrams-Simpson
Rebecca Elizabeth Gibbs

Editorial Management
Charlie Panayiotou
Jane Hughes
Bartley Shaw

Finance
Jasdip Nandra
Nick Gibson
Sue Baker

Marketing
Corinne Jean-Jacques

Publicity
Sian Baldwin

Production
Ruth Sharvell

Sales

Dave Murphy
Sammy Luton
Victoria Laws
Rachael Hum
Ellie Kyrke-Smith
Frances Doyle
Georgina Cutler

Operations

Jo Jacobs